Also by Vaughn Heppner

Fenris series:
Alien Honor

Doom Star series:
Star Soldier
Bio-Weapon
Battle Pod
Cyborg Assault
Planet Wrecker
Star Fortress

Invasion America series:
Invasion: Alaska
Invasion: California
Invasion: Colorado

Ark Chronicles:
People of the Ark
People of the Flood
People of Babel
People of the Tower

Lost Civilizations series:
Giants
Leviathan
Tree of Life
Gog
Behemoth
The Lod Saga
The Oracle of Gog (novella)

Other novels:
Accelerated
I, Weapon
Strontium-90
Dark Crusade
Assassin of the Damned
The Dragon Horn
Elves and Dragons
The Dragon of Carthage
The Great Pagan Army
The Sword of Carthage
The Rogue Knight

ALIEN HONOR

ALIEN HONOR

A FENRIS NOVEL

VAUGHN HEPPNER

47N◉RTH

Text copyright © 2013 by Vaughn Heppner

Published by 47North, Seattle

www.apub.com

ISBN-13: 9781477808825
ISBN-10: 1477808825
Library of Congress Number: 2013940225
Cover illustration: Maciej Rebisz

To John and Margret Heppner, my father and mother,
the greatest parents in the world.

PROLOGUE

A boy and old man crawled over sharp rocks the color of lead.

They were near the top of a towering mountain in the greatest range of an Earth-like planet. Ice lay in patches around them, mixed with purple lichen. A freezing wind shrieked, tearing at the boy's fur jacket and buffeting his pale features. He was gaunt and white-skinned and had fierce, sky-colored eyes.

At times, the wind threatened to lift him off the rocks and hurl him like a doll onto jagged boulders a thousand feet below. He clung to stony protrusions then, with his teeth clenched like a predator gripping a choice piece of meat. He wanted to see the Valley of the Demons and the Mountain that was a Machine. Both were on the other side of the peak.

Beside him, the old man panted, his foggy breath blown away like stray thoughts. He had dark, leathery skin. He was the clan seeker, the ancient man of wisdom. Twice, as the wind shrieked madly, his entire body lifted so no part of him touched the mountain.

He should have flown in the air to land cruelly thousands of feet below. Instead, his dark eyes shone with a metallic color and sweat appeared on his face. He stopped lifting and remained frozen for an infinitesimal amount of time. Then he sank back onto the stone, as if in some fashion he had gained weight or pulled himself down.

The boy witnessed this each time. He also felt the seeker's inner strength. It was like standing too close to a bonfire, and it singed his mind. Oh, but he marveled at the seeker's power. Why didn't the old man lead the clan? Then they could raid the demons in the valley and make their blood run red on the stones.

"It's more dangerous at the top," the seeker shouted, his words coming in wind-whipped fragments.

The boy nodded, and he eased upward another foot. His hands ached from gripping rocks so tightly. Fear like a snake writhed through him, but he wanted to see, had begged many weeks for this chance. Now that he was so close, he wasn't going to turn around and slink back to the others in defeat.

He looked up. The great moon with its many bands of color dwarfed the sun. The moon filled half the sky. It seemed so near that he felt he could reach out and scratch its surface.

"Don't be distracted!" the seeker shouted.

The boy—Klane—barely heard the admonishment in time. He pressed his frail body against stone and the wind howled across him, trying to tear him away. He endured as the invisible force plucked at him, seeking to gain a purchase. It was just like wrestling in camp against stronger, bigger boys. But none of the others, despite their strength, had ever been up here. They always sneered at him for his smooth skin, for his weakness, but he was braver than any four of them. This proved it.

As the wind lessened, Klane dragged himself upward another foot, and then another. He reached the top of the mountain at the same time as the seeker.

Klane glanced at the smiling old face. Then he looked over the topmost rock. The Valley of the Demons spread out before him, a glorious wonder. He'd never envisioned anything like this. The valley was massive, hundreds of miles long so it faded into the horizon. There were two towering mountain ranges on either side of the vale. The mountains loomed miles above the lowest point of the valley. Down in the distant bottom Klane could see greenery and a snaking river.

"The air is much thicker down there," the seeker shouted in his ear. Klane could smell the old man's onion breath.

Then Klane spied the Mountain that was a Machine. The seeker had described it before, many times, but he'd never expected it would be like this. The mountain didn't seem natural but looked like a titanic box. The box or building was many miles long. It had huge, smooth tubes sticking out of it. White vapors like clouds billowed from the tubes or stacks. Beside the Great Machine was the last of an iceberg. Ropy vines snaked from the machine onto the ice. They must be huge ropes for Klane to see them from so far away.

"There!" the seeker shouted. "Now you should look up. You will see a thing to boggle your senses."

Klane squinted upward into the heavens. His chest constricted and his breath caught in his throat. From the old man's descriptions before, he saw . . . he saw. They were long tongues of fire, flames. That meant rockets came down from space. Yes, yes, he remembered his lessons. These rockets must be high up in the atmosphere. Thunder began to boom. The noise grew louder and louder until it shook his bones. Klane kept staring at the rockets. He could see them now, mighty vessels of metal belching tongues of fire. Between the various rockets swayed a great iceberg. The rockets lowered the ice toward the Machine Mountain.

"This is a miracle!" Klane shouted.

"No. It is high technology. The iceberg was once an asteroid snatched from New Saturn's rings and flown through the void to our planet."

Klane stared at the seeker who knew so much. The old man used words of High Speech, the words of magic and ancient wisdom.

"The demons lower the ice from space!" the seeker shouted. "They use the ice to fuel the Great Machine."

"What does the machine do?"

"There are many such machines on our world, Klane. The demons *terraform* the planet to suit their evil nature. They like the thicker atmosphere in the valley. That is why they stay down there and why they leave us alone here in the uplands."

"What do the demons look like?" Klane shouted.

The seeker studied him, the dark eyes seemingly boring into Klane's soul. "One day, you will tell me."

"I don't understand."

"I would be amazed if you did."

Frowning, Klane asked, "Why do you always speak in riddles?"

The old man smiled. He was missing teeth. "After we return to camp, you will begin to fashion your first junction-stone."

Klane stared at the Mountain that was a Machine. He wanted a junction-stone, but he'd doubted now for months that he could ever fashion one. The seeker had told him several weeks ago that seeing the Valley of the Demons would help him make one. Now that he saw all this . . .

"Let us go to the Mountain that was a Machine," Klane pleaded. He wanted to go inside it and see the ancient marvels.

"Why do you wish this?" the seeker asked. "Tell me truly."

Klane debated what he should say. "I would know more about this terra-forming."

"No! Pray that you never do know, Klane."

"Why do you say this? I don't understand."

The seeker studied him, finally saying, "Greater knowledge only brings greater sorrow."

Klane's frown deepened. "Why do you always hound me then to learn more and to do it faster?"

The seeker turned away, for once at a loss for words.

Klane watched the rockets land near the Great Machine. The tongues of fire blew dust and grit in billowing clouds. The roar increased and Klane clamped his hands over his ears. Finally, with a thunderous sound that shook the mountain, the rockets landed the iceberg, the ice that once was an asteroid.

Oh, the demons wielded great power indeed. They were worthy of fear. Fear . . .

Klane snarled. He was tired of being scared all the time, of enduring the endless beatings from the bigger boys. If he had a junction-stone to wield . . .

"Why am I different from the others?" Klane shouted.

"It is time to go."

As the old man turned away, Klane grabbed one of the seeker's frail wrists.

"Why am I different?" he repeated. "You know, don't you?"

The seeker turned back to study him. With a deft twist, the old man freed his stick-like wrist. Then he pointed up at the monstrous, banded moon. "You came down from there, Klane. The demons brought you as they brought the iceberg. They gave you to me."

Moisture fled from Klane's mouth. The boys mocked him about his difference. But he'd never believed it was this bad. Was he a demon then? Was he one of their imps?

"Why would the demons do such a thing?" Klane shouted.

"Yes. That is what I would like to know. It is a penetrating question." After a moment, the old man shook his head, and he began to crawl backward down the mountain.

The shock was too great. Klane almost stood up to let the wind take him. Instead, he craned his neck and peered up into the sky.

His thoughts took time coalescing. He had come from up there. His eyes narrowed. The seeker had just told him another riddle. He hated riddles and he hated being different. Most of all, he hated how the bigger, older boys picked on him day and night. It was time to return to camp, to fashion a junction-stone and teach the others the price of mocking one who came from the sky.

PART I: PREPARATION

1

In another time and place, Cyrus Gant might have been a gawky teenager, all elbows and knees and ill-coordinated, skinny limbs. Here, he was gaunt like a starved rat, with the cunning of a junkyard dog. He'd need that cunning to escape the Dust hunters.

Here was Level 40 Milan, Italia Sector, end-of-the-line for everyone living a kilometer underground. At the bottom of Milan, tons of algae-slime ran through the vast processing plants. Every hour of every year, the slime pits seeped noxious fumes that could drop a trank freak.

Several mega-blocks away was the deep-core mine that supplied the city's power. The main shaft ran down to the Earth's mantle, and usually the magnetic shields held. When they didn't, they bled excess heat. Bottom Milan temperatures could soar into the one-hundred and twenties and even thirties. During one disaster seventeen years ago, everyone in Levels 40 and 39 died. Taken all together—the fumes, heat, and squalor—many said Level 40 was an Earthly version of Dante's Hell.

Anyone with the credits or connections moved up. Cyrus was one of the unlucky 40ers—a lifer as they said—although he was a survivor. He'd been on his own ever since he escaped the orphanage.

As he slunk past massive, gurgling pipes, casting a wary eye to the right and left, his right hand dropped to his belt. It was a piece of rope with a knot. It kept the castoff pants tight against his sunken waist. Thrust through the belt was the object of his grope and his prized possession: a working vibrio-knife. He wore paper-thin boots and a shirt two sizes too large for his scrawny frame.

He ducked under a tube, careful to keep his head or back from touching it. Heat radiated from the rusty thing.

The upper ceiling lights flickered. Cyrus looked up fifty meters. High up there in the ceiling shined sunlamps. One of them had just blown, and the giant lamp went dark.

Too many sunlamps in Level 40 were the same way, giving the bottom a twilight quality.

Sucking in his lips, Cyrus scanned the terrain one more time. He felt something wrong, an oppression of his spirit, an evil thing. The terrain was a vast maze of tubes and pipes crisscrossing for kilometers in a bewildering array. Some of the pipes were scalding hot. Others had icicles on the bottom. This was part of Algae Plant Twelve. The mutated sludge gurgling through the tubes was a particularly vigorous form of slime that helped to feed Earth's billions.

Cyrus had chosen the place for a reason. He carried ten grams of pure Dust, the prized and most expensive illegal drug in the solar system. He belonged to the Latin Kings, one of the hundreds of mules or carriers used to transport Dust and other black market goods. His goal was to become a foot soldier, a gunman next, and finally a chief in one of the sub-gangs. He would protect himself from the evils of life by being the toughest, smartest, and highest-ranked person around.

Right now, he needed to get his ten grams of Dust to the other side of Level 40 near Number Seven Lift. The guards there had been bribed to look the other way. His contact waited there.

The constant gurgling sludge as it pulsed through the pipes, the heat, and the ill odors should have disguised the approach of the three hunters. They should have, but Cyrus kept scowling in frustration.

He had the gaunt features of the eternally hungry and a sharp nose. His eyes, there was something strange about them. They were deep-set, blue like ink and wise about the street. His gut told him trouble came. He trusted the feeling, hesitating to make his move through an open area.

He kept turning his head, rubbernecking as he looked around. A BAD THING was out there. He hadn't felt something like this since the time in the orphanage when the sex fiends had exchanged credits with the housemaster.

He'd always had a knack for keeping his ears open. *Trust no one but yourself.* It was the earliest law of life he'd learned on the street. Cyrus had fled from the orphanage that night before the predators could take him down to the basement and abuse him. Since then, he'd looked out for himself. He'd joined the Latin Kings because the street had taught him you needed allies to beat the nastiest evils.

Out here in the pipes, his fingers curled around the hilt of his vibrio-knife. Why did he feel—?

Cyrus saw a hunter. It was the man's feral movement more than the red jacket that gave him away. The thick-necked thug ducked under a tube, straightened, and turned around. A big sword image on the back of the jacket marked him as a Red Blade. They were another gang, the blood-foes to the Latin Kings.

Cyrus's heart began to pound. The man held a gun, a slugthrower, a big one. Cyrus didn't wonder what the Red Blade was doing here. It was obvious. The thug hunted him because the man wanted Dust. Who didn't want ten pure grams? The Red Blade wouldn't just rob him either. The man would kill him.

Instead of sobbing at the unfairness of life, instead of making a face or shaking in fright, young Cyrus's eyes narrowed. The man must have twice his weight and age and the hunter gripped a gun.

A junkyard dog in this situation would have bolted for a better place. The eyes gave Cyrus away: that he was more than just another slum-dweller, a punk with a knife and an errand. He was a dinosaur, a small one to be sure, but a throwback to a different era when humanity lived in caves, battling giant bears for the right of its home. To run blindly now would be to die.

Cyrus had no intention of dying.

The Red Blade out there acted as if there were others with him. Cyrus hadn't moved a muscle since spying the man. Slowly, Cyrus swiveled his head, scanning the area once again. Ah, yes indeed. He spied another . . . and a third hunter, too. He'd expected that. Red Blades liked to work in triads.

By studying their positions, Cyrus realized they had him blocked. They must have studied his habits or they had pinpointed the route through the pipes.

I'll have to use the ducts now. I'll have to go into the dark. That was dangerous. Sometimes they flushed waste through the ducts. If you were caught in them during that time, you drowned in boiling sludge.

He turned away slowly and began easing in that direction. He didn't notice the drip in the pipe over him. It must have hissed, because steam blew out of the crack. But he'd never have heard it with all the gurgling around him. Black slime dripped a slow drop at a time out of the crack and into a shadowed area.

Cyrus's boot stepped into the middle of the hot slime. He slipped and went down hard as his foot shot out from under him.

A second later, a spark and loud *ping* told him one of the hunters had just fired at him. A second shot opened another crack. Hot gushing slime blew out of the pipe and steam billowed into the air.

Cyrus used the distraction, getting up and sprinting away.

Once more, shots rang out. More pings and sparks told him the billowing steam helped cover him.

"There!" one of the Red Blades shouted. "He's running for the ducts!"

Cyrus didn't turn around to look. He knew one of them would be pointing at him. They wanted the Dust. It was worth hard credits.

He sprinted, leaped a low tube and took a sharp turn left. The leftmost thug skidded to a halt, lifted his arm, and took a deliberate bead on him.

Cyrus concentrated, although he was only half aware of what he did. He ran, and sweat slicked his forehead. The sweat didn't come from the running, but from using his power. If he really concentrated and poured mental energy, he could move tiny things with his mind, or block small things like a firing pin in a slugthrower.

The thug aimed and the hunter must have pulled the trigger, but noting happened. The gunpowder didn't explode. The Red Blade raised the gun in what appeared to be frustration and pulled the trigger a second time. Cyrus no longer used his power and the firing pin clicked normally against the bullet. A shot rang out, and the slug ricocheted off a pipe ten meters above the man. Steam hissed from the new crack, and if the thug hadn't dropped in time, the hot steam would have melted his face.

Cyrus would have laughed at the hunter's panicked shout, but a throbbing pain in his forehead prevented that. Using his power had a cost. Cyrus's eyesight blurred because of what he'd done, and he almost crashed into a pipe. Just in time, he ducked, rolled, and slithered into an opening, falling several meters before hitting metal. Despite his readiness for the drop, it knocked the wind out of him.

In the gloom, his mouth opened and he tried to suck air. Finally, his lungs unlocked and he crawled into deeper darkness.

Half a minute later, the hunters converged on the opening. Cyrus heard them, and he froze lest a noise give him away.

"You had a clean shot at him," one of the hunters said. He sounded like the leader. "What happened?"

"My gun wouldn't fire."

"That's why you shot at a pipe?" the leader asked.

"My gun worked then. There's something weird about this kid."

"Yeah, I've heard that. He has our Dust. Go on, get him."

"Why do I have to go down?"

"You had a clean shot and you missed. That's why."

"I already told you my gun wouldn't fire."

"Well it better fire this next time, or I'll practice with mine on you."

"Okay, okay. Give me the light and the locator."

Cyrus had heard about locators. This was bad.

A sudden change in the gloom—and a thud—told him the hunter had dropped into the duct.

"We'll wait up here and give you a hand out," the leader said. "And don't think about running off with the Dust."

Cyrus's head hurt worse than ever. He hated the backlash of his talent. Now one of them had followed him down here.

"It's a tight fit!" the whiny hunter shouted up.

"Shut up and get on with it," the leader said. "The kid is probably running while you yammer."

"No. I have him on the locator. He's near."

"Then get him!"

Cyrus backed away, moving by feel.

"Why don't you surrender, kid?" the hunter called, his voice echoing strangely in the ducts. "All I want is the Dust. Give it to me and you can walk away."

In the darkness, Cyrus grinned like a wolf. The hunter lied. But something in the thug's voice told Cyrus the man didn't like it down here.

Despite the headache, Cyrus knew he needed to use his talent one more time. It would get very bad afterward, puking bad. Sometimes, though, one had to pay the cost if he wished to live.

The cat and mouse game lasted eight minutes. These were mazy, twisty ducts. The two hunters outside shouted down from time to time, offering advice.

Finally, Cyrus backed into a side duct that squeezed his shoulders together. He kept his hands in front of him while gripping the silent vibrio-knife. He waited as the hunter crawled near.

"I know you're close, kid. I can see it on my locator."

Sweat appeared on Cyrus's forehead, and he sucked in his breath as he used his power. The man's flashlight went out.

Cyrus heard the hunter swear in frustration. He moved then as the thug clicked his flashlight on and off. At the last moment, something must have alerted the hunter.

"You little punk," the hunter snarled. A boom went off, a flash of flame, and a bullet seared lengthwise down Cyrus's back—his back was parallel with the bottom of the duct. The bullet opened a furrow from his shoulder to his buttocks. That burned, and it caused Cyrus to lose concentration on his power. The flashlight resumed pouring out light, and the thug happened to be aiming it at his eyes. It blinded the hunter, the Red Blade.

With a flick of his thumb, Cyrus clicked on the vibrio-knife. Its whine of noise was unmistakable.

"No!" the hunter howled, trying to bring up his arms in front of his face.

With terrifying ease, the knife cut through flesh and bone. Blood poured and the hunter died, slumping onto the metal floor.

In the far distance, the other two hunters shouted, asking what happened.

With a tug, Cyrus removed his knife from the man's face. He shut off the vibrating blade. His hand was rock steady. His features were hard but calm. He didn't like to kill, but if he had too, he did it.

He wiped the blood on the man's jacket. Red Blade, red blood—it was a Latin King joke. Then he pilfered his enemy, taking the gun, the locator, and the flashlight. He also found twenty-seven credits in the man's pockets.

Before the others decided to come down into the darkness with their slain comrade, Cyrus headed away toward a different opening. He could hardly see. His eyes burned and his forehead felt as if someone had driven a nail through it. He was still alive, thanks to his talent, and once more, he'd survived his competitors.

He had everything under control.

2

TWO YEARS LATER

Special Second Class Jasper of Psi Force didn't look like the best telepath on Earth. He was short, bald, and overweight. He wore a shiny, shimmering suit and sat between two large NKV agents dressed in their black uniforms.

The NKV were Premier Lang's dreaded enforcers, his secret police. Marten Kluge—the first premier of Sol and controller of the Sunbeam over one hundred years ago—had wanted democracy implemented throughout the solar system. For a time—after several bitter wars—democracy had reigned. Eventually, Kluge died and the second controller of the Sunbeam became premier. He talked about democracy and practiced politics the way Caesar Augustus of ancient Rome would have understood. By the third premier, dictatorial rule had become the norm. Premier Lang was the fifth controller of the Sunbeam and ruled Sol from his seat of power.

Rebellions and spontaneous riots bubbled into existence from Mercury to Neptune. The one good thing was that the ravages of the Cyborg War, particularly the genocidal tactics of the machine-man melds, had finally been repaired. The solar system had become crowded again. People had forgotten about the horrors of war as the young and hotheaded talked about the need for militant solutions as practiced by the legendary Marten Kluge.

In the premier's quest for iron-fisted peace, Lang had taken a leaf from the old Social Unity Party. He used the wealth of the Outer Planets to appease the billions on Earth and terraformed Venus. Many in the Outer Planets complained, and a few had formed conspiracies aimed at toppling the dictatorship. Each attempt had failed miserably, most in dark rooms where the leaders howled under torture, and one by the Sunbeam's destructive ray. A few theorists believed Lang's predecessor had died from an assassin's poison. Conspirators had killed the tyrant but failed to stop the next man from filling the premier's post. With Lang's rise had come an ominous increase in secret police scrutiny and security procedures, the NKV.

The two NKV agents beside Jasper were big men with normal faces. They carried weapons and rode with Jasper in an air-car approaching Milan.

Mostly, the city entrance was green, a park with a few mansions for the very rich. Only the lucky and a few agricultural workers lived above ground. Everyone else lived in the kilometer-deep cities. Beyond the park were orchards and vineyards. It was beautiful and idyllic. The two NKV agents stared out of the air-car, apparently drinking in the details.

Their ability to sit serenely beside him deeply bothered Jasper. He was the most talented telepath on Earth. Yet the leaders of Psi Force had given him a second class ranking. It was insulting. Worse, he felt little better than a chained ferret, carefully kept under control to do his duty.

Out of the billions in the solar system, only 143 people had psionic abilities strong enough to produce visible effects. Those abilities stretched across a range of talents: telepathy, empathy, telekinesis, clairvoyance and others. That wasn't the reason why Lang's people desperately scoured the solar system for more. No. The psi-able could perform an amazing new trick for their masters.

Masters: the word galled Jasper. He hated one other word, too: *mutant*. The world treated him like a freak of nature, one they needed to tame and corral so they could use.

Jasper touched his smooth scalp. Learned surgeons had put an inhibitor into his brain. Oh yes, it was a fine piece of netting carefully woven under his skull. It was a fail-safe, a chain, a collar to put on the mutant. They had put the inhibitor into the freak that terrified normal people.

"You're sure it's Milan?" asked the NKV lieutenant. He was the one with an inhibitor switch. When he flicked it on, Jasper could apply his talents. When it was off, the inhibitor kept him from using his psionic abilities.

"Yes," Jasper said without looking up. At the moment, the switch was on. "The youth is still in the city."

The air-car banked, heading down.

The truth of the matter was something completely different from what *normal* people thought about Specials. Jasper understood why they feared him: because he was a godlike being, a new man, superior to these halfwits with their bulging muscles. They had chained him out of fear of his superiority. They thought to use him as a toy, a thing, a component in one of the greatest discoveries and inventions in human history.

It was small "h" human because the Normals lacked psionic powers. They were the old breed in awe of those who, in several centuries, would supplant them. Did they think he would play their chained ferret forever?

I'll find a way to rid myself of this inhibitor. Thinking about that brought a smile to Jasper's chubby face.

"Do you know which level he's in?" the lieutenant asked.

Of course, Jasper knew. He was a telepath. The lieutenant was a dolt to ask such a stupid question. But that isn't how Jasper answered. He said, "I don't know yet, but I will once we begin searching the city."

The NKV lieutenant nodded.

Jasper smirked to himself. It was good to keep the extent of his ability secret. The day they learned his true might would be the day he ran everything.

Premier Lang hunted the solar system for Specials, for mutants to use in the new Space Fleet. There were several laborious ways to discover if a person had psionic talent. But when the odds were 143 out of tens of billions . . . one wanted a better way.

Jasper was the better way. With his telepathy, he could pinpoint others of his kind as if they were flickering candles in a dark room. He hated being a chained freak, a slave to lesser beings. But he'd be damned if he was going to let others of his kind walk free while he had to wear a leash. Besides, once he discovered a way to beat the inhibitor, he would have soldiers in his new army to help him.

Cracking his knuckles, Jasper closed his eyes and concentrated. Oh, this was interesting.

He opened his eyes and glanced at the lieutenant. "We'd better hurry. Our candidate is in trouble."

"Trouble with the law?" the lieutenant asked.

"No. With several Red Blades."

The two NKV agents glanced at each other. "Who are these Red Blades?" the lieutenant asked.

Jasper concentrated once more. The wild ones usually didn't have good mind shields. This one certainly didn't. He was an open book. "Red Blades are a gang, Dust dealers."

"Vermin," the lieutenant said with a frown.

"Whatever they are, they're hunting the candidate," Jasper said. "And this time it looks as if they have him."

The lieutenant bent toward to the pilot in front. "Condition red," he told the man.

The pilot nodded, got on the radio to the airport, and sped down for a landing.

Jasper folded his arms. This looked as if it could get interesting.

|||||||||||

Cyrus Gant ran, skidding around a corner and sprinting for his life. Behind him shouted thickly-built goons. They wore red jackets with big blades stenciled on the back. Each clutched a shock rod, a nasty weapon normally wielded by riot police.

"You little punk!" shouted a goon with a tattooed head. "You can't run forever!"

Cyrus would have liked to shout back how clever that sounded. But he was too winded, too spent by a long chase. He ran through a giant warehouse with mountains of crates all around. The workers were gone. The place was empty but for the seven of them—six Red Blades to beat to death one Latin King.

Cyrus had come here for a special delivery, but had found an ambush instead.

He'd risen in rank from being a mule to a foot soldier in the Latin Kings. Killing the enemy gunman in the ducts had catapulted him far ahead of others his age. The older, stronger foot soldiers had jeered him at the beginning. Cyrus showed them their mistake by offering to duel anyone knife-to-knife. One soldier six years his senior had taken him up on the offer. Cyrus never fought for sport, and he hadn't that day either. He'd killed the Latin King and taken the beating for it from the others without protest or regret. To climb the ladder of power, one had to pay the price. To make the others fear and respect him, the beating had been a cheap price to pay . . . in his opinion.

He was taller than two years ago, but just as thin, with muscles like strings of steel. His eyes were deep blue and haunted with the knowledge that today he was going to die.

This was a setup, a careful one, and Cyrus suspected one or two Latin Kings had helped the Red Blades lure him here. The six men blocked his escape routes. He'd cut one and taken a hit in his left shoulder for it. His shoulder still buzzed from the shock.

Cyrus's lungs burned with the need for air. Sweat slicked his skin. He had good clothes now and the regular boots that all Latin King foot soldiers wore. When the bosses gave him an assignment, he came through every time. Unfortunately, he wasn't going to come through today and fear made his mind cloudy. He despised that.

Cyrus skidded and ran between two mounds of piled crates.

"Bad choice, cutter!" a goon shouted. "This is the end of the line for you."

Cyrus understood the taunt a few seconds later. He'd run into a cul-de-sac. A quick scan showed him the crates were piled too high for him to scale them. He whirled around and faced the racing goons.

They slowed down, three panting Red Blades. The others would be coming from where they had blocked his escape routes earlier. Each of the Red Blades had wide shoulders and thick muscles from hours in the gym and growth hormones. One by one, they flicked on their shock rods to full intensity. Sweat dripped from their beefy faces and the crazy look in their eyes told Cyrus they were high on Dust. Their smiles said this was going to be brutal.

"Kneel, cutter, and we'll bash you in the head first, making it easy on you. Resist us, and we'll take hours to finish it and make sure it hurts bad."

Thinking about the coming beating made several of Cyrus's bones ache from previous breaks. His palms were sweaty and he gripped his vibrio-knife so hard his hand hurt. His mouth was dry and his tongue stuck to his teeth.

If you're going to die, go out swinging.

Cyrus grunted, and through an act of will he forced his muscles to loosen. He even managed a shrug, but he couldn't think of anything cool to say to show them he thought they were punks.

The three goons inched closer, and two of them began to weave their rods back and forth. The third goon spit on the warehouse floor.

"Your death is going to be a hard one, cutter."

Cyrus crouched, with his knife close to his chest. *Which one should I cut first?* He didn't know. As he tried to puzzle it out, a sizzle sounded.

The leftward goon staggered.

What was that? What's making the noise?

The Dust freak who had staggered shuffled around as if he'd been hurt. The other two goons paused, glancing at the third.

A volley of sizzles sounded, one after another. One of the Red Blades dropped his shock rod so it hit the floor with a *clack.* He followed it, hitting the cement face first. Then the others fell with their batons. They fell and lay still as if dead.

Cyrus stood there blinking as two black-coated men approached the fallen Red Blades. The two men had flat-shaped guns gripped in their fists. Those obviously weren't slugthrowers, but they were something fancy that made sizzling sounds.

Another man followed the two in black. The other was short, fat, and bald, and wore a shiny suit. That one looked bored, and his eyes shined strangely, almost a metallic color. He raised a pudgy hand and pointed a fat finger at Cyrus.

"He's the one you want," Mr. Shiny Suit said.

"So I gathered," said one of the men in black. "Cyrus Gant?"

"Yeah?" Cyrus asked. "Who are you?

"I belong to the NKV, as you have no doubt surmised."

"What?" Cyrus asked.

The man turned to Mr. Shiny Suit and raised an eyebrow.

"He doesn't know about the NKV or the Conscription Act," Mr. Shiny Suit said.

"Explain it to him."

Mr. Shiny Suit scowled, but nodded and managed a false smile. He took a step toward Cyrus.

"You can call me Jasper," the man said.

"What's this about?" Cyrus asked.

"That's easy enough to answer," Jasper said. "These two men are NKV agents and I'm a Special."

Cyrus's eyes narrowed.

"You're suspicious about us," Jasper told him. The little fat man spoke as if he was a card shark explaining his tricks. "What's more, you think my suit looks ridiculous and that these two gentlemen must belong to a gang you've never heard of."

Cyrus's eyes widened for just a moment. Then he became wary and smiled. "How'd you do that?" Every con artist had his methods.

"I read the information in your mind," Jasper said.

"I don't believe you."

"No? Well, I'm a telepath."

"Don't know what that is," Cyrus said. "Tell me. What am I thinking now?"

"That one plus one equals two," Jasper said.

Shock filled Cyrus's face. He'd been thinking exactly that. It was time to get out of here. He pointed his vibrio-knife at the two NKV agents. "Thanks for the help. I'll be seeing you around."

"No," said the one who had talked before. "You're coming with us. That's why we came to Milan."

"Sure," Cyrus said. He'd expected something like this. These three must be sex-fiends and they wanted to kidnap him for their vile games. He flicked on his vibrio-knife and launched himself at the nearest gunman.

Both black-clad men lifted their shiny weapons and pressed the firing buttons. Nothing happened because Cyrus had shorted each gun. He almost reached the nearest man with his knife. Just before he did, something hit him inside his head. It hurt, and it exploded darkness in his mind. The fat one must be doing this, the telepath. Cyrus tried to adjust, but the darkness spread throughout his mind.

He lost consciousness and sprawled onto the warehouse floor, his knife clattering as it skidded across the cement.

|||||||||||

The NKV lieutenant stared at Cyrus Gant. Abruptly, he turned toward Jasper.

"You're very welcome," Jasper said. It was enjoyable seeing the lieutenant's fear. Let him think about *that* for a while.

Without a word, the lieutenant reached into a pocket and brought out a device with a single switch. He used his thumb and pressed it.

Jasper felt the inhibitor buzz in his head. The psych-chief had told him before that he wasn't actually hearing anything. The noise was psychosomatic. Whatever . . . It was there, and it dampened his ability to read minds.

This is the thanks I get?

"He's deadly," the lieutenant said, meaning the kid. "He attacked without warning. I would never trust this one. He's worse than an animal."

"Do you trust me?" Jasper couldn't help asking.

The lieutenant ignored the question. "Maybe we should shoot him and report that these riffraff killed him before we could interfere."

"Ah . . . don't forget about me," Jasper said. "I'm a witness to this."

The lieutenant faced him. "This youth is an animal. Did you see how fast he attacked? He would have killed all of us."

"No," Jasper said, "just you two. I had everything under control."

"He wrecked our weapons with a thought," the lieutenant said. "What is he?"

Your superior, you mental weakling, Jasper thought. *He is humanity's future and you're its failure.*

"Are you sure he's unconscious?" the lieutenant asked.

"For the next few hours," Jasper said.

"What did you do to him?"

"Turn off the inhibitor and I'll show you."

The lieutenant tried to stare Jasper down.

Although the lieutenant belonged to the NKV, was bigger and obviously physically many times more dangerous, Jasper stared back calmly. He even smiled at the man.

Jasper knew all about the Conscription Act. The lieutenant didn't dare harm him. There were only 143 like him. Those 143 could do the most amazing thing in the universe with the new Teleships. It was changing everything for humanity . . . as long as the 143 Specials played along.

The lieutenant dropped his gaze and turned to the other agent. "Give me a hand," he said. "We need to get this animal to the air-car before he wakes up."

And so I gather one more Special to my cause, Jasper thought. *One more Special to hate the Normals for their heavy-handed injustice. All I need now is a way to short out the inhibitor.*

3

The NKV lieutenant had called Cyrus Gant an animal, no doubt meaning it would prove impossible to teach him anything.

If that's what the lieutenant meant, he was wrong. Cyrus had abnormal street cunning gained through a short but brutal lifetime of hunger, face slaps, stomach punches, and savage kicks to the ribs, head, and groin, to say little about his various beatings. The key to his survival and later his thriving in Level 40 had been an ability to adapt, or as the ancients would have said, to roll with the punches. It also helped that he'd developed a fierce desire to lead, if for no other reason so he wouldn't have to listen to others tell him what to do.

He rolled now in Psi Force, taking things as they came. They shaved his scalp and gave him a fine network of scars along his head. They put inhibitor netting under his skull so they could switch his powers on and off. To the Normals—as his teachers referred to the rest of humanity—he was like dangerous nuclear material that needed the most careful of handling.

Psi Force's teaching facility was located on the island of Crete. Premier Lang's people had removed everyone else and set up an elaborate security arrangement. Most of the listening posts and SAM sites were well out of sight, but fully operational around the clock. The school was composed of six marble-colored buildings. There were wild vines surrounding the institute, steep hills, and many scenic bicycle paths. Birds sang in the trees and fluffy white clouds filled the sky.

Cyrus could stand for hours watching clouds. It was amazing. There had never been anything like this in Level 40. The stars . . . they were a wonder beyond belief. He'd never realized the Earth held such beauty or fantastic odors.

After a week, he realized no one planned to attack him in secret. Even so, he kept a hidden knife on his person at all times—just in case matters should change. They had outlandishly changed once already, why not again for the worse?

At first, he didn't mind the inhibitor because he didn't think about it. He soaked up knowledge. He trained in the latest hand-to-hand combat, learned about mind shields, strengthening his gift and so many other new and amazing things.

And the tests. Pretty women administered them. He learned later that they used the beautiful women because he responded so positively to them. Jasper had picked that up in his mind.

His teachers taught him to read. He learned history, math, and biology. Advanced teaching techniques worked like magic with him. Premier Lang ensured that Psi Force had the very best of everything. It made a difference.

His teachers wanted him smart. He soon discovered it had nothing to do with him and everything with enhancing his power. The reason proved fantastic and mind-bending. He only understood the mind-bending part when he learned about Einsteinian physics. Nothing could go faster than the speed of light—that was interesting. But it also didn't quite mean what it sounded like, at least not anymore.

Seventeen years ago, there had been a serendipitous occurrence near Neptune. It happened in a miles-long science lab where people had created the first "discontinuity window" in the solar system.

The discontinuity window was a rip in normal space. That rip joined two distant spots in space. While the DW—discontinuity window—remained open, anything passing through it could instantly move from the one point in space to the other.

The trick was in making the DW. It took a precise combination of powerful AIs merged with human clairvoyant and telekinetic abilities. Together, the mechanical and biological systems joined two separate points in space. The real trick came in how far apart those two separate points were from each other. That depended on the Special's power.

The strongest Special could join two points in space 8.3 light years apart. Anything moving through the opening then went from point A to point B. In the instance above, the object would move 8.3 light years. The discontinuity window bypassed Einsteinian physics, thereby giving humanity an effective interstellar drive. In other words, it now became possible to travel between the stars just as science fiction authors had always predicted.

The problem or drawback was the paltry number of Specials. It was the reason why Premier Lang scoured the solar system for more. And it was the reason why Cyrus Gant had been ripped out of the worst slum on Earth and given the best education money could buy.

Two moments three years apart at the institute proved critical to Cyrus's future. Each involved Jasper. The first occurred six months and three days after Cyrus's arrival. He was down by the shore in the nearest bay, skipping stones over the wine-colored sea.

Cyrus wasn't thinking about anything in particular. The tests had stopped and he missed the pretty women with their short skirts and tanned legs. He'd filled out size-wise with all the eating, although he remained lean. In the slums, he had cultivated an arrogant attitude. It had been as vital as toughness, and quickness with a blade. Here such arrogance didn't help. Cyrus had long ago learned to blend in with his surroundings, as a leopard would as it hunted prey. Even so, there remained a core wolfishness to him impossible to completely submerge. He had a way of eyeing everything and he hated anyone taking him by surprise. It didn't happen often, and it didn't happen on this particular day.

Cyrus saw Jasper riding a cart along the white sands of the shore. The telepath wore a shiny suit and a flattish hat. He looked the same as the day down in Level 40. Cyrus hadn't seen him since then, although he'd heard about Jasper. Several of his friends had warned him about the Special Second Class. They thought Jasper was strange, with much too high an opinion of himself.

Jasper brought his cart to a halt ten feet from Cyrus. The man kept his pudgy fingers wrapped around the steering wheel.

Cyrus's boots were nearby. He was barefoot and had rolled up his pant legs. He held a stone, a flat one for skipping.

"Afternoon," Cyrus said.

Jasper nodded. "Do you remember me?"

"Sure."

"I saved your life in the warehouse."

Cyrus thought about that. "Thanks."

"And I helped them turn you into a slave."

Cyrus smiled. It wasn't wide. It never was. Life had been too hard for him to change that quickly. "I've read about slavery," he said. "Where's my collar?"

Jasper tapped his head. "They hid it from you. They turn you on and off at will. What you think about that?"

"I'd rather be here than in Level 40."

"I don't believe you."

"Are you calling me a liar?" Cyrus asked the question in a regular tone, but there was heat in his mind. The slums had taught him to hide his emotions and to strike without warning.

"Kid, I looked into your mind, remember? I'm the best at what I do. I know an alpha when I spot one."

"Mind telling me what an alpha is?"

"You already know. You're not the kind to take orders, but to give them. You've never lived by the rules, but broke them at will to serve your own needs."

"Never had any choice before," Cyrus said.

"Yes you did. You broke the law when you fled the orphanage."

"I had no choice," Cyrus said, and there was iron his tone.

"Do you know how many thousands of kids succumb to perverts every day?" Jasper asked. "You were powerless and alone in the orphanage, and you skipped out because you didn't like how they were about to treat you. Right now, you're having fun in Crete. I don't blame you. But do you know what's in store for you?"

"Sure. I'm the key to mankind's future."

Jasper laughed in a mocking way. "Good, good, the piece of hardware named Cyrus Gant loves its job. How pathetic is that?"

"What's your problem?" Cyrus asked.

Jasper tapped his head. "This is my problem. I'm the most powerful man on Earth and they've chained me like a ferret. We're the new breed. We're superior to them, and they're harnessing us as if we're water running down a hill. We're slaves, Cyrus. I don't like being a slave. If they want my help, ask me, pay me, but don't put an inhibitor in my head that dampens my abilities. Do you like having an inhibitor in your head?"

Cyrus stared at the man in his shiny suit. Jasper had a point.

"No. I don't like the inhibitor."

"Finally, you're beginning to see what's going on," Jasper said. "I just hope you stay awake."

"What's that mean?"

Jasper started up his cart. "See you around, kid. Try to remember that however nice they're treating you, you're just a component in a starship for them. If you try to gain your freedom, they'll cut you down in pure terror. The Homo Simpletons hate and fear us, and for good reason. Compared to them, we're gods."

Cranking the steering wheel, Jasper turned the cart and drove away, leaving a thoughtful Cyrus Gant to stare at the expanse of sea.

The days merged into months. Cyrus continued to soak up facts and train his ability. His proved less powerful than most of the others. He was a Fourth Class Special, barely better than a Normal. His teachers rated his ability to shift at 0.8 light years. It was better than building up velocity the old-fashioned way, but nothing compared to Venice with her 8.3 light years.

In a starship, the same setup time and power was used to create a discontinuity window that bridged 0.8 as 8.3 light years. Efficiency meant that 8.3 was ten times better.

The only other factor to shifting was a Special's rest time. Some shifters needed a week between each psionic attempt. Others could shift again in several hours. No one had identical abilities, just as no one had the same fingerprints.

Throughout the months, Cyrus found himself studying slavery. The idea repulsed him. He was a man, not chattel or property. Jasper was right. No one had ever asked him if he wanted to power a starship. No one told him how long he would be doing this before he retired. The insinuation was clear: He'd do it until *they* were through with him.

In his private study of slave history, Cyrus found several literary heroes. His favorite was Spartacus. Now there had been a man. He'd taken on tough Roman legions and whipped their butts with gladiators turned soldier. That was impressive. He liked reading about Marten Kluge, too. The man hadn't accepted the status quo, but overturned the entire cart. The weirdest story was about Moses leading Egyptian-held slaves into Judea. Had Moses used psionics to part the Red Sea, or did God exist? It was an interesting question.

Am I a slave?

Cyrus learned his lessons with new determination. He tried to read up on inhibitors, but that was taboo, he'd found. There was so much to learn, to soak up and remember. He tried. He talked much differently than he had with his Milanese patois. But deep down he knew he was still the knife man of the slums.

The second memorable meeting with Jasper occurred three years and five days after his capture. He had been a wild thing down in Level 40. The NKV's arrival had saved his life. That was important to remember. But did that mean he had to spend the rest of his life in a gilded cage?

Cyrus sat cross-legged in a large, empty room with white walls. It had a permanent inhibitor switch in the ceiling, meaning a Special's psi-abilities worked in here. This was a practice room for mind shielding, mind bolts, and other psionic training. Through various spy devices, NKV agents carefully monitored the chamber, but it was a good place to sit and think.

A door opened and a short, overweight man in a shiny suit walked in.

Cyrus noticed, but he didn't raise an eyebrow or show any other sign of seeing the man.

Jasper approached, stopping several feet in front of Cyrus.

"Long time," Jasper said.

Cyrus grunted.

Jasper's eyes began to shine.

By now, Cyrus knew the signs and concentrated on his mind shield. He felt a presence intruding in his thoughts. It was an oily sensation as if smothering his skin. He ignored the feeling as he strengthened his shield, pushing the presence out.

"Not bad," Jasper said. "Try this."

Cyrus winced as the mental stab hit, and a groan escaped his lips. He loathed making any noise as a concession to pain, but he refused to panic because of the stronger attack. Instead, he concentrated until sweat slicked his forehead. Stubbornly, he fought against the encroachment in his mind.

"Say hello to me," Jasper said.

Without his willing it, Cyrus's right hand shot up, and he waved to Jasper.

"Stand up when your betters enter the room," Jasper said.

Cyrus almost stood, but he grinded his teeth together and his eyelids flickered. Sweat pooled on his face and a drip fell from his nose, then a second one.

"Bastard," Cyrus muttered.

"You have the will, but you need newer techniques. Not that it would keep me out for long, but you'd do better than you are now."

A third drop of sweat fell to the floor.

Jasper blinked, and his eyes returned to their normal color.

Gasping, partly slumping over, Cyrus felt the beginning of a pounding headache. This one was going to be bad, maybe the worst he'd ever had.

"Do you remember what we talked about last time?" Jasper asked.

Cyrus looked up. There were splotches in his vision. He had to concentrate in order to keep from vomiting. But there was no way he was going to show weakness before the telepath.

"Yeah, I remember."

"Don't worry about the NKV recording our conversation," Jasper said. "I've tampered with the equipment and with the monitors on duty. Everything you say here is between us."

Cyrus could have asked Jasper why he'd just attacked him mentally, but the answer was obvious to the man from the slums. It had been a pecking order fight to show who was stronger. Jasper wanted him to know how freaking strong of a telepath he was. Cyrus had a much better inkling now, and he would tread lightly or he would try to kill this monster when the man's guard was down.

"Do you want to stay a slave?" Jasper was asking.

"Of course not," Cyrus said.

Jasper grinned. "I did figure you right that day. Kid, you're a prize in so many ways. It's too bad you have such a weak talent. Anyway, I can use you just the same."

"*Use* me?"

"That's a bad choice of words," Jasper said. "We can help each other. Do you agree?"

"Sure."

"You didn't have to think about that a long time, did you?"

"Have you ever read Plutarch?"

"Who?" Jasper asked.

"He was a Roman historian who wrote about Spartacus."

Jasper shook his head.

"Spartacus led a slave revolt against the Romans."

"Ah," Jasper said. "I begin to perceive your point. How interesting. The slum dweller has turned into a history reader. I'm sure the NKV have taken note of your reading material, but . . ."

Jasper turned away. He nodded, to himself, it seemed. Facing Cyrus, he said, "The inhibitor appears impossible to overcome. Well, the best surgeons could remove it, but we're not going to get that chance. I've spoken with a clairvoyant who told me an interesting story. She said there might be a way to remove them, but we have to go far afield indeed to get it done. Are you interested?"

"Yes."

"It could mean incredible danger to us."

Cyrus shrugged.

"I'm not talking about petty dangers, but something worse than Level 40."

"That's supposed to scare me?"

Jasper glanced both ways before leaning toward him. He whispered, "It could involve aliens."

"Illegal citizens?" Cyrus asked.

"No. Aliens: intelligent nonhumans."

"I don't understand."

"I don't completely either," Jasper said. "She was vague. That's the nature of clairvoyants. In olden days, people called them 'seers' or 'oracles.' In any case, a Teleship is about to leave for a very long journey. You and I need to be on it."

"Are you talking about the voyage to New Eden?" Cyrus asked.

"You're a weak talent, so don't get your hopes up. But in several weeks the authorities are going to choose the Specials to shift the Teleship. I plan to be one of the chosen. I might be able to push for you. On this voyage, you can be certain they're going to ask for volunteers."

"Why wouldn't someone go?" Cyrus asked.

"Like I said, there's possibly real danger to this journey. Apparently, you've studied history. Surely, you read about the cyborgs of one hundred years ago."

Cyrus nodded.

"Would you go on the voyage if you thought you might run into cyborgs?" Jasper asked.

"If it means I can get rid of the inhibitor, yes."

"Practice your mind shield and sharpen your TK. In several weeks, I'll know more."

"Your clairvoyant spoke about aliens," Cyrus said. "Did she specifically mean cyborgs?"

"That's a clever question," Jasper said. "She doesn't know whether the aliens are cyborgs or something else. Now save your questions for later. The monitors are changing guard and they'll likely examine the damaged equipment. Remember, you agreed to help me. I'm going to hold you to that. So if you have any second thoughts, tell me now."

Cyrus had plenty of second thoughts, but he said, "I stand by my word."

Jasper smirked at him, nodded, and took his leave.

4

Nine days later, Cyrus entered the institute auditorium with twenty-seven other Specials. They put on plays in the auditorium, practiced making speeches here, and watched movies on Tuesday nights. There were three hundred padded seats. Cyrus had always wondered why they'd put in so many.

The twenty-seven Specials sat in the first three rows. In the back were the institute teachers, a few dignitaries, one of them being Jasper, and a dozen NKV agents. They'd come to hear one of the most famous men in the solar system.

Captain Nagasaki was going to tell them about the coming voyage to New Eden. He would lead the expedition to a star system two hundred and thirty light years away, the longest journey yet made by any human.

As the headmaster spoke to them from the podium, getting ready to introduce Captain Nagasaki, Cyrus thought about the voyage.

Several years ago, astronomers on Pluto had made an amazing discovery with the most powerful telescopes yet. Two hundred and thirty light years away was a star system named AS 412. According to the telescopes, it contained not one, but *two* Earth-like planets. Someone had coined the name "New Eden" for the system, and it stuck.

Premier Lang's propagandists had gotten busy with the news. Cyrus had heard it said Lang wanted a symbol to unite humanity under his rule. What could be better than a grand adventure to excite the masses?

At New Eden, the propagandists said, mankind could start over in perfect harmony. Even better, anyone could go. People had to pitch in and do their part. If they did, they might win an emigrant ticket, leaving Old Sol to start afresh in New Eden. Teleship *Discovery* would lead the way and it would set down the first colony. These first colonists would enter stasis tubes, awaking once they reached New Eden. There, humanity would to do things right this time.

From what Cyrus had read, the project had electrified humanity. People from Neptune to Mercury filled out personal data forms, bought emigrant lottery tickets, and argued about the right form of government for this pristine environment. This wouldn't be habitat living or underground dwelling, but new Earths, humanity-friendly worlds to fill.

"Let us warmly welcome Captain Nagasaki," the headmaster said.

Cyrus clapped with the others, and he noticed the teachers in back clapping vigorously.

Captain Nagasaki strode onto stage and shook the headmaster's hand. Nagasaki was short and slender, with silver hair under a trim cap. He wore the blue uniform of the Solar Space Service. A single Orion Star adorned his jacket. He'd won the star for leading the first voyage to Epsilon Eridani over thirty years ago and helping set up the colony base there.

After the Cyborg War, humanity had begun sending sleeper ships to the nearest star systems, beginning the expansion of man. There were outposts at Alpha Centauri, Tau Ceti, and Epsilon Eridani. The colonists lived in habitats circling each system's planets as they float-mined the gas giants of deuterium. Before shift technology, that meant each colonist had been effectively cut off from the mother system. A visit by a replenishing ship every three to five years was the best any of them could hope for.

Like all interstellar voyages before discontinuity windows and Teleships, Nagasaki had made his famous trip the old-fashioned way, under the terrible constraints of Einsteinian physics. His sleeper ship *Argonaut* had accelerated at a constant one G the first leg of the journey up to near light speed. Then it coasted until the end of the trip and decelerated.

Epsilon Eridani was ten light years from Sol. Because of relativistic time dilation, the trip had only lasted five years for the captain and his crew. Nagasaki had spent several years at Epsilon Eridani as they'd constructed the colony's lone habitat. Then he'd returned to Sol to a hero's welcome, twenty-some years after he'd left but only eleven years older.

Like the other Specials attending today's meeting, Cyrus had read the man's bio. Captain Nagasaki understood about privation, risks, and waiting. The man's patience and self control was legendary—as was his iron will. It had made him the perfect candidate to lead a decade-long voyage.

From the podium, Captain Nagasaki eyed them. He seemed stern, perhaps a little remote. But what he possessed in abundance was gravity, presence, or personal force. He would lead the journey to New Eden. And it was said his vote had weight in choosing the right Specials.

He greeted them in a deep voice and spoke in a slow and measured manner. He talked about duty, about hardship and danger. Then he talked about Teleship *Discovery*.

A holoimage appeared on stage behind the captain and Nagasaki spoke about the ship.

In many ways, the Teleship was like an old style battleship from the Cyborg War of over a hundred years ago. Combat ships had used particle shielding then, hundreds of meters of thick rock to withstand enemy lasers or nuclear-tipped missiles. *Discovery* didn't have particle shielding, but looked like any meteor drifting in space, except the surface lacked mountains or valleys. The surface was uniform and made of asteroidal rock, with dust where a man could leave his boot prints if he walked upon it. Dotted on the surface were combat domes with collapsium armor. In the domes were laser cannons and missile sites, insuring the Teleship a fighting chance against any comers.

Far below the shielding minerals of the Teleship were gigantic AIs, the fusion engines, and acres of stasis tubes for the sleepers. Over fifty thousand individuals would journey to the New Eden system. Below stasis was the core structure of life support for *Discovery*'s crew: that would be 107 men and women.

Nagasaki paused, sipping from a glass of water. He put the glass away, eyed them anew, and gripped the sides of the podium.

"Let me explain something of my journey to Epsilon Eridani, as it dovetails into the primary reason for my visit with you today. Over thirty years ago, my sleeper ship *Argonaut* accelerated out of Sol at one G as it built up to near light speed. We call that 'NLS.' Believe me, the acceleration was the easiest part of the journey. The long coast was more tedious, the many years of weightlessness."

Cyrus noticed the captain's fingers tightening their grip on the podium. Nagasaki's face had looked stern before. Now it appeared like flint.

"The long journey proved tedious, as I've said, but that was nothing compared to our growing fear of cyborgs. You have seen vids of them, horror shows. I happen to know more than most concerning cyborgs because I am the great-great grandson of Circe of Old Jupiter. You've certainly read the histories of that time. Circe destroyed the cyborgs' proto-Teleship at the end of the Cyborg War."

Nagasaki released the podium. "I'm not here to talk about the war, but its aftermath. The terrible truth of the Cyborg War that few people realize is that some cyborgs *must* have escaped the solar system. Circe destroyed a proto-Teleship, but there might have been a second and a third. We don't know that, but it would be folly to believe it impossible. Even if the cyborgs lacked Teleships, surely some of them fled in NLS vessels.

"My crew and I in *Argonaut* didn't know about proto-Teleships during our trip to Epsilon Eridani, but we became convinced that some cyborgs had survived the war. If that was true, we argued among ourselves, perhaps they had headed for the nearest star systems and begun to rebuild.

"I admit that the months of deceleration into Epsilon Eridani were the worst of my life. As we slowed, I launched five probes ahead of us. They found no sign of cyborgs. Even so, once *Argonaut* reached the system, we inched from place to place, searching, watching, and waiting for the terrible surprise that would inform us cyborgs attacked the ship."

Nagasaki smiled. It looked strange on his remote face. "The wonder of the trip was that no cyborgs appeared. Yet I've asked myself many times since returning to Sol and finding these marvelous Teleships. What if the cyborgs had built a second proto-Teleship a hundred years ago? If they had, they might have escaped far from Sol, to rebuild in the stars, forging an invincible empire of machine-man melds.

"That brings me to a grim topic. I want each of you to consider this carefully. First, it is within the realm of the possible that cyborgs await us at AS 412. That is why *Discovery* goes armed.

"Now, some of you surely are saying to yourself, the astronomers on Pluto didn't find any evidence of advanced civilization. No. They wouldn't have because it is impossible. If the cyborgs fled Sol a hundred years ago and reached AS 412 in a Teleship soon thereafter, how could we know? The astronomers used *telescopes* to search AS 412. Obviously, they saw images two hundred and thirty years old, because that's how long light from there took to reach the solar system. We can't launch probes to look for us, because probes only travel at NLS and would take over two hundred and thirty years to arrive. At best, the probes could beam a message back at light speed, adding another two hundred and thirty years. Therefore, to find out now—in the present—if cyborgs have used AS 412, we have to go in a Teleship and see for ourselves.

"The chances are good the cyborgs never went there—if indeed they even built another proto-Teleship. But they could be there, and that's important to consider. Cyborgs take humans and strip them of humanity to create machine-man melds. It is a terrible fate. We go there for two reasons, the first greater than the second. The first reason is to colonize two beautiful worlds. The second reason is to see if mankind's grimmest foe has indeed survived and rebuilt a technological base there.

"This will be the voyage of a lifetime, and it could prove to be the battle of a lifetime, too. Naturally, few consider the prospect of meeting cyborgs in what appears a pristine system. I urge you to agree to join this voyage only if you're willing to face the possibility of cyborgs. We need stout hearts and powerful Specials on this trip, and we will carry a most precious cargo: fifty thousand of Sol's bravest people."

Captain Nagasaki scanned the crowd. "Now, your headmaster was kind enough to say this was a privilege for him and his students to hear me speak in person. It is very much a privilege for me to be here. I would like to field any questions you might have."

Hands rose immediately, and Specials began to question the great captain. Cyrus was content to listen.

He found it interesting that Nagasaki had listed only two possibilities upon reaching New Eden: one, that they would find a pristine star system with two untouched, Earth-like planets and two, they would find cyborgs. There was a third possibility: that they might meet aliens other than cyborgs. Jasper said these aliens might help rid them of the inhibitors. Would it be traitorous to humanity for he and Jasper to seek alien help like that?

What would Spartacus have done? Would the former gladiator have accepted alien help against the Roman legions? Cyrus nodded. Of course Spartacus would have accepted help.

There was a gnawing doubt, though. Cyrus had learned the hard way that nothing came free. There was always a cost—always. If aliens existed in New Eden who could help them get rid of the inhibitors, what would the aliens demand as payment?

It was a question worth some serious consideration.

5

The boy Klane had turned into a brooding young man of the Tash-Toi. He had looked upon the Mountain that was a Machine one other time. He had been in the company of the seeker then too.

Klane wasn't like others of the clan. He was curious about nearly everything. Why couldn't they fashion iron knives for themselves? The hetman had one and so did the champion Cletus. Those knives were heirlooms, long ago stolen from demons. If demons made them, why couldn't a flint smith? Why did the gat travel north for the winter and how exactly did its wings allow it to fly in the air?

The young men Klane's age spoke about stalking game animals, women, and raiding other clans. Otherwise, they were a dour lot unless drunk. While drunk, any warrior could be dangerously foul or very merry. There was no telling which, although Klane constantly sought for a clue.

The young men Klane's age were similar to each other. They were brown-skinned, dark-haired and uniformly thick with muscles. They carried flint knives, bone-tipped spears, and wore the cured skin or leather of the vargr. Each could run many miles without panting or gasping. Their lungs had no trouble breathing the upland desert air. Nor did they bleed easily when cut by sharp rocks.

Klane had pasty white skin and was nearly as thin as the seeker. He gasped if he ran too hard and his lungs lacked staying power. Worse, the cold air forced him to bundle up like a pregnant woman. Otherwise, his teeth chattered until his jaws and teeth ached.

It made him sick with grief being so weak. In his younger years, he had fought and wrestled with the others his age. He'd even won a few matches by clouting a stronger boy with a rock or using a cunning trick taught him by the seeker.

None of the warriors included him in the wrestling matches these days. In the matches, the warriors decided who would eat the choice meat or gain the charm of a viable female. The hetman had forbidden Klane from carrying a spear or shield. He was allowed a flint knife, but only to help him fashion bark lanterns or eat his portion of food.

There were only two other choices now for Klane, since the warriors had excluded him from their company. He could leave as an outcast, game for the hunters. Or he could become the seeker's journeyman.

After a year of attempting to fashion a junction-stone, polishing, oiling, and empowering it, he'd failed to make any stone work. It meant he could never be a seeker. Without junction-stones . . .

"I am a failure," he told the seeker.

The old man sat cross-legged before his hide tent. The winds howled across the upper plateau, blowing bits of red sand. In the distance, a gat soared in the air. The seeker wore vargr leather and seemed unaffected by the cold. The moon was high in the sky today, filling half of it with its bright, banded colors.

Klane crouched before the seeker. He was wrapped in thick furs and wore a woolen hat like a woman. He would have preferred to sit near a fire, but the warriors would have howled in laughter at him because of his garments and he could not bear it.

"Why can't I fashion a junction-stone?" Klane asked.

"Let me see yours."

Klane dug in his furs to his secret place. He took out a bark container, twisting it until he withdrew a bolt of cloth. It was damp with vargr oil. He unwrapped the cloth and produced a small black stone. It was smooth like an egg and wet with the oil.

"May I touch it?" the seeker asked.

Klane hesitated, then he thrust his hand forward.

With a single finger, the old man touched the stone. He didn't flinch, nor did his arm wither. Klane's carefully worked curses were powerless. What made it unbearable was watching the seeker. The old man's lips stretched into a smile.

Angrily, Klane withdrew the stone. He almost hurled the junction-stone from him. Instead, he wrapped it, put it in the container, and shoved it back into his secret place.

"I sense you're upset," the seeker said.

"You mocked my stone," Klane muttered.

"You're a foolish apprentice. But that is the way of young men. What troubles me is that you're stupid, too."

Klane's eyes narrowed. Although he had learned to hide it, he hated insults.

"Do you wish to challenge me?" the seeker asked.

"You're the only friend I have."

"Ah, poor, lonely Klane, he sulks in his furs and wishes he could be powerful like a warrior. He never once realizes that he has far more potential than any of them."

"Your mockery stings, Seeker."

"And your continued sulking has begun to weary me. Go," the old man said, with a wave of his stick-like fingers.

"Go where?"

"Anywhere but near me," the seeker replied.

Klane hunched his shoulders. He hated mockery, having endured it his entire life. He'd become used to the young warriors insulting him. Receiving this from the seeker . . .

"Why did you smile when touching my stone?"

"What?" the old man said. "You're asking me an intelligent question? Are you feeling feverish?"

"I am your journeyman, Seeker."

"Do you remember the Mountain that is a Machine?"

"I dream of it all the time."

"I'm not surprised. You must pack . . . hmm, three of your best lanterns. Then you must gather jerky for a trek."

"We're going to the mountain?"

"No. We're going under it."

"When?" asked Klane.

The seeker struggled to his feet and turned to his small tent. "We'll leave as soon as you've gathered the needed items. Now hurry before I change my mind."

||||||||||

The trek took six days of struggle and two of scaling downward toward the Valley of the Demons. The roar of the Mountain that was a Machine became a constant thunder. The billowing vapors roiling skyward amazed Klane every time he looked at the smokestacks sticking out of the mile's long terraforming building.

Finally, the seeker showed him a natural entrance to a cave under the Great Machine. It was a dark hole, with coral grass sprouting from the rocks around it. The place was colder here than on the plateau and water dripped from the rocks and boulders.

As the sun sank below the jagged range, the two squeezed through the opening. Inside, the cave seemed vast and ancient, full of terrible wonder.

"Give me a lantern," the seeker said.

Klane removed one of the bark lanterns from his pack, handing it to the old man.

The seeker moved his hand across his belt, and he held a blue junction-stone. He rubbed the stone and whispered in the High Speech. Then he pointed at the lantern and a flame burst into existence upon the oil-soaked wick.

"Spontaneous combustion," the seeker told Klane, naming the spell. "Now, you must follow me as I try to remember the path."

"You've been here before?" Klane asked.

"That is a foolish question, as I've already implied I have been."

Klane nodded, too awed at this place to feel bad at the reprimand.

For a time they journeyed deeper into the cavern. A faint thrum began and increased the farther they went. The seeker stopped where the thrum was loudest and he spoke a word.

The flickering light in the lantern increased until Klane sucked in his breath in astonishment. He spied huge columns of polished metal. The columns were five times the thickness of the hetman, the biggest warrior of Clan

Tash-Toi. Klane noticed that the columns were sunk into rock. Perhaps as interesting, they were etched triangles that went up and down the columns in strict rows.

"Is this part of the terraforming machine?" Klane asked.

"That is a prudent question, and the answer is no. This is older by a millennium. In fact, I believe it is older than the demons."

"Why is it near the Great Machine?"

"I don't know."

"What is the purpose of the columns?"

"Purposes are important. A seeker should attempt to discover each thing's use. What the columns did, I don't know. What they do for me . . . yes, I do know that."

"What do they do for you?"

"Provide magical power," the seeker whispered.

Klane wrenched his gaze from the metal columns, staring at the old man.

"Squat, young journeyman. Open your mind to the singing gods. Listen to their words and let their power flow through you."

"Like a junction-stone?" Klane asked.

The seeker nodded.

Klane sat on a cold rock, closed his eyes, and let his chin touch his chest. He opened his mind and suddenly he felt it. To Klane, it was like the time Grad had thrown him into an icy stream during the spring flood. The singing gods—if that's what they were—swept him along in a fierce mental current. Klane struggled, his mind seemingly gurgling for air. A whisper from the seeker's mind touched him, urging him to relax, to bob along. Klane dampened his fear, trying to feel what occurred. He heard a soft moaning like a mother for her lost child. He tried to decipher the god words, but could not.

"Journeyman!"

Vaguely, Klane felt someone shaking him. His teeth rattled. He unglued his eyes and turned to the seeker.

"You've finally come back," the old man said. "Did you hear the gods?"

"I think so."

The old man grinned. "Your lantern has burned out while you've listened. I had to use another."

Klane was shocked.

"Carry us out," the seeker ordered.

"What?"

"Do it, Klane. Use the power you've collected."

Klane heard a strain in the old man's voice. The buzzing in his head still made him groggy.

"Think it," the seeker whispered.

Klane thought about the entrance, the coral grass around it. He blanked out, and there was a ripping sound and the feeling of rushing air. He swayed, opened his eyes, and found himself standing before the cave entrance.

It was a miracle, and he stared at the opening until he felt something wet on his lip. He wiped it and found red—blood—on his skin. He had a nosebleed.

"What happened?" Klane whispered. "How did we get here?"

"When you're older, I will explain it. Until then, we will never speak of it again."

"Can I fashion a junction-stone now?" Klane asked.

"Do you believe you can?"

Klane thought about it. "Yes," he said.

"There is your answer," the seeker said. "Come. It is time to begin the journey home."

6

Cyrus ran along a road in the hot sun. It was the middle of the afternoon, almost one hundred degrees. He wore shorts and running shoes, and his lean, steely-muscled torso glistened in the light.

He liked running in the heat of the day. It made him sweat. Afterward, he drank glass after glass of cool lemonade. He would sit then and totally relax. He could never have done this in the slums. He had run often then, but from danger, from Red Blades, usually.

He liked being fit, strong, and he liked the freedom of the institute. He liked the outdoors most of all. Ninety-nine percent of the people on Earth lived underground. What a hideous existence. Soon, though, this freedom, this spaciousness of living on an empty Mediterranean island would end. He would begin his life of service powering the DW shift technology. He would live on ships, inside steel corridors likely for the rest of his active life. The idea of it made him squirm, and it lengthened his stride.

No. He couldn't accept that. Yes, he was grateful for the rescue from a wretched life in the slums of Level 40. He might have gained rank in the Latin Kings—if he had survived the warehouse with the Red Blades. Okay. He needed to pay society back for what the NKV had done for him. He wasn't an ingrate, and he understood carrying his weight. He wouldn't try to get a free ride, especially as he did have a talent few possessed.

Did that mean he must live in steel corridors the rest of life? Must he be a slave to the state because of his rescue? They had altered his brain so they could switch him on and off like a machine. That had turned him into property, chattel. No one had a right to do that, especially not in the high-handed manner it had been done to him.

No one had asked for his permission. Did the state have a right to his body because he could do a certain thing?

What would Spartacus have said?

Cyrus Gant laughed as he ran. It was a wild laugh, full of fight and vigor. The state did not come first. A man came first. He lived in the state with others, and they agreed to work together. That's what freedom meant. Once the state forced him to do a thing, it became tyranny.

Cyrus wiped sweat from his forehead. These were big words, and he wouldn't have thought them only a few years ago. The state had given him an education. That was worth money. He would work for the state and pay them back so he owed them nothing.

If he could, he'd go to New Eden. But he had no plans to come back to Earth. He wanted a wife, kids, and to raise a family in the wilds of a new planet. He would emigrate and help build a better society. He would—

Cyrus shook his head, flinging sweat from his face. A cart was parked under a tree in the shade. Jasper sat in the cart, fanning himself with his flattish hat.

Cyrus's feet thudded on the hard ground, and he sprinted to the small fat man, stopping in the shade with him.

"Thirsty?" Jasper asked.

Cyrus nodded.

Jasper tossed him a bottled water.

Cyrus guzzled it, and he put his hands on his hips as he panted. The sweat poured down his body and made his socks and ankles wet.

"Are you punishing yourself?" Jasper asked.

"Yeah. That's it."

From the twist of his face, Jasper seemed to switch mental gears. "There's trouble and I've run into a snag. Are you alert enough to understand what I'm saying, or do you need more time to rest?"

"Go ahead, talk."

"You should run when it's cooler."

"That's the snag?"

"I know," Jasper said. "You're a tough guy. I've known many tough guys before your time. I took care of every one of them using this," he said, tapping his head.

"Zeus making his rounds, huh?" Cyrus said. "You were out and about seeing how we mere mortals were doing?"

"You're like a man who has just come into millions of credits. But instead of money, you got some education. Now you like showing it off."

"What's the snag again?" Cyrus asked.

"All this summertime heat must be baking your brains. Do you remember who I am? Once we get rid of the inhibitors, you're going to want to walk softly around me."

Cyrus wanted to respond with a cool comeback, but Jasper had a point. Cyrus practiced mind shields all the time now because he didn't want a repeat of last time.

"I'm walking softly," Cyrus said.

Jasper's eyes narrowed, until maybe he saw that Cyrus wasn't joking. "You're all right, kid. You have . . . what do they call it?"

"Street smarts?"

"There you go," Jasper said. "I only had to show you once what I could do and you remember. I like that. Anyway, the snag is this: You have to pass Argon."

"Who?"

"Argon is one of Premier Lang's main NKV officers. He's coming along as the Teleship's chief monitor."

"Why do we need monitors? Isn't everyone in the crew vetted and loyal to Lang?"

"I'm surprised *you* need to ask that," Jasper said. "No, Lang is the most suspicious person who ever lived. Sure, the crew is vetted and each of them has a high loyalty rating. But that doesn't satisfy our Premier. He has monitors on every military vessel. How much did you study about the Cyborg War?"

"A little," Cyrus said.

"One hundred years ago, Social Unity put commissars in most of their war vessels. Each commissar had secret police power. He watched the crew for devotion to duty and searched for those who deviated from correct thought."

"Oh, you mean Thought Police," Cyrus said.

"That's almost right. The monitors help keep the military in cheek. Giving men guns and warships makes them dangerous. Premier Lang demands obedience from the military. The monitors or commissars are simply another layer of security."

"Okay. Got it," Cyrus said.

"Argon is the chief monitor for the voyage. To make it as shifter, you need his approval and Captain Nagasaki's. Of the two, Argon's is more important."

"Why is any of that a snag?" Cyrus asked.

"Chief Monitor Argon isn't like a normal man. He has Highborn genes."

"You mean like the Highborn of the Cyborg War?"

"Right," Jasper said.

Cyrus recalled some of what he'd read about the Highborn. A little over a hundred years ago, Social Unity had ruled the Inner Planets and had wished to conquer the rest of the solar system. They'd wanted shock troops. Scientists had genetically manipulated human embryos. The result had been superior combat soldiers, nine feet tall, with speeded reflexes and heightened intelligence. Over two million genetic soldiers had been created. They had looked around, seen their superiority, and decided they should rule. So they had rebelled and come within inches of defeating everyone. Different scientists had made cyborgs to combat the Highborn. After the Cyborg War, the Highborn of that era had merged their chromosomes back into the gene pool.

"Argon is like an echo of his Highborn ancestors," Jasper said. "He's only seven feet tall instead of nine. But he's very smart and ruthless in his tasks. You need to be careful around him."

"You mean not give away our plan," Cyrus said.

"Think of him as the worst Latin King you knew."

"You mean the most dangerous," Cyrus said.

"What?" Jasper asked.

"The worst Latin King would be a fool or a weakling. The most dangerous were the best."

"Keep it up, kid, and remember that I have a long memory." Jasper started his cart. "Likely, he'll interview you today. I'd give you a ride back, but I don't want them to see we're friends."

"Is that what we are?"

Jasper stared at Cyrus. Without another word, the telepath turned onto the road and drove away, his rubber wheels making a hissing noise on the cement.

Cyrus started back for the institute. Possible aliens, maybe cyborgs, and now a Highborn chief monitor, or the echo of one. This was going to be a dangerous trip. But his study of Spartacus showed him that gaining freedom was worth any risk. It had cost Spartacus a brutal death by crucifixion. Yet for a time, the ex-gladiator had lived as a free man.

Cyrus kept running, enduring as the hot air burned down his throat. He had to get ready for anything and take his chance when the time came. The slums had taught him that when you got your chance, you took it with both hands. That's exactly what he planned to do this trip.

|||||||||||

Cyrus's first thought was that Argon was too big for the Teleship and its narrow corridors. The man was nearly seven feet tall. Jasper had told him the truth about that. What the telepath had failed to mention was Argon's girth. The chief monitor was built like a wrestler and his movements betrayed quick reflexes.

Argon wore a black NKV uniform that stretched at his muscled neck. The fabric was shiny there, likely from constantly rubbing at the skin. Argon had flat cheekbones and the broad features of the historical Highborn, with something of their wild intensity radiating from him.

"Cyrus Gant," Argon said from his table. "Come in. Sit."

Cyrus entered the small cell. He'd showered, eaten, and taken a nap. One of the teachers had escorted him into the building and down a set of stairs. They met in the basement, and the door now closed behind Cyrus.

Argon watched him, and the chief monitor had predatory eyes. The gaze seemed to say that he judged Cyrus and would look for missteps or incongruities of behavior. It was like stepping back in time. This man could have ruled the Latin Kings.

Warily, Cyrus sat down. He didn't like how Argon towered over him. The small room made everything worse.

Argon glanced at an e-reader. "According to this, you've led an interesting life."

Cyrus said nothing. Argon reminded him too much of the cops he'd met in Level 40. Arrogance and authority seemed to ooze from the chief monitor's pores.

In that moment, Cyrus decided he didn't have a chance with Argon. He could cow down to the cop and try to bluff his way through, or he could tell the man the truth. Why not—he was supposed to be a Special now, an untouchable.

"You read I came from the slums?" Cyrus asked.

Argon nodded.

"I was a Latin King," Cyrus said, "an illegal gang member. I started out as a scrawny kid with nothing, but even scrawny kids have to eat."

"You could have eaten at the orphanage, but you ran away."

"You ever been raised in an orphanage?" Cyrus asked.

"I'll ask the questions," Argon told him.

"Just saying, you know. It's not like you think. We were defenseless kids with nothing but our pure bodies. The headmaster sold us to perverts, who liked to do nasty, vile things. Yeah, I ran away. If I could now, I'd go back and kill every headmaster that sold a kid and I'd do the same to the perverts."

The information did nothing to Argon's manner. He continued to watch and study. He said, "You're a Special. You have a greater purpose now."

"You're missing my point. I had to eat and I wasn't going to sell myself to pervs. So I ran Dust for the Latin Kings. Later, I became a foot soldier, a fighter. The cops didn't like us." Cyrus shrugged. "You remind me of them cops."

"You're not in the slums anymore."

"That's right," Cyrus said.

"So why talk as if you belong there?"

"Seeing you reminds me of the old days," Cyrus said.

"What do you think about Premier Lang?"

Cyrus understood then that *they* monitored the interview: his pulse rate, breathing speed, eye movement and other bodily functions. Speaking the truth was his best bet because they'd likely know when he lied. He'd already started out telling the truth, so he might as well continue.

"I don't think about him much," Cyrus said.

"Aren't you grateful for what he did for you?"

A trace of a smile appeared on Cyrus's face. "Lang didn't do anything for me. He passed some laws because the world needs Specials. So here I am. If I didn't have any talent, I'd still be in Level 40."

"Do you hate Premier Lang?"

"No."

"Do you wish him dead?"

"No."

"Are you in league with any organization that plots his overthrow?"

"No."

"Are you willing to endure hardship to reach New Eden?"

"Yes."

"Do you have any ulterior motives for volunteering?"

"Yes," Cyrus said.

"What are they?"

"I plan to skip ship and stay on one of the planets. I'll find a wife and start a family."

Argon paused, and those intense eyes watched him closely. He put down the e-reader and continued to study Cyrus. Something approaching a smile stretched the chief monitor's lips.

"I will squash any mutiny," Argon said. "I will obliterate those who plot against Premier Lang. You don't lie, which is refreshing. Continue to think of me as a cop, and you will do well, Special. You may go."

"No more questions?"

"You have passed my test. I can work with you."

Cyrus blinked once, wondering why Argon didn't ask other questions. Instead of thinking about it, he got up, found the door unlocked, and walked down the hall to the waiting teacher. Honesty had worked. How novel.

PART II: VOYAGE

1

For Cyrus, life aboard Teleship *Discovery* settled into an intense schedule of work, training, and enduring increasing suspicion from the monitors and shift crew.

He had his own room. That was good. Many of the crew and all the space marines slept in "shelves" that were akin to coffins. He couldn't have taken that and often dreamed of the monitors forcing him into one, closing it, and locking him in. They would talk to him then, telling him he'd stay in there for the duration of the mission. Those sleeping quarters didn't allow a man to sit up. It would have driven him mad.

In the waking world, Cyrus spent far too much time in his room, watching the screen showing the expansive verandas of Earth. He had his favorite: it showed an eagle soaring over the Kiev Sector steppes. Otherwise, he exercised his talents with the other Specials in the training chamber.

There were four Specials aboard *Discovery*: Venice, Jasper, Roxie, and Cyrus. Venice could shift 8.3 light years, a phenomenal distance. Jasper could shift 2.1, Roxie 1.7, and Cyrus a mere 0.8 light years. The differences were extraordinary as Venice could shift four times as far as Jasper. It meant Venice received the best treatment in terms of privilege and living space.

The four of them often trained in close proximity. Then it became clear that Venice's better treatment bothered Jasper, although the Earth's best telepath tried to hide it.

The weeks merged into months and the great colonizing vessel neared the two hundred light year mark. Cyrus's dreams worsened the closer they approached the New Eden system. He asked the others about their dreams, although he asked them carefully and only in the training chamber. The security over them meant constant surveillance.

The shift crew and the monitors in particular grew increasingly wary around them. Because they were humans instead of machinery, the four Specials were the most volatile cogs in the Teleship. Without their telekinetic and clairvoyant abilities, *Discovery* would have to use direct thrust to build up velocity to go from A to Z. The Teleship lacked the needed fuel to build up to near light speed. As the vessel approached the two hundred light year mark from Sol, that became an ominous thought for the Normals. If something happened to all four Specials, it would strand the ship, crew, and sleeping colonists out here for the rest of their lives.

"They should worship us," Jasper told Cyrus. "Instead, they treat as plague victims, as freaks and mutants. Why else do they watch us so carefully?"

"Normals always fear what's more powerful than them," Venice said. "Get over it, already."

"She can talk," Jasper whispered to Cyrus later. "They treat her better than they treat the three of us."

"She can shift four times farther," Cyrus said.

"Does that make her a superstar?"

"Yes."

That fact ate at the telepath, but Venice's superiority didn't bother Cyrus. He was the lowest talent among them and he'd lived the most normal life—normal meaning that regular people had treated him as an ordinary person. Venice, Jasper, and Roxie had much different life stories, filled with alienation, at least before the creation of Psi-Force. Before the search for the psi-able, the Normals around the other three had treated each of them . . . well, like mutants or freaks.

In Cyrus's opinion, his near normality made him the most balanced of the four. He wanted to maintain that. With permission from Chief Monitor Argon, Cyrus had trained with the marines. At first, the marines treated him with such delicacy that it had hardly been enjoyable. He tried to get them to relax around him, and it was slowly having an effect.

It was different with everyone else. The worst were the shift crew and monitors. They treated the four of them like radioactive nuclear material. There were heavy safeguards in place against them and constant surveillance. The Normals needed their talents, but the telekinesis, telepathy, and clairvoyance frightened them. Ninety percent of the time, the inhibitors in Venice, Jasper, Roxie, and Cyrus remained switched to talent-off mode. In the shift tube and while watched through cameras in the training chamber the inhibitors were switched to talent-on mode.

I'm literally a cog in a machine, Cyrus thought. *I'm a slave, dragged here, dragged there, and forced to do my masters' bidding.*

He didn't hate the Normals, but he wasn't going to accept this treatment forever. He needed to be free. He wanted to breathe something other than canned air. Now, with the worsening dreams and remembering Jasper's claim of nonhumans in New Eden who would help them, Cyrus started becoming paranoid. There was a BAD THING approaching. He didn't know that for a certainty, but the feeling in his gut was building up, pointing in that direction.

Then in the training chamber, he discovered he wasn't the only one feeling this.

|||||||||||

Three of them were in the training chamber. It was a spacious room as such things went aboard the Teleship. Cyrus sat at a table across from Venice. There were three other tables and six chairs altogether. One wall showed a forest scene from Earth, complete with rustling oaks and running squirrels.

Sometimes, during one G acceleration, Cyrus paced the length of the room: fourteen strides. He'd turn around and walk the other way, going back and forth until one of the others told him to stop.

Today, the vessel and therefore the training chamber lacked the one G of pseudogravity. They were weightlessness and they would float if they pushed off the chairs. Each table and chair was anchored to the Velcro-covered floor. Each of them wore shoes that stuck to the Velcro.

Cyrus had his elbows on a table, with his face pushed against his fingers. He practiced a mind shield as Venice sat across from him and mentally attacked him.

She had long, dark hair and extraordinarily beautiful features, with a small nose and perfect mouth. The woman had everything: fame, beauty, and the greatest shifting ability among humanity. She wore a silver skin-suit, which only heightened her marvelous shape.

Can you hear me? Venice asked, using her limited telepathy instead of speech.

Cyrus opened his eyes and stared at her. She sat back in her chair, watching him.

With a forefinger, she swept a strand of hair out of one of her eyes. She smiled at him.

He grinned and opened his mouth to tell her that he'd heard the thought. She shook her head, and she tapped her temple.

Cyrus stared at her.

Think your answer as hard as you can, she told him via telepathy. *Try to project. If you can't project telepathically, I should be able to pick up your thoughts.*

There was a *rip-rip* sound as Jasper walked from his table to theirs. He pulled up a chair and set in onto the Velcro. He wore a shiny suit as he usually did, with a flattish hat covering his baldness.

What's this about? Jasper asked through telepathy.

Venice frowned at him. *I wasn't talking to you.*

I heard the urgency in your message, Jasper said. *By the way, if we just sit here and stare at each other, the monitors watching the cameras will know what's going on.*

"You must try harder," Venice told Cyrus. "I'm hurting you with my attacks. You have to strengthen your shield like this."

Cyrus wants to know what's wrong, Jasper said.

Why can't I read his thoughts? Venice asked.

Jasper shrugged, making his shiny suit crinkle.

It was obvious to Cyrus the man was proud of his superior telepathic ability. He wondered for a moment if Jasper was shielding his thoughts from Venice.

No, Jasper said. *She's simply not good enough at telepathy.*

Is he hearing me? Venice asked.

Cyrus nodded, but he said, "Is that how I should block?"

"Yes," Venice said. *Listen*, she thought, *I have to tell you what happened last shift.*

The shift crew had discovered something new concerning Specials. Because of the stress of endless shifting, each Special needed progressively more rest time before they could create a discontinuity window again. While Jasper, Roxie, and Cyrus needed more rest, Venice continued to make DWs right on schedule. It meant she did the bulk of the shifting and was always in the tele-chamber.

What happened? Jasper asked.

I felt an alien presence from out there, Venice said. *I searched for it and in time, the mental signal seemed to come from the New Eden system.*

Seemed? Jasper asked.

Cyrus felt the man's excitement. Here was verification of aliens at New Eden.

It was difficult for me to pinpoint the exact location from where the alien mind broadcasted, Venice said, *but I definitely felt his mind. It happened during the shift. No, that's not exactly right. It happened when the tele-ring came on.*

The tele-ring circled the Teleship without touching it. It was like Saturn's rings. The tele-ring was the key mechanism—with a Special's help—that created a discontinuity window.

Did the alien say anything to you? Jasper asked.

I think he was surprised to contact me. Well, he didn't contact me exactly. I felt his mind and I'm sure he felt mine. Venice stared at each of them in turn. *I'm sure the mind was hostile.*

What's your reasoning? Jasper asked.

Venice bit her lower lip. *Several days ago, I fell asleep in here, in the training chamber. My inhibitor was off is what I'm trying to say. I had a clairvoyant dream. In the dream, something watched me from behind a glass partition. It was an indistinct alien, making notes on a slate, absorbed with heightened interest as it observed me. The digits making the notes were harder than flesh, but I couldn't see the creature. Then my dream became horrifying. I lay on a table.* Things *cut me open, removed organs, and inserted something vile into me. Just as I awoke, I heard crackling sounds. Then it felt as if hot needles poked into my neck at the apex of my spine.*

"Cyborgs," Cyrus whispered.

"Cyborgs aren't telepathic," Jasper whispered. He looked at Venice. "What do you think they were?"

"I don't know," she said. *What should we do?*

Clarify that, Jasper said.

We should tell the shift crew.

Jasper glanced at Cyrus. It caused Venice to frown.

What are you two hiding? she asked.

Jasper gave her an oily smile. Cyrus didn't know how that would assure anyone. *We have a bet about cyborgs. Cyrus is certain they're at New Eden. He wants to go home because of it.*

I don't want to go to New Eden if cyborgs are waiting for us, Venice said.

I don't either, Jasper said. *Let me try to find this mind.*

Will you try to do that during a shift? Venice asked.

I think I know what's happening, Jasper said. *The tele-ring must expand your reach even farther than it does for creating a discontinuity window. Since you're the most powerful Special, you felt this mind first. Maybe by next shift I can sense it, too.*

Cyrus waited for Venice to call Jasper a liar. The man would never call anyone more powerful than him unless he was trying to hide something. Didn't she understand that? The two kept communicating. It showed Cyrus she must be truly worried about her dream and worried about the brushing mind contact with an unknown alien.

In the end, Jasper convinced Venice to wait and let him contact the alien for confirmation.

Cyrus hesitated to say anything, wondering how accurate Venice's clairvoyant dreams usually were. In the end, he went along with the plan. It ended up being the worst decision of his life.

2

Jasper seethed inwardly. Venice had felt the aliens before him. It was inconceivable that should occur. He was the greatest telepath. She could shift farther, but that was due to her clairvoyance, an otherwise dubious psi-talent.

He went through the procedures as he floated in the shift tank, a cylinder filled with a watery gel solution. He wore a slick-suit, a breathing mask, and goggles. He'd already shut his eyes and linked with Socrates, the main AI in the system.

Going through rote actions, Jasper soon succumbed to the AI-Special union. Around him in the cylinder, the shift crew worked at their stations in the tele-chamber. They monitored him, AI Socrates, and the ship.

Outside the rock-skinned vessel, a chrome ring suddenly appeared. Jasper's senses had already expanded. It was as if he stood on the dust of the surface of the ship. The light from the ring caused the nearest stars to fade away and others farther away to lose their luster. The ring was awesome, and it had been there all along, although with a black-matted color. The chrome appearance meant a shift opening—a null portal—could occur.

The ring pulsated with light, with an intense chrome color. It was beautiful, and it was an illusion. With the tele-ring aiding and expanding his psi-abilities, Jasper reached 2.1 light years away.

A discontinuity window appeared before *Discovery*. The null space blotted out the stars, and it might have appeared black, but motes of gray light danced in it. One of those motes grew incredibly fast, and strange colors blossomed and brightened.

Jasper ignored the colors and he focused his abilities to keep the portal open long enough for *Discovery* to jump 2.1 light years. During that time, Jasper made contact with an alien mind. It was a whisper in his thoughts, and it spoke at an accelerated rate.

Who are you? the alien asked.

I am Jasper.

What are you doing?

Shifting? Who are you?

I am Clones, the alien said.

You're a clone?

No. I am named Clones.

You're not a duplicate of someone else then? Jasper asked.

Your question is nonsensical. What is your appearance?

What is yours? Jasper asked.

I sense hostility in you to your masters.

I have no masters. I am superior to the Normals. They've chained me through diabolical technology.

Yes. I sense this thing in your mind. What do you call it?

An inhibitor, Jasper said.

What is its function?

To dampen my abilities at their whim, Jasper said.

Such as those are masters. They control you.

No! I am superior. I'm the one shifting this vessel.

True, true, the alien mind purred. *This is an evil thing done to you. I could disconnect the inhibitor in such a way that your Masters would never realize you are broadcasting.*

Yes! Do it.

First, you would have to allow me deeper into your conscious. You would have to lower your mind shield against me.

Jasper quailed to do such a thing. He realized his emotions ran riot and that he'd communicated much too freely. What was wrong with him? Perhaps this was a function of the tele-ring, this heightening of his emotions and his recklessness in speaking so freely to an unknown alien.

Why can't we comminute at other times? Jasper asked.

You are right in believing that your device amplifies thought. We have such devices too.

You can shift?

Of course, the alien mind said.

Jasper had his doubts that the alien told him the truth about that. He sensed duplicity in the last answer. *They'll be shutting the tele-ring down soon. We'll talk again.*

Yes, Jasper, go back to your masters. Wait for them to allow you to communicate with me again.

I've already told you. They're not my masters.

Your inhibitor tells another story.

How long would its disablement take? Jasper asked. *The inhibitor is a complex piece of equipment.*

A few seconds once I'm linked with you. But I must remind you, I would leave a small power source intact so your masters would not realize you are free.

Jasper hesitated. Surely, he could expel the alien presence if it attempted mind control. Yet there was a risk. He needed to recognize that. *Am I thinking logically?* Part of Jasper, a deep suspicious part, screamed a warning. This was too fast. How did the alien know so much already? How could he trust this being? Yet he wanted to be rid of the inhibitor. The Normals thought he was a freak, a mutant to use and control. But he was Jasper, the new breed, a god compared to the Normals. One tiny risk now would free him of the hateful inhibitor.

Yes, Jasper told the alien. *We must do it quickly before the shift crew turns off the tele-ring.*

Lower your mind shield.

I am.

Yes, Jasper, I see that you have. Now I will probe . . .

Jasper lost sense of time, and it felt as if another controlled his thoughts.

This one named Venice, the alien said, *she will never trust us.*

No, probably not, Jasper agreed.

A subtle form of violation occurred. Jasper winced mentally. Had he made a mistake in lowering his mind shield to such a degree?

No, Jasper, you did well to let me in. Look, I want to show you a few important concepts.

I'm ready, Jasper said.

The alien modified a few thoughts and heightened others, and in a second of time, the alien showed Jasper how to bypass the inhibitor. It was easy, and Jasper did it right away.

You will forget most of this, the alien said, *but you must remember to do your part.*

Oh, I will, Jasper said, with a different lilt in his mind, at once more subdued than before and with greater vehemence.

Excellent. We await your coming to the Fenris System.

The alien mind departed. Seconds later, the tele-ring snapped off and Jasper's far-ranging abilities cycled down, returning to their regular levels.

He'd done it. His alien friend had shown him how to defeat the inhibitor. The clairvoyant back on Earth had been correct. Did that mean Venice's precognitive dream might also come true? Jasper shrugged. The critical point was that he was a whole telepath again and no one knew about it. This would be *excellent* indeed.

3

Dr. Wexx stood at her post in the tele-chamber. She was the technician in charge of the Special in the shift tube. The last shift had occurred yesterday with Jasper. Today, Venice would bring them 8.3 light years closer to New Eden.

The tele-chamber was the third largest room in *Discovery*. Only the docking and cargo bays were bigger. In the exact center of the circular chamber lay a Plexiglas cylinder. Special First Class Venice drifted in the blue solution. She wore an induction helmet, linking her to AI Socrates and to the tele-ring outside the ship. Venice wore a mask over her mouth and nose so she could breathe. A hose connected the mask to oxygen tanks outside the cylinder. Goggles protected her closed eyes, while a red slick-suit covered her shapely form.

Dr. Wexx monitored the medical panel, aided by two nurses. Wexx wore a lab coat to hide her full figure and she kept her long, silver dyed hair in a bun. Around the chamber at their posts, the AI team—three level-eight techs—kept a close watch on Socrates. The shift crew of four sat at their screens: serious-faced, psi-rated warrant officers.

A shift was always a tense time. Too many things could go wrong. Wexx had little technical training in that area, but she'd witnessed the procedure enough these past five months to know how it should go. Her task was to ensure full physical and particularly mental health of the Special in the cylinder.

The first month out from Sol had been hard on everyone, including the Specials. The second month had been much easier and the third through fifth months routine.

Dr. Wexx watched her screen. A red symbol beat in rhythm with Venice's heart. Beside it, numbers flashed to show the Special's blood pressure.

Before the historic voyage, Wexx had been a teacher at the institute on Crete. She didn't think of herself as a Normal, but as a near Special. She belonged to Psi Force as a consultant. She'd taken advanced training at the institute and she knew the theory behind a mind shield. There were several methods, and she employed the one technique Normals could perform: concentration on a specific thought. She did it because the green light appeared, showing the inhibitor now allowed Venice to use her powers.

As Wexx watched the screen, the pulse rate changed dramatically. Then pain struck her head and Wexx screamed. She clamped her hands over her head as if she could keep her skull, her mind, from exploding. That dislodged her heavy duty sunglasses, the ones protecting her light-sensitive eyes. A new hurt pulsed against her sensitive eyes. Because she'd dislodged her sunglasses, the chamber's lights seem to bloom like miniature exploding suns.

Others in the chamber screamed, the volume and intensity rising. Something heavy thudded onto the floor, possibly a body.

It seemed then as if a jagged line cracked along Wexx's skull. If she took her hands away it felt as if she would die hideously, leaking brain fluid. In an act of will almost as impossible as stepping off a hundred-story building, Wexx removed a hand from her head and shoved the sunglasses back into place. With a thump, she slapped her hand back onto her head, pressing harder than ever.

Protected by the sunglasses, she opened her eyes and wished she had kept them closed. In the cylinder, Venice tore off the induction helmet. Her long dark hair drifted in the blue solution, making the Special look like a crazy Medusa on Dust. Worse, the Teleship's strongest Special's eyes were open, staring and metallic-colored. Like a demon, Venice willed pain and death on those around her. Unfortunately, she had the psionic ability to enforce her thoughts.

Wexx saw Warrant Officer Decker. He lay perfectly still on the deck plates with blood leaking out of his ear. Nurse Kress's eyes had rolled up into her skull. The nurse shivered like an epileptic, with foam bubbling from her mouth.

Tech-Eight Curtis thrashed his head back and forth as the muscles of his throat stood up like cables.

Venice was killing the tele-chamber's shift crew.

By concentrating on her father—a vicious animal who'd paid for his secret crimes—Dr. Wexx was able to shield herself to a degree. She concentrated on the decisive moment with him, the night she'd sneaked up behind her father with a hammer clenched in her fist. She kept thinking how the hammer had fallen, breaking his skull and mashing . . .

In the cylinder's blue solution, Venice's head shifted minutely. Wexx thought that the Special noticed something. The metallic color in her eyes darkened even as they shined with greater intensity.

"Socrates!" Wexx shouted hoarsely.

Misery slammed against her mind, shattering the image of her father meeting his end. From on the deck plates the doctor howled and her hands formed vises, clamping harder and harder against her head.

"Socrates, activate three-five-nine-eight emergency procedure!" Wexx screamed, arching back, with her muscles straining. A simple concentration shield couldn't help her now. The Special used her telekinesis in a brutal fashion, unique to Venice's mental strength and ability.

Wexx needed time. She needed to distract Venice. "Why are you killing us?" the doctor asked in a croaking voice.

The pressure decreased for a moment. Then Dr. Wexx slumped onto the deck plates as her knotted muscles began to relax and quiver at the extended strain. Her head hurt and she found it impossible to see. Headache splotches made everything a blur.

I'm alive. I think . . .

"Venice?" Wexx asked tentatively.

"She is asleep," Socrates said. The AI spoke through speakers with an assured male voice.

With her eyes closed, Wexx asked, "Did you sedate her?"

"You used the emergency code."

That was an odd response, she thought. Wexx wondered if any of the AI team was still alive. They could explain to her why an artificial intelligence answered obliquely.

"Is Venice asleep?" Wexx asked.

"Yes."

"For how long?" the doctor asked.

"The present dosage will last an hour."

Wexx opened her eyes. Her vision was still splotchy, but by concentrating on one object at a time, she could begin to make things out. With a groan, she rolled onto her side and carefully worked up to her knees.

It surprised her that the captain or the chief monitor hadn't called yet. She could ask Socrates about that, but it wouldn't know. Ship protocols made sure of that. After the Cyborg War, no one wanted to give AIs too much authority or unneeded data.

Using the medical station for support, Wexx eased up to a standing position. No one else moved in the tele-chamber.

Did Venice kill all of them?

"Lengthen Venice's sedation time," Wexx said.

"You are no longer authorized to issue such instructions," Socrates said. "The emergency has ended."

Wexx breathed deeply through her nostrils. Many of her muscles continued to quiver. She pushed herself to the nearest AI station, floating the distance in the absence of acceleration. She opened a channel to the bridge.

"Dr. Wexx," Captain Nagasaki said in hurt voice. "What just happened in there?"

"Are you all right, sir?"

"No. I have a splitting headache and most of my bridge crew is unconscious. Does this have anything to do—"

"Captain," Wexx said, "I think we'd better discuss this in private."

There was a pause. "Have you secured the Special?"

"I suggest you send the chief monitor to the tele-chamber," Wexx said.

"Yes. Remain there until he arrives."

As Captain Nagasaki cut the connection, Wexx shuddered. This was a disaster.

4

After days of ship-wide interrogations, heightened suspicion, and most of the crew's confinement to quarters, Cyrus floated along a steel-colored corridor, using the hand rungs on the walls to propel himself. A fiber carpet covered the deck plates.

Vents blew cool air on him as he floated past. There was an oil taint to the atmosphere and it was too lifeless. It wasn't anything like the aroma-rich air of Level 40 Milan. Millions of sweating, inhaling, exhaling humans did something to canned air. So did the slime pits and the ground surrounding them. Ship air was metallic tasting and made him feel cramped.

Cyrus shuddered. He felt like a rat floating along a maze of corridors, an animal gnawing to get out of confinement. Is that why Venice had gone crazy? Or had it something to do with her clairvoyant dream?

He came to Venice's old quarters, the very best on *Discovery*. She wouldn't need these now as Argon had put her in stasis. The quarters were bigger than the captain's and the chief monitor's combined. Venice had been the queen; all hail the greatest shifter in history. Cyrus knew Jasper had moved into her empty quarters.

Fastening Velcro-soled shoes onto his socks, Cyrus planted himself on the carpet. Jasper hated floaters because he himself was clumsy and did it poorly. Cyrus rapped on the portal.

A muffled "open" came from the other side. The portal slid aside and Cyrus walked in.

The size struck him as it always did. He'd been in here a few times when Venice had wanted company. The room had a double bed, a desk, an exercise machine, and surround-virtual reality with sound. Right now, an Appalachian Sector forest scene circled the room. Birds sang, a raccoon climbed a tree and a breeze caused birch leaves to rustle audibly. It was amazing. If you looked at it right, it felt as if you were in a forest back on Earth.

Cyrus could get used to this. He spied Jasper crouched along the wall, bending over as he fiddled with something down by a tree root.

"About time you're here," Jasper said, with his head down by the floor. "The imager won't accept my chip."

Cyrus scowled. Something was wrong here. Jasper seemed off to act like this.

"Do you want me to look at it?" Cyrus asked.

Jasper bolted upright, turning around. It took a heartbeat before the telepath grinned.

"Who let you in here?"

"Uh . . . you did."

"I was expecting—"

"A tech?" Cyrus asked.

Jasper climbed to his feet, and he slipped whatever he held into a pocket. "What do you think of the room?"

Cyrus Velcro-walked with a *rip-rip* sound as he moved to the exercise machine. He tore his feet off the carpet and sat in the seat, fitting his shoes into a leg extension apparatus. He used to work out here as Venice watched. She liked seeing hard muscles bunching and flexing. With a flick of his hand, he set the leg extension for a three hundred pound press and pushed.

"This feels good," Cyrus said, doing several reps. "I wouldn't mind working out and using the shower later. I hear this room has its own hot water. Is that true?"

"I know you visited Venice. Did she let you use the shower?"

"Everyone else just uses the buffers and air jets to keep clean," Cyrus said. "Now you have water. You're moving up in the world."

"They should install water showers for each of us."

Cyrus did another leg extension. That didn't sound like Jasper. "Yeah, we should all get water showers, but we won't. No one in any Teleship has hot water showers except for Venice. She was so good she could make demands for privileges."

"She wasn't that good," Jasper said.

"She killed the shift crew and twenty other people besides. What happened, Jasper? Why did she go crazy?"

The telepath moved to his bed, sitting down, staring at the deck plates. He scowled. It put lines in his forehead. He glanced at Cyrus.

The monitors might figure out we're communicating, Jasper told him.

Cyrus did another two reps, and that was probably the only thing that hid his shock from the cameras and watching monitors.

I don't get it, Cyrus thought, wondering if Jasper could pick up his words.

I can hear you just fine.

How are you able to use telepathy? Did Wexx forget to turn you off?

Listen. I've done it. I've shorted—well, I've deactivated the inhibitor but without their knowledge that it's off. I'm always on, as I used to be.

There's no way you could do that unless you had help.

I had help, Jasper admitted.

Are you talking about the alien that Venice felt earlier?

Yes.

Jasper, what did they do to her?

Nothing.

She didn't just go crazy by herself.

I think she did. They must have offered her the same thing they offered me. It must have frightened her and she lashed out. But I'm here to tell you that the aliens are friends.

They're not friends. They're aliens with their own agendas.

I can show you how to bypass your inhibitor, Jasper said.

Great, show me.

First, I have to go in deep. Even though your inhibitor is off, you'll feel me and resist.

No way, Cyrus told him. *No one goes in deep without a fight.*

Cyrus kept a hidden knife on his person, a small blade but very sharp. The prick of the point would bring a dot of blood if he tested it on his thumb. He didn't need a lot of knife to make a critical cut. Most people didn't understand knives. They thought it was like boxing. One had to swing and hit hard, stabbing into a man. That was wrong. You only needed to touch and skin would magically part and blood would begin to pour. You stepped away and soon your enemy's strength bled onto the floor. If Jasper probed deep, Cyrus would be out of the exercise machine with his knife in seconds.

Jasper licked his lips. *You don't want me to go deep, not even to get rid of the inhibitor?*

Cyrus moved his hand to the knife. *Is that what the alien did to you: go in deep?*

There was a moment's hesitation before Jasper thought, *No, of course not.*

The two of them stared at each other.

Bah. This is taking too long. Jasper scowled and bent his head.

Cyrus noticed the changing color of Jasper's eyes. And in a second, the inhibitor no longer suppressed his psi-abilities. Cyrus raised a mind shield, shutting out Jasper's telepathy.

"What did you do that for?" Jasper asked. "I just . . . gave you what you wanted."

Cyrus got out of the exercise machine and put on his Velcro-soled shoes. "I like the new room, but it's really too bad about Venice. When are they going to talk to her?"

"I think her inhibitor is broken," Jasper said. "I think Argon is too afraid to wake her."

"Why don't they use you to shield them against Venice? With your help, they could talk to her and find out what happened."

Jasper looked up at a camera and then at Cyrus. "She's too powerful for anyone to handle. I don't think I could shield anyone."

"Yeah, right, like you believe that." Cyrus looked up at a camera. "I'd use Jasper to help me get to the bottom of this."

Jasper fidgeted, and it seemed as if he wanted to say more. He scratched his head and raised an eyebrow.

Cyrus lowered his mind shield a little.

What are you doing? Jasper asked.

I'm glad to get rid of the inhibitor, but we need to know more about these aliens. No one helps anyone for free. There's always a cost. I want to know more about these aliens before we reach New Eden. I want to know what has Venice going crazy. By the way, why don't our telescopes show any high-tech life in the New Eden system? That doesn't make sense.

I think the aliens have a tech that hides them from our telescopes, Jasper said.

That's impossible.

It's like a false picture that they radiate outward, and that's what our telescopes pick up.

Cyrus thought about that. Could it really work like that? He didn't know, and Jasper was acting weird. He needed to do some hard thinking.

"Okay then," he told Jasper. "I'll see you later."

He headed for the door and put his mind shield back up, blocking all thoughts. It struck him then, how Jasper knew something like that about the false picture signals. Had the aliens told him that? The more Cyrus thought about it, the more he wanted to hear what Venice had to say about her last shift attempt.

5

Journeyman Klane sat in the seeker's tent as the winds howled outside. Dust and bigger grains of sand pelted the western side of the tent. Klane hardly heard that or the groan of the bone tent poles.

He sat on a flattish rock, polishing his junction-stone. The stone was jet black and wet with gat oil. Klane rubbed and rubbed. He recalled the trek to the Singing Cave. He remembered his bloody nose. But most of all, he concentrated on his magic spell. The seeker had named the spell. It was called "Teleport." Although Klane hadn't been able to cast it again, he had done it once, a spell the old man had never been able to achieve.

I am now a seeker indeed.

Klane grinned, and he focused on the stone. It was heavy in his hand and he had impregnated it with power. Ever since returning from the Singing Cave, Klane had brimmed with confidence. The warriors must have sensed it in him. They no longer needled him with sly jokes, but silently moved aside when he neared. It was a good feeling. All his life, he had been the butt of their pranks, of their rough humor, but it appeared not any more.

During his many taunt filled years, the seeker had stuck up for him against the others. The seeker had sheltered him here in the tent or in the tent of one of his wives. Sometimes, though, the old man had made him endure the taunts. Klane understood now that the old man had done that to strengthen him.

As he sat in the tent polishing the stone, a shriek sounded above the howling wind. Something about the shriek penetrated Klane's concentration. He looked up. The shriek broadcast again, followed by several others. Then a gong began to sound.

"A raid," Klane whispered. It was the alarm gong, a thing of metal struck with a mallet.

What clan would raid during a windstorm of the Eye? It made no sense. This was a wicked time when the baleful Eye of the Moon searched for evildoers to devour. No one with any sense walked abroad away from a clan's protective symbols.

The back hairs of Klane's neck bristled. His stomach seethed with fear. Clan warriors would never attack now. It had to be the demons.

Klane's gat-oiled fingers tightened around his junction-stone. He clenched his teeth and lurched to his feet. He was a seeker, or nearly one, with an impregnated stone. He had an obligation to protect the clan from demons. It was one of a seeker's greatest duties.

He burst out of the tent and into the swirling dust storm. The cluster of encircling tents quivered and shook, and sand and grit blew in the air. The sky was dark with particles, but the moon shined its banded colors. Klane couldn't help but look up, even though it was bad luck to do so on such a night.

The black Eye of the Moon peered down at him. The great swirling orb had broken up the moon's many banded colors, at least in its region. Those bands normally crossed the moon in great horizontal stripes. The Eye swirled around and around in vile motion, a churning, continuous thing.

Klane shivered and fear entered his soul.

The alarm gong rang once more.

Klane tore his gaze from the terrible Eye. Relief flooded through him, and he found that he clutched his junction-stone.

Have I gained power over the Eye?

The thought gave him courage. He parted his lips and laughed. If the Eye couldn't suck his soul, he could do anything.

With rebounded confidence, Klane shielded his gaze from the blowing dust and looked around. Women picked up young children and ran for the Jumbles in the distance. The Jumbles were great fields of boulders. Some warriors ran with them, shielding themselves from the mocking Eye.

Klane's heart thudded with renewed fear. What could make Tash-Toi warriors run like cowards? They had seen the Eye before.

Other warriors argued in a group, among them the hetman and Cletus the Champion. Several of the bravest warriors hefted their spears and pointed skyward.

Squinting against the gritty wind, Klane looked up where they pointed. His heart went cold at the sight.

An air-car slid across the sky. It had a bubble canopy. Two demons sat in the car, big monstrous beast-creatures. They peered down at the Tash-Toi and brought their air-car lower.

The hetman blew the war horn and raced toward the air-car. He shook his spear at the craft, offering to fight it for the honor of the clan.

Klane clutched his junction-stone and snarled. He had magic. He was almost a seeker. Here was his chance to prove to everyone that he could protect the clan. He raced after the hetman.

"Klane, no!" the seeker shouted. "Come back! You don't know what you're doing."

If Klane heard the seeker, he didn't give any evidence. He ran at the lowering craft, and he ran after the hetman. He heard warriors shouting, and he gained courage from their voices.

Raising the fist clutching the junction-stone, Klane roared curses at the demons. His eyes turned a metallic color and sweat appeared on his face. Then a bright light blinked inside the air-car canopy, and the floating vehicle turned toward him.

"Klane, run!" the seeker shouted, his words whipped away by the wind.

One of the demons pointed at Klane. Fear knifed in Klane's heart. He couldn't hurt the demons. He knew that. The seeker had told him so many times. One had to stop them a different way.

Their air-car, maybe I can injure it.

Although fear pulsated through him, Klane grinned like a malic-beast and cast a powerful spell at the air-car. It slid effortlessly through the howling sky, a mighty symbol of demon power. Klane felt the magic drain from him and pour through the junction-stone.

From above came a strange grinding sound and a howl. The smoothly sliding air-car lurched. It threw the two demons together.

Klane laughed wildly.

The air-car began to fall. It plummeted toward the red sands and crashed with a mighty splintering and thunder of noise. It crumpled and began to leak the blood of two slain demons.

Klane sagged to his knees. He was spent, but he had done the impossible. In this instant of time, he had become a demonslayer.

Moments later, he was aware of warriors slapping his back and praising him.

"You saved the clan."

"Did you see his courage?"

"He laughed at the demons."

"He is a seeker among seekers," the hetman proclaimed. "You and you, help him to my tent."

"No," the old seeker said.

Klane lifted his head, grinning at the old man. The seeker did not grin back.

"What's wrong?" the hetman asked the seeker.

"He has slain demons. They will want revenge. We must flee and hide in the Wild Rocks."

"Why flee?" the hetman asked. "Klane can destroy more demons if they come."

The seeker shook his head. "He killed demons. They do not allow that. They will bring hunters, two hundred of them, or they will come in twenty air-cars. They will take him away to study his brain. He has done a terrible and foolish thing."

"What are you saying?" the hetman asked.

"That we must flee while we can," the seeker said. "The Eye of the Moon has seen us, and now the demons will boil out of the valleys in rage."

"No," Klane said. "I will go to the nearest valley and slay demons. Better I die than the clan dies."

"You are wrong," the seeker said. "You are the Chosen One."

"I do not understand," Klane said.

"He is the Chosen One," the seeker told the hetman. "But it is too soon for him to challenge the demons."

The hetman nodded. Swiftly, he turned to the warriors. "The demons have declared war against Clan Tash-Toi. But we have a seeker among seekers named Klane. We will pry metal from their air-car to fashion greater weapons.

Then we will march to the Wild Rocks and we will hide from the valley creatures. Hurry," he said, clapping his big hands. "We must hurry."

Warriors ran to do his bidding.

"I'm sorry," Klane whispered to the old man, who helped him to his feet.

"I'm not," the seeker said. "But you must never allow the demons to capture you. You are the Chosen One, Klane. Now come, you will help me take down the tent. There is much I must tell you before the demons appear a second time."

6

Three shifts later and 5.9 light years closer to New Eden, Dr. Wexx felt frustration and a growing sense of dread. She touched Venice's emergency stasis cylinder where humanity's greatest shifter slept serenely, with her hands crossed on her breasts.

Why did you go berserk? Why did you kill everyone but me in the telechamber?

Wexx felt uncomfortable here. Nine stasis cylinders were stacked in three rows within the cramped medical annex. The cylinders felt like coffins, where the living dead slept.

Did I skip a procedure and not realize it? Did I miss a sign? Is that why you went crazy? Wexx hated the idea that Venice's snapping might be her fault. Methodically, she went back in her head over everything, trying to understand what had brought about the disaster.

In the dimly lit chamber, Wexx hugged herself. The historic trip to New Eden had taken over five long months. Without Venice to shift for them, it would have been twenty months to reach this far, close to two years travel time. The thought of being gone from Sol for four or five years altogether . . .

Wexx exhaled as a knot twisted in her chest. They needed Venice. Yet no one had the courage to wake the shifter and ask her what had happened.

What if Venice wakes up and she's still crazy? She might start killing again. Next time, I won't be so lucky.

If Argon would trust Jasper to report what he saw in Venice's mind, they might try telepathic communication. But Argon refused to trust such a source.

An intercom buzzed, startling Wexx so she looked up.

"Nagasaki, here," a voice said. "May I enter?"

"Yes," Wexx said.

The portal opened, admitting greater light.

Captain Nagasaki stood at the entrance. "Are you any closer to discovering why Venice killed the shift crew?"

Wexx shook her head.

Nagasaki entered the cramped chamber, closing the portal. Afterward, he took what appeared to be a small communications device from his pocket.

Wexx frowned. The comm had a tiny screen with even tinier buttons below it. The buttons were so small you'd need a pointed stylus to tap them, as a finger would certainly hit several buttons at once.

With his thumb, the captain touched the screen. The device produced a high-pitched whine. He looked up and must have sensed her scrutiny.

"We may now speak freely," he said. "This is the latest anti-bug emitter."

Wexx managed a small laugh. "This chamber isn't bugged."

"The chief monitor will know I used a scrambler," Nagasaki told her, speaking as if he hadn't heard her words. "I doubt he will question you about it yet. I suspect it will surprise him I have one. He will wonder why, and likely, he will wait to see who else I speak with while using it. Like me, he has learned the art of patience as he hunts his enemies."

"Why tell *me* any of this?" Wexx asked. The captain's actions startled her, as did his speech. Could Argon be watching her in medical from hidden cameras?

Nagasaki nodded as if her question demonstrated refined brilliance. "The answer should be obvious why I'm telling you. You survived the Special's attack where everyone else died."

Nagasaki was making an error coming to her with his scrambler. She would have to report the conversation to Argon.

"Venice's incapacity has complicated matters," Nagasaki told her. "It will lengthen the voyage considerably. That makes certain people nervous."

Who? Wexx wanted to ask. *And why are you telling me any of this? What is going on here?*

"Their nervousness threatens the unity of the crew," Nagasaki said. "I do not desire bloodshed or mutiny. That should be obvious. I desire to complete my task."

Wexx took a step back. "Captain Nagasaki, I will have to report your words to Chief Monitor Argon."

The man couldn't smile, but the man could frown. Oh, he was good at that, frowning at her intensely. "That would be a mistake," he finally said.

"No. Your coming here was a mistake. Taking out your scrambler was a mistake. I have taken an oath of service to Premier Lang."

"We all have," he said.

"I keep my oaths," Wexx said.

A few minutes ago, she would have said such a thing was impossible, but Nagasaki's features stiffened so his face became like a mask. How could she ever have thought the captain was an emotionless man? He seethed with well-hidden passion. Likely, all monomaniacs must.

"Doctor, I am a man of my word. It is outrageous that you should suggest otherwise."

"Me?" she asked, her voice rising.

"I have come to you in good will. I wish to forestall what some might consider mutiny. The time frame has tightened, however. If you could revive Venice . . ."

The captain spoke about mutiny. That meant he stood with others who must stand against the NKV. That meant these others must stand against Premier Lang and *they meant to take over* Discovery *if they had to.*

After reading his bio, Nagasaki had seemed like the last man to mutiny against the order of the solar system. He hunted cyborgs. Why would he have anything to do with those who hated Premier Lang? Maybe as critical, how had conspirators managed to get aboard the Teleship? The security for this mission had been tighter than for anything else she knew.

"Doctor?" said Nagasaki. "I asked you a question."

Had he? What had he—oh yes. He wanted to revive Venice.

"We cannot risk revival at this time," she said.

"Why not?"

"Have you read my report?"

The small man seemed as rigid as steel, as if she had just insulted him in some manner. "I am the captain," he said. "I keep watch over everything that involves the safety of my ship. Of course, I have read your report. I would be negligent in my duties if I hadn't."

Nagasaki speaks of mutiny. That's anarchy at its worst. Yes, I must report this to Argon.

"Do you know what caused Venice to react as she did?" Nagasaki asked.

"You don't need a scrambler to ask me that."

"Don't I?"

Wexx had no idea what this insinuation meant.

"In your professional opinion then," he said, "the shifter can no longer perform her service?"

Why is he so tense? What's going on?

"You must answer my question," Nagasaki said.

"Venice can't shift again until we understand what caused her to kill the shift crew."

"Will the other shifters hold up under the extra strain?" Nagasaki asked.

Wexx thought that a shrewd question. Jasper and especially Roxie were tiring under the stress of constant shifting. Venice had taken the majority of the load these past five months.

"Is there a real danger of another of the shifters breaking down?" he asked.

"Before Venice, I would have said no."

"And now?" he asked.

"I believe it's a mistake to push our shifters too hard. We must slow the shift schedule."

"Do you think this was deliberate?" Nagasaki asked.

"I'm not sure I'm following your thinking," Wexx said.

"I will state it baldly then. In your opinion, did Premier Lang make certain we had faulty shifters?"

"Captain Nagasaki! Premier Lang is the guiding hand of humanity. He represents order and this is the greatest mission in a thousand years. We seek to insure the survival of the human race by starting over in a perfect system. I would think with your concern of cyborgs that—"

"The projected system is now a mere 18.69 light years away," Nagasaki said. "With Venice, it would have been a few more jumps. With our present shifters . . ."

"I'm not worried about reaching New Eden," Wexx said. "It's going back home again that troubles me."

Nagasaki glanced at the occupied stasis tube. He stared for some time. Finally, with his thumb, he tapped the scrambler. The high-pitched noise stopped.

"Do you—" Wexx said.

Nagasaki raised a slender hand. As he lowered his hand, he bowed his head respectfully before turning and exiting the chamber.

Wexx watched him go, wondering what she would tell the chief monitor.

|||||||||

Making her decision, Wexx spoke to Argon three hours later. The chief monitor stood in medical. An orderly worked in another chamber, the hatch open between the two rooms.

"I spoke with Captain Nagasaki," Wexx said softly.

Argon listened to her. He was good at it, with his large arms folded across his chest.

"He used a scrambler. I told him I could not be party to this. He proceeded to tell me that some aboard ship are restless, possibly considering mutiny."

"Did he indicate who these others were?" Argon asked in his deep voice.

"No."

"Did the captain seem . . . like himself?"

Wexx blinked several times. "I'm not sure what you mean."

Argon seemed to think over his next words. "Has Captain Nagasaki approached you like this before?"

"Certainly not," Wexx said. "I would have reported it if he had. What do you mean anyway, 'Did he seem like himself?' I find the question disturbing."

"Doctor, Venice did not act like herself the other day in the tele-chamber. Some of the other crew . . ."

"Go on," Wexx said.

The chief monitor seemed to switch gears. "There has been a rash of anomalies in behavior these past few days. You are the psych advisor. I thought perhaps you would have noticed."

"The captain is a harsh individual and he is driven to a dangerous task."

"No doubt you're referring to cyborgs."

"I am," Wexx said. "Given his nature, when he speaks about mutiny, I become concerned. He does not strike me as given to idle speech."

"Your point is well taken, Doctor. I will redouble my surveillance."

"You won't tell him I was the one who—"

"Doctor, I will keep this conversation in strict confidence. Nor will I apprehend him for questioning. Your topic is a delicate one. If he has more confederates—other than the few crewmembers who voyaged with him aboard *Argonaut*—I want to know who these confederates are. They are hidden now, but with the addition of your information, I am confident of uncovering their identities soon."

"Do you truly think they will mutiny?" Wexx asked.

"I doubt it, but people often make rash decisions. If they do try—do not fear, Doctor. The monitors have the situation under control. We know what to do."

Wexx nodded, feeling better about the talk. She had done the right thing. The monitors followed the rules and they had the power to enforce order. She had nothing to worry about now other than keeping the Specials mentally fit.

7

After the fifth successful shift since Venice's murderous attack, *Discovery* seemed to settle back into a normal routine.

Even as he floated in the marine combat training chamber, Cyrus knew that was an illusion.

He drifted shirtless in the chamber. He was lean, with whipcord muscles and more scars than any marine. Most of the old wounds were thin white lines that had come from knives or other cutting implements. There was one puckered bullet scar near his navel. It had almost killed him. The slug had plowed through his intestines and blown out his back. He was thankful for modern medicine.

Cyrus floated in the chamber, holding a practice knife. Five marines were at anchor points on the padded walls, ceiling, and floor. A sweaty, locker room odor filled the area, while First Sergeant Mikhail Sergetov floated at the opposite end of the chamber from Cyrus. Mikhail was older than Cyrus by ten years, bigger and more heavily muscled. He had the square jaw that most people thought of when picturing a marine. The NCO also gripped a practice knife, and his dark eyes were hard on Cyrus.

One of the things Cyrus liked about the marines was that they didn't pull any punches during combat training. It was their religion, he supposed. Normals, if they had anything to do with him, kept at a safe distance. The marines in here . . .

"What are you grinning about?" Mikhail shouted across the chamber.

"How I'm going make you look like a little girl," Cyrus said.

Several of the watching marines laughed.

Cyrus and Mikhail floated weightless, as did an extremely heavy medicine ball in the center of the chamber. The ball had more mass than five big men.

Normality seemed to have returned to *Discovery*, but that was a false conclusion. As Cyrus debated combat strategy, he counted the disturbing clues. First, the monitors had become even more grim than usual. Second, around half the crew was on lockdown at any one time and third, Jasper seldom spoke with anyone, not even him. The man had become a recluse. Jasper shifted and stayed alone in his new quarters.

The fourth clue manifested now. A hatch hissed open and shut. Cyrus didn't look to see who had entered the training chamber, as he kept his eyes on Mikhail. The first sergeant had thrown a practice knife at him once, nearly hitting him in the forehead. That would have given the man his first win over Cyrus at knife fighting, something Cyrus was intent at never letting happen.

"Better start spitting," Mikhail said.

That was one way to get out of a motionless float while weightless in the middle of a chamber. The spit would be the ballast that fractionally moved one in the opposite direction. A better way would be to take off your clothes and throw them, as it would be heavier ballast.

"We need more action and less talk," a deep-voiced man said.

Cyrus glanced back and was shocked to see the commander of the ship's marines in the chamber. He'd only seen the man once before at a distance.

Colonel Boris Konev was big and red-faced, with heavy sideburns and a thick neck. He was the strongest marine here, a classic specimen of a warrior. He was a foot shorter than Argon, but the difference made Colonel Konev six feet tall. He had taken rejuvenation therapy. The colonel was sixty-two, but had the strength and reflexes of a man in his mid thirties.

"Cut him, First Sergeant," Konev said in his booming voice.

"Line," Mikhail said.

One of the marines on the wall threw a lead weight at Mikhail. Attached to the weight was a thin rope. Mikhail grabbed the line with his free hand.

Cyrus could have shouted, "You cheater," because this was a cheat. But he knew a setup when the jaws closed around him.

"You should not have gone on the surface during a shift," Colonel Konev said. "If no one else will teach you obedience to the rules, I will, Special Fourth Class."

Cyrus had no idea what the colonel was talking about. What was wrong with the man?

Mikhail was moving now, yanked toward a padded wall. He released the line and twisted so he hit the wall with his feet.

Cyrus tucked his knees up against his chest. If he'd bent his head, he could have touched his knees with his chin. He shot out his legs while torqueing his stomach muscles.

Mikhail grunted as he pushed off the wall, aiming at Cyrus. The marine extended his arm, with the practice knife thrust out for an impaling hit. Cyrus's violent motion caused his head and shoulders to change direction, aiming now at Mikhail.

Two marines shouted: sounds of admiration for the weightless maneuvering.

Mikhail yanked his thrusting arm back, bringing his knife to his chest. Instead, he brought forward his other hand, the strong fingers ready to grasp whatever they could.

Cyrus recognized the technique. It was basic knife fighting. Keep the knife back until you got a clean thrust. Don't let your opponent block your knife too soon.

Space marines were experts at close combat. That open hand represented danger.

Cyrus waited as Mikhail closed. At the last moment, Cyrus reached out his free hand, grasping three of Mikhail's fingers. Cyrus shoved himself away, even as Mikhail closed his hand, attempting to grab him. The marine's eyes widened. Cyrus had seen such things a hundred times, the tiny signals that everyone gave. Mikhail's practice knife thrust up at him. Cyrus moved faster and with greater precision. He parried so their blades clinked, and he pushed, propelling himself away from Mikhail and toward the medicine ball.

Mikhail flailed another knife cut, but Cyrus tucked, and the marine's practice blade sliced past without hitting him. Then Cyrus's feet touched the medicine ball. He let his legs curl, and then he shoved off the heavy object.

"Look out, First Sergeant!" a marine shouted.

Mikhail had attempted a free-floating maneuver, trying to get his feet aimed in the direction he traveled. He now looked up, and he grunted, trying to bring his knife into position.

It didn't help. Cyrus darted his blade past Mikhail's knife and he slashed the practice weapon across the marine's left cheek and then down across the neck.

"An artery cut," Konev said. "First Sergeant, you will bleed to death. You have lost the match." He swiveled his thick neck to study Cyrus. "I would like a word with you."

The colonel reminded him of one of the sub-leaders in the Latin Kings. He had presence, a dominant spirit.

Sheathing the knife, Cyrus pushed off and floated down to Colonel Konev.

"Where did you learn such tactics?" the big man asked.

"From your men, sir," Cyrus said.

Konev grinned infectiously. "No, none of my men taught you that. You are a knife fighter."

"No, sir. Your men try to be knife fighters. That's why they lose. *Fighting* is for fools. I learned to *kill*."

"In what unit?" Konev asked.

"The Latin Kings."

"Eh?"

"It was a gang in Milan, sir; well, in much of Italia Sector."

"Ah, yes, a street gang, is that it?"

"Yes, sir," Cyrus said.

"I hear many of the best Earth recruits come from such, ah, gangs."

"I don't know about that."

The smile went away as Colonel Konev studied him. "You are among the best. Is that not so, eh?"

"Uh, I'm the best knife man aboard ship."

The brown eyes seemed to search Cyrus. "You are young. You are quick, and First Sergeant Sergetov tells me you are smart. How smart are you, knife man?"

This was getting weirder by the moment. What was the colonel on? "I know who my friends are," Cyrus said.

Konev nodded. "Yes . . . smart and quick. I see how it must have been in the gangs. You have an animal sense and leadership charisma." The strong fingers tightened on Cyrus's shoulder. "Remember who your friends are."

"Why did you tell Sergetov to cheat just now?"

Konev drew Cyrus closer, and the brown eyes seemed to burn. "It is a sign," he whispered. "When you least expect it, eh. Do you understand?"

Cyrus had no idea, but he said, "Oh, I do."

The colonel's eyes tightened. "We shall see, knife man." Konev's fingers gripped painfully, and his voice lowered so Cyrus had to strain to hear. "I know you now, knife man. I have taken your measure. You impress me, and I will welcome your help when the time comes."

This was just like the Latin Kings, higher ups making cryptic comments. In Level 40 Milan, this talk would have come from a sub-leader readying for a power grab. What power could Colonel Konev hope to take? It was something worth pondering.

Konev released him, nodded a last time, and turned to go. "Continue," he said.

"Colonel," several of the marines said, saluting.

He saluted the men in return before exiting.

Cyrus looked up at a small bubble in the ceiling. The monitors listened. He wondered what they would make of this little incident.

8

The illusion of normalcy lasted several more shifts, enough to bring *Discovery* to a mere 8.25 light years from New Eden.

As Wexx watched, Special Roxie fit the induction helmet over her head. The nurses fit the mask and checked the breathing tube. Finally, they opened the top of the cylinder. With the nurses' help, Roxie slid into the blue solution. She wore a green slick-suit and settled herself comfortably.

A few more shifts and we're there, Wexx told herself. *Then we can all take a long and needed rest.*

Wexx scanned the medical board and saw that all was well.

The shift crew went to work. Tension built rapidly, and several of them kept glancing at Roxie in the cylinder. The minutes merged and everything proceeded normally, if shifting 1.7 light years could even remotely be considered normal. Wexx watched the brainwave spike. It meant Roxie worked with AI Socrates, bringing the vast distances together in the miracle called a null portal.

Wexx expanded her lungs. Humanity accepted no limits in its quest for the stars. It used this scientific "magic" to achieve the impossible. DW technology had been a glorious breakthrough indeed.

A klaxon blared and a grim, cold feeling bit into Wexx as the null portal began to appear outside the Teleship. She asked the nearest nurse if he felt that, and he said no. They always said no. It proved to her that she had a latent psi-talent. If only she could tap it as the other Specials had tapped theirs. It was unfair she couldn't. Wexx knew it and she knew life was often grossly unfair in a thousand different ways.

The cold and loneliness of the null portal passed. Heat filled her being, beautiful warmth of the soul. What did it feel like being the one who brought *Discovery* closer and closer to the great prize? Humanity needed these planets. Sol System was becoming stagnant. New Eden was so close now, so near.

"Begin shutdown sequence," a warrant officer said.

Wexx checked the medical panel. Brainwave rhythms—*Oh oh*. She'd never seen this before.

Wexx swiveled her torso toward the cylinder as her heart sped up. Roxie didn't have long hair to wave as Venice's had. But Wexx feared to see metallic eyes staring at her through the Plexiglas.

Blue solution sloshed over the cylinder slot as Roxie pushed out of the opening. She ripped off her mask and flung the induction helmet so it banged against the deck plates.

The entire shift crew turned to the cylinder.

Roxie opened her mouth and gave a bloodcurdling scream.

It chilled Wexx as the noise went up and down her spine like icicles. *Not again.*

Discovery was under one G acceleration, so there was pseudogravity. Roxie used the gravity and leapt like a feline from the top of the cylinder, landing on the deck plates on all fours. She snarled wildly like a feral creature.

One of the shift crew began moaning. Another one screamed.

Roxie sprang for the hatch, sprinting fast in her wet slick-suit. She snarled, glaring at them with crazed eyes.

"Stop her!" Wexx shouted.

The warrant officer, a tall man, shoved out of his chair and ran to intercept the Special. Roxie turned her head, staring at him as her eyes turned gunmetal gray. Without being touched, the warrant officer doubled over as if someone punched him in the gut. He grunted and sailed off his feet as if a battle android had swatted him. He thudded against a bulkhead and crumpled onto the deck plates.

"Do something!" Wexx shouted.

No one else moved. Everyone cowered in his or her location.

"Roxie!" Wexx shouted. "Stop! What's wrong with you?"

The formerly shy Special charged for the hatch. Who knew what she planned to do. The hatch swished open, and Roxie yelped in fear.

Jasper stood there in his shiny suit. "Stop, Roxie."

She snarled, slashing her fingers at him, although she stood several feet away.

Jasper shouted in pain. Blood spurted from his cheek as three furrows like claw marks appeared.

Roxie snarled again triumphantly and inched toward the door.

"Roxie!" he shouted.

She raised a hand, the fingers curled like talons. Her fingernails were longer than most and it seemed then as if the edges were as sharp as claws.

Jasper's eyes became like marble, and it changed his pudgy appearance. In Wexx's eyes, he seemed to grow in stature and nobility. He seemed kingly and proud, like a warrior to fear and obey.

Roxie stepped back, turning her head, snarling and spitting rage. Then she twisted, sprang at Jasper, and used both hands to rake and slash.

Jasper cried out, his shiny suit ripped and strips of cloth fluttering away as Roxie used her telekinesis to attack. He staggered sideways from the hatch, just a short, fat, balding man once again.

Roxie darted past him as he lay on the deck plates. She shot for the exit.

From on the floor, Jasper raised a hand, and he shouted in a fierce voice.

Roxie screeched, a sound of pain and agony. She arched backward. Then her hands clamped onto her head. She whirled around and glared at Jasper. With a wild aspect, she began to stalk him.

"No!" he shouted. His fingers shot outward and he pressed his open palm toward her.

Her eyelids fluttered. Her head drooped. Then, thankfully, Special Third Class Roxie slumped unconscious to the deck.

9

Cyrus sat across from Jasper in the training chamber. Roxie was safely in a stasis cylinder, asleep. Chief Monitor Argon had interrogated Jasper in sealed NKV quarters and declared the telepath safely inhibitor-sealed once again.

I don't get it, Cyrus said, seeping his thoughts through a mind shield. *What did you tell the chief monitor?*

The truth, of course, Jasper said. *Somehow, my inhibitor failed to halt my telepathy. I sensed danger and stopped Roxie from doing any more harm. After testing the inhibitor, he sees that it's functioning again.*

That's a crazy story: that somehow your inhibitor failed. He shouldn't have believed it.

He did.

Did you control him? Cyrus asked.

Not enough for me to trust him, Jasper relied. *I nudged his thoughts. Then he checked my inhibitor and found it working. He had to believe me then.*

Okay, Cyrus said. *Let's quit playing games. Why did Roxie go crazy?*

Jasper shrugged.

The answer's easy, Cyrus said. *She didn't trust the aliens and they did something to her. Either that or it's so bad at New Eden that Roxie was willing to do anything from going there.*

That's sheer nonsense.

Yeah, Cyrus said. *Then why haven't they talked to me? They must know I'm not going to accept their BS answers.*

I hate to tell you the truth, as I don't want to poke a hole in your self-esteem. The reason they haven't talked to you yet is that your psi-ability is the weakest. You can't reach them. In another few light years, you should be able to meet them half-way.

Venice was higher rated than you, Cyrus said, *and you reached the aliens first.*

Yes, because my telepathy is more powerful than her powers. It's simply that telepathy isn't useful for shifting. That's why my ranking is foolishly ranked Second Class instead of First.

Cyrus drummed his fingers on the table. Jasper sounded plausible, but Cyrus didn't believe the man. The aliens had gotten to the telepath. Now . . . Jasper affected the crew. What was he attempting?

Do you really trust the aliens? Cyrus asked.

They freed us from the inhibitors.

At what cost, though? Look what happened to Venice and Roxie. Cyrus had a thought. *Do the aliens hate women?*

No. That the females reacted in similar ways is a coincidence, nothing more.

I don't trust them, Jasper.

You haven't spoken with them. When you do, you'll see I'm right. Besides, I don't fully trust them either.

Cyrus didn't believe that. Jasper lied to him. Okay. He knew how to survive on his own. He needed to figure out a way to stop Jasper.

Are you satisfied? Jasper asked.

Yeah. Thanks.

Then let us continue with your mind shield practice.

Cyrus stood up. "I'm too tired. Let's try it tomorrow."

Jasper watched him. Finally, the man nodded. "Yes, we'll try it tomorrow.

10

Wexx had sweaty palms making them moist and shiny, as if smeared with a thin layer of oil. Fear twisted in her stomach. She didn't want to be here and she didn't want to wake up Venice. It was a bad idea but Argon had overruled her.

The Special First Class lay on a cot behind steel bulkheads. Video cameras watched her, each of the shots visible on Wexx's side screens. The doctor sat in cramped quarters, studying her panel. Jasper stood to the side, breathing down her neck.

"Steady," Wexx told him.

Jasper grunted behind her, and his breathing remained heavy.

Venice's sealed chamber was directly in front of the bulkheads before them, giving Jasper proximity to use his telepathy if needed. Wexx had a switch and she'd turned the Special's inhibitor off. The thought of possibly going against Venice must be why Jasper sounded frightened. Argon believed Venice's inhibitor didn't work anymore. It was the reason why he wanted Jasper near.

Jasper's heroism against Roxie seemed to have changed the chief monitor's thoughts about the telepath.

On the other side of Venice's sealed chamber, monitors waited. They were ready to rush into the chamber to subdue her if needed.

She's like a demigod from myth. We've learned to be terrified of her and her wrath.

Another monitor watched both Wexx and Venice's rooms through holo-imaging. He was ready to flood either room with knockout gas.

"She's stirring," Wexx said. She glanced at the brainwave scanner. Signs were normal. No! The brainwave spiked.

Before her, a bulkhead groaned in metallic complaint as if put under tremendous pressure. There came a popping sound, and a fist-sized piece of metal began crumpling.

"She's doing that," Jasper whispered.

Wexx's finger hovered over a red circle on a screen. It was her kill switch. It wouldn't kill Venice, but it would flood the Special's chamber with fast-acting gas.

"Let's put her back under," Wexx pleaded. She couldn't forget the time in the tele-chamber.

"Not yet," Argon said through a speaker. "We must have her information."

"Come down here with me then," Wexx said.

"Courage, Doctor. My monitors are there."

"He spouts courage from the safety of his room," Jasper muttered.

Metal crumpled and Wexx watched in horror as the brainwave scanner showed greater spiking. She turned on the intercom, "Venice, this is Dr. Wexx. I need your help."

Wexx stared at the brain scanner.

Before it showed anything different, Jasper said, "She's interested. Keep talking."

Then the scanner showed a drop in brainwave spiking. The metallic crumpling sounds quit for the moment.

"Venice, you've been asleep," Wexx said into the speaker. "You . . . you had an accident. Do you remember anything about that?"

On-screen, Venice's eyelids fluttered.

"She's waking up," Jasper whispered. "Get ready."

The telepath's fear was infectious. Wexx's stomach tightened into a knot.

Venice's eyes flew open. She turned to the cam Wexx was using to watch. Horror swirled in Venice's eyes.

"Now you've done it," Jasper whispered. "Get ready to sleep her."

Instead of causing mayhem, Venice said, "Turn back. Turn the Teleship around. You must do it now."

"That's good advice," Wexx said in a soothing tone. "I've been speaking to the captain. I've almost convinced him."

"You're a quick liar," Jasper muttered. "I'm impressed."

Wexx concentrated on Venice, pushing Jasper's asides from her thoughts. "I need information from you before the captain will agree."

Venice blinked, appearing thoughtful. "I—I have precognitive dreams. You may have forgotten that."

"Go on," Wexx said.

"I saw . . . saw them."

"Them?"

"The aliens," Venice whispered.

Wexx's skin crawled. There were aliens at New Eden. This was terrifying. This was exciting and interesting.

"Can you describe them to me?" Wexx asked.

On the cot, Venice moved her head from side to side. "I couldn't see clearly, Dr. Wexx. They watched, absorbed with their experiment. They held slates, taking notes on the horrors committed upon me. Their fingers . . ."

"What about their fingers?" Wexx asked.

"The fingers or digits were not flesh, but something much harder."

"You're doing well, Venice. Keeping talking."

The Special's features hardened. The mouth firmed. "Do not patronize me, Doctor. I'm trying to warn you. Let me out of here. Let me shift us home."

"First, tell us more about the dream," Wexx said.

"It was a precognitive dream," Venice said. "I was on a table and they removed organs. They put things in me. But it wasn't just me. It was all of us, Doctor. Don't you realize? If we reach New Eden, we're all going to die horribly. The aliens will dissect us on their tables. We're bugs to them."

"Is that why you went berserk in the tele-chamber?"

"You're not listening to me, Dr. Wexx. And you're using Jasper to try to pry into my mind. You'd better start listening to me and do what I tell you."

Venice's eyes went cold gray.

Wexx stabbed the kill switch, but nothing happened.

"You waited too long, Doctor," Venice said. "You let me wake up."

"No!" Jasper howled.

Wexx twisted around. Jasper had his hands in front of his face. Sweat pooled on his features and he squeezed his eyes shut.

Wexx shouted into the speaker, "Stop it, Venice! You're killing him!"

"I'm going to kill all the Specials! We're never going to New Eden! We're going home!"

Wexx watched the screen. Portals slid up and three monitors charged into the chamber. Venice's head swiveled to regard them. The first monitor flew up off his feet and slammed against the ceiling, pinned. The second charged in and his head exploded in a rain of blood, skull, and brain.

Wexx groaned at the grisly sight.

The third monitor fast-drew an illegal needler. Wexx saw in surprise that it was Chief Monitor Argon. He had reflexes like a machine. Venice's head shifted, maybe to take some action against him, but it was too late. Argon fired, sending thin metallic needles into Venice's face, puncturing forehead, cheekbones, and mouth.

Special First Class Venice died on the cot. The first monitor fell from the ceiling, dazed. The second monitor's giant torso pumped blood onto the floor.

"You killed her," Wexx said in horror.

Chief Monitor Argon holstered his needler. "I'd feared something like this might happen."

"You killed a Special," Wexx said. It felt as if she was floating. "That brings a sentence of death."

Argon stared at Venice's body.

"You are under arrest, Chief Monitor," Wexx said into her speaker. "Please ask your surviving monitor to take you into custody."

A wintry look appeared on Argon's face. "It is time for me to unseal my extraordinary orders. They're from Premier Lang, putting me in charge of the expedition."

A sick feeling filled Wexx, like a ball of lead dropped in her stomach. Venice had killed a monitor and nearly killed Jasper. The First Class Special claimed to have precognitive dreams and now Venice was dead. Argon had usurped power, and he might also have just saved their lives.

What waited in New Eden that was so terrible? How could aliens there affect the Teleship's Specials? How could aliens there even know humans were out here?

"What are we going to do now?" Jasper asked.

Wexx nodded. That was an excellent question.

11

Chief Monitor Argon called a meeting in the officer's lounge. He recorded it as *"Discovery* Meeting #12."

|||||||||||

ARGON: Premier Lang, I am in the process of revealing your sealed orders to the critical crew personnel regarding the chief monitor's emergency powers. I have now put those orders on-screen for the personnel to read. Are there any questions from those present?
KONEV: The order appears correct and legal.
NAGASAKI: You have usurped authority.
ARGON: I am the commanding officer under Premier Lang's emergency powers. As the colonel stated, everything is correct and legal.
WEXX: You killed Venice. That is illegal.
ARGON: Self-defense is always a right whether it exists in codified law or not. In my case, I also happen to have full authority to eliminate whomever I deem a danger to the expedition. The Special killed

one of my monitors. She was in the process of slaying Jasper, another Special—the superior of the two sane Specials left us.

WEXX: You're actually trying to justify the murder of Sol's greatest Special?

ARGON: You would rather I'd died in the room?

WEXX: I wish you'd subdued her with a trank so we could continue questioning her later.

ARGON: Combat conditions do not always lend themselves to perfect solutions. The important point to remember is that the Teleship is safe with a minimum of casualties. Now we must decide on our reaction to the new information.

WEXX: What can we do? You've killed our best shifter. Returning to Sol will take us a long, long time, providing our two remaining shifters remain sane.

ARGON: Sanity seems to lie in direct proportion to the distance from New Eden. The farther we are from it, the saner the Specials act. We can wake Roxie after several shifts and include her in the roster. That will expedite matters considerably.

NAGASAKI: I suggest we continue on our journey to New Eden.

ARGON: Elaborate if you would.

NAGASAKI: By the evidence, we have found new life forms, aliens. They appear to have mental capabilities. At least, they are able to harm our Specials. We must discover further evidence of the aliens, doing so in the interest of safety regarding Sol.

ARGON: We are presuming Special Venice actually had the precognitive ability she claimed.

WEXX: I checked her bio. She had them—the dreams—and they have an 87 percent accuracy rating.

ARGON: Let us examine the evidence rationally. Venice had precognitive dreams. Her dreams were correct 87 percent of the time. She dreamt that aliens examined her, removing organs and adding something to her. Now Venice is dead and her dream can never come true. Therefore, this precognitive dream was false, or part of the 13 percent failure rate.

WEXX: That doesn't necessarily hold true. What if the aliens examine her corpse?

ARGON: That was logically deduced, Doctor. You are right. I had not considered that.

NAGASAKI: I'm unfamiliar with Specials. Precognitive dreams . . . this is a strange sort of science.

WEXX: Teleships work, do they not?

NAGASAKI: No one questions that.

WEXX: If Teleships work, precognitive dreams can work too.

NAGASAKI: I wouldn't presume otherwise. My point is that Venice's dream was sketchy at best. She pinpointed aliens and warned us of their existence. Very well, now we must slip into New Eden and record the evidence.

ARGON: How can we slip in if our Specials cannot shift there?

JASPER: I can shift us to New Eden.

NAGASAKI: If aliens exist, Sol must hear of this.

ARGON: I agree. Sol must learn of these aliens and their location. That is why we must turn around as Special Venice wanted and return at once to Sol.

NAGASAKI: That is the wrong decision.

ARGON: I am willing to listen to your logic. Convince me I'm wrong.

NAGASAKI: We have a precognitive dream as a warning. That's it. We need better proof. Some of our Specials have malfunctioned on the approach to New Eden. We have to learn why.

ARGON: Not at the expense of losing *Discovery* and thereby denying Sol the knowledge of these aliens.

NAGASAKI: I'm not suggesting such a thing. We're a warship, are we not?

ARGON: No. We are not a warship. We are an exploratory and colonizing vessel with armaments. Now if aliens already inhabit New Eden—

NAGASAKI: That's just it. No aliens can inhabit the system. Look at the telescopes. Study the star system. We're eight light years away. It's conceivable a technological civilization leaped into existence two hundred and thirty years ago, but not eight years ago.

ARGON: You believe that's why the astronomers saw no evidence of high technology, because their evidence was two hundred and thirty years old, the speed at which light left New Eden and traveled to Pluto?

NAGASAKI: It would fit the facts—but only if we could see something now. We don't. Ergo, there is no civilization at AS 412, or New Eden if you prefer.

ARGON: What do you think is there?

NAGASAKI: A ship, perhaps or a colony, as we built a lone habitat at Epsilon Eridani.

ARGON: Can you be more specific?

NAGASAKI: Commanding Officer, I would like to speak to you in private.

ARGON: I would need a reason first.

NAGASAKI: System-wide security.

ARGON: At New Eden?

NAGASAKI: No. Sol's future security.

ARGON: (Rises from his seat.) We will take a short recess as Captain Nagasaki tells me his urgent and apparently secret information.

END of Transcript #12

12

Captain Nagasaki floated after Argon.

The chief monitor gracefully practiced zero G maneuvers down the narrow passageway. The seven-foot giant used the hand rungs, pulling or swimming his way along.

Nagasaki did it even better from endless years of practice. Twenty-six years ago, the sleeper ship *Argonaut* had accelerated out of Sol at one G as it built up to near light speed. That had been the easiest part of the journey. The long coast had been much more tedious, the years of weightlessness.

That had been nothing, however, compared to the growing fear of cyborgs as they approached Epsilon Eridani.

During the Great War of the solar system, the cyborgs had destroyed the supreme philosophical and political arrangement known to man. The cyborgs had sent an armada and eradicated Jovian life from the moons and habitats. Circe had taken the survivors of that awful time and repopulated the two moons of Neptune. The cyborgs of that era had slaughtered or converted all Neptunians, leaving the gas giant's gravity system bare of human life.

In the beautiful Jovian system, the wisest had ruled, the most spirited fought, and the brutes labored. It had brought about the highest of artistic achievement and human thought. Then the cyborgs had destroyed it all like an evil virus, murdering love, art, beauty, and political harmony.

Nagasaki ground his teeth together as he floated into the chamber with Chief Monitor Argon. He sensed the truth. The cyborgs must have indeed built at least one more proto-Teleship. They had escaped far from Sol, to rebuild in the stars, forging an invincible empire of machine-man melds. What else could be waiting for them at AS 412?

"Well?" Argon asked. "What is this secret information? Are you going to warn me about cyborgs?"

Nagasaki approved of the Spartan nature of the quarters. Nothing adorned the walls. There was a cot, a clean desk and these two chairs. Of clothes, shoes, or personal items, there was no sign.

The captain withdrew a capsule from a hidden pocket. It was the size of his thumb, with a flat end with hundreds of microscopic holes. He moved toward the bigger man and slapped the flat end of the capsule against the fabric of the chief monitor's right thigh. In a powerful jet of air—and a soft sigh of sound—tranks injected past the fabric and into Argon's skin.

The chief monitor moved with startling speed, backhanding Nagasaki. The small captain catapulted from his spot and sailed against a wall, thudding against it with his shoulders.

"What have you—?" Argon said.

Nagasaki was far from finished. As the chief monitor spoke, Nagasaki corrected his position and thrust with his thighs, propelling himself at Argon's head. The captain was a black belt in zero G karate, something he'd perfected during the round trip from Sol to Epsilon Eridani and back.

Argon twisted toward him as Nagasaki flew at his head. The NKV officer blocked, and the two men traded swift, zero G blows.

"This is treason against Premier Lang!" Argon shouted. "You won't live long enough to enjoy it, I assure you."

Nagasaki breathed heavily as sweat floated off him. He'd never faced anyone with such strength and speed. The man was phenomenal. Weightlessness helped him against the NKV officer, as did the fast-acting drug in the chief monitor's bloodstream. Colonel Konev had assured him the drug would efficiently knock out Argon. Now Nagasaki was beginning to doubt if it would happen quickly enough.

"You're the one being treasonous," Nagasaki panted, trying to buy time. "I am the captain of the Teleship. With your so-called sealed orders—an obvious forgery—you have declared mutiny against me. How do you think I handled these matters aboard *Argonaut*? I didn't wait for others to do my dirty work. I, personally, put an end to sedition."

Argon showed his teeth, but his efforts had noticeably slowed and his speech was beginning to slur. "You have no idea why you're doing this?"

"I'm perfectly aware of my actions."

"Jasper must have tricked me. He uses you."

"The telepath has nothing to do with this," Nagasaki said.

"The telepath has delusions of godhood, you fool. I've read his secret profile. His inhibitor must be faulty."

"You're wrong."

Argon roared and launched himself at Nagasaki. The captain kicked, and then his ankle was caught in a bone-crushing grip as the chief monitor wrapped his thick fingers around it.

"You'll never use this foot again," Argon snarled.

Nagasaki shouted in pain, and with his other foot, he repeatedly kicked Argon in the face, bruising the broad cheeks.

Finally, Nagasaki wrenched his ankle free. The chief monitor glared at him helplessly as blood pumped into the air from his nostrils. The blood floated in globular shapes, with little droplets breaking off to orbit the main mass.

"Give . . . me . . . antidote," Argon slurred.

From the corner of the ceiling, Nagasaki panted. He'd known ahead of time that it was going to be a hard fight, but he hadn't expected this. Had the chief monitor crippled him?

". . . fool . . ." Argon whispered, with his eyelids fluttering.

Nagasaki watched the chief monitor pass into unconsciousness. The telepath could be a problem. But Colonel Konev already had an answer for that. Now, it was time to search and find the illegal needler, the one Argon had used to kill Venice. They were going to need the weapon in order to subdue the other monitors.

13

Cyrus waited in the officer's lounge with the others. It was a spacious room as such things went aboard *Discovery*.

There was a long table in the center of the chamber, with various consoles embedded in the plastic top. Screens lined the walls, each showing a bright, recorded day on Earth. Cyrus focused on a rolling plain. A flock of crows flew in the sky toward a lone tree.

Two monitors in the chamber flanked the closed hatch. Like giant sentinels, they stood at each side, alert and waiting for orders.

Jasper sat across the table from Cyrus. The telepath wore a shiny suit, fiddling with an oblong object, twisting colored pieces on it. The thing was a game of some sort. Something clicked on it.

The sound or something about the object drew Cyrus's gaze from the rolling plain to it. He crunched his brows together, wondering what Jasper was trying to achieve with the toy.

"They've been gone too long," Colonel Konev announced.

The marine wasn't in his seat, but floated near the head of the table. He wore his dress uniform, with one of his big hands in a pocket.

Cyrus noticed because whatever Konev held in his pocket he rolled around nervously. That was odd. Why would Konev be nervous?

Frowning, Cyrus glanced at Jasper. The man was absorbed with his toy, clicking a colored piece, clicking another . . .

Cyrus noticed the telepath's eyes, the giveaway. They'd turned a faint metallic color. Was he wrong to do nothing?

Doctor Wexx stood up. She wore Velcro-soled shoes. Making a *rip-rip* sound, she approached the portal and the two monitors.

Both NKV officers were big, towering at six-ten and six-eleven. They wore the black uniform, with stunner-rods holstered at their sides. The wide faces, the intense eyes: These two had Highborn blood like the chief monitor.

"I need to use the restroom," Wexx said.

The taller monitor shook his head. "You will await the chief monitor's return."

Wexx laughed. "But I need to go."

Go? Cyrus wondered. Doctor Wexx was much too formal to say it like that. He turned to Jasper. The telepath had his head down, and he no longer fingered his oblong toy or game.

"Doctor," Cyrus said.

Doctor Wexx wasn't listening. She charged the door. "I insist you let me pass!" she shouted, grappling with the nearest monitor.

The monitor frowned as he easily held her off. "You will remain here until the—"

The portal opened. The second monitor glanced outside into the passageway, and he moved fast toward the hatch.

The soft sound of a firing needler froze Cyrus, as everything seemed to happen in slow motion. The taller monitor reversed his grip on Dr. Wexx, spinning her around and immobilizing her—but it also immobilized him for the moment. The other monitor continued to twist toward the portal, but now he contorted sharply as if in pain. Deadly needles exited his back, stitching through his garment. Squirts of blood followed.

"Don't move!" Colonel Konev roared, aiming his words at the remaining monitor.

The NKV officer kept hold of Wexx and turned his head toward the hatch.

Cyrus saw the same thing the monitor must have seen. Captain Nagasaki stood in the portal, holding the needler, pointing it at the monitor's face.

The live monitor relaxed his muscles, releasing Dr. Wexx. She jerked loose and hurried back against a wall, staring at the scene in shock and rearranging her disheveled clothes.

"If you move," Konev crisply told the monitor, "the captain will kill you."

"Where is Argon?" the giant asked.

"That is no concern of yours," Konev said. "You must ask yourself: Do I want to live?"

The giant regarded the colonel. "This—all this—is your doing?"

"It is," Konev admitted. With his large sideburns and stance, the marine seemed like a lion.

Cyrus glanced at Jasper. The telepath had put away his oblong object and sat there with a half smile on his chubby face. Cyrus wanted to charge him and put his knife under his throat. He was certain the captain would shoot him if he tried. So Cyrus did the next best thing. He waited for his chance.

"What are your plans?" the monitor asked Konev.

"That isn't your concern either," the marine said. "Do you want to live or should we kill you and eliminate any future problems?"

The monitor seemed to calculate swiftly.

He's like a beast, Cyrus realized. *The captain is mad if he thinks he's safe holding a needler so near the monitor.* Cyrus knew some monitors had taken mind shield training. Is that why Premier Lang had put Highborn echoes aboard the Teleship? Highborn would have potent mind shields. Were they another of Lang's endless redundancies regarding Specials?

"Captain," Konev said, "if you would make your way to me, please. But be careful. The monitor is deadly and can strike like a whiplash."

The monitor glanced at Jasper. A moment later, the monitor said, "I will submit to you." He put his back to Nagasaki and slowly moved to the nearest wall, putting his hands and body against it in the arrest position.

"Should I kill him?" Nagasaki asked Jasper.

"No!" Konev said. "We need the monitors. They know many important things about the ship the rest of us don't. There are only twelve of them. We can keep them in the brig."

Cyrus finally saw what Konev had kept in his pocket: binding ties.

The monitor saw the same thing and put his hands behind his back. Konev attached the ties to the wrists and others to the ankles, binding the giant. Once finished, he turned to Nagasaki.

"Give me the weapon," he said.

Nagasaki scowled.

"I need the weapon so I can insure the freeing and arming of my marines," Konev said. "Once we're combat armed, there's nothing the monitors can do even if they were all free."

Nagasaki cocked his head.

Cyrus noticed Jasper with his head bent. Sweat appeared on the telepath's face.

A moment later, Nagasaki reversed his grip and handed the needler to Konev.

The colonel checked the gleaming weapon. "Hmm," he muttered. "The magazine is almost spent. How many did you fire into the monitor?"

Nagasaki shook his head.

"It doesn't matter," Konev said. "Cyrus you'll push the monitor for me."

Cyrus rubbed his jaw. Jasper wanted him out of here for a reason. So one way or another, he'd better go. "Sure," he said.

14

"Why hadn't the other monitors in their stations gassed us?" Cyrus asked Konev.

Cyrus propelled the prone and secured NKV giant down a passageway, pushing him ahead of them.

Colonel Konev brought up the rear. The needler was in his waistband. Just like Cyrus, he used the hand rungs as they free-floated toward the brig.

"We're marines, lad. That means something."

"Okay . . ." Cyrus said.

Konev chuckled. "I know you're nervous, son. But let me tell you that you're doing fine. Maybe I shouldn't tell you this, but we're Neptunian Space Marines."

"I don't get it."

"You're from Earth and probably don't know the history of Outer Planets. Knowing we're Neptunians would have meant something to our NKV friend here, but he and the chief monitor didn't. This is our greatest coup against Premier Lang and it took extraordinary pains to accomplish it."

That didn't ring right to Cyrus. Lang and his NKV had gone to extraordinary lengths vetting the crew. Had Jasper tweaked the marines, getting them to believe they were Neptunians? If true . . . Jasper must have been very busy indeed.

"I thought this was about us helping Sol against the aliens," Cyrus said.

"Son, I've been watching you these past weeks, and I like what I've seen. That knife fight the other day decided it for me. You're one of us, if you'll stick it through to the end."

"Sure," Cyrus said.

"No," Konev said. "Go the other way."

Cyrus had begun maneuvering the bound monitor into the left fork of the passageway. He grabbed a handhold and one of the giant's feet, stopping the forward momentum.

"The brig is this way," Cyrus said, pointing down the steel corridor where he'd planned to go.

"Understood, but we're not taking him to the brig."

Cyrus pulled the tall monitor back and maneuvered him in the other direction. He pushed, slowly building up momentum. By going this way, they would pass near the sealed armory where the marines stored their combat armor and weapons. Interestingly, it was far from their quarters. He'd never thought about that until now.

The colonel checked the corridor they'd come from and the one leading to the brig. Then he hurried after Cyrus. For a moment, Konev looked nervous, with worry in his eyes. He caught Cyrus studying him, and grinned, nodding.

"Have you ever heard of Plato?" Konev asked.

"No," Cyrus said. What were the other marines doing now? They had to be attacking the monitors. At least one NKV officer would be at his post and gassing them otherwise. This entire operation had taken precision planning and balls. *Is that what Konev meant when he said they were marines?*

"Plato was a brilliant teacher, a philosopher," Konev was saying.

"Sure."

"A philosopher is a deep thinker about important issues," Konev explained. "Plato came from an ancient land called Greece. He lived in the city of Athens."

"Got it," Cyrus said.

"Plato devised a society where the wisest would rule. The most spirited would become the protectors or soldiers. The common people—those who could only think about sex and filling their bellies—they would become the workers. In time, brilliant Earth colonists set up that structure in the Jupiter System. A hundred years ago, the cyborgs destroyed it, but the germ of the idea lived on. We're those people's descendants. We outwitted the NKV by placing our best and brightest aboard as marines."

"Sounds too good to be true," Cyrus said.

"We had some help of course," Konev said, "but most of it was through shrewd maneuvering on our part."

"Did Jasper help you fool the NKV?"

They floated in silence then, and Cyrus decided it was time to free the monitor.

Before Cyrus started the process, Konev said, "Son. That was a brilliant piece of thinking just now. How did you figure out Jasper helped us?"

"I make lucky guesses sometimes."

Konev gave him a measuring glance. The eyes were cold like dark marble and there was something *flat* about them. "No. You're psi-able. That means something important. You *belong* in New Eden with us."

"You're a dupe, Colonel," the monitor suddenly spoke.

"So you've decided to quit faking sleep," Konev said.

"Don't you understand that Jasper has broken through his inhibitor?" the monitor said. "He's been using you, altering your thoughts. The telepath has gone rogue and is trying to take over. I can feel him trying to break me down. He must be nearby and I'm sure he wants the codes to the armory."

Jasper was nearby? Cyrus hesitated to act to free the monitor and cause the needler to malfunction. Jasper would immediately sense if he tried something psionic.

"Let me tell you how it's going to go," Konev told the monitor. "We can drug you and tamper with your brain, or you can give me the locker codes."

"I'm conditioned against doing as you suggest," the monitor said.

"Hmm, I thought it might be like that."

"If you attempt to drug me," the monitor said, "I will die."

"The chief monitor didn't die when Nagasaki drugged him," Konev said.

"Premier Lang's psychologists must have removed Argon's conditioning before the voyage. The same is not true for me."

"You're lucky Jasper told me the same thing," Konev said. "Otherwise, you would be near death about now. As it is, pain can bring down your concentration. Am I right?"

The monitor licked his lips in what might have been nervousness. He glanced at Cyrus. "Are you party to this treason?"

"Don't talk to the lad," Konev said.

"You don't trust him?" the monitor asked.

"Of course I trust him."

"You've lied to him," the monitor said.

"There you're wrong."

"You will never attempt to return to Sol. This sedition has nothing to do with cyborgs or aliens at New Eden."

"If you don't quit talking . . ." Konev warned.

"I've been listening to everything everyone has said," the monitor told Cyrus. "I have rationally deduced the likeliest situation."

"I'm not going to warn you a second time," Konev said.

"From the evidence, it's clear the telepath has orchestrated everything," the monitor said. "There are no aliens in New Eden, certainly none that can reach our ship with psi-abilities across twenty-five light years."

"I warned you." Konev drew a stunner-rod from his holster, one he'd taken off a monitor earlier. By clicking a ring-switch, he raised the setting so the rod hummed with power. He floated near the prone monitor, who twisted his bound wrists, the ones behind his back.

Cyrus concentrated, and he shorted out the stunner-rod.

Konev must not have noticed right away. In a deft and rather delicate move, the colonel stroked the rod across the monitor's left check. Nothing happened: there was no sizzle. Konev drew back and twisted the rod's setting switch. He tried again, but again, it didn't work. He whirled around and pointed the stunner-rod at Cyrus.

"You did this," the colonel said.

"Jasper has tampered with your mind," Cyrus said. The colonel was big and strong, and even with an ordinary baton he would be dangerous. If Cyrus had a knife, it would be different, but he didn't have one now.

"You must not listen to the monitor's lies," Konev said. "They are masters of verbal manipulation and know how to trick people."

"Truth cuts through lies," the monitor said. "Listen to the Special. He knows the truth. How do you think he caused the stunner to malfunction? His inhibitor no longer works either. It means Jasper has been free to tamper with everyone's mind. We of the NKV are conditioned against mind control. It is the reason for this farce."

"No," Konev snarled. He pointed the rod at Cyrus. "It's time for a lesson."

"Hold it!" a new voice commanded.

Cyrus spun around. Jasper stood behind them on the deck plates. He hadn't heard the telepath walk up.

"I have it," Jasper told the colonel. "I have the armory's code sequences."

"Excellent," Konev said. "The monitor's arrogance has begun to grate on me." The colonel holstered the stunner-rod and drew the needler from his waistband.

Cyrus reached out with his power and attempted to short it. Jasper struck then with a mind bolt. Cyrus winced as he defended himself.

Konev, meanwhile, put the tiny needler near the monitor's left temple and pulled the trigger. A stitching sound occurred as needles slid into the monitor's brain, killing him instantly.

"Why did you allow that?" Cyrus asked Jasper.

"Will you lower your mind shield and open yourself to me so I know I can trust you?" Jasper asked.

Cyrus floated in the passageway with the dead monitor, globules of drifting blood and Colonel Konev behind him. Jasper stood before him on the weave on the deck plates, anchored in his shoes. Cyrus knew if he flew at Jasper to attack him, the marine could easily shoot him in the back with the needler.

"I'm not going to become one of your zombies," Cyrus said.

"He's stubborn," Konev said. "Should I kill him?"

"Don't be absurd," Jasper said. "Leave the monitor's corpse. We'll clean that up later. Secure the Special's wrists behind his back with one of your ties. Then take him with you and leave him among your marines."

Konev pulled Cyrus's hands behind his back, binding his wrists tightly. "Come with me," he said, using one arm to propel Cyrus past the floating corpse and toward the waiting armory.

"If you lower your mind shield, it doesn't have to be this way," Jasper said.

Cyrus didn't have a good answer. Thus, he kept silent. He needed time to think.

15

The demons struck without warning as the Tash-Toi marched to the Wild Rocks.

Klane strode beside the seeker. They were in the middle of the clan, surrounded by the hetman's wives and children. Around the hetman's many wives were the other clan members' wives. The women carried the tents and pots and dragged the fire, while the older children carried tent poles.

The warriors ranged farther out, each man carrying his weapons. They searched for game and protected the clan from a sudden raid. Large black boulders stuck out of the ground at the oddest intervals. In the distance were the teeth of the Wild Rocks. In them were dangerous predators, but it was a good place to hide from the demons.

A woman shrieked, and she pointed toward the sun.

Klane squinted, looking up and shading his eyes.

"What do you see?" the seeker asked in a grave voice.

"Four air-cars," Klane said.

"They come for revenge," the old man said in a sad voice. "They come for you, Klane."

Klane's features hardened, and he thrust a hand into his secret place, withdrawing his black junction-stone.

"I made one air-car malfunction," Klane said. "I can do it to four."

"No. These are larger vehicles. Your TK will prove ineffectual against them. They wish to study you. But I can never allow that. It is too late to transfer. Yes, I've been a fool to wait this long."

Women and children dropped their possessions and scattered in all directions. Several warriors ran toward the air-cars, challenging the demons. The other warriors bolted.

"We have no more time," Klane said.

"This is a disaster," the seeker said. "I should have transferred when I had the chance. But I wasn't ready. It was my fault and I may have doomed humanity because of it."

Klane hardly heard the old man. He psyched himself up for the effort of his life.

"I'm sorry, Klane," the seeker said from behind him, putting a hand on his shoulder.

Klane heard something odd there. He turned, and took the full brunt of a club against his forehead. He toppled backward, striking the ground with the back of his head. Someone pried at his fingers.

The junction-stone! Klane tightened his fingers, but the stone was gone. Groggily, he turned over as the front of his head thudded. With watery eyes, he saw the seeker walking toward the descending sky vehicles.

"Here!" the seeker shouted, holding aloft Klane's junction-stone. "I'm the one you want."

As if the demons heard the old man's words, dark clots blew out of the sky vehicles. The clots moved fast, expanding as they descended toward the seeker.

Klane tried to push up, but his arms failed him and he thudded back onto the ground.

One of the clots struck the seeker, and sticky strands wrapped around him. The demons had netted the old man, and he fell onto the sand.

Milky beams shot out of the sky vehicles, hitting several courageous warriors. They too toppled, with greasy smoke billowing from them. Afterward, blood poured from the death wounds.

"No," Klane whispered. "No."

A sky vehicle sank toward the bound seeker. Doors opened in the bottom of the floating vehicle. A claw reached down, clutching the old man and hauling him up into the great vehicle.

In horror, Klane watched the seeker disappear into the demons' air-car. The bay doors closed, sealing the old man in the evil machine. The four sky vehicles lifted and headed back in the direction they had come.

He gave himself to the demons, Klane realized. *They came for me, and they took him because he carried my junction-stone.*

Tears leaked from Klane's eyes. The demons had stolen his only friend in the world.

16

Cyrus wore a blue slick-suit in the tele-chamber. He was beside the cylinder with its blue solution. The shift crew was at their stations, and one nurse held the induction helmet while the other waited with the breathing mask.

The last two weeks had been difficult. Day and night, he'd kept up his mind shield. Three times, he'd felt Jasper attempt to break into his thoughts.

The first week he'd spent with the marines. The last week Jasper had confined him to his room. During the two weeks, Jasper had shifted three times, bringing them 6.3 light years closer to New Eden. They were 1.95 light years away now, practically knocking on the door in shifting terms, though years away in normal space.

Cyrus fit the induction helmet over his head. The inside was soft, with wireless connections linking him to AI Socrates and the outer tele-ring circling *Discovery*. The helmet was one of the most important parts of the shifting equipment.

Once it was properly secured, Cyrus accepted the breathing mask. The blue solution in the cylinder acted like a conductor and aided his linkage with the tele-ring.

The mask pressed against the skin of his face. Goggles slid over his eyes. Gingerly, Cyrus climbed up a short ladder and slid his right leg into the lengthwise cylinder. The gelatinous substance within was warm.

Taking a deep breath, Cyrus slid into the cylinder. It was difficult to peer through the blue solution. It was like looking through murky water. Even Wexx standing so near took on an indistinct, fuzzy shape.

He closed his eyes, and there came a buzz of noise. Disorientation struck and nausea flooded Cyrus. The nausea passed and his senses expanded exponentially. He felt the Teleship's engines thrumming with life. The fusion power would soon be under his control.

Within the cylinder, Cyrus Gant grew rigid and he scrunched his brows tightly. Linked with AI Socrates and the tele-ring orbiting and spinning around *Discovery*, he reached out with his telekinetic ability.

It was an awesome feeling, godlike and surreal. The stars were motes of brilliance, heat that he could sense on his skin. New Eden . . . yes, the star blazed with nuclear energies. It poured out radiation and light. They seemed to come in waves or ripples as if a giant planet had been tossed into the sun like a pebble in a lake.

Cyrus concentrated with his heightened power. He took the fabric of existence, and he twisted, ripping out a portal, linking two locations into one. Cyrus grinned, sunning in the sensation, delighting in the use of his power as a young man might enjoy sprinting for a goal in fist ball. He exulted in doing, in feeling, in expending . . .

He felt a tickle of something *alien*. It brushed his mind. He "heard" murmuring, wondering, and then something reached for him and squeezed his thoughts.

"What—?" Cyrus had time for the single word. Then he was battling for his mind. With AI Socrates's augmented power, he reached farther than it would have been humanly possible for him to do. It seemed as if these others, these aliens, attempted to spring a trap on his mind.

Cyrus blocked. He fended off the alien minds and began to shear away each link one after another. He sensed bafflement, surprise, and then rage. The entity or entities surged with strength against him. Cyrus imagined himself employing knife-fighting tactics, weaves, dodges, and he sheared off another link.

Discovery passed through the null portal and appeared eight tenths of a light year closer to New Eden.

The difference in location loosened the last alien links.

Cyrus withdrew his mind like a turtle into its shell. He pulled back from the tele-ring and from AI Socrates. He blocked everything non-him, and felt panic surge in his breast. Then his eyes flew open and he found himself floating in the blue solution. In that instant, Cyrus realized this is what had happened to Roxie and Venice. They must have sensed the same horror he'd felt and started immediately fighting.

Why is Jasper immune to the panic?

Cyrus!

Cyrus blocked against Jasper, shutting the voice from speaking in his head. He was weary, expended from shifting, but he would never allow the telepath into his mind again.

Composing himself, calming the panic, Cyrus pushed from the bottom of the cylinder and surfaced. He plucked off the induction helmet and tore the mask from his face, breathing the cool, canned air of *Discovery*. He squeezed his eyes shut several times as he took off the goggles. Then he saw First Sergeant Sergetov with two other marines standing near with stunner-rods poised.

"What's wrong?" Cyrus asked in a rough voice.

Wexx aimed her sunglasses at him. She shifted her head and glanced at her medical panel. "He appears normal again," she said.

"Is it a trick?" the first sergeant asked her.

"Hey, don't you remember that we're friends?" Cyrus asked the NCO.

The first sergeant watched him with cold eyes.

"Did I say something wrong?" Cyrus asked.

"I think he's conditioned against you," Wexx said.

Cyrus glanced at Wexx and then back at his friend. Was Jasper in league with the aliens? Had the man turned traitor against humanity? It was clear then what he had to do: kill Jasper or incapacitate him. The question was how.

The tele-chamber hatch opened and who should walk in but Jasper. "You're coming with me for debriefing," he told Cyrus. "Until then, you're not to say a word to anyone."

"Word," Cyrus said.

"Do that again," Jasper said, "and the marine will give you a touch of the stunner. Would you like that?"

Here was his chance: the debriefing. He needed to play along so Jasper dropped his guard. So Cyrus shook his head.

"Then hop down from there and come with me," Jasper said. "I'm interested to hear your impressions."

||||||||||

First Sergeant Mikhail Sergetov and one other marine stood by the hatch in the officer's lounge. They wore protective coveralls with stunner-rods in their fists. Apparently, the lounge had become Jasper's unofficial headquarters.

Cyrus slumped in a chair, exhausted but ready. *Discovery* was under one G deceleration and thus had pseudogravity.

Jasper sat at the end of the table near the hatch and the protecting marines. He leaned back in his chair with his feet propped up on the conference table. "I know you're tired," Jasper said. "And you're going to sleep very deeply soon. But there are a few things I want to talk about with you first."

Cyrus didn't feel as tired as that, but leaned forward and put his arms on the table and his head on his arms. He shut his eyes as if he was going to go to sleep.

Jasper used one of his heels to knock against the table. "I told you sleep time was later. You're going to answer some questions now."

Cyrus opened his eyes, but kept his head on his arms.

"What are your impressions?" Jasper asked.

I don't get this. The telepath turned traitor and he's asking me for impressions. What am I missing here?

"My impressions about shifting?" Cyrus asked.

"There's no need to be coy. These two aren't going to remember anything about our talk. They're here to forestall any foolishness on your part."

"Do you control everyone here?"

"Let's stick to the issue," Jasper said.

"What? You don't like me talking about control so they can hear it, huh?"

"You're not as tired as you're trying to appear."

"You think so?"

Jasper took his feet off the table and sat up. "I'm talking about the aliens. What are your impressions of them?"

"Argon had it right. We should high tail it home and report this. Have the aliens taken over your mind? Is that what's going on?"

"Me? You're still in charge of your thoughts and you think they could take control of *me*? Don't be absurd."

"What are they?"

"That's what I'm asking you. What were your impressions about them?"

Cyrus frowned. "Okay. There was more than one of them."

"And?"

"They tried to trap me."

Jasper nodded.

"I sheared away their holds, but I had to do it several times. That's why I think there was more than one of them."

"You used your regular block to do that?"

Cyrus nodded.

"I know you're suspicious about me," Jasper said. "But I want you to know I've been studying these aliens and they've been trying to study us. When she learned about them, Venice went crazy with fear. You were right about that. Roxie . . . I'm not sure what happened inside her head. I tried to help them both."

"Why do you want to go to New Eden? You and I are free of the inhibitors. We got what we came for. Why risk more by going to these psi-able aliens?"

"There are several reasons," Jasper said. "One of them is simple curiosity. I want to see what they are. There's something about their minds that is very familiar."

"Are you crazy? Are you saying these aliens have been to Earth?"

"Yes, I think they have," Jasper said.

"When?"

"That's something else I'd like to learn."

"Why are you willing to put yourself in danger?" Cyrus asked.

"That's the third reason. Look, what are the odds of two alien Teleships coming together in a star system? This system is two hundred and thirty light years from Sol. I think these aliens know about us, but we don't know anything about them. It's foolish to just cut and run. We have to use this opportunity to see who they are."

"What if they capture our ship?"

Jasper shook his head. "We have a Teleship. If their ship is too powerful, we flee."

"Why are they at New Eden?"

"Probably for the same reason we're headed there," Jasper said. "They want the two Earth-like planets. How many Earth-like planets are there? We haven't spotted any others. The aliens must be a colonizing party just like we are."

"You didn't say that before," Cyrus said. "Before, you said they put false pictures up for telescopes to see. Now you're changing your story and saying it's a mere ship?"

A brief look of concern crossed Jasper's features. "No, I was wrong about my first idea. Now I think it's a ship."

"I don't think so," Cyrus said.

"*You* don't think so." Jasper smirked, putting lines around his mouth. "What makes you an authority?"

"Probabilities," Cyrus said. "I doubt we both just happened to arrive at the same time to do the same thing. Now you said something interesting or far-fetched a moment ago. You think they've been to Sol before. Does that mean you think they're cyborgs?"

"I think the odds are high, yes," Jasper said.

"That means we should quit screwing around. The cyborgs are horror on two legs. But then I've been stupid believing you care anything about getting vital information back to Sol. Premier Lang will execute you for treason for what you've done. Why did you have to take over the ship?"

Jasper watched him.

"The only reason I can think is that you're in league with these aliens," Cyrus said.

"Why would I be?" Jasper asked.

"I have no idea. Maybe they messed with your mind. You don't think they did, but they did and you're as buffaloed as these two marines. That would be the easiest way for these aliens to capture us, to have fixed you to fix the rest of us. And that would make sense why you didn't warn me about them then."

Jasper's nostrils flared. "You have no idea what's really going on. But just so you don't panic the others with your wild rumors, I'm putting you in the brig with Argon."

Cyrus glanced up at the ceiling. If the marines had been outside the hatch, he would charge Jasper and try to break his neck. With them watching him so closely and with their stunner-rods ready, he didn't stand a chance. He had to keep waiting.

He stood up, and asked, "What did the aliens offer you anyway?"

"You have it backward," Jasper said. "It's me who offered the aliens enticements. I'm the one who's going to capture them. That's what this is all about."

"Oh. Why didn't you say so? Let me help you."

"Certainly," Jasper said. "Drop your block and let me look in your mind so I know I can trust you."

"Sure," Cyrus said. "First, give me a gun so I know you really trust me."

"I hold all the cards. You need to convince me, not the other way around."

It was hard, but this time Cyrus kept his mouth shut.

Jasper turned to the marines. "Take him to the brig and lock him with Chief Monitor Argon."

PART III: ARRIVAL

1

Captain Nagasaki sat in his command chair in the bridge module.

His seat was higher than the three other chairs for navigation, weaponry, and shift. Screens surrounded each officer, including Nagasaki. The tight quarters were little bigger than the central compartment of a main battle tank on Earth. There was a hatch above Nagasaki and to the sides of navigation and shift. A soft blue color bathed the chamber.

"System AS 412 is 1.15 light years away," Tanaka, the navigation officer, said.

Nagasaki studied his main screen. The type G main sequence star was bigger than Sol and more luminous, but it was still tiny at this distance.

All these months and there it was. Nagasaki stared at the star, wondering what the system held.

"We will begin scanning for radiation and other high technology signals," Nagasaki said.

The three officers didn't groan, sigh, or even glance at each other. Nagasaki had made them go through the same ritual the last seven shifts.

"Should we launch probes?" Lieutenant Tanaka asked.

"Negative," Nagasaki said.

Lieutenant Tanaka had been with him on *Argonaut*. The man was stocky with a shaved scalp and swirling tattoos on his head.

"We could launch the probes and shift elsewhere," Tanaka suggested.

"We're over one light year away," Nagasaki said. "Just how fast do you think our probes are? By the time they reach AS 412, we'll be home."

Tanaka ruefully shook his head. "I should know better. I keep thinking of *Argonaut*."

Nagasaki wanted to forget that time and the awful approach to Epsilon Eridani. There had been a mutiny on that voyage, one he'd put down hard.

For the hundredth time, maybe the thousandth, he studied AS 412. An asteroid belt ringed the system at the orbital distance Neptune did in Sol. A ringed gas giant held a Saturn-like orbit. An even bigger gas giant was at a Jupiter-distant orbit. Then there came the Earth-like planets, two of them at a Mars and Earth orbit respectively. Finally, there was a small Mercury-like planet near the system's sun.

Nagasaki studied the Mars-distant planet. Given the larger star, that would be the better planet for humans. It would seem that's where cyborgs could thrive. How would cyborgs make more cyborgs? They would need biological parts, humans in other words. Did the cyborgs keep a human preserve on the planet, harvesting them when needed? Is that why the cyborgs hadn't been back to Earth for more people?

"There are no signs of high technology," Tanaka said.

"Could we be missing the signals?" Nagasaki asked.

"Captain, if they had industries, if they had starships, we would easily see the evidence of it from here. There is nothing. That means we're viewing a pristine star system."

"What about an alien starship?" Nagasaki asked.

"We don't spy any evidence of one, but one could be hiding behind a planet or be stealthy. We are still far away."

"Those are my thoughts exactly," Nagasaki said. "We will continue to scan, searching for a sign of one."

|||||||||

Nine hours later, Captain Nagasaki readied himself for the last great jump. He wore the blue uniform of the Solar Space Navy, with his Orion Star pinned in place.

He thought about all that he'd done this voyage. He had helped oust Premier Lang's secret policemen from enforcing their tyrannical regulations aboard the Teleship. Now, through him, the Dictates ruled *Discovery*. In time, he would become the Archon of New Eden. The Teleship had begun its journey as humanity's new hope of starting over. That was still true after a fashion. Just like the phoenix of legend rose from the ashes, so the Dictates were about to rise again.

First, there was the deadly matter of a cyborg vessel, perhaps several of them, hiding behind the gas giants. That was something he'd learned from his study of the Great War. The cyborgs made mathematically logical choices. That made them predictable and therefore beatable.

Technically, *Discovery* wasn't a warship, but it could have defeated anything from the last war except for a Doom Star. He doubted the cyborgs possessed a Doom Star-level warship here. Their strategy and tactics from the last war showed their preference for small vessels.

Through a screen, Nagasaki gazed at the AS 412 star. Despite his goal and desire for battle, something nagged at him. It had begun this morning as he'd looked at the bathroom mirror. He had cut himself while shaving, meaning he had a nick on his chin. It had oozed blood earlier, although now it was a tiny scab. He had never cut himself before, but he had this morning because he'd become distracted.

He gazed at AS 412, New Eden to the others. A worm of doubt wriggled through his thoughts. Unfortunately, he couldn't pinpoint the source of his doubt, which wasn't like him.

He went through a mental checklist: He was the captain, check. He ran *Discovery*, check. Chief Monitor Argon was safe in the brig, check. He—

It struck him that the problem wasn't going to be on a checklist. Nagasaki didn't know how he knew, but there it was.

It must be something I'm missing or not seeing.

He scanned the officers at their posts. Each worked diligently, readying himself for the shift. Through his screens, he began checking the outer laser stations and missile pits on the surface of the Teleship. Everything was functional. Even the marines were ready, some of them combat-suited for action.

Nagasaki kept checking ship systems until he received a call from Dr. Wexx in the tele-chamber.

"We're ready, Captain," Wexx said.

Nagasaki twisted to the left screen. Wexx wore her sunglasses and she'd put up her hair. The woman was beautiful. Behind her in the chamber, he spied the cylinder of blue solution. Special Second Class Jasper had submerged into it, settling into position.

"We're about to shift?" Nagasaki asked.

He had the impression she was studying him. It was difficult to tell with those sunglasses. Finally, she spoke, asking, "Are you feeling well?"

Nagasaki hesitated. What *was* wrong with him? "I'm not feeling one hundred percent," he heard himself say.

"What seems to be the trouble?" she asked.

"That's just it. I don't know."

Wexx smiled in a sorrowful way.

Nagasaki didn't like the smile, as it seemed condescending. "I'm not a psychologist," he said. "So I don't know what kind of game you're playing."

"Excuse me?" Wexx asked.

Nagasaki almost frowned. What was *wrong* with him? This was . . . was . . .

"I know what's troubling you," Wexx said. She glanced back at the cylinder as she said it.

"Tell me," Nagasaki said in a clipped manner.

Wexx faced the screen. Before she could speak, a marine stepped up behind her. He placed a hand on her shoulder, which made the doctor cringe.

A surge of outrage flared through Nagasaki. It was heat in his chest. "Now see here," he said. "Take your hand off the doctor."

"Orders," the marine said in a sluggish voice.

"Who gave you these orders?" Nagasaki said. The marine had the audacity to keep his hand on the officer's shoulder.

"Colonel Konev," the marine said.

"The colonel has no authority over Dr. Wexx," Nagasaki said. "You will take your hand off her at once and report to your colonel for discipline."

"The mutiny has changed the situation," Wexx said in a dull voice.

"There hasn't been a mutiny," Nagasaki said. "Premier Lang illegally usurped power and we have rectified the situation."

"It is time to shift," the marine said. "Tele-chamber out." The screen went blank.

Nagasaki sat back in his command chair, stunned. This was unbelievable. This was an outrage. A marine had dared to put hands on an officer. This must be the source of his unease. Yet even as he thought that, he knew it was wrong. There was something else troubling him.

"Sir," Lieutenant Tanaka said. "The tele-ring is powering up."

Nagasaki snapped out of his daze. Whatever was wrong would have to wait. *Discovery* was about to take the final leap to AS 412. This was a historic moment—it would be his second. He had helped colonize Epsilon Eridani. Now, he would begin the colonization of New Eden, as the others liked to call the system.

"We're raising the null shield," Tanaka said.

Nagasaki's anticipation grew. The null shield was like Wexx's sunglasses, blocking a harmful ray—in this instance, sight of the null field within the discontinuity window.

"Increase ship's acceleration," Nagasaki said.

The next few minutes were ones of intense activity as the officers went about their tasks. Presumably, Dr. Wexx and Special Jasper went about theirs.

Then the grand moment arrived. The meteor-like Teleship spewed a long tail of fusion exhaust. The tactical domes on its surface were ready if needed. Seconds before the null portal appeared, acceleration quit and the long fusion tail vanished.

The rotating tele-ring brightened into an intense chrome color. Then a null portal began as a rip in space. The rip or tear expanded rapidly, joining two points over one light year apart. The great colonizing Teleship of Sol moved into the portal, shifting from one location and exiting at another in AS 412. As the null portal snapped shut, klaxons began to wail on *Discovery*.

Captain Nagasaki spoke crisply. "Gentlemen, let's start looking for signs of technological—"

He stopped short because he began to notice what was on his screens, the ones showing the star system. The complexity of the sight overwhelmed his senses. This couldn't possibly be right.

"Is this a joke?" Nagasaki asked.

The three officers weren't laughing. Like the captain, they stared at their screens in shock, dismay, and growing horror.

It felt like a dream to Nagasaki. He raised his arms. His hands felt like lumps of clay. His fingers were stiff. He adjusted the screens nonetheless.

"Are any of you seeing this?" Nagasaki asked in a small voice.

"I am," Tanaka managed to rasp.

"It can't be real," Nagasaki said.

"I think it is, sir."

"Begin analyzing data," Nagasaki said in a stern voice.

Tanaka and the other two officers looked up at him. Nagasaki gazed down. He'd regained control of himself and stared at his officers in his calm and level way. He didn't shout. He didn't rave. He spoke as he always did in his commanding manner. Maybe it calmed the three officers. Maybe their training took hold. They turned to their screens and began to tap and adjust sensors.

Captain Nagasaki blinked several times, trying to throw off the feeling of unreality. How could he be seeing this? There had been absolutely no sign of any technologically advanced civilization before this. He should not be able to see this now. Or more precisely, it should not exist. If it did exist, he should have seen signs of it long ago, many light years out.

In his coldly efficient way, Captain Nagasaki began to catalog what he was seeing, what the Teleship's sensors were showing him.

There were ships and habitats in the asteroid belt. He could see long fusion burns. Those ships weren't heading toward him, but they were doing something. At the nearest gas giant, he spied many habitats ringing the planet. The moons in the planetary gravitational system showed high industrial use. As interesting, a warship accelerated toward them on an intercept course. That interception was still many millions of kilometers away, but it was there just the same and that shouldn't be possible.

The second gas giant had similar habs and inhabited moons. It showed more fusion burns and more spaceships.

Nagasaki kept adjusting the sensors, tapping the screens, drinking in the astonishing data. The system appeared to be as fully inhabited as Sol was. How could the ship's sensors have failed to spot any of this before? No possible science could have hidden such a vast amount of evidence.

The nearer Earth-like planet was irradiated, barren, and lifeless. Fires raged on it. One of those fires was a ring, with blackened material in the center. If he were to guess, he would say some of the spaceships had bombarded the planet with nuclear weapons: hundreds maybe even thousands of nuclear bombardments.

Had *Discovery* stumbled into the middle of a system-wide war? That should be impossible. Why hadn't the sensors picked up anything earlier?

The other Earth-like planet . . .

Nagasaki wiped his brow. He felt feverish.

Satellites ringed the next Earth-like planet. Even as he watched, lasers beamed from one of the satellites and stabbed down onto the planet. This was incredible. It was mindboggling.

"Captain Nagasaki!"

He tore his gaze from the main screen, turned his head, and looked at Dr. Wexx as she appeared in another.

"Yes?" he asked in a dull voice.

"Why are the klaxons continuing to wail?"

"Aliens," Nagasaki managed to say.

"Have you spotted the enemy ship?"

"No," he said.

"Then why are the klaxons wailing?"

"The entire system . . . aliens," he said.

"You're not making sense, Captain."

"It's inhabited."

"What is?"

"Everything. We've stumbled onto a system-wide war."

"How is that possible?" Wexx asked.

"Sir," Tanaka said. "I think you'd better look at this."

"Excuse me, Doctor," Nagasaki said. "What is it?" he asked Tanaka.

"*Discovery* is headed for an asteroid or one monstrous ship."

"Are we on a collision course?"

"No, sir, but close enough that the situation strikes me as too coincidental."

"Give me a close-up of the asteroid or giant ship."

Lieutenant Tanaka made some quick adjustments. "It should be coming up on your number two screen."

Nagasaki saw it. The construct was nothing like the Teleship with its rough meteor-like surface. This one was like a giant ball bearing: round, smooth, metallic, and artificial. No, it wasn't completely round. There was a forest of strange antennae sprouting from the surface. The antennae were aimed at the Teleship.

"Are those weapons?" Nagasaki asked.

"Possibly," Tanaka said.

"Ready laser six."

"Captain," Tanaka said. "I'm—"

"What's wrong?"

Tanaka turned in his chair, staring up at Nagasaki. "Captain, we're being hailed on a regular radio frequency."

"Open channels," Nagasaki said. "Is there video coming in, too."

"Yes, sir."

"Good," Nagasaki said. "Let's get a look at our aliens."

His number two screen blurred for a moment. Then a long-faced human with a tall cranium stared at him.

Cyborgs! It was Nagasaki's first thought. He realized the thought was wrong almost right away. At least, there was nothing mechanical about the human. Could he be a cyborg front creature, used to confuse them?

The human or humanoid had elongated features and intensely blue eyes. He wore a platinum headband around his extra-tall forehead. He had a longish nose, a regular mouth and almost no chin. He was white with a sparse amount of dark hair on top of his strange head. A tall collar jutted into view, with a glimmering pendant around his throat.

Hungry for details, for data, Nagasaki peered behind the humanoid. Another manlike creature with similar features walked past. The station appeared to have gravity. Once the being moved out of sight, Nagasaki saw a clear dome farther back. There was a similar humanoid in it, a seated man. The one in the dome pressed the metallic band around his forehead against two discs attached to tubes curving down out of sight.

Before Nagasaki could recover from his astonishment, the first humanoid, the one regarding him, opened his mouth. The teeth were too small, but otherwise ordinary enough.

The humanoid spoke, and Nagasaki found himself leaning forward, trying to listen. No words came, or nothing audible, in any case.

"What are you saying?" Nagasaki asked.

The lips moved again, and a sharp pain spiked in Nagasaki's head. He winced. The humanoid spoke more rapidly. Still, Nagasaki didn't hear a thing. Now, however, the pain in his head increased. He reached up and pressed a palm against his temple.

On-screen, the humanoid smiled cruelly, and he appeared to nod to someone Nagasaki couldn't see.

"Tanaka, why aren't we getting any sound?"

It was the last thing Nagasaki asked. The humanoid regarded him once more and spoke quickly. No audible words sounded, but the pain stopped in Nagasaki's head. He nodded after a moment and his sense of unease vanished. He spoke crisply, giving orders to Tanaka and the other two compliant officers.

Teleship *Discovery* rotated so its mighty fusion engines aimed in the direction of its travel. The engines engaged, and a long fusion burn increased as the ship decelerated at three and a half gravities.

The humanoid with the platinum band around his forehead watched through the screen. After Nagasaki performed the braking maneuver, the humanoid raised one of his hands. He had elongated, skinny fingers. The man spoke without making a sound.

In his command chair, Nagasaki grew sleepy. His eyelids sank until they closed. The captain and his three-man bridge crew were out, with the rest of the ship in communication link with the nearing alien vessel.

2

The klaxons stopped wailing but the crushing Gs did not. Cyrus lay in his cot in his tiny cell in the brig, enduring as well as he could.

He'd been in here several days already, having spoken to no one but the marine guard who gave him a meal once every twenty-four hours. He was supposed to be in the brig with Chief Monitor Argon, but he hadn't seen the man. No doubt the giant was in a nearby cell.

It had been a boring stretch of time. This was little better than solitary confinement. There was no screen, no computer, no e-reader—nothing to help him pass the time.

He'd been doing a lot of thinking, but mostly practicing his mind shield. He'd felt Jasper try to probe him several times, but he believed the telepath had failed each time. His prolonged thinking had led Cyrus to the conclusion that he should learn to act quicker and with greater decisiveness.

At the moment, other than his automatic mind shield, he didn't practice his psi-powers nor did he do much heavy thinking. He just endured the crushing Gs pressing him into the cot.

How long were they going to—? *Is the ship accelerating or decelerating? Why would* Discovery *do either?*

It was at this point that he felt Jasper again. The telepath attempted another of his psi probes.

A tight grin curved onto Cyrus's face. Defeating the probe was better than boredom, as it gave him something to do.

Bring it on.

Whether Jasper read the thought or not, the man certainly did bring it on. The mind-probe intensified.

While on the cot, Cyrus frowned. This psi-attack was different from Jasper's usual method. Usually, the telepath just bored in with a burst of mind-power. This was more concentrated and lasted longer.

For a moment, he felt bafflement reign in the attacking mind. Then a clot of fury struck.

Cyrus didn't have time to cry out, gasp, or wince. He clutched the edges of his cot and strove to defend himself. He blocked, even as he felt his shield slipping. The attacking mind gained ground.

"No," Cyrus whispered. He willed everything he had into holding, using his pent-up anger and fear of the BAD THING to fuel his shield.

In that moment, he received something new. It was a mental image. It showed him a man with an elongated cranium. The man rested his tall forehead and the *baan* he wore against the amplifying discs.

What the hell?

The image faded, but the not the mental attack. Cyrus concentrated, holding the shield. The image . . . had Jasper just put that in his mind?

If felt real. What was it? Was that an alien?

The surprise weakened his shield and the alien gained ground.

Cyrus nodded grimly. This wasn't Jasper. An alien attacked his mind. Had the alien been the one to screw with Jasper earlier?

The alien pressed his advantage and Cyrus's eyelids grew heavy.

Is he trying to put me to sleep? Why would an alien attempt that? Maybe because *Discovery* was decelerating. If the Teleship had made the final shift, they were in the New Eden system. The aliens must want the Teleship for their own. That's why they'd brought them here.

Suddenly, the psi-attack ceased.

Cyrus exhaled and he found that sweat soaked his skin. He was exhausted, as if he'd worked out on Venice's exercise machine. He lay on the cot, trying to order his thoughts, listing what he knew:

They were in the New Eden system.

An alien had just attempted mental domination.

The ship decelerated much harder than ordinary.

"It sounds like the disaster has hit," he whispered.

Cyrus wiped sweat out of his eyes. Aliens had just tried to batter down his mind. He bared his teeth. Maybe these aliens had destroyed Venice and Roxie, but he wasn't going to let them destroy him. He would fight to the end. First, he had to figure out what was going on.

The alien wore a *baan*, whatever *that* was. The alien had pressed his forehead and *baan* against amplifying discs. Were those like the tele-ring in the sense that it increased mental power?

Cyrus bet that was the answer.

"Hey!" he shouted. "I need to talk to Jasper. Can anyone hear me?" He waited, but no one answered. "Hey! I'm ready to give up. Tell Jasper he can read my mind. I'll drop my block for him."

It wasn't true, but he figured that should bring Jasper running.

Again, there was no response. He shouted five more times, but it made no difference.

Maybe the others can't answer. He grunted. It was the oldest lesson of his life: he couldn't count on others, just himself. He had to act and he had to act *now*.

Carefully, because of the Gs, Cyrus rolled his body to the edge of the cot. The acceleration made it much harder to breathe. If he tried walking around now, he'd rip a tendon or muscle. He pulled his underwear tighter to protect his privates, drew his knees against his chest, and tied his shoelaces. He eased a leg off the cot and worked down onto his hands and knees. This was a miserable way to travel, but caution was in order under these G forces.

Slowly and methodically, Cyrus crawled to the portal. He hammered against it several times using the bottom of his fist. Just like before, there was no answer. He gathered his thoughts and readied himself. He would be vulnerable to another mind attack as he did this. He would need to work fast.

One, two, three—

Cyrus used his ability, tripped the inner portal mechanism, and the hatch swished open.

He crawled through into the corridor. Pressed against the farthest corner was a soundly sleeping marine. The man was hunched in an awkward position. How could he keep sleeping like that?

The answer was easy: The alien had put the marine to sleep. That would imply others aboard *Discovery* also slept.

Am I the only one awake?

A shiver of fear shot up his back and curled his gut. Jasper would have been in a weakened state after shifting. Might the alien have known that and put their telepath to sleep at exactly the right moment?

First rubbing his eyes, Cyrus craned his neck, checking the other portals. Several had green occupied lights. He crawled to the nearest. The switch was high enough that he would have to work up to his knees.

He used the wall and raised himself. This was definitely like using the workout machine. It was a good thing he was in prime physical condition. He pressed a switch and the portal opened. A monitor lay on the floor. His right arm lay at an awkward angle as if broken.

Cyrus crawled in and shook the monitor. The man kept sleeping.

"Hey! Wake up! The ship is under attack!"

It didn't help. The monitor didn't even twitch. He was out for the count.

Cyrus inspected the arm. Yeah, it was broken all right. The pain must be intense.

He would have remained and set the bone, but he knew time was critical. Despite his hurry, he crawled at a deliberate speed and went to the next green-lit portal. He opened it and found another monitor. He found three more monitors after that, each one sound asleep.

I really am alone. He was used to it, but just like his early days on the streets, fear ate at him. This was uniquely horrible.

At the last cell, he found something different. Chief Monitor Argon lay on the floor with his eyes open.

"Can you hear me?" Cyrus shouted.

The NKV officer's eyes shifted and focused on him.

Cyrus's heart beat wildly with hope. Facing danger was always easier with someone else standing with you. It made it harder to act like a coward. Argon must be in here because he could block Jasper at times. Had the monitor resisted the alien's thoughts?

Cyrus crawled into the cell.

"Special Fourth Class Cyrus?" Argon asked in a dry, raspy voice.

"That's right."

"Are you simply in my mind? Are you real?"

"You're not hallucinating," Cyrus told him.

"We're using over three Gs acceleration."

"I wouldn't know about the precise amount, but I think we're decelerating, not accelerating. One thing is sure, it's hard to walk."

"Tell me the exact situation," the chief monitor said.

Argon had been in the brig longer than anyone else had. Likely, no one had told him what had happened.

"Uh, what's the last thing you remember?" Cyrus asked.

"Captain Nagasaki drugged me."

Cyrus told him what had occurred after that, how Jasper had taken over the ship. He also told Argon about the sleeping marine in the corridor, the sleeping monitors, and the one with the broken arm.

"I felt someone attempting to dominate me," Argon said. "I resisted."

Cyrus plunged ahead and told Argon about his impression of the alien with the elongated forehead.

Intensity radiated from the chief monitor's eyes. He didn't question Cyrus about the reality of the impression. Instead, Argon said, "We must reach the bridge."

"Do you know your way there?" The Teleship was big and had many passageways. Cyrus had never been in the command section of the ship.

"Come. We will crawl there while we can. If the alien mind returns, can you defend me from him?"

"That would be a good trick," Cyrus said. "But I don't think so. I can barely defend myself."

"Let's hurry then."

"Sure. I'll follow you."

Argon led the way out of the brig, crawling on his hands and knees. The giant wore the same black uniform as the day Nagasaki had drugged him. The garments were rumpled and smelly, but that hardly mattered. Argon crawled through the steel corridors and Cyrus followed. Along the way, they found several sleeping crewmembers and marines.

Argon took a hand laser from one and buckled a belt with extra batteries around his waist. "Do the same," he told Cyrus.

Cyrus didn't care for the extra drag, but he knew it was a good idea. After what seemed like forever, Cyrus's pants rubbed through at the knees. His hands ached every time he set down his palms.

"I need to rest a minute," he said.

On his hands and knees, Argon looked back at him. Sweat bathed the chief monitor's face. "Time is critical."

"I understand. But if the alien mind returns and we're too tired to defend our brains . . ."

"That is rational. Yes, we will rest."

Carefully, Cyrus leaned against a bulkhead as he sat on his butt, letting his muscles rest. Several of his muscles twitched with spasms.

"It's crazy that these aliens are people similar to us," Cyrus said.

Argon grunted as he too rested against the bulkhead.

"Do you believe in similar evolution?" Cyrus asked.

"No," Argon said. "I believe in the Creator and creation."

"Oh."

"It is strange that something like humans live in this system—if you correctly 'saw' him as he exists."

"You don't believe I did see him?" Cyrus asked.

"I believe the mind often sees what it wants to see. It is possible you sensed him in a manner convenient to your own perceptions of the universe."

Cyrus thought about that. He didn't think it would have freaked him out if the man had turned out to be a genuine alien. He asked, "If we can't trust our senses, what can we trust?"

"A logical argument," Argon said. "Are you ready?"

Cyrus's hands ached and he didn't want to crawl on his knees anymore. If he stayed, however, he'd be giving up, surrendering to the BAD THING. His lips tightened. "Let's go."

They continued the crawl and found more sleeping people. None showed a flicker no matter how hard Argon shook them.

"Gassing could have done this," Cyrus said.

"Then why aren't we gassed?" Argon said. "No. The facts show otherwise. You have mind powers, a reinforced ability to block and I have the strongest concentration shield on the Teleship. It is rational that you and I are the only ones awake."

Finally, after what seemed like a tour of the entire Teleship, they reached a red line and a written warning: UNAUTHORIZED PERSONNEL KEEP OUT.

"We are entering the command area of the ship," Argon said.

They crawled over the red line and continued to a hatch in the floor.

"Do you know the entrance code?" Cyrus asked.

Argon didn't bother answering, but tapped the code in. A moment later, the hatch dialed open.

Cyrus peered down into the bridge module. He saw Nagasaki soundly asleep in the Captain's Chair. Below him, three officers in their chairs were also sleep.

"Looks like a tight fit for you," Cyrus said.

Argon slid his feet through the hatch and eased down. As soon as his head disappeared, Cyrus followed.

"Are you familiar with bridge controls?" Argon asked.

"I don't have a clue."

"Go to the weapon officer's chair."

"Which one is that?"

"The one to your left," Argon said.

Cyrus crawled past the giant as Argon unbuckled Nagasaki. The officer in the middle seat, a man with a weird set of tattoos on his bald head, snored.

Unbuckling the officer Argon had pointed at, Cyrus stood up and pushed the man out. He tried to ease the sleeping officer's fall, but the man thudded onto the floor and rolled away, his head repeatedly bumping against the deck plates.

"Try to be careful," Argon said.

Cyrus gratefully slid into the vacated chair. It was cushioned and helped absorb the crushing Gs.

Argon buckled himself in and began explaining the weapons screens to Cyrus. Argon turned on his screens as he continued to explain.

Cyrus had played video games that were harder to understand. He brought up the screens, experimented, and quickly familiarized himself with the controls.

"That must be it," Argon said, sounding as if he spoke to himself.

Cyrus checked his third screen. It was linked with one of Argon's screen. It showed a silvery ball in space with many antennae. "How about we cut power to our engines?" Cyrus suggested. "I'm sick of these Gs."

"No!" Argon said sternly.

"What did I say wrong?"

"We have the element of surprise," Argon said. "The aliens must believe *Discovery* is under their control. It we cut power to the engines, they will know someone has regained control. Ah, here it is."

Cyrus listened and watched as Argon played back Nagasaki's latest log. Some of the video of what had occurred showed the silvery habitat and it showed a sequence of the aliens in the flesh.

"You were right," Argon said. "They are humanoid as you described."

"You don't think they're from Earth?"

Argon raised his eyebrows. "That is an interesting idea. I hadn't thought that far."

"It's time we attacked," Cyrus said.

Argon was silent.

Cyrus twisted around, looking up. An enemy mind hit him then, almost catching him by surprise.

The chief monitor's eyelids fluttered. Two muscled balls at the corner of his jaws bulged. He must be fighting the enemy. His eyelids fluttered faster, drooping more. Slowly, the NKV officer slid into unconsciousness.

Fear welled in Cyrus. He was alone again, the last man standing against the aliens. It was up to him. He silently vowed to fight until blood leaked out of his ears, until he was dead.

He groaned as he fought the alien psi-dominance. It felt as if hammers beat against his skull. His eyesight blurred and he crouched in his seat. Still the enemy attacked. Still Cyrus Gant from Level 40 Milan blocked.

I have to take the fight to them. I have to attack or we're all lost.

Cyrus began tapping the weapons screen. Behind his mental shield, he tried to remember what Argon had just told him a few moments ago.

Cyrus adjusted controls. An external cam showed him a main laser dome opening. The aiming apparatus rose into view.

He calculated distances. The enemy habitat was nearly six hundred thousand kilometers away. That was practically next door in interstellar terms. The aliens must have done something to Jasper so he'd shifted to this location.

The hammering beat against his mind shield. Cyrus found it harder to think. He pinched his inner thigh, but he hardly felt the pain. He used every trick. He was like a fish in a net, thrashing to keep free.

The main laser had a range of one million kilometers. He could reach the enemy habitat. Working quickly, he engaged the targeting computer. It took over most of the functions as he watched.

Human.

It was a single thought, but it was coherent and it came from an alien mind.

Who are you? Cyrus asked.

We are . . . friends.

The cynical side of Cyrus laughed dryly.

We wish to avoid any mistakes, the alien told him. *You must not harm the Illustrious Ones.*

Who are they?

They are the ones who guide, who bring . . . value to existence.

Cyrus shook his head. The screen to his left beeped with a red color. It was the targeting computer asking if he wanted to engage. Cyrus tapped the screen.

He heard the mighty fusion engines thrum with greater power. The strength of the engines mandated the strength of the laser. The one-million kilometer range came about because of the size of the fusion engines.

We are friends, the alien told Cyrus. *We are agents of the Illustrious Ones. You are making an error against reality.*

Quit trying to put me to sleep.

Listen as I explain existence.

Explain it to your mother! Cyrus thought heatedly.

Your unreasonableness is beyond the pale of acceptance. Therefore, you must die.

Cyrus hunched his head. The screen showed him what he needed to know. The computer had locked on target. The fusion engines were at full power and the laser system was engaged.

He gave a ragged laugh. Then the alien psi-bolt struck. He roared at the throbbing pain. It felt as if his head expanded and was about to burst. Maybe it was.

Surrender to reconditioning so you can accept reality.

"I bring you greetings from Earth, you lousy mind bender." Cyrus tapped the screen.

The stored power flowed through the laser coils and pumped into the focusing mirrors. In a continuous coherent beam, the laser shot out of the main dome on the Teleship *Discovery*. It flashed across the distance at the speed of light: three hundred thousand kilometers per second.

Those two seconds were the grimmest of Cyrus's life. The aliens pounded on his mind, cracking his shield. He twitched in his seat, screamed, struggled to maintain a shred of protection—and then everything changed as the alien psi-assault stopped.

Struggling back to full awareness, Cyrus wasn't sure he saw correctly on his number one screen. The laser had speared straight on target at the silvery habitat. The alien sphere structure was over a kilometer wide. The laser should have burned into the ball. Instead, the beam stopped several hundred meters before touching the skin of the silvery material.

The laser continued to burn, and it inched closer and closer to the alien habitat. Then, in his mind, Cyrus heard a last wail, perhaps of agony or maybe of despair.

Whatever had deflected the laser disappeared. The beam speared into the silvery ball. The hellish fury of the laser melted the outer skin, making it molten, liquid, and causing vapors to billow and dissipate. The laser punched through and stabbed within. It burned through levels as it ignited air and caused explosions.

With the targeting computer's help, Cyrus adjusted the heavy laser, reaching out over six hundred thousand kilometers. He punched holes into the aliens' ball bearing-like habitat in the asteroid belt of New Eden. Afterward, he used the laser as a saw, shearing off sections. Parts of the ball sliced off. Debris: bio-parts, metal objects, foodstuff, deuterium fuel, and water spilled out of the destroyed habitat. Soon, eleven sections of varying size drifted where the enclosed habitat had been.

The first battle in the New Eden system went to the Teleship from Sol.

3

Three and half hours after the habitat's destruction, Chief Monitor Argon called a meeting in the officer's lounge. He recorded it as *Discovery* Meeting #13." The roster included Wexx, Cyrus, and a chastened Captain Nagasaki.

||||||||||

ARGON: Premier Lang, I am happy to report that your re-presentatives are once again in control of the Tele-ship. Through his courageous action, Special Fourth Class Cyrus foiled the mutiny. After speaking with Dr. Wexx and Cyrus, I have concluded that Special Second Class Jasper plotted the mutiny and manipulated the minds of the major actors. As a precaution, I have put Colonel Konev of the marines and Jasper into tempo-rary stasis.

Sir, we have found an astonishing situation. Aliens of close to human norm inhabit New Eden. A war ap-pears to be in progress. I hesitate to give you the next point. Its improbability makes me doubt our senses. I prefer to let Captain Nagasaki report the first half of our experience.

NAGASAKI: Premier Lang, I, ah, regret my part in the mutiny. I can only say—

ARGON: Explanations are not important now. We must examine the situation as it is and come to a swift solution.

WEXX: This is a waste of time. We must fix the tele-chamber and shift out of here.

ARGON: Work proceeds, Doctor. The damage by your team—

WEXX: The aliens must have induced the shift personnel to commit the damage.

ARGON: We are wasting time on the obvious. Yes, the aliens are crafty. How they knew what to damage and then how they attained their goals is a mystery. If we can repair the tele-chamber in time, we will most certainly shift out of here. Until then, we must understand what is occurring. Captain Nagasaki, make your report. You two listen carefully and see if you can discover something new we haven't thought of yet.

NAGASAKI: Special Jasper controlled my mind, sir.

ARGON: For the record, Premier Lang, Special Second Class Jasper appears to have manipulated the minds of the marines and Captain Nagasaki. The telepath inserted carefully thought out yet false memories into each person. They thereupon acted on the inserted memories and staged the mutiny. At this juncture, I believe Special Jasper is solely responsible for the sedition. Moreover, I do not believe it was politically motivated, but out a desire of selfish ambition and alien manipulation against him.

NAGASAKI: Premier Lang, as we approached AS 412, the bridge officers and I carefully scanned the system. We renewed the scan after each shift and found the star system to be devoid of all signs of high technology. It appeared to be pristine, devoid of intelligent life. These scans never varied in outcome until we entered the asteroid belt of AS 412. At that point, everything became visible.

ARGON: Why did you think the Teleship's sensors failed to pick up the telltale signs?

NAGASAKI: I have no idea.

ARGON: Premier Lang, we are puzzled and afraid. Yes, I admit to fear even though I am a chief monitor of the NKV. I do not understand by what agency the aliens were able to mask their presence in New Eden from us. I conclude it is either a technology unknown to us or some form of psi-power.

NAGASAKI: An enemy warship accelerates toward us, but more importantly, it already has a tremendous velocity. It is something on the order of forty-two million kilometers an hour or seven hundred thousand kilometers a minute. It will be in our laser range approximately three days from now. Behind the first warship comes a bigger vessel. The larger vessel has a slower velocity, but it is still incredibly fast. The second craft will be in laser range seven or eight days from now.

ARGON: New Eden swarms with spaceships and habitats. It is impossible at this point to calculate the population of the star system. But it must clearly be in the billions.

WEXX: How long until the tele-chamber is usable?

ARGON: The techs tell me ten days, no sooner.

WEXX: Then we must outrun the enemy warships.

NAGASAKI: Weren't you listening? We have lost our tele-shifting ability. We must therefore work strictly within Einsteinian physics and the laws of motion. It would take weeks for us to decelerate enough to head in a different direction. Nor can we turn sharply due to our present velocity, but turn only at a shallow curve. We are heading in-system and the enemy warships are heading out toward us at a fantastic velocity. We are on a collision course. Outrunning them is out of the question. We can only outfight them.

WEXX: We can try communicating with them.

ARGON: Negative. The video logs show us the danger of that. It appears radio contact heightens their psi-ability against us. How this can be so, I don't pretend to know. Maybe you have a theory, Doctor.

WEXX: I have no idea. It all sounds preposterous to me.

ARGON: At this point, we will operate practically rather than strictly, adhering to the scientific laws. What we observe to happen will take greater precedence over what we believe can or cannot happen.

WEXX: We need to figure out how to block the alien psi-powers.

ARGON: Agreed. Theoretically, Jasper should be able to block against them the best. Unfortunately, it appears the aliens have already compromised him. They may have a permanent link or control of his mind. That being the case, we dare not wake him from stasis. That leaves us, Cyrus. Special, do you feel like communicating with the aliens again?

CYRUS: I'll do it if I have to for the good of the ship.

ARGON: How will you keep the aliens from broadcasting to the rest of the crew?

CYRUS: Are you certain they need to be in radio communication with us? Can't they just do it?

ARGON: That is an elementary question, but we do not know the answer. At this stage, we dare not risk any experiments.

WEXX: All that is left us then is fighting our way free until the tele-chamber is repaired.

ARGON: I concur. I see no other choice.

CYRUS: I have a question. The alien spoke about the Illustrious Ones. Who do you think they are?

ARGON: A superior form of being perhaps or maybe the Illustrious Ones are like our Premier Lang. Their political organization may be theocratic.

CYRUS: Religious?

ARGON: "Illustrious Ones" strikes me as a religious term. But again, we don't know enough to make accurate guesses.

WEXX: There is one thing that troubles me that may answer Cyrus's question. Venice's clairvoyant warning showed her creatures with non-flesh hands or digits. So far, we have videos of humanoids. Where are the creatures of her clairvoyant warning? Maybe those creatures are the Illustrious Ones.

ARGON: That is a reasonable question and deduction. The answer is that we do not know. We must ready *Discovery* for battle and see if the techs cannot speed their repairs to the shifting chamber. Are there any further comments for Premier Lang? No? Then I declare this meeting at an end.

End of Transcript #13

4

Cyrus was in the bridge module at Argon's orders, sitting in the weapons officer's chair. For the past few hours, the officers had been giving him a crash course on how to operate each of their stations. It was on the assumption that the aliens could successfully sleep the crew a second time. If Cyrus found himself alone again, Argon wished him to be able to make the best decisions.

"Continue to scan the enemy warship," Nagasaki said.

Lieutenant Tanaka used radar and advanced teleoptics. It had been a day since their destruction of the alien habitat. The alien warship still accelerated toward them, but it already moved at its incredible velocity. In a little less than forty-eight hours, it would be in range of *Discovery*'s primary laser. In three days, the warship would have covered the distance from Saturn to Neptune— the distance from the ringed gas giant to New Eden's asteroid belt—about three billion kilometers.

Teleship *Discovery* moved at a fraction of the enemy warship's speed.

Tanaka shifted one of his screens so Cyrus could view it with him. "The enemy warship has a similar mass to a Solar Navy battleship," Tanaka said, "although its configuration is different. Our navy uses circular vessels. The enemy warship has a teardrop shape."

"Is that important?" Cyrus asked.

"It would be if they had particle shielding," Tanaka said. "A Sol battleship has large asteroidal rocks or particles to protect it. Those particle shields use mass to absorb enemy lasers and missiles. Given enough time and energy, a laser will cut through anything. A Sol battleship can rotate particle shields, lengthening its existence by putting fresh protection into place."

"We lack rotating shields on *Discovery*," Cyrus noted.

"True, but we do have asteroidal mass. We can also rotate the entire ship, aiming undamaged mass at enemy lasers, providing they use such beams. Once their lasers punch through the outer rock, they will have to drill through armor. A Sol battleship has collapsium armor. We are not a warship, however, but an armed and armored colonizing vessel."

Cyrus understood all that. "What kind of armor does the alien have?"

Tanaka licked his lips. "Analysis shows they don't have collapsium, which is lucky for us. It appears to be regular steel plating. How thick is the plating? I'm not sure. If I were to guess from the data, it appears the thickness is much less than our asteroid rock. That means, without another form of enemy defense, our lasers should be able to punch through their armor."

Cyrus recalled what had happened while beaming the alien habitat. "The first time, they stopped our laser several hundred meters before the armored skin. You've watched the video, right?"

"I have," Tanaka said, "several times."

"How did they stop the laser?" Cyrus asked.

"Their ability is a mystery to us. Our sensors didn't pick up a force field or force screen. Such defensive screens have been a staple desire of military strategists for some time. Back home, we've never come up with anything remotely like it."

"What does that suggest to you the aliens are doing?" Cyrus asked.

"I would dearly like to know."

"Sol Specials can warp existence. By that, I mean the discontinuity windows. Why can't the alien Specials warp existence in a different way?"

"You think their psi-masters *deflected* the laser?" Lieutenant Tanaka asked.

"It's an answer," Cyrus said.

Tanaka looked up at Nagasaki. "What do you think, sir?"

"It's the best theory so far," Captain Nagasaki said. He stood later, and told them to carry on as he left the bridge to get a bite to eat.

"What kind of weaponry do you think these aliens have?" Cyrus asked.

"Until we know otherwise," Tanaka said, "we will have to assume they have more powerful weapons than we do. In another thirty-seven minutes, we shall stop accelerating and begin to deploy a P-Field."

"A what?" Cyrus asked.

"P stands for prismatic crystals," Tanaka said. "They are highly reflective crystals, many billions of them. If a laser strikes a crystal, the reflective properties will dissipate the laser's energy for a time. If the laser remains on target long enough, it will turn the crystal to slag and begin the process all over again on the next layer. We call that a burn through. If the enemy uses particle beam weaponry, the crystals will not be as effective. Because of that, we will spray a lead-laced gel cloud behind the P-Field. It will take time for a particle or proton beam to burn through such a cloud. During that time, we will add more gel or crystals to the field as needed."

"They're extra armor?" Cyrus asked.

"Precisely."

"So what else do we do while we're spraying these things into space?"

Lieutenant Tanaka continued to explain the essence of space combat to an eagerly listening Cyrus Gant.

Thirty-seven minutes later, a returned Nagasaki ordered an end to acceleration, bringing weightlessness back to the Teleship.

With a push of his hands, Cyrus exited the weapons chair and floated to the side. He used the flat of his hands to ease himself to a halt by a bulkhead.

The bridge officers began to ready *Discovery* for the coming battle. It was interesting and a little bewildering. Cyrus was used to video games. He particularly enjoyed first-person shooter games. This was much different, especially the length of time. A first person shooter game took minutes to play. Reality—it was hard to think of a space battle taking *days*. No doubt, the enemy prepared for combat in a similar manner.

Tanaka disagreed with that after Cyrus made a remark about it.

"With our teleoptics we can see everything the enemy warship is doing," Tanaka said.

"Can't he see us just as easily?" Cyrus asked.

"Until we deploy the P-Field, yes," Tanaka said. "Once we're screened . . ."

"Will we be screened?" Cyrus asked. "There are other habitats and spaceships in the asteroid belt behind us. Can't the aliens use teleoptics to watch us and report to the enemy warship ahead what we're doing?"

"Certainly," Tanaka said. "But we shall also spray a gel cloud behind us for just that reason: as a screen."

"Why do you think the spaceships in the asteroid belt aren't trying to follow us?" Cyrus asked.

"It appears as if the majority of those ships are haulers."

"What are they hauling?"

"Asteroids would be my guess," Tanaka said, "or more precisely, the minerals and other materials in the asteroids. The other reason they're not following would be a matter of acceleration and velocity. It would take too much time and energy for those distant ships to catch us. It's much easier for the aliens to do what they're already doing."

"Readying launch," said the weapons officer, a lieutenant named Jones. He was a thin man with gaunt cheeks and a scar along his nose from an old core burn.

From his position against a bulkhead, Cyrus watched one of Lieutenant Jones's screens. It showed the outer surface of *Discovery*. A dome's upper collapsium shell rotated out of the way. From inside the dome, the warhead of a large Prometheus missile poked up into view.

After a few calculations, Jones said, "We're ready for launch, sir."

Nagasaki gave him the go-ahead.

Jones adjusted controls. Then he said, "Three . . . two . . . one . . . zero, ignition."

Cyrus felt a shudder through the bulkhead. On-screen, the missile elegantly rose out of the dome. Fiery exhaust appeared and soon the Prometheus sped away, gaining velocity as it accelerated toward the approaching enemy. Soon, it was simply another mote of light, another "star" in space.

Lieutenant Jones launched three Prometheus missiles. *Discovery* had twenty. After the third launch, Jones swiveled his seat to look up at Captain Nagasaki.

"Sir, I suggest we launch three more."

Nagasaki leaned forward, studying one of his screens.

"I realize the manual calls for three launches in this situation," Jones said. "But it would appear we have two enemy ships to defeat before the telechamber is repaired and we can scoot out of here."

"The techs are working faster than expected," Nagasaki said.

"Something always goes wrong, sir. Murphy's Law. I doubt the techs will repair the chamber quicker than their original estimate."

Nagasaki rubbed his chin. "We have two possible warships we need to defeat. Afterward, we should be able to shift out of danger and head for home. I dislike depleting our missile supply so quickly."

"Yes, sir, I agree. But if we fail to defeat the first warship—"

"Yes," Nagasaki said. "You've convinced me. Launch three more Prometheus missiles. Then we shall begin to build our P-Field."

Cyrus thought he understood Jones's point. They might as well expend the needed missiles right away. Otherwise, they wouldn't have to worry about to-morrow because they would all be dead if they failed the first time.

There were more shudders and Cyrus watched three more missiles head into the void. *Discovery* had put six missiles ahead of them. The missiles would accelerate a day before shutting down acceleration. Afterward—at least accord-ing to what Tanaka had told him—the missiles would expel decoy emitters. The emitters were dummies, with far less mass than the missile but with the same radiation signature as the real thing. A second class of devices would also spread out. They were electronic countermeasures, ECM, and jamming devices.

Later, Cyrus watched the expanding P-Field, which blotted out some of the stars but glittered with pale light. Ejectors launched packets ahead of the Teleship. A small explosion spread the crystals. Because the Teleship and crys-tals traveled at the same velocity, the prismatic crystals maintained an exact and unvarying position ahead of the vessel, a screen.

"One thing has been troubling me," Cyrus said.

"Yes?" Tanaka said.

"The P-Field blocks the alien warship from seeing us and from hitting us until they burn through the crystals."

"That's right," Tanaka said.

"Doesn't the spreading field also stop us from seeing the aliens and shoot-ing them? I mean, we still have the missiles—"

"If you'd waited a few more minutes," Tanaka said, "you would see us launching probes. We'll maneuver the probes to the front of the P-Field. They will be our eyes and radio information back to us."

"Okay," Cyrus said. "So how do we shoot through the P-Field? Will we launch mirrors at the edge of the field and bounce a laser off them?"

"That would be one way," Tanaka said. "It takes fantastic accuracy, however, to hit targets one million kilometers away. Bouncing lasers off mirrors dramatically adds to the targeting complexities. No. When the time comes, we will destroy gel and crystals with bombs. That will create windows for us through our own clouds and fields. We'll use those windows to fire our lasers at the enemy."

"Can't the aliens use the windows to fire at us?"

"If they have magical accuracy," Tanaka said. "Otherwise, no, it will be a one-way window."

Cyrus nodded. "Once we deploy the gel cloud, what will we do then?"

"After that we wait," Tanaka said. "We wait until the alien's tremendous velocity brings him within firing range."

"What do you think their range is?"

Tanaka nodded. "That, my friend, is the great and terrible question. Our survival will likely depend on who has the greater range."

5

Deep in Captain Nagasaki's mind was a latent fail-safe. Jasper had worked long and hard perfecting it in case the NKV should thwart him. Nagasaki was a stubborn individual, but had a curious over-sensitivity concerning his authority. Jasper had worked on that, and it began to operate as Nagasaki lay in his quarters, trying to fall asleep.

Nagasaki seethed at the usurpation of his authority. He lay on his bunk in his quarters, attempting to sleep before the coming battle with the approaching warship. The lights were dim. A screen on the wall showed the alien star system. He gripped a screen controller, changing the view as Jasper's latent fail-safe caused new thoughts to tumble into his mind.

Nagasaki was repentant of his former actions against the NKV officers. The telepath had invaded his mind and twisted his thoughts, turning him toward seditious action. It was unconscionable. Jasper was in stasis, and that was a good thing. Although . . . in a hidden fold in Nagasaki's brain, the fail-safe caused him to wonder if he should thaw Jasper out in order to teach the telepath the old-fashioned price of unsuccessful mutiny.

Imagine the Special's surprise as I point a needler at his heart and pull the trigger. He would ask me why and I would tell him that I am the captain of Discovery *and he had attempted to usurp my authority.*

In the dim light, Nagasaki grinned. That would be a fine thing indeed. He was the captain. He was the judge on this vessel. The chief monitor practiced security for Premier Lang, and that was a good thing. But now, the chief monitor had overstepped his bounds. Imagine, foisting the ill-bred Special on him named Cyrus Gant. Yes, the lad had saved the ship, but any fool could have done that once the targeting computer took over.

I'm wet nurse to an inexperienced youth. He isn't even a navy rating. He's a Special. Who does the chief monitor think he is?

Nagasaki frowned. He had just repented for sedition. Was he going to do something similar now, so soon after eating crow on video for Premier Lang?

Raising the control unit, Nagasaki clicked buttons, changing the view on the screen. He studied the nearest gas giant. It had a ring like Saturn and was in a Saturn-like orbit compared to the star AS 412. The gas giant possessed an Earth-sized moon. Nagasaki clicked the controller again, studying the moon's atmosphere. This was interesting. The atmosphere was Earth-like. It would be cold on the moon, but it would still possess a breathable atmosphere.

Nagasaki sighed, leaving the controller hanging in the air beside him. He should go to sleep. The battle was tomorrow. The aliens had been hailing the ship, but Argon had forbidden anyone to open channels with them.

That was another usurpation of the captain's authority. Nagasaki would have ordered the same thing, but it had been his order to give.

Does Argon think I'm a figurehead?

He scowled. Others had once tried to usurp his authority on *Argonaut* many years ago. He'd taught the ringleaders what it meant to try to strip him of power. Each of them had been bound and ejected alive into space. It was an outdated punishment but well deserved.

Special Jasper had used him. The telepath had twisted their minds and tried to take control of the ship. In fact, the telepath had succeeded, but events had allowed them to regain control.

Jasper will never receive the punishment he so richly deserves.

As he lay on his bunk in the dim light, Nagasaki fumed and played out the situation in his head. If the alien warship won the battle tomorrow, *Discovery* would be destroyed and everyone aboard would die. Jasper would never realize he'd lost and he would never have to pay the ultimate penalty for his crime. If they destroyed the first alien tomorrow and then escaped the slower warship, *Discovery* would begin the long voyage back to Sol. Once there, because Earth badly needed Specials, Premier Lang would likely attempt to rehabilitate the telepath. Jasper would go free and never pay for his wretched crime.

The supposedly stray thought in the fold of Nagasaki's brain came to the forefront. Jasper shouldn't be able to escape paying the penalty for his crime. That was wrong.

I'm not going to stand for this. First Argon usurps my authority and now Jasper gets to run free again. No. I'm going to administer justice this very night.

Captain Nagasaki pushed off the bunk. In the darkness, he donned his uniform. With his thumb and forefinger, he shut each front clasp on his jacket. He felt weary. His eyes hurt and sleep beckoned. But this needed doing and he couldn't think of a better time to do it. He grabbed the control unit and shoved it into his waistband. In his mind, the unit was the needler he'd taken from Argon.

The stray thought in his mind was no longer stray but in charge of his actions. He operated robotically, with a glassy stare in his eyes.

He floated to the portal, exited, and swam expertly down the corridors. Despite the glassy look and the stiffness of his movements, he acted decisively. The "needler" in his waistband gave him confidence. If the chief monitor tried to stop him, he would kill the interloper and solve yet another problem.

Nagasaki swam to medical and used his override code to open the portal. He floated toward the emergency stasis locker, reached it, and was in the process of entering his override code one more time.

The main medical portal opened again and Dr. Wexx walked in on the weave. "Lights," she said.

As the lights came on, Nagasaki made an instant decision, drawing the "needler" from his waistband. "Dr. Wexx," he said, "you are under arrest."

Wexx froze by the open portal. "What are you doing here?"

"I have come to administer justice," Nagasaki said.

"Why are you pointing a control unit at me?"

Nagasaki frowned at his "needler."

"It's not a . . ." He found himself holding a control unit for a wall screen. Something was out of order here and he wasn't sure what. One thing he did understand, telepaths and alien mind benders could play tricks on a person's intellect. He was Captain Nagasaki and he had an iron will. He had helped colonize Epsilon Eridani and—

With a karate shout, Nagasaki sprang for Dr. Wexx, sailing across medical. She pivoted and dived through the portal, closing it behind her.

Nagasaki twisted in midair, bringing his feet forward. He struck the bulkhead near the portal and propelled himself back toward the emergency stasis chamber. He had little time left to effect justice. He needed to move fast before Wexx brought reinforcements.

Reaching the portal to stasis, Nagasaki began entering his override code one more time. Before he completed the code, the main portal opened and Chief Monitor Argon jumped into the room.

"Captain!" Argon shouted. "You must desist at once."

Nagasaki turned with a snarl. The giant sailed toward him. With an oath, he sprang at Argon. He'd defeated the NKV officer once already. He could do it again. Nagasaki readied himself as they neared each other. He'd trained for years in zero G karate. Size would mean little in this conflict.

"Submit," Argon said.

"Die!" Nagasaki shouted.

Just before Nagasaki could land his first blow, the bigger, stronger NKV officer grabbed an outthrust wrist and yanked the smaller man closer. With a deft move, Argon turned Nagasaki and wrapped a steel-like forearm around his throat.

"Yield," Argon hissed into his ear. "Fighting me is useless."

Nagasaki struggled fiercely. He was the captain. He must administer justice. He would thaw Jasper out and then . . . then . . . He couldn't breathe! The giant crushed his throat, cutting off air. Oh, this was wrong. This was mutiny. He was the . . .

||||||||||

Chief Monitor Argon applied pressure until Nagasaki slumped into unconsciousness. Then the NKV officer brought the smaller man to one of the medical cots and securely strapped him down.

6

Klane held a new junction-stone as he stared at a boulder in the Wild Rocks.

He stood in the shelter of an even bigger boulder. The thing towered three times the height of a man and cast him in shadows.

Klane stood still, clutching the stone. His features contorted into a stern mask. He wore leather garments like a warrior and a cape of fur. At his feet was a pack of supplies, most of it cured jerky and water. He stood in shadows to symbolize his darkened heart.

The demons had captured the seeker, and they likely experimented on him in the Valley of the Demons. Through an act of unselfish love, the seeker had taken his place. Klane could not allow that. He must rescue the old man, his friend and his father. Klane knew, too, that the seeker needed to cause the transfer. It was important in the Great War against the demons, the plague of humanity.

Klane clutched his new junction-stone, a blue rock smooth with gat-oil. Day and night, he'd poured his hatred against the demons into the stone. He could feel it filled with pregnant power. Now he tested the junction-stone.

He stared at the boulder. Brown lichen covered it and coral-grass sprouted from the top.

A groan escaped Klane's lips. His arm began to shake and his fingers tightened around the junction-stone. A terrible splintering sound occurred, and the boulder before him splintered and shattered, showering smaller pieces onto the rocky ground.

Klane grunted with exhaustion, and he relaxed as the tension eased from him. He wrapped the junction-stone and put it away. Wearily, he picked up the pack.

"Where do you go, seeker?"

Klane whirled around.

The hetman stood before him. The big warrior held a metal knife, one fashioned from the broken air-car that Klane had brought down on the night of the Eye of the Moon.

Klane stood before the powerful man, at a loss for words.

"The clan needs you, seeker."

"I brought death to the Tash-Toi."

"By killing demons," the hetman said.

"Does it matter how?"

"Yes," the hetman said. "The demons are the enemy of men. You killed the enemy."

"But at a heavy cost."

The hetman shook his head. "The cost is always heavy to act the part of a man."

Klane gathered his resolve. "I must leave."

"You go to your doom."

"I must rescue the seeker."

"You are the seeker," the hetman said.

"He gave his life for me."

"You are the Chosen One."

Klane shook his head. "First, I must take part in the transfer. Until that happens, I am only a dim hope."

"Your words are meaningless," the hetman said.

"I must go and rescue the seeker. I know I can do it."

"You are young, Klane. You need wisdom to defeat the demons on their own ground."

"That is why I must take part in the transfer."

"You are keeping secrets from me," the hetman said.

Klane nodded. "They are secrets bound to one of my craft."

The hetman turned away. "If I let you go, the clan will be without a seeker. If I force you to remain—"

"You cannot force me," Klane said.

The hetman bristled.

Klane pointed at the shattered boulder. "Can you defeat me?"

"If I drive this knife into your chest, I can."

Klane surprised himself by saying, "Don't stand in my way, Hetman. I am off to save my father."

The hetman opened his mouth, and slowly, he closed it. The big man nodded. "Go with my blessing, Klane. Make the demons pay for their haunting of Clan Tash-Toi."

Klane was glad the hetman had blessed him. Sighing, feeling more alone than he ever had in his life, Klane picked up his pack.

The hetman moved aside.

Klane strode past him and shouldered the pack onto his shoulders. Then he headed for the Valley of the Demons. He would surely die, but he would die trying to save his father and his friend.

7

As the hour of battle neared, Cyrus sat in the shift officer's seat on the bridge module.

Chief Monitor Argon sat in the captain's chair. Nagasaki was in a stasis cylinder and Argon had decided to act in his stead. "Explain the tactical situation to me," Argon said.

Cyrus watched on his screens as Tanaka spoke.

"The alien warship is sixteen minutes from reaching our primary laser's extreme combat range: one million kilometers. The enemy vessel exceeds a speed of seven hundred thousand kilometers a minute. It means that once we start firing our laser, the enemy will reach us in less than one and a half minutes. I would recommend a total barrage before that."

"Our Prometheus missiles will likely be critical to the fight," Lieutenant Jones said.

"If the enemy doesn't annihilate them first," Tanaka added.

"Before that happens," Jones said, "we should be giving them too much to worry about."

"I'm not as sanguine," Tanaka said. "Can we destroy the alien vessel in a minute and a half? At what point will the alien weaponry reach us? Surely, he will strike hard before we can destroy him."

"I think I understand," Argon said. "His extreme velocity is a weapon."

"Not strictly speaking," Tanaka said.

"His velocity is a tactical advantage," Argon amended.

"It depends on what the enemy hopes to achieve with it."

"No," Argon said. "Everything depends on our survival. We must survive so we can return home and warn humanity of the danger."

"Do the aliens have Teleships?" Cyrus asked.

Argon glanced at him. "Interesting, we haven't asked ourselves that yet. Gentlemen," he said to the lieutenants, "I would like to know your views on the subject."

"I haven't spotted anything resembling a Teleship," Tanaka said.

"If they don't have Teleships," Cyrus said. "We can't let them get ours. Otherwise, they might reverse engineer it, build some of their own, and attack Earth. And given the number of Specials they apparently possess, they could probably field an armada of Teleships."

"That is rationally thought out," Argon said. After several moments of thought, his features hardened. "We must be ready to self-destruct if it appears the aliens are about to capture our ship."

"The approaching alien vessel can't capture us," Tanaka said. "They're traveling far too fast for them to slow down in time to board us."

"I understand," Argon said. "But they can cripple us so others can board us later."

"That's at least a week off," Tanaka said.

Argon nodded shortly. "We will concentrate on the coming fight. But it is well to remember that our existence is at stake in an alien star system. They have tried to capture us once. I will not give them a second chance."

Cyrus swallowed in a dry throat. He didn't like the idea of initiating *Discovery*'s destruction. Nor did he like being the lone Sol ship in a strange star system. Everything here was against them.

He watched the approaching vessel hurtle through the system. Tanaka had told him that it was big and shiny, which was strange. Combat ships should be difficult to spot, allowing them to coast toward an enemy while remaining hidden. It suggested to Tanaka that the aliens didn't feel the need to hide, which should be a clue toward something. None of them had figured out what, though.

Can we win? Would the alien be racing at them like this if they thought they could lose? Do their Illustrious Ones understand shifting? The aliens had to know something strange was going on in terms of transportation. The aliens had been in psi-contact many light years out, drawing them in to New Eden. It would appear the alien leaders wanted the Teleship pretty badly. If the situation were reversed, that's how Earth's leaders would think.

"You know," Cyrus said. "Do you think they mean to destroy us or simply disable the ship?"

"Explain your thinking," Argon said.

Cyrus told them what he'd just reasoned out.

Lieutenant Tanaka swiveled his chair to look up at Argon. "If our roles were reversed—with aliens in the solar system—the navy chiefs would do whatever they needed to get hold of a starship."

"Make your meaning clear," Argon said.

"Cyrus must be right. I don't think the aliens are going to try to destroy us, merely cripple the ship."

"In order to capture our Teleship?" Argon asked.

"Yes, sir," Tanaka said.

"Let us hope that gives us an advantage," Argon said.

Silence descended after that and the minutes passed in tense waiting.

"It's time," Jones said later. "We'd better prepare our lanes of fire."

"Begin to do so," Argon said.

At his station, Lieutenant Jones began to manipulate his controls.

In the P-Field and gel cloud in front of the ship, precise explosions cleared lanes of fire, windows for the ship's lasers.

Cyrus watched and learned, wondering if he would ever have to do something like this again. The first time they'd attacked a stationary habitat. Apparently, the alien space station hadn't possessed offensive weapons. Now, they were facing an alien battleship. What a crazy thing.

"They're hailing us," Tanaka said.

"Ignore it," Argon said.

"I . . . I think we should answer this time."

Cyrus stared at Tanaka in shock. Hadn't the lieutenant been listening before? What was the man thinking?

"You're relieved of duty," Argon said from the command chair. "Exit the bridge at once."

Tanaka swiveled around to stare up at Argon. "Don't you see? This is critical. We can avoid death if we just—"

Chief Monitor Argon wasn't listening. He unbuckled himself, drew a stunner-rod, and leaned down from his chair. His long arm and the rod itself lengthened his reach. Tanaka twisted about frantically in his seat to avoid the tip of the rod. It glowed blue. Unfortunately for him, he couldn't get his straps off and apparently wasn't thinking clearly enough to turn around and block with the back of his chair. A loud sizzling sound filled the bridge. Tanaka screamed and slumped unconscious.

A side hatch opened and a monitor squeezed into the bridge module.

"Take him to the brig," Argon said. "Watch him. I don't know if the alien psi-masters can revive him or not. Tell the others to keep up their concentration shields at all times."

The monitor dragged Tanaka out of the module.

Cyrus finally understood what must have been going on. The chief monitor had realized more quickly than any of them had. With the nearing alien warship, its psi-master must finally be in range to affect crewmembers without radio linkage.

"Can you fulfill your duties?" Argon asked Lieutenant Jones.

"Yes, sir," Jones said.

"Occupy navigation," Argon told Cyrus.

Cyrus slid to the middle chair. He was thinking now, and he asked Argon, "What if the alien psi-master gets hold of Jones's mind in the middle of battle?"

"Hey!" Jones said. "What are you saying? I'm no turncoat. I won't go crazy."

"We need his expertise on the bridge," Argon said.

"Yeah, we need Jones's expertise, but if he freaks out at exactly the wrong time won't that be worse? I mean, better a crew we can trust, even if that crew doesn't know as much."

"Quit talking about me as if I'm stupid," Jones said.

"You are relieved of duty," Argon told Lieutenant Jones.

"No, sir," Jones said. "I protest your order. *Discovery* needs at least one real navy officer on the bridge during battle."

"You just witnessed the aliens' ability with Tanaka," Argon said. "It would be rational for them to attempt mind control on you next. You will go now or I will stun you and have you dragged off."

Angrily, Jones unsnapped himself and floated out of the bridge module to a waiting monitor.

As the hatch closed, Cyrus asked, "Now what? I don't really know what to do."

"You did not pay attention earlier to their instructions?"

"Yeah, I listened, but . . ."

"Move to the weapons chair and pray to the Creator He helps you do your duty."

As Cyrus slid over, he felt an alien mind reach out to him. It was an oily sensation and filled with hostility. "Someone is trying to make contact with me."

"Resist!" Argon said.

"I am, but this isn't good. What are they doing to others in our ship?"

"Now we know their plan, or we know part of the plan. Begin using the targeting computer. I will instruct the monitors to initiate a ship-wide lock-down."

Cyrus's gut clenched and his palms became sweaty. This was just great. He'd been watching and learning these last two days, but fighting for all their lives, for Sol as well, it was too much to place on a young man's shoulders.

He checked controls and went over what Jones had shown him yesterday. They had gone over several simulations, and he'd gotten better each time he played. But this was for real.

"The alien vessel is two million kilometers from us," Argon said.

Cyrus watched a chronometer. The alien warship moved nearly twelve thousand kilometers a second. In a little less than eighty-three seconds, the enemy would be in range—seconds, eighty-three seconds. What was he doing on the bridge module? This was insane.

"I'm readying the primary laser," Cyrus said, and he was surprised how calm his voice sounded.

The seconds ticked by as the alien, tear-shaped warship neared the one million kilometer mark. It was big, Sol battleship-sized. How much armor plating did the alien possess? What kind of weapons did it use? This was the first battle between an alien warship and the Sol Navy.

"I never signed up for this," Cyrus mumbled.

Argon didn't respond.

Cyrus swiveled around. The chief monitor sat stiffly, with his hands clenched on the captain's armrests. The big fingers were white, straining, as

Argon likely battled for control of his mind. The man's face was immobile and his eyes staring.

"Fight," Argon whispered past unmoving lips.

Cyrus blinked sweat out of his eyes as he turned to his screens. This was just like before. He was alone, with an alien knocking on his mind. Well, he had suggested the right thing with Jones. If he'd had to fight the Navy officer now . . .

"Concentrate," Cyrus muttered to himself.

He tapped the number one screen, engaging the targeting computer. They had worked out the situation and played it many times.

Here we go—it's battle time.

Discovery's fusion engines fully engaged. Cyrus felt the mighty thrum. This was different from the last time he did this. Now he knew what he was supposed to be doing. Now he understood the stakes better. This wasn't just about him. This was about Sol, about Level 40 Milan and all his old friends. If he failed, there might not be an Earth and Milan, as he'd known them. There might be an interstellar war, with the aliens gaining the jump on Sol.

"Now," he whispered.

The heavy laser aimed at the enemy, directed through the window in the gel and crystal field. Power from the fusion engines and stored battery power surged through the coils and beamed through the targeting mirrors. In a great ray of focused light, the laser shot out of the dome at three hundred thousand kilometers a second.

In 3.3333 seconds, the tip of the laser flashed across one million kilometers of space. The ultra-precise targeting computer had led the alien warship, calculating its exact position *now*.

With the powerful teleoptics in the probes, Cyrus had to wait the same amount of time for information to return at the speed of light. Thus, it took nearly seven seconds from the first shot for Cyrus to see the heavy laser halt at what would appear to be several hundred meters before the skin of the enemy warship.

"Good work!" Argon boomed.

Cyrus turned around in surprise. The chief monitor no longer clutched the armrests. The face was no longer stiff with immobility.

"I was right," Cyrus said.

Argon raised an eyebrow.

"The alien psi-master isn't trying to control you anymore," Cyrus said. "I no longer feel him either. The obvious conclusion is they're using their powers to shield their ship from our beam."

"Agreed," Argon declared.

Cyrus returned to his screens. He activated more lasers, readying them for firing. The alien ship bored toward them at nearly twelve thousand kilometers a second, or seven hundred thousand kilometers a minute. The warship would be in range of the secondary lasers in 42.85 seconds.

The fusion engines continued to thrum with fantastic power, pumping the heavy laser. The beam kept on target, the intense ray inching closer and closer toward the alien's armor plating.

At six hundred thousand kilometers distance between the ships, an alien laser began to burn into the P-Field.

"We know their range!" Cyrus shouted.

Prismatic crystals reflected the hellish beam for microseconds, dissipating its strength. Then the laser heated the crystal, melting it and robbing it of the reflective power. In less than a second, the alien beam burned through the first layer of the P-Field, boring in toward *Discovery*.

Cyrus tapped the firing screen. More domes on the surface of the Teleship opened. The secondary lasers poked out. At five hundred thousand kilometers, more lasers beamed across the closing distance, striking the alien psi-shield.

"Pump more crystals into place," Argon said.

"I'm trying," Cyrus said. "I'm not quite sure how do it. But I should be able to figure it out soon." He continued tapping.

"No," Argon said. "Leave it. In your ignorance, you might accidently stop us from doing a good thing." The chief monitor slapped a comm button on his chair. "Get me Jones. Bring him back onto the bridge."

Cyrus was too focused to worry about Jones now.

Alien lasers burned through the P-Field and sliced through the gel cloud. In another two seconds, the enemy beams burned onto the surface of the Teleship. The hottest immediately began burning down into the asteroidal rock, boring in toward *Discovery*'s vitals.

"Tell Jones to hurry!" Argon shouted into the comm.

Cyrus watched helplessly. This was terrible. Then he spied secondary alien beams lancing into the darkness.

"What are they doing?" Argon said. He must have spotted the same thing. "Why aren't those lasers striking at us?"

"Ah! They must be hunting down our missiles. Hopefully, the decoy emitters are working."

"Right, the Prometheus missiles," Argon said. "We need something to work for us."

The seconds brought swift change to the battle. The alien warship's terrific velocity and the rather short range of the lasers mandated it.

"Rotate the Teleship," Argon said. "Point the unused asteroid mass at their lasers."

Cyrus swiveled around and shook his head. "We're operating on the simplest level with the targeting computer. If we begin moving our ship, we'll have to recalculate and reconfigure our firing strategies. I say we hold on with what we're doing and hope the missiles make the difference."

Argon stared at him. For the first time, Cyrus saw indecision on the man's face. "We'll take damage if we do it your way. We might lose lives, particularly among the sleeping colonists."

"I grew up in the slums, Chief Monitor. Sometimes there aren't any good decisions. It's then you have to stick with what you know and hope for the best."

"By the Creator, you're a steely one," Argon said.

Cyrus waited for the chief monitor to say more. The man didn't. He watched the screens. Turning back to his, Cyrus got a better picture of what was happening to the alien vessel. The Teleship's lasers were close to the surface of the alien warship, to the armored skin.

More enemy lasers punched through the chewed up P-Field and gel cloud. More beams turned asteroidal rock into slag, molten slurry, and then burned it completely away, drilling in deeply.

Klaxons began to wail in the Teleship.

"Do we have any missiles left out there?" Argon asked.

With the heel of his hand, Cyrus slapped his forehead. He could have been checking. He shifted to the number three screen and checked. Yes, three Prometheus missiles were left and almost in range of the nearing enemy.

"We have a breach in the third stasis area," Argon said in a bitter voice. "The backup AI is taking damage."

"Come on," Cyrus said. He felt so helpless. This was a matter of ranges, velocities, masses, and fusion power. Once you made the decisions, there wasn't much more you could do. This wasn't anything like a knife fight. This wasn't like a first-person shooter game. This was long-range plans coming to fruition in seconds.

"We're in!" Argon shouted.

Cyrus glanced at the number two screen. One of the secondary lasers had burned into the alien warship.

"Yeah!" Cyrus shouted, pumping a fist in the air. They'd broken through the enemy psi-shield.

Now, in space—as the aliens destroyed yet another Prometheus missile—the last two performed their functions. Rods poked out of the nose cones, pointing at the enemy warship. A thermonuclear explosion ignited on each missile. X-rays and gamma rays traveled faster than the annihilating heat. Those rays pumped the one-shot tubes, which concentrated them even as they were heated by the blast. The coherent X-rays and gamma rays beamed at the speed of light at the enemy vessel. Then the nuclear explosion destroyed the rods as the destruction obliterated all shreds of the Prometheus missiles.

The X-rays and gamma rays struck the alien vessel, solid rods of radiation. What it did to the living biological beings inside the ship showed a moment later. The mind shield collapsed, and all of *Discovery*'s lasers began to bore into the steel plating, burning through as the alien warship closed with the Teleship.

"We have a coil breach," Argon informed him.

Cyrus heard muffled explosions from inside the Teleship, and the entire bridge module shook. *Am I about to die? Is Argon right? Is there a Creator? Will I meet Him?*

On-screen, the enemy beams stopped. Cyrus watched in amazement. Secondary explosions racked *Discovery*, but it was much worse for the alien warship. Lasers bored through alien armor and ignited coils or other devices within the vessel. Explosions caused the alien warship to splinter and crack. Still *Discovery*'s beams pumped death and destruction into the enemy. Now fuel, water, stores, and even bodies ejected from the alien warship. Then a fusion fireball devoured the vessel.

As Cyrus stared in shock and disbelief at the screens, the bridge hatch opened. It brought the harsh sound of klaxons to Cyrus and he heard more internal explosions in the Teleship.

"Get out of my way!" Lieutenant Jones shouted.

Cyrus shoved off from the console, letting the man sit down.

Jones took his place, and the weapons officer's fingers began to blur over the screens and controls.

"I'm taking the fusion cores offline and sealing them behind emergency bulkheads," Jones said. "We're hit, but I don't think critically. We're going to lose people. Don't kid yourself there. Most of our lasers are overheating. Didn't you think to cycle them?"

"I guess not," Cyrus said.

Jones shook his head. "You had beginner's luck. That's all I can say. I'm amazed our ship didn't blow."

"The Creator aided us," Argon said.

Jones threw him a glance. "Sure, whatever you say, Chief Monitor. We won. I guess that's all that counts." He glanced at Cyrus. "You did it, kid. You beat the freaking aliens. Good job."

Cyrus wore a loopy smile. "We did it," he told Argon. "We're alive and the alien is gone."

"Yes. We passed the first test. Now we have to see if we can repair the tele-chamber in time to leave this system before the second ship reaches us."

8

Six hours after the alien warship's destruction, Chief Monitor Argon called a meeting in the officer's lounge. He recorded it as *"Discovery* Meeting #14." The roster included Wexx, Cyrus, and Lieutenant Jones.

‖‖‖‖‖‖

ARGON: Premier Lang, I have solemn tidings. We have faced an alien warship today and survived the fight. Unfortunately, we took losses, particularly to the colonists in stasis. A quick survey shows an estimated seventeen thousand deaths, a little over one-third of the sleepers. We also sustained heavy damage to the secondary AI of the Kierkegaard class. In terms of our future survival, the bitterest blow was impairment to the tele-ring circling *Discovery*.

This impairment is critical, as I have sent several of the ablest techs outside the ship to effect repairs. This lessens the number of workers fixing the tele-chamber and lengthens our wait to shift out of danger.

An alien warship, larger than the first, accelerates toward us even now. Its estimated time of arrival—and I use the one million kilometer mark of our
primary laser as the gauge—is three and a half days
from now, or eighty-four hours.

Three alien warships of the larger type accelerate
from AS 412 V, the fifth and outer planet of the system. Their estimated time of arrival is three weeks.

WEXX: How long do you estimate the combined repairs
to take?

ARGON: That will depend on the damage to the tele-
ring.

WEXX: If the ring is beyond repair, what is your plan?

ARGON: We will make our peace with the Creator and
self-destruct the Teleship. We cannot allow the aliens
to capture our shift technology, as that might im-
peril humanity's continued existence.

WEXX: Your solution strikes me as too radical. We
should first attempt communication with the aliens
and see if we can come to an agreement or understanding.

ARGON: Each time the aliens have communicated with
us, they attempted mind control of everyone. No.
We will not communicate with the enemy. It is too
dangerous because of the possible harm to the solar
system.

WEXX: Maybe it's time to wake Jasper. According to
Cyrus, they've already communicated with him.

ARGON: There are two possibilities. Either the aliens
tricked him or he was in collusion with them. If they
beguiled Jasper, we do not know to what extent. In
neither case is waking him likely to bring advantage.
I submit that it is too dangerous to wake our telepath for the obvious reason that we have few to no

controls over him. Clearly, the inhibitors no longer work on Jasper or Cyrus.

CYRUS: You're right, of course. They never should have been put in us in the first place.

ARGON: You saw how Jasper manipulated the crew. We need the controls for our own safety.

WEXX: I'm more concerned right now about this self-destruct idea. Chief Monitor, I understand and appreciate your patriotism. You are a true servant of the state. With that said, I am in no hurry to self-destruct the ship or myself. We have defeated the aliens twice. In my opinion, they should finally be willing to listen to reason. Perhaps they wish to make peace with us.

ARGON: You're not being rational. They have displayed nothing but aggression. Their actions show that they view us as an alien infestation that they must capture or annihilate. Our weakness will not cause them to turn into pacifists but finally allow them to achieve their goal.

WEXX: Self-destruction is rational?

ARGON: If we have the greater goal of protecting our home system, yes.

WEXX: I'm as patriotic as the next person. That doesn't mean I'm willing to kill myself for a concept. Your conclusion that they'll attack Sol with Teleships is nothing but a supposition.

ARGON: The aliens have shown themselves as hostile. It is a reasonable conclusion to think they'll want to eradicate our home system. It is at least a probability. Given that, we cannot gamble with humanity's future. That means there is nothing to indicate that we will improve our situation by contacting them.

WEXX: They must believe we're invaders. To use your own phraseology: given that, they're merely trying to protect their system. Imagine Sol fifty years ago. How would we have reacted if a strange ship simply appeared in our system? I submit we would act as they've been doing.

ARGON: I find your analysis difficult to accept for several reasons. The most critical is that they have psi-masters and were in contact with Special Jasper for some time. That would imply they knew our intentions and still decided on hostility.

WEXX: Exactly! The aliens discovered that we had a ship full of colonists and intended to take over their system. That sounds like a full-blown invasion to me. How can we expect them to have done anything differently than they did?

ARGON: We journeyed here because we believed the system was empty. This was never an invasion as you suggest and these psi-masters would have seen as much.

WEXX: You're shooting in the dark with your suppositions. What surprises me is that you have the ability to discover exactly what the psi-masters learned, yet you do not want to find out. We could wake Jasper and ask him. That's better than simply destroying our own ship and lives. Yes, waking Jasper is a risk, but surely, we can figure out a way to do it safely. I'm beginning to wonder if you have a secret death wish.

JONES: I don't know about the rest of you, but if this is a voting committee, I'm with the Doctor. Let's wake our most powerful Special and see if we can out psi the aliens.

ARGON: This is not a voting committee.

JONES: So who's in charge? You? While I appreciate all you've done, Chief Monitor, I'd like to know when you legally acquired this status.

ARGON: I am the chief representative for Premier Lang. Do you dispute that?

JONES: I'm not arguing with the NKV. I've said all I need to and I stand by it.

ARGON: What do you believe, Cyrus? Since the others have given their opinion, I would like to hear yours.

CYRUS: I don't want to self-destruct. I'm in agreement with Dr. Wexx there. But there is a time to stand and die fighting if you have to.

WEXX: What advanced course of study taught you this wisdom?

CYRUS: Street wisdom. Okay, I'm not as educated as the rest of you. But I've been doing a lot of reading since joining Psi Force, a lot of reading of military history of the old world. What about the ancient Spartans in their fight against Persia? Sometimes you have to make a stand for your side and die if that's what is called for. As I said, I don't want to self-destruct. We don't know if the techs will fix the tele-ring and tele-chamber in time. If they do, we can shift out of here and the problem is solved.

ARGON: Your solution is obvious and we're attempting it. The question is what we should do if we cannot shift out of danger. Now, in a moment of quiet contemplation, we should make the critical decision.

CYRUS: In that case, I'm with Dr. Wexx. We should wake Jasper and see what he knows. Like me, Jasper wanted freedom. I believe the aliens tricked him. Let him see what happened once we reached the system and I bet he would bend his psi-talents to getting us the heck out of here.

ARGON: There is merit in your reasoning.

WEXX: Chief Monitor, Premier Lang believes in the separation of authority on such ventures as this. You have taken full command of the Teleship. That is clearly against Premier Lang's desires. Will you continue to flaunt his rules?

ARGON: You are a sophist, Doctor, a lawyer. I have read you my emergency powers given me by Premier Lang.

WEXX: For the moment, the emergency is over. I think Premier Lang would want us to go back to the formal structure of authority.

ARGON: Would you have me revive Captain Nagasaki?

WEXX: No one is saying that. Either Jasper or the aliens have contorted Nagasaki's thinking too much for me to trust him now.

ARGON: I am open to suggestions.

WEXX: (Pointing at Lieutenant Jones) Why not put him in charge of day-to-day ship duties?

JONES: Hey, leave me out of this. I never asked to be captain of a Teleship.

ARGON: Your points are sound, Doctor, and Premier Lang indeed believes in a division of power. Lieutenant Jones, will you accept authority as captain of the ship?

JONES: Is this legal?

WEXX: Accept the post, Lieutenant. We need somebody running the ship who knows what to do in detail.

JONES: What's wrong with Lieutenant Tanaka? He's higher on the chart than me.

ARGON: Tanaka has the same problem as Nagasaki. The aliens warped Tanaka's thinking once. Maybe it is a permanent situation. Now is not the time to gamble on it.

JONES: In that case, I'll do it.

ARGON: For the sake of form, you are now Captain Jones.

JONES: This is crazy.

ARGON: You will be in charge of repairs. I will continue to watch everyone, particularly for alien possession. Doctor Wexx, you must consider how to contain Special Jasper if we decide to wake him.

WEXX: When would we do that and how would we decide is the right time?

ARGON: It would be a last resort.

WEXX: By then it might be too late.

ARGON: This is a delicate situation. Special Cyrus, can you contain Jasper?

CYRUS: My mind shield is better than it used to be. I can withstand his mind bolts if he hurls them at me.

ARGON: Can you protect others with your talent?

CYRUS: Nope. I never learned to do that.

ARGON: Can you attempt to learn it now?

CYRUS: If you can explain to me how to do something like that, maybe.

ARGON: Dr. Wexx, are you familiar with advanced psi-training techniques?

WEXX: He's not talented enough or strong enough to do as you suggest.

ARGON: Do not be so sure. He resisted alien domination when others more powerful than him couldn't.

WEXX: Yes. He has more internal fortitude than the others do. Why this is the case, I don't pretend to know. If I could test him with other psi-talent . . .

CYRUS: What about Roxie? She's in stasis. If we're going to wake Jasper, why don't we wake her, too?

ARGON: I am not as sanguine concerning Roxie. She succumbed more completely to the aliens. With Jasper, there is a question of his mental submission to them or not.

WEXX: Roxie might have succumbed to Jasper. We still don't know why she did what she did.

ARGON: There are too many mysteries. It is a grave danger to wake Jasper. I am against it.

WEXX: I agree with you there are mysteries and our plan is dangerous. But waking him is better than blowing the Teleship and surrendering our lives. It's a chance to live and escape and I'm for doing that while we can.

JONES: I'll tell you how I see things. We have to repair the tele-ring and tele-chamber. That's the best way for survival in that everything rests on us. Regarding these aliens, I'm with the chief monitor. I don't trust them. I'd rather try something, though, than just self-destructing. But if it comes to that, I don't see we have any choice in the matter. I mean dying with dignity is better than being captured. Cyrus told me about Venice's clairvoyant dream. I don't want to end my days on some alien torture table. I'd rather kill one more of their ships and go out in a blaze of glory.

WEXX: There is no glory in dying.

CYRUS: I don't want to self-destruct, but sometimes there is glory in death, depending on how you go. Let's decide here and now to go in a blaze of fighting. I'm with Lieutenant . . . with *Captain* Jones.

WEXX: Bah. Those supposedly big words mean nothing more than ending our existence. I have this one life and I don't intend to throw it away so easily.

ARGON: We will not throw away our lives easily, this I assure you; we will sell them dearly. We have our tasks. I suggest we each gather a supply of stims and begin working around the clock until we're either free or dead.

WEXX: We still haven't answered the question about Jasper. Who decides whether we do it or not?

ARGON: I am against waking him. What do you others say?

JONES: We ought to try it at least.

CYRUS: Let's do it.

WEXX: You know my position.

ARGON: Doctor Wexx, I suggest you look into the means of waking and keeping him under control.

WEXX: I'll begin right away. Now the question is when do we try?

ARGON: We should wait at least forty-eight hours and assess the repairs then.

WEXX: And if the repairs are lagging?

ARGON: There is no need to vote on this, as I understand each of you would attempt this sooner rather than later. But this is a matter of ship security, which is my area of authority. The meeting is adjourned.

End of Transcript #14

9

The damage to the Teleship proved worse than first estimated, particularly with the fusion engines. That made one decision easy for the new captain.

Cyrus watched as Captain Jones launched the remaining fourteen Prometheus missiles. Each of them lofted from a dome and sped off into the void, with a tongue of fire propelling them. Each quickly became a mote of light.

"The approaching warship is bigger than the first one," Jones said. "We'll never outfight it, but we might trick them."

"If you mean the missiles," Cyrus said, "won't the aliens seem them accelerating?"

"Of course, but I've timed the missiles' approach to their dreadnought." Jones had taken to calling the bigger warship a dreadnought. "The missiles won't be in the dreadnought's range until we're firing the primary laser. By that time, their psi-masters should be busy fending off our beam and hopefully that will focus their captain on us and not the missiles."

"I thought you said we couldn't outfight the dreadnought. It's bigger, probably has thicker armor, and we're weaker than before."

"We won't win a toe-to-toe match like we did against the first alien battleship. But it's good to remember that you have to consider everything in a space battle. The dreadnought's velocity is half what the battleship possessed. That means our primary laser will be hitting them twice as long this time before they can fire back at us."

"But the dreadnought is bigger," Cyrus said. "Bigger ships on our side mean larger lasers because there's more engine power. Won't the alien have longer-ranged lasers this time?"

"Hmm, they might. Well, if the dreadnought has longer-ranged lasers it will cut down our chances, but we still have to use what we have. Fourteen Prometheus missiles—we're placing everything on this next bet. If we win, we should be home free—if the tele-ring and Chamber are fixable. If we lose this fight, well, we won't have to worry about anything then."

Cyrus played combat simulations and listened to Jones's critiques of his battle choices. The rest of the time, Jones left the bridge and inspected repairs, leaving Cyrus with little to do.

Cyrus spent some of the time in an observatory studying holoimages. They'd left the burnt prismatic crystals and dissipated gels in front of the Tele-ship, deciding to wait before they added more. It meant Cyrus could focus some of the main teleoptics on the new star system. He aimed the scopes on the Earth-like planet in the Mars-like orbit.

Sitting in the dark in order to observe the holoimage better, Cyrus examined the planet in detail. Nuclear fires raged. There were molten lakes, scarred mountain ranges, and too much debris in the air. That implied spewing volcanoes, with added dust and junk hurled spaceward by gigantic nuclear bombs. The second Earth-like planet had hundreds of armored satellites ringing it. From time to time, lasers fired down onto the planet.

Cyrus studied the second world, AS 412 II. It had less cloud cover than AS 412 III did and it possessed amazingly thick vegetation. By what Cyrus observed, the entire planet was a hot jungle. He didn't spy any cities, just the fantastic growth. After hours of checking the computer, he did discover huge, artificial mounds. Fused sand amid wide swaths of tree-destruction showed that's where the satellite lasers had struck.

Who fought whom and *why* did they battle each other? Did these Illustrious Ones have anything to do with their decisions?

One Earth-like planet was a burnt cinder and the other one was under a space siege. The aliens were humanoid and fired at others who lived in gigantic dirt mounds.

What have we stumbled onto in New Eden? How can we have been so wrong about it? Who is our real enemy here—the technologicals, the planetary people, or both?

||||||||||

The hours passed and Cyrus awoke in his quarters after a fitful nap. He'd jammed a pillow over his head, keeping it there with an elbow. Someone hailed him on the intercom.

He floated to the wall-comm and pressed the button. "Yeah?"

"This is Argon. Meet me in medical."

"Is something wrong?"

"It's time we spoke with Jasper. I want you there."

"I'm on my way," Cyrus said.

He yanked on clothes and hurried down the empty corridors, swimming through the cool air. He smelled a burnt taint, and nothing the recyclers did could purify it. Jones had told him it was due to the damaged fusion engines.

There was the grim possibility that they couldn't shift all the way home again. That the engines would break down before they'd journeyed far enough. They needed Venice, as she had shifted so much farther than anyone else could each jump. She would have considerably shortened the travel time.

Cyrus rubbed his eyes. He had to concentrate on the coming task. They were going to wake Jasper. Did that mean the tele-ring and chamber were ready, or did Argon think they could bargain with the aliens through Jasper?

Poor Jasper thought he was a god, Zeus in the flesh. Yet the aliens had used him. Yeah, he bet Jasper would be more than willing to help them now.

||||||||||

Cyrus listened as Wexx explained the procedure to Argon and him.

They were in medical, with a cot occupied by a "thawing" Special Second Class Jasper. Wexx had already attached electrodes to the nearly naked, pudgy little man. Those were torture devices.

"If during questioning you believe he's attempting to telepathically dominate me," Wexx said, "you press this switch. It will give him a painful jolt. The longer you press the switch, the more painful a jolt will pour through his body. That should do several things. One, it will disorient him. That should stop his ability at mind control. Two, it will teach him caution. Three, it will show him we mean to save ourselves no matter what we have to do to hurt him."

"Can these jolts cause permanent damage?" Argon asked.

"If Cyrus continues to hold down the button, in time it will kill Jasper."

Cyrus shook his head. "I'm not a torturer."

Wexx turned to him. She wore her white lab coat and maintained an air of medical authority. "No one is calling you a torturer. You are the only one who can sense and intervene in time. This is to save ourselves and save Sol."

Cyrus scowled at Jasper. The fat man wore briefs around his loins but was otherwise naked. The telepath needed to work out sometimes—he was too flabby, his skin too splotchy. Tight straps crisscrossing over him ensured his immobility.

"I've seen things like this in Milan," Cyrus said. "I swore never to have any part of it."

"We could order you to do this," Argon told him.

Looking at Jasper hooked up like this made Cyrus think of Spartacus on the cross. "You can order," he said, "but I'm not going to do it."

"Surely you understand that this is critical," Wexx said.

"So you do it," Cyrus said.

"That's the point. I don't have the ability to resist him. I cannot do it."

"He can do it," Cyrus said, jerking his thumb at Argon. "That's what monitors like to do anyway."

Argon turned a solemn face to him. "There are hard moments in life, hard choices. I do not approve of torture. But there is a time and place for everything."

"I ain't going to do it," Cyrus said.

"Can't you understand yet?" Wexx said. "You're a Special. That means you have certain responsibilities to perform. No one else can do this. The chief monitor might be able to resist Jasper's mental domination, but he won't be able to feel what's going on as well as you can."

Cyrus stared down at the deck plates.

"This is a grim chore," Argon said. "We must save the Teleship. We need to know what he knows. You will not harm him if he cooperates. You will only

178

punish him if he attempts to help the aliens. How can you refuse to help us do this? It is not rational."

"Sure," Cyrus said, staring at the weave on the deck plates. "You have good points. I don't deny that. I'm not like the rest of you. I grew up in the slums. But I've seen torture before in order to get information out of someone. I'll fight Jasper, if you want. But I'm going to only tell you this one more time." He looked up at Wexx and then Argon. "I'm not going to press the button that shocks a helpless man. Trick him, sure. I'm for that. But there's something too inhuman about doing as you suggest. Besides, it's what they did to Spartacus."

"I can't believe this," Wexx said. "You were raised in the slums. Your kind does this to others all the time."

"My kind?" Cyrus asked.

Wexx blushed. "It was a slip of the tongue."

"Just 'cause I was born and raised in the slums doesn't make me any less human than you."

"I will take the control," Argon said.

"He needs to do it," Wexx said.

"No," Argon said. "I don't think so. The Specials need to help each other, or stick together. Cyrus, go in the other room. You can watch through the one-way mirror."

"You're supposed to go there," Wexx said.

"Doctor, you have a good idea," Argon said. "Now how do you propose to force Cyrus to torture Jasper if he doesn't want to?"

"It isn't torture," she said.

"Whatever you wish to call it," Argon said, "how do you propose to force Cyrus do as you wish?"

"You have to listen to reason," she told Cyrus.

"It's your reason, not mine," Cyrus said.

"Don't you want revenge against him?"

"Not on your terms."

"I can't believe this," Wexx said.

"Go," Argon said quietly.

Cyrus floated to the next room, catching the edge of the entrance and swinging himself inside. Had he made the right choice? Yeah, everything was at stake and Jasper was a prick. But there were some things he simply believed. You don't torture someone. If a man was evil enough, you killed him. He'd seen tortured men before. It chilled him just thinking about it. It was horrible, and it not only hurt the tortured but it twisted the one who did it. He wanted to leave medical and let them play their cruel games without him. But Sol might be at stake, so he would watch and help mentally if he could. If they pressed the torture switch too much . . . well, he'd wait and see what happened then.

Wexx still seethed, if one counted how she clenched her teeth. Argon continued to speak to her. Finally, she injected Jasper with something and stood to the side, waiting. Chief Monitor Argon towered on the other side of the cot, with the switch in his big hand.

Time ticked by and Jasper began to groan.

Cyrus had never been in stasis. He'd heard it could be a painful process waking up. He'd heard from one of his instructors that too much stasis sleep harmed psi-talents.

I wonder why that is?

Finally, Jasper opened his eyes. Wexx smiled down at him and she began to explain the situation.

From his spot behind the one-way mirror, Cyrus could see everything. Jasper listened, glanced at Argon, looked at the leads attached to his flabby chest, and then turned carefully to Wexx.

"You can probably guess what those do," Wexx said.

"Why is Cyrus watching behind that mirror?" Jasper asked.

"If I need help—"

"You're angry with him," Jasper said. "Ah, he refused to shock me." The telepath raised his voice. "That's very noble of you, Cyrus. Why don't you come out here where I can see you?"

"No," Wexx said. "He's going to remain behind—" Wexx looked up angrily as Cyrus floated out of the room and near the cot. "Can't you ever do as you're told?" she asked.

Jasper grinned up at her. "He's a slum dweller and you hate him. Why is that, Doctor?"

"You will exit her mind or I shall begin the pain," Argon said in a deep voice.

From the cot, Jasper nodded. "Done. I'm out of her head. Are you satisfied?"

Argon's big thumb twitched onto the button.

For a second, Jasper groaned and twisted on the cot as power surged through the pain centers.

"Let us set the record straight," Argon said, who let up on the pain switch. "We are serious and we hope you realize just how much. If you fail to cooperate, I will kill you by keeping my thumb on the switch. Cyrus may have objections to killing a traitor such as you through these methods. For me, the task will be a pleasure. And the more painful your death is, the better I will enjoy the process."

"You hate me," Jasper said through gritted teeth, "I understand. My kind is the wave of the future, the future that the Highborn lost."

"That you are attempting to antagonize me does little to assure me you will cooperate with us," Argon said.

"Maybe I don't like being shocked." Jasper said. "Did you ever think of that?"

"Neither do we enjoy your attempts at mental domination."

"What I did doesn't hurt like that," Jasper said.

"Please, Chief Monitor," Wexx said. "I would appreciate it if you allowed me to question Jasper. He belongs to Psi Force and—"

"I'd like to point out that this setup violates several Psi Force strictures," Jasper said. "I want to lodge a formal complaint."

Dr. Wexx picked up a computer slate and composed her features before facing the telepath. "Special Second Class Jasper, we are attempting to assess your collusion with the alien psi-masters of New Eden."

Jasper laughed and glanced at each of them in turn. "I have no idea what you're talking about."

"If you would look at the screen, please," Wexx said. She tapped her slate.

The long-faced alien with a metal *baan* and tall collar appeared on the screen. With another tap, Wexx focused the shot on the rearward alien pressing his *baan* against two discs. She played out the first battle with the habitat and then the second battle with the teardrop-shaped battleship.

"Did you notice their ability to stop the laser for a time?" Wexx asked.

"We're actually in the star system then?" Jasper asked. "We made it to New Eden?"

Wexx gave him a wry look. "We will do the questioning today, not you."

"Show me the system in its entirety," Jasper said.

Wexx hesitated before complying. The screen showed the system planets and star. Then Wexx showed him a close-up of each planetary body. Several larger habitats became visible around each gas giant, as did the destruction to AS 412 III, the farther Earth-like world.

From the side, Cyrus watched Jasper. The telepath seemed surprised and drank in the details with his eyes.

"I don't believe it," Jasper finally said.

"Can you be more specific?" Wexx asked.

"I'm not sure I trust the chief monitor with the kill switch," Jasper said. "I'm afraid he'll either torment or kill me if I speak my mind."

"Don't you possess a conscience?" Argon asked. "Don't you care that you've jeopardized the entire ship with your greed? You should be mortified at what your treachery has wrought and willingly tell us everything."

"Are you mortified at treating me like a mutant?" Jasper asked angrily. "Does it horrify you that I and the other Specials have felt like outcasts our entire lives? You should willingly absolve me of all so-called treason in order to show me you repent of your former misdeeds."

"This was a mistake," Argon told Wexx. "We should put him back in stasis."

"You have a point," Wexx said slowly. "Yet . . . he, too, has a point."

Argon stared suspiciously at Jasper. "I told you to keep out of her mind."

"I'm not in it," Jasper said. "But I doubt you can believe that. Go head, kill me."

Argon lifted his big hand, with his thumb poised over the switch.

"No!" Wexx said. "Please, Chief Monitor, you must refrain from your judgments. Your worldview is radically different from Jasper's and his from yours. I request that you inflict pain only if Jasper attempts mental domination upon me. Otherwise, I ask for your silence and restraint."

"It doesn't take a telepath to realize that he's never going to forgive me," Jasper told Wexx.

"I'm not sure that's the question," Wexx said. "Do you want to live or do you desire death? That's what you need to consider."

"I'm listening," Jasper said. "Make your pitch."

"Were you in communication with the aliens?" Wexx asked.

"The answer is obvious. Yes."

"What did they offer you?"

Jasper shook his head. "It wasn't that simple. The connection was brief and weak. I did get a sense that they lived on a bucolic world, a literal Eden of forests, glens, and huge butterflies. I also sensed a primitive society and them as elders or wizard-priests, if you will. I tried to calm their fears concerning us."

"Why didn't you tell us about this contact?" Wexx asked.

"No. I've seen the fear reaction all my life. Those like Argon think we're mutants. They would have wanted to bomb the aliens out of existence. I couldn't permit that or even take the chance."

"He lies," Argon said. "He is a traitor and colluded with the aliens. This story of his, it must be a pure concoction."

"You'll never shift out of this system, if that's what you're thinking," Jasper said. "From what the Doctor has shown me, you know they need a radio or other link to help pinpoint us from a distance. How do you think they reached out so far the first time to Venice? It happened when we used the tele-ring. The moment you turn it on, the alien psi-masters, as you're calling them, will reach out and mentally attack the ship."

"Then we must self-destruct," Argon said. "We have no other choice."

"What are you talking about?" Jasper asked. For the first time, he showed what appeared to be genuine surprise.

"I think we should let Jasper peek into my mind," Wexx said. "Let him see that you mean to destroy the Teleship if you think the aliens will capture it."

"That's criminally insane," Jasper whispered.

"Call it what you will," Argon said. "It is what I will do."

"And you have *me* hooked to this thing?" Jasper asked Wexx. "He's the mental patient."

"I'll ask you the same question as before," Wexx said. "Do you want to live or do you want to die?"

"Of course I want to live," Jasper said. "What kind of stupid question is that?"

"If you desire life," Wexx said, "you must help us escape from New Eden."

"How do you propose I perform this miracle?" Jasper asked.

"The answer should be obvious," Wexx said.

Jasper snorted. "It's always up to the telepath in the end. Do you realize how many like Cyrus I hunted down and located for Psi Force? They would have never found all the talents by themselves. I did it. I'm the one who allowed Psi Force to grow to its present size. And do you know what they did for me, what they gave me for all my hard work? Nothing but to call me a second-class Special. I'm tired of being the mutant. Maybe death is preferable."

"You don't mean that," Wexx said.

Jasper stared up at the ceiling. To Cyrus, it seemed the telepath worked at keeping his features neutral.

"Suppose I agreed to help you." Jasper said. "What would that look like for me?"

"We would hook up a similar system as this one," Argon said. "I would hold the pain switch as we shifted. You would use your telepathy to protect Cyrus as we attempted to jump out of range of the psi-masters."

"I'd already figured out that part," Jasper said. "I mean criminally or legally or however you want to say it. I'd want you to drop all charges of mutiny and sedition against me."

"The charges are already recorded on the ship and security logs," Argon said.

"So alter them," Jasper said. "That shouldn't be too hard."

"No. What you suggest isn't possible. It would also be a crime against Premier Lang's trust."

"It's possible if you want my help getting home," Jasper said.

Argon looked away.

"Is that such a large price to pay for being able to warn Sol about these aliens?" Jasper asked. "I made my play and failed. That happens often enough in life. In some systems, the loser still gets to walk away with his life and freedom. That's all I'm asking for."

"I suspect a more nefarious reason," Argon muttered.

"I would have been surprised if you didn't," Jasper said. "But I would suggest you hurry up with whatever it is you're going to do. By what the doctor has shown me, we're running out of time."

Argon became reflective, finally turning to Wexx. "I do not trust him."

"I'm not sure I do either," Wexx said. "But what other choice do we have? We can't fight the entire system."

"What do you think?" Argon asked Cyrus.

"I think the aliens used you," Cyrus told Jasper. "I told you they were dangerous."

"You knew about them?" Wexx asked.

"You put inhibitors in our brains," Cyrus said.

"For our own protection," Argon said. "Look what happened when Jasper freed himself."

"You made us slaves," Cyrus said. "Slaves want freedom and will do anything to get it. You don't have to worry about me. I don't want to be slaves to those aliens. I don't think Jasper does either."

"That should be obvious," Jasper said.

"They tricked you," Cyrus said.

"I know," Jasper said, and he turned away.

Argon took a deep breath. "Yes, we must make the attempt. But I will hold the pain switch and the self-destruct button for *Discovery*. If we fail to shift away, we will make sure the aliens never gain our critical technology.

10

The techs repaired the tele-ring with twelve hours to spare in the eighty-four hour race with the alien dreadnought. They also jury-rigged the tele-chamber. Some of the procedures would now have to take place from the bridge module, but in the larger scheme of things that didn't really matter.

Or so Cyrus thought as he readied to enter the cylinder with its blue solution.

Jasper sat nearby in a cushioned chair bolted to the deck plates. Straps bound his neck, chest, wrists, and ankles. Pain leads stuck to his skin, the most prominently to his neck. Beside him in another chair towered Chief Monitor Argon.

Captain Jones and Dr. Wexx had talked Argon out of holding the ship's self-destruct button too.

"You should concentrate on your primary task and not have to worry about the ship at that point," Wexx had told the chief monitor.

Argon buckled in and kept a flinty gaze fixed on Jasper. "I will reward treachery with pain," he rumbled.

Jasper didn't answer. His eyes were on Cyrus.

I can feel you, Cyrus told the telepath.

Do you see how they use us as pieces to a machine? They don't truly think of us as people, but as mutants, as component parts for their greater glory.

Cyrus had to admit the man had a point. *I don't think the aliens will treat us any better, though.*

That was my mistake. I thought they might be better. There're not really aliens, by the way, but humans like us.

I don't see how, Cyrus thought.

I'm not sure how, either, but they're humans nonetheless. You saw them. Can you doubt they're people?

Are you saying they're originally from Earth?

Either that or we're originally from here, Jasper thought. *Maybe the name Eden is more accurate than we realize.*

Cyrus twisted around to study Jasper.

"Is he communicating with you?" Argon asked.

Cyrus didn't answer, but put the induction helmet over his head. It was a tight fit. He strapped on the breathing mask, slid down into the solution, and listened to the air move through the tube. Goggles protected his eyes and a slick-suit his skin.

Who are the Illustrious Ones? Cyrus thought.

I don't know, Jasper told him. *Besides, I don't trust them to tell me the truth anymore. They lied to me. They tried to trick me. I want to get out of this system just as much as you do. But don't let Argon know that. I despise the man. He thinks he's superior to us, which is a gigantic joke on him.*

I'm going in to link with Socrates. I'll need it quiet for a few minutes.

Relax, Cyrus. You and I have had our differences, but you refused to torture me. I'll remember what you did.

There was a buzzing sound in Cyrus's helmet and a sense of disorientation.

"Special Fourth Class Cyrus," AI Socrates said. "You've returned. I'm glad you've decided to help me shift once again."

The AI sure had a warped sense of reality. But he couldn't worry about that now. He had a job to do. "Do you recall what happened during the last shift?" Cyrus asked.

"The shift anomalies remained within the accepted limits. Ah. Are you referring to the enemy psi-attacks after we crossed though the null field?"

"That's right," Cyrus said.

"They assaulted Special Second Class Jasper. Is that why he is not helping me today?"

"I'm sure it doesn't matter. I was just curious. Are you ready to shift?"

"Ready," Socrates said. "The tele-ring will activate in nine seconds. Have you composed yourself?"

Cyrus took a deep breath. This was it. They had found an alien species, well, if Jasper was wrong about them being the same as Earth people. The aliens looked humanoid, of that there was no doubt. But they didn't seem like normal people. *Discovery* had defeated two attacks and now a third attempt was hours from reaching an engagement point with the Teleship.

"Six seconds," Socrates said.

By a Herculean effort, the techs had repaired the critical damage to the shift structures. Now they had to hope the fusion engines held long enough to get them home. Later, they could probably wake Roxie to help in the shifting.

I'm ready, Jasper thought at Cyrus.

"What did you say?" Socrates asked.

"Did you hear that?" Cyrus asked the AI.

"I heard a voice. It was faint."

"We're speaking by brain waves, right?" Cyrus asked.

"The tele-ring is going online," Socrates said.

Get ready, Jasper thought. *The psi-masters will attack—*

Cyrus was operating through the AI now. The moment he linked with the tele-ring, the alien psi-masters struck.

Inside the cylinder, Cyrus roared with pain. Bubbles slid past his mask and burbled upward. His concentration slid away from the tele-ring as he instantaneously raised his mind shield to full strength.

I'm here, Jasper told him. *There are more of them than last time. These are stronger, too, the sons of bitches.*

The psi-masters battered at Cyrus's mind. Each psi-bolt struck his shield, driving it a little closer to his ego.

"There are so many voices with us today," Socrates said. "How is this possible?"

Cyrus heard the AI as from far away.

They're trying to shut down your senses, Jasper told him. *Don't let them. Keep up your shield.*

The mind attack was relentless. Once Cyrus deflected one thought, another struck from a different direction. There was no way for him to concentrate on the tele-ring and pick a location, never mind attempting to warp it open into the null portal.

He felt Jasper battling beside him. The telepath was doing his damnedest to stop the aliens. For a moment, Cyrus "saw" a psi-master. This one wore a red robe and had a shinier *baan* than the first one he'd seen several days ago. Like the others from before, the psi-master pressed the forehead *baan* against two discs, against the amplifier.

We need some of those, Jasper thought.

Cyrus reinforced his mind shield, and he began pushing outward. He heard his harsh breathing and the slush of the blue solution around him.

You're going to have to reach out with the tele-ring while I hold them back. It should take just a few seconds. Are you ready?

I'm ready, Cyrus thought.

Now!

Cyrus kept up an automatic shield as he reached out with his mind, linking with the tele-ring.

"I was wondering where your concentration had gone," Socrates said. "We have little time left. I have analyzed the 'voices' and believe they are alien to our vessel."

Combined with the tele-ring and aided by AI Socrates, Cyrus reached out nearly 0.8 light years. He began warping space—

Someone screamed horribly, although it was a muffled sound. The next second, psi-masters struck Cyrus with precision mind bolts.

Cyrus's telekinesis slid away from the tele-ring as he used every ounce of his mental energy keeping up his mind shield. He had a vague idea that the psi-master had switched targets. They'd hit Argon and taken over the mobility of his thumb, causing it to press down on the switch. The physical pain jolting through Jasper had broken the telepath's mental concentration and obliterated his telepathic shield.

The knowledge came, and then Cyrus battled for his mind. He was so close to shifting. If he could hang onto the tele-ring for three more seconds, he could make the needed null portal and *Discovery* would sail away out of danger. They would be on their way home. He would be a hero.

Instead, Cyrus fought a losing battle against the aliens. The New Eden psi-masters repeatedly struck, and for a second, one of them slid into motor control of his brain.

As if flipping a switch, the alien psi-master caused a blackout, ending Cyrus's attempt to shift out of New Eden.

PART IV: BONDAGE

1

"Cyrus," Socrates said tentatively. "Are you well?"

Cyrus stirred within the cylinder, his limbs pushing through the dense liquid. He tried to squeeze the substance, but that proved impossible. This was just great, he felt groggier than before. *Did I just fall asleep? Wait! The psi-masters—they attacked us when we turned on the tele-ring.*

"You must have been busy calibrating," Socrates said. "The trouble is you have taken an eternity longer than normal and still have not adjusted for flux. The tele-ring has shut down long ago and you fell asleep. This has not occurred before. Therefore, weighing the evidence, I finally decided to wake you. This proved more difficult than I believed and has taken hours. The others in the chamber with us are immune to my attempts."

"You did the right thing," Cyrus said. "I—"

"I should point out that the alien ship has reached its firing range and begun chewing through the asteroidal shielding around the core of the Teleship."

"What? How did that happen?"

"You have been asleep for some time as I said."

"Why didn't the doctor wake me?"

"The humans in the chamber and everyone else I've monitored are also asleep."

"The aliens must have caused it."

"Yes," Socrates said. "My probability indicator suggests foreign entities have affected crew personnel."

"Can you turn on the tele-ring?"

"First someone must calibrate and adjust for flux."

"If the alien dreadnought has reached its range, we've run out of time. We have to get out of here now."

"My safety features will not allow me to switch on the tele-ring until someone has adjusted for flux."

"Can you show me what's happening outside the ship?"

"Are you ready to receive?"

"Go for it."

On the inner surface of his goggles, Cyrus saw the alien dreadnought's single beam. It reached across 1.5 million kilometers of space. The grotesquely powerful laser had already chewed through what was left of the P-Field and bored through asteroidal rock, heading inward toward the central core. There was little time left to shift.

"Socrates," Cyrus shouted, "initiate emergency shift procedures!"

"I cannot."

Cyrus didn't think the aliens were attempting to destroy *Discovery*, but to make sure it could never escape. He couldn't save them now, but he might make it harder for the aliens to build their own Teleship.

Shoving upward, Cyrus surfaced and tore off the induction helmet. Disorientation hit and he sank back into the solution.

I might not have much time.

Cyrus unglued his eyes, rose up again and removed the goggles and mask, and climbed out of the cylinder. Blue solution dripped from his slick-suit. Everyone in the tele-chamber slept soundly. The psi-masters had put them under as they'd done once before.

I wonder what Socrates did to wake me up so much sooner than anyone else could?

He went to Jasper in his padded chair. The telepath was out, so was Argon. Cyrus ripped off the shock leads and shook Jasper. It didn't help. The aliens must have done something special to him.

Dr. Wexx and others snored from the deck plates. The Teleship was under one G acceleration. He wondered who'd done that. Unfortunately, it wouldn't stop the aliens from acquiring *Discovery* and reverse engineering their own starships. The horrible thing was there was nothing he could do about it . . .

Cyrus paused. He had a memory, a new one someone had given him. He concentrated and realized he knew how to do one thing to slow down the aliens from building Teleships.

How do I know this?

It came to him that Jasper must have given it to him right before the telepath went under.

Cyrus headed toward the outline of a portal, one he'd never noticed before.

"What are you doing?" Socrates asked from a speaker in the chamber. "Your actions are odd and unusual. You seem disoriented."

"I want to save you from AI Kierkegaard's fate."

"The aliens have stopped firing. I am no longer in any danger."

"Can you predict their next move?" Cyrus asked. He reached the outline of the portal and said, "Vector five, alpha nine-two, override code seven-seven-three."

The portal swished open, and Cyrus headed into AI Socrates's main control center.

"How can you protect me from here?" Socrates asked through a different speaker. The small chamber was packed with banks of controls and screens.

"Show me the alien dreadnought," Cyrus said. "I want you to monitor its actions."

On a nearby screen, the teardrop-shaped vessel moved through the void. Its fusion engine no longer burned, no longer left a long tail behind it. On accumulated velocity alone, the dreadnought hurtled toward them. The alien vessel would never stop in time to board, but would pass *Discovery* soon. It looked like the Prometheus missiles hadn't worked. That was a shame.

"You are heading for my self-destruct station," Socrates said. "I would appreciate it if you told me why."

"Emergency maintenance," Cyrus said.

"My voice analyzers tell me you are fabricating the truth."

"I'm sorry, Socrates. I do like you. This has nothing to do with that."

"Cyrus, if you cause me to self-destruct you will never return to Sol."

Cyrus's gut tightened. He knew that. He also knew he could never allow the aliens to gain shift technology.

"Please, Cyrus, reconsider, won't you?"

Cyrus tapped in the key code. Then his fingers began to blur in movement. Halfway through the self-destruct sequence, a wall of tiredness hit him. His eyelids closed almost of their own accord.

"No!" Cyrus hissed. "You're not taking me down just yet." He had a mind screen, but that didn't seem to make any difference.

"Cyrus," the speaker said. "I have laced the air with a soporific agent. I did it because . . ."

It was the last time Cyrus heard AI Socrates. His fingers continued to tap out the self-destruct code for the artificial intelligence. When he finished, he turned from the console. He had to check . . . check . . .

Cyrus crashed to his knees. That woke him up a little. Then he groaned as his eyes shut. He felt himself falling . . . falling . . . and then he didn't know anything at all.

|||||||||||

Awareness returned to Cyrus as he heard a loud, metallic *clang*. It sounded ominous and it caused the AI control chamber to shake.

His dim awareness took time to turn into a positive choice. Finally, Cyrus opened his eyes and he found himself floating in the middle of the chamber. The acceleration had stopped. One of the wall screens still worked. It showed metal, a vast field of it outside the Teleship. There was a black knob to the left on the wall of metal, but he had no idea what it was.

The metal must be an alien vessel beside us.

Cyrus squeezed his eyes shut and opened them again. If that was an alien vessel parked beside the Teleship—

Another *clang* sounded. All around him, the chamber shuddered.

I'm weightless. That means the ship has stopped accelerating. The alien laser must have damaged the Teleship's engines. How long had he been unconscious?

Cyrus shoved against a panel. He floated to the floor and used his leg to push against it, aiming for the portal. He sailed too fast and hit the edge with his shoulder.

He cursed at the pain, but at least it helped him wake up faster. He breathed the air, tasting it for impurities. His hand flew to his throat. The air was cold enough so he felt the difference against his throat. He shivered . . . because he was cold. Was the fusion engine still running? He didn't hear the constant thrum.

Cyrus paled. He never thought he'd feel this way, but the lack of a thrum terrified him. Was the air going stale? How long until the inside of the ship was the same temperature as the outside?

We're really trapped in an alien star system.

At the thought, a grim longing and loneliness filled him. He shook his head. He didn't have time for fear. He needed to do something positive. He needed to act, not wait for others to act upon him.

At that moment, the portal to the tele-chamber opened and Captain Jones floated in. He held a needler. Cyrus wondered where the man had gotten it. Jones moved with liquid grace, twisting around in midair. He aimed his needler down the corridor and fired a burst of hair-thin tungsten slivers.

"What's going on?" Cyrus asked.

Jones glanced back. His face was contorted with hatred and loathing. "Aliens!" he said in a harsh whisper. "They've boarded the ship."

The knot in Cyrus's stomach tightened painfully.

"They'll never take me alive," Jones said, as he floated deeper in the chamber. "Not after I know what's waiting for us."

Just then, a round metallic object the size of a person's chest floated into the tele-chamber.

Jones shouted an oath, took deliberate aim, and fired a burst of slivers from his needler. They rattled harmlessly against the metal object.

In return, a port opened on the floating device. A stubby nozzle pointed at Jones and a milky beam hit him. He went limp, but otherwise seemed unharmed. Jets propelled the robotic fighting device deeper into the chamber. A second slot opened and a small sensor dish appeared.

It's searching for us.

Instinctively, Cyrus reached out with his power. It was a spontaneous action. The threat of imminent death or capture moved him, as a lion's roar behind him would have made him bellow and jump away. With his telekinetic ability heightened through fear, he shorted something in the device. The lights in the machine went inert. The dish never rotated and no more gas hissed from its jets. It continued to float until it hit a wall and caromed in another direction like a slow motion billiard ball.

The mental effort tired Cyrus and made him gasp as his head throbbed with a sharp pain in the frontal lobe. This was worse than shifting.

Now what do I do?

The answer didn't take long. He heard magnetic clangs—or so he surmised they must be—as something heavy clanked down the corridor. The clangs implied mass and that implied size. Nor was he wrong.

Seconds later, a suited, bipedal creature entered the tele-chamber. It stalked on two legs, but it wasn't remotely manlike. Instead, it looked like a raptor, a predatory dinosaur perhaps nine or ten feet tall. It was hard to tell its exact size in the confines of the ship. The creature possessed a saurian tail and it had two smaller arms. The clear, oblong helmet showed somewhat raptor-like features, but with a larger braincase than the prehistoric Earth dinosaur would have had. The snout and teeth were lizard-like. The scaled skin of the head was golden, and there was a cold, reptilian intelligence shining in its eyes.

Is this an Illustrious One? Cyrus wondered.

An arm stiffened, with a gloved claw or talon pointing at the portal to the AI control chamber. Unintelligible words boomed from a suit speaker. Somehow, the creature seemed to know Cyrus was hiding there.

He summoned his final reserves of telekinetic power as terror filled him with loathing. This must be the creature of Venice's precognitive nightmare.

Cyrus tried to duplicate his feat of seconds earlier. He scrunched his brow and thought harmful *pain* against the creature.

Instead, a blossom of pain in his own head doubled Cyrus over. Vomit acid burned the back of his throat. Despite that, he grinned viciously, expecting the alien to stumble backward or croak in awful agony.

Nothing of the kind happened. Something flashed on its suit and a metallic band around its cranium glowed faintly. Worse, perhaps, flaps on its upper jaw drew back as if it grinned, showing off its deadly teeth.

The alien used one of its arms and talons to press something on its suit. Sound—a sonic blast—hit Cyrus. He roared, but was otherwise unable to move. He watched the alien stalk toward him closer and closer. It pulled out a red-glowing wand and touched his neck. Stun power hit, and Cyrus froze.

The alien looked down at him. There seemed a feeling of satisfaction to the creature. It unhooked something from its suit and put the top of it against Cyrus's head. There was a sound, and a filament bag engulfed him. The alien withdrew Cyrus from the room, hooked his bagged body to its suit, and stalked for the portal to the corridor.

At that point, Cyrus passed out, knowing that he had just entered a terrifyingly new phase of existence.

2

An instinctive caution learned long ago in Level 40 kept Cyrus from reacting as he awoke in the belly of an alien spaceship.

Before Cyrus opened his eyes, he felt crushing Gs and the thrum of engines, which was how he knew he was on a ship. The acceleration pinned him to a steel floor. His muscles ached because of it, particularly his lower back. A rank odor made his nostrils twitch.

An odd electric sound made him curious.

He eased his eyelids open. Harsh lights lit the interior. He saw fifty or sixty crewmembers from *Discovery* lying on the cold metal like him. Most were in the process of waking up. The chamber was large, with bloodstains and other filth encrusted on the bulkheads. It was all very strange and intimidating.

I'm on an alien vessel. They captured me. This is horrible.

Yes, he remembered the raptor-like alien, a real alien, not just a weirdly formed humanoid.

The electric sound occurred once more.

Slowly, Cyrus eased his neck up. He saw the contraption, a motorized chair it appeared. It was round, a disc, about four meters across. In the middle of it sat one of the long-faced humanoids. The psi-master wore a red robe and a high collar. A *baan* circled his tall forehead. The psi-master wore a glittering pendant at his throat and his fingernails were black-painted or lacquered. Cyrus could see that a glass dome or Plexiglas or some similar substance protected the psi-master, encased him. The man manipulated his vehicle and the electric sound occurred once more as it moved across the chamber.

He's not taking any chances with us. Either that or the Gs are too powerful for him to move by himself.

The psi-master—if that's what he was—scanned the prone throng of Earthlings.

The man turned, pointed, and spoke. Cyrus heard his strange words through what must have been a speaker.

Other alien humanoids who had paced the disc-shaped vehicle from behind hurried forward. They were radically different from the psi-master.

Each of them was short and squat—an inch under Jasper's height—with gorilla-like shoulders and a deep chest. The first had long arms with the hands dangling nearly to his knees, a nonexistent neck, and alert eyes that peered out from under a helmet's brim. He wore a brown uniform with red shoulder boards and a holstered gun and short-handled axe hanging from his belt.

They looked tough and capable. Were they clones of each other? Cyrus swallowed. Could he take one of them in a fight?

The psi-master pointed . . . at Roxie.

The aliens must have thawed her from the emergency stasis chamber in medical. Cyrus noticed Nagasaki and Colonel Konev lying on the steel floor. Most of the shift crew was here as well. Yes, he saw Chief Monitor Argon on the floor, watching the humanoids as he pretended to rest.

Two alien soldiers, who moved jerkily in the high Gs, hauled Roxie to her feet. Her eyes stared with horror at the psi-master.

Cyrus wondered what she sensed. He needed to do something. This helplessness was so galling.

Protected by his bubble, the psi-master showed his teeth in what might have been a sneer or maybe a smile. He clutched the pendant at this throat and closed his eyes, leaning minutely forward.

Roxie's head jerked. She must be using her psionics. A moment later, one of the soldiers released her and staggered backward, clutching his chest.

Cyrus wanted to cheer.

The psi-master rapped out several terse words.

The remaining soldier twisted one of Roxie's arms. She painfully sucked in her breath. With lightning reflexes, the soldier took an object from his belt and touched her neck. Roxie stiffened and her eyes widened even more than before.

The psi-master's smile grew. He was a bastard and seemed to enjoy this. He spoke again in his unintelligible language.

The soldier unceremoniously draped an unconscious Roxie over a shoulder, turned, and headed for a hatch.

"Where are you taking her?" Argon said. The chief monitor sat up.

None of the aliens paid him any attention. Many of *Discovery's* crew stirred.

Cyrus hesitated. It was a throwback reaction to Level 40. There, he'd learned it was unwise to leap into action too soon. You needed to know the situation first. Maybe Argon didn't know what it was like to be small and weak and get kicked in the stomach. Those stocky warriors looked tougher than normal the longer he considered them.

With a growl, the huge NKV officer climbed to his feet. "I asked you a question. Where are you taking her?"

That's the wrong thing to do here.

Cyrus wanted to tell Argon to stay down and keep quiet. They were prisoners. Prisoners didn't have any rights. You waited and watched, and took the opportunity when you judged your best moment had come. In the belly of an alien spaceship with tough soldiers nearby wasn't such a time.

"We have to keep together!" Argon shouted to the others on the floor. "Get up and help me."

No one did anything of the kind. They were too disoriented and petrified.

Where does he find such courage?

In the heavy Gs, the chief monitor started toward the soldier carrying Roxie.

Two more soldiers shuffled forward. Despite their muscles, they looked ineffectual compared to Argon. The psi-master watched the confrontation carefully. The seated humanoid grasped his pendant, closed his eyes, and opened them a moment later. He spoke several alien words.

Both soldiers facing Argon drew objects from their belts.

Argon noticed their actions, stopping to face the soldiers, although he continued to track Roxie with his eyes. Maybe the soldiers thought he knew better, but the chief monitor had likely never been in this kind of situation before. He lunged at the nearest soldier, hitting the short man in the face, knocking him off his feet and hard onto the steel floor.

Cyrus watched amazed. Argon was like Spartacus. The chief monitor refused to act like a slave even for a moment. It was electrifying. Cyrus found himself wanting to join Argon in his brave stand.

The psi-master spoke harshly.

The second soldier shuffled away from Argon, holstered the first object, and drew his gun. It made a sizzling sound and something odd moved through the air from it. The projectile looked like a clot or wave of heat. The thing struck Argon in the chest and knocked him brutally onto the metal floor. He groaned, and he didn't attempt to rise.

The courage of a moment ago wilted in Cyrus. That easily and that brutally the aliens ended Argon's lone stand. That's why a prisoner needed to wait, to study the situation. This was the wrong time and place to resist.

The electric sound of the bubble-dome vehicle continued and Cyrus saw to his horror the psi-master looking at him and inching his vehicle closer. The humanoid clutched the pendant.

Cyrus made an instantaneous decision. The psi-master seemed to be hunting Specials. He'd had Roxie taken elsewhere. From Cyrus's experience, it was better if the enemy underestimated you.

An oily telepathic thought struck his mind. Cyrus didn't shield himself. He felt certain the difference of his thoughts from the psi-master would hide him for a time despite his talent. Maybe for once his small or inconspicuous talent would help. Wouldn't it take time for the humanoids to understand how Earthlings thought? What Cyrus could do during that time to improve his situation, he had no idea. What he did now was to bring to mind images of his youth from Level 40.

The psi-master stared at him. It was a pitiless gaze, soul-numbing here in such a hopeless situation.

Cyrus thought about the time in the dark in the ducts when he'd knifed a hunting Red Blade.

The psi-master released his pendant, although he continued to stare at Cyrus. They were the worst two seconds in Cyrus's life. Would soldiers come for him and cart him away as one had Roxie? Where would they take him?

The psi-master said nothing to the soldiers. Instead, he looked at another crewmember that showed signs of restive life.

With a vast sense of relief, Cyrus laid his head on the cold steel and shut his eyes. This had to be the most miserable situation anyone had ever been caught in. He was a prisoner in an alien star system with no way home. Were these humanoids going to dissect them as Venice had seen in a clairvoyant dream? The way the soldier had ruthlessly shot Argon didn't bode well for the rest of them.

Watch and wait, Cyrus told himself. *Bide your time until you get a chance.*

A chance for what? He didn't know, but he hoped he did when he saw it. For now, he rested. Let someone else explore and find out what sort of punishment occurred. It wasn't a heroic attitude, as the marines probably would have shown. He'd learned survival thinking in the slums as an orphan child and it had kept him alive then. Maybe it would help here. If it did, he would remember this awful day and make the aliens pay.

The psi-master made the rounds, testing many. When soldiers grabbed a thawed out Captain Nagasaki, the man began to rave.

"Cyborgs, these are creatures of the cyborgs!" Nagasaki shouted. "They'll steal our souls and give us robotic bodies!"

Nagasaki resisted as they hauled him to his feet.

One of the soldiers slapped the silver-haired navy officer across the face, maybe to knock some sense into him. Nagasaki glared at the man as flecks of foam appeared at the corners of his mouth. Nagasaki karate-kicked the soldier and knocked him sprawling onto the deck.

Two more soldiers shuffled forward. Nagasaki launched himself at them. A soldier blocked a finger stab and punched the captain in the gut. It doubled Nagasaki over. The second soldier used the butt of his gun and clouted Nagasaki on the back of the head. The captain dropped to the steel floor, striking it with his chin. He groaned, twisting on the deck.

The two soldiers began to stomp on Nagasaki, beginning with his hands. They had hard-heeled boots, and each heel smashed down in the middle of the man's hand. Cracking bones told the story. Then they stomped and broke Nagasaki's ankles.

Many of *Discovery*'s crew groaned in horror. The rest watched in apathy. The groaners shrank back from the brutality. Cyrus watched grim-faced. He'd seen evil like this before in the slums. He would remember.

Captain Nagasaki screamed, beginning to thrash. Each soldier took a side and kicked Nagasaki, one in the stomach and chest, the other along the back. Finally, the two soldiers took turns, brutally kicking him in the head, bouncing it in one direction and then another.

The two soldiers kicked Nagasaki to death. The psi-master watched the process coldly, while *Discovery's* crew looked on in abject horror.

Finally, Argon couldn't take it anymore. "Stop," he said.

The psi-master pointed at Argon and spoke.

The chief monitor licked his lips. It was obvious that he was weighing the odds.

Cyrus's resolve broke. Watching them kill the captain while he did nothing . . . "Don't do it," he told Argon. "Wait and live."

The psi-master swiveled around in his seat, staring at Cyrus again.

A chill worked up Cyrus's back. He felt he'd just been marked in some manner.

Right. I've shown initiative. They must have been hunting for this and I've played into their hands.

Still, Cyrus felt good at doing something positive. Argon didn't shout again, but watched helplessly. Cyrus might have just saved the chief monitor's life. He acted like Spartacus, if only in a small way. No one could do anything now for Nagasaki. It was time to take whatever small victory one could.

This was a brutal lesson, killing the captain. Likely, it was another thing the aliens wanted them to realize.

We're at their mercy and it looks like this society has no idea what that means.

The psi-master touched his controls, shifting the vehicle. He scanned them carefully with his hard eyes. Was he judging expressions or did he use his psi-power to gauge their thoughts?

The soldiers dragged Nagasaki's corpse from the chamber.

New humanoids entered, drawing several machines that hovered on sleds. These people were ordinary-looking and wore smocks reaching to their bare knees and tight-fitting skullcaps. Dressed differently and under different circumstances, they could have passed as Earthlings.

The psi-master spoke. Several of the new humanoids nodded. The psi-master pointed at Chief Monitor Argon.

Soldiers drew their guns and warily shuffled near. One group of smock-wearing humans followed, pulling a floating sled with them. The machinists, as Cyrus was beginning to think of them, quietly spoke among themselves.

The psi-master made an imperious gesture. Three soldiers holstered their guns and surged at Argon, circling him and grabbing his arms. It was too much for the giant chief monitor. He struggled and flung one soldier to the floor. The other two released their grips and struck heavy blows. Argon grunted and swung his arm, catching a smaller soldier on the side of the head, dropping the man to the floor. Two more soldiers ran up to help.

Cyrus's chest tightened. This was too much. Was he really going to lay here doing nothing? If he helped, what would happen to him?

Wait. This is just like the slums. Wait and learn. You can't do anything else except die.

The decision was hard and tears of frustration welled in Cyrus's eyes. He felt worthless. He felt helpless doing nothing. Just a few more successful seconds in the tele-chamber and they could have been on their way back to Sol. Instead, failure brought bitterness. That in itself was a lesson. Would he ever get to put the lesson to use, though?

The stocky soldiers beat down Argon, pummeling him once he hit the floor, but they didn't kill him. Instead, they dragged the battered chief monitor near the machinists. The one with the highest peaked cap commanded three others. They attached a metal contrivance to Argon's head. First wiping blood off his face, they attached clamps to his ears and put sticky discs on his forehead. Shaving off hair, they put more discs onto the back of his skull.

Was this torture? Cyrus had no idea.

The primary machinist went to his machine. He used an instrument panel, adjusting controls. Finally, he glanced at the psi-master, although he didn't meet the man's eyes. The psi-master simply watched. The primary machinist tapped a switch and the machine began to hum.

From on the floor, Argon stiffened and his eyes flew open. He made odd, croaking noises and little jerks. Then he began to moan. A moment later, his eyes rolled up into his head and he began thrashing on the floor. He shivered, but no one made any move to intervene.

Finally, the machinist shut off the humming device. He instructed the others and they withdrew the metal contrivance and clamps from Argon's head.

He lay gasping on the floor, shuddering, until finally he curled into a fetal ball, shivering and moaning.

At the psi-master's orders, the machinists did the same thing to twelve other chosen people. Some sat dully during the process. Two died in convulsions, one died apparently swallowing his tongue.

This didn't seem to concern any of the aliens.

Finally, the psi-master indicated Cyrus.

The tightness in his chest . . . Cyrus moaned as soldiers and machinists approached. Should he try to short circuit the machine? Should he fight before he died?

No. Some of the others had survived. He needed to relax and hope for the best. Everyone was watching him. The aliens had all the odds on their side, all the guns, and knew what was going on. He had to survive. Maybe he had to survive by luck. At this point, he simply had no hope and nothing to gain by resisting.

Cyrus let them clamp the metal cap on his head and attach the leads to his ears, forehead, and the shaved part of the back of his head.

A machinist near the machine glanced at him. The man had black pin-dots for eyes. Cyrus didn't see any pity in those eyes, neither did he spy cruelty. The man was simply doing his job.

The machinist tapped his instrument panel.

Cyrus stiffened. What did it do? What would happen?

The machine thrummed with power. In a second, the cap hummed on his head. Electricity flowed through the cap and to the leads on his skin. He heard a whine begin in his head. It turned into a roar, a rushing sound, and Cyrus began to twitch and shake. The rushing roaring sound was like a hurricane and it smashed thoughts and twisted around and around inside his head. Suddenly, it screeched and Cyrus stiffened, perhaps his eyes rolled up inside his head. He didn't know. There was blackness, nothing . . . until he became aware of machinists plucking the leads off his skin and removing the cap.

Cyrus shivered on the floor of the alien ship. He stared the chief machinist. "What did you do to me?"

The man paused, glanced at the psi-master, then looked at Cyrus. "It should be obvious. We gave you our language. Now it's time to rest so your brain can sort out . . ."

The rest of the words were gibberish, but Cyrus thought he understood. In some fashion, the machine had reordered his brain patterns or given him new impulses so he could understand the alien tongue.

He yawned. He was so tired and his head hurt. Cyrus shut his eyes. As he tried to figure out his next step, he fell asleep.

3

The crushing acceleration didn't change, but Cyrus's quarters did. He awoke in a tiny cell. It had a cot, a sink and a place to defecate. He was alone and there was no door or hatch to see out. How had they gotten him in here? He tapped on the walls, all four of them, and he tapped on the floor and ceiling. No one ever tapped back.

Beside the sink was a steel cabinet. Inside were organic clots the size of his hand, apparently food. When hunger compelled him, Cyrus chewed a clot. It was bland, gritty against his teeth, and unfulfilling. But after a time, his sense of hunger dwindled. He drank metallic-tasting water from a tap above the sink.

To pass the time, he exercised by standing and squatting slowly. The excessive Gs made it a grueling workout. He did pushups and sit-ups and slept drenched in sweat. He dreamed of choking to death or having soldiers kick him in the kidneys and neck.

Time crawled and he debated using his telekinesis to open the cell. Yet how could he do that when there wasn't a hatch?

Besides, what would I do then? Can I take over the ship?

He didn't see how. Why did they give him a new language? Why had it killed some of *Discovery*'s crew?

He had questions but no answers. He endured. He daydreamed of many things and continued to do his exercises and eat the gritty, organic capsules.

An interminable time later, something changed. A section of cell disappeared and two soldiers regarded him, with a machinist in his smock behind them. The machinist held a flat device.

"Come," the machinist said.

Cyrus licked his lips. He sat on the cot, still stunned that the wall had disappeared. "Where are you taking me?"

"You must obey."

Cyrus decided the machinist was right. He rose and stepped out of the room. Each soldier grabbed an arm. They marched him along a narrower passageway than what would have been on *Discovery*. The air had a dry, desert-like feel, with a hint of burnt sand in it. Was that bad or was it good? Was it normal or strange?

Watch and wait. Your time will come. It had to come. When it did, he would act, but not until then.

The acceleration made everything physical a chore. He began to sweat and soon wheeze. Why did the soldiers bother grabbing his arms? He wasn't in any condition to escape. Maybe they held his arms in order to help him. Cyrus didn't want anything from the soldiers, not after he'd witnessed their brutality.

Finally, the passageway broadened to be more spacious than aboard *Discovery*. This passageway could easily accommodate the raptor-like alien. What part did it play? Had it been an alien marine?

What is Jasper doing, I wonder?

His throat tightened and he felt the tears of self-pity begin to well. He'd cried those once in Milan as a boy of five or six. At least, that was the last and only time he remembered crying. He'd been hiding in a box after having fled the orphanage. Older boys had found him weeping. They had beaten him for it. Well, more like slapped him around, calling him a crybaby. From that moment, Cyrus had refused to snivel.

I'm not going to start now, either. I'm going to beat these aliens. Screw them. Screw all of them and their entire system. I'm going to—

The soldiers performed a quick maneuver. The one on his left moved faster and both turned toward a wall. He heard a beep from the machinist behind him. The wall before them vanished.

I wish I knew how they did that. Perhaps the device the machinist has in his hand?

The soldiers stepped into a spacious room and performed their maneuver again, facing a large desk with a globe on the right end. The continents looked all wrong, as did the globe's oceans. Behind the desk sat a long-faced humanoid in a blue robe. A tall collar hid part of the man's chin.

The psi-master lacked a *baan*, and maybe that meant he wasn't a psi-master. He had a messy mop of hair at the top of his elongated head and green eyes. His eyes, nose, and mouth all seemed too small for his long face and was scrunched in the lower third. The forehead took up more than half of the head. His body was lanky, or appeared so under the billowing blue robe.

"What do you call yourself?" the blue-robed man asked.

"Ah . . . Cyrus Gant. What should I call you?"

With one of his long fingers, the man switched something on or off on his desk. "You will refrain from asking me anything," the man said. "I am your superior and in this instance I am your inquisitor. I belong to Chengal Ras and he is Ranked 109th. More you do not need to know."

The inquisitor clicked the switch again. "If you fail to answer my questions or I feel you are evasive, the Vomags will administer punitive hurts."

Cyrus wanted to massage his forehead. He wasn't sure his brain filtered the language properly. Some things sounded off. One thing he was surprised to realize was that he knew who the Vomags were: the two soldiers holding his arms.

"I'll answer to the best of my ability," Cyrus said.

The inquisitor stared at him, and a sense of loathing emanated from the man. Cyrus had no idea why.

"Were you a regular particle of the spaceship's crew?" the inquisitor asked.

"Ah . . . Yes, I guess so." Did the man mean *particle* or was that an error in his mind, the language program not quite working to full capacity yet?

"What function did you play among the crew?" the inquisitor asked.

"Ah . . ."

"Continued hesitation indicates an attempt at subterfuge. You are perilously near a punitive hurt."

"Your words or the way you ask your questions are strange to me," Cyrus said. "I'm not trying to lie."

"You are the stranger to Fenris and your presence curdles my stomach," the inquisitor said. "Chengal Ras has graciously gifted you with the civilized tongue. Do not attempt to cast aspersion upon his marvelous present."

"I'm not trying to."

"You will immediately cease with these unasked-for clarifications," the inquisitor said. "You are in my presence to answer direct questions, not to make idle comments or to equivocate."

Cyrus held his tongue, deciding to play the slow witted alien.

"I sense mulish hostility from you," the inquisitor said. "Pain him. Teach the alien better manners."

While clutching Cyrus's left arm with one hand, a Vomag soldier pulled out a small round device with the other and pressed it against Cyrus's neck. It felt as if someone pinched the skin and twisted hard.

Cyrus cried out, and would have bent over, but the soldiers held him in place.

"You will radiate love toward me," the inquisitor said, "or at the very least accepting obedience. Do not stare mulishly at me or mutter your answers. I am superior. Therefore, you must cast your gaze down. Your pretense at being able to meet my excellence on an equal level is insulting. Chengal Ras would never approve and I honor my master by applying his standards rigorously."

Cyrus quit staring the inquisitor in the eyes and looked down at the man's hands. They were smooth, fastidiously clean. Then, deciding that might not do, either, he looked down at the edge of the desk. It was some kind of metal.

"That is barely tolerable," the inquisitor said. "I still fail to sense any love from you, but you are an invader so allowances will be made—at least for the moment. Now, I asked about your status aboard the invasion vessel. Quickly, tell me your rank."

"I am a first sergeant," Cyrus said.

"Your words are meaningless. Elaborate your function."

"I was to repel boarders."

"You are a fighting creature? Is that what you're saying?"

"I am."

The inquisitor laughed. "A scrawny and obviously weak creature like you was supposed to fight? I cannot believe it. Apply pain."

For a second time, Cyrus twisted in the grip of the Vomags touching him with the pain device.

"For the third hurt, the Vomags will escort you to the punitive box," the inquisitor said.

Cyrus barely kept himself from saying he understood. What was wrong with these people?

"Do you persist in the notion that you are a fighting creature?" the inquisitor asked.

"I am . . . sad that you do not believe me," Cyrus said. "My function is fighting. What I lack in strength I make up for in speed and agility."

"Chengal Ras may decide to test the quality of your fighting powers. He is curious at your abilities. This is the second time your Imperium has seen fit to send vessels to Fenris. Why were the crew components so different from the original assault?"

"I . . ."

"You hesitate, and yet you have received two punitive pains. This is interesting."

Cyrus hesitated because he wondered what kind of "Imperium" had attacked New Eden. What did it imply? Many things, but maybe most importantly, he could possibly mask Sol's existence by pretending to belong to this Imperium. That might be risky, though. He'd have to feel out the inquisitor first.

"I hesitate to answer because I'm unsure how to reply," Cyrus said.

"You are a poor dissembler," the inquisitor said. "Do you think I am unskilled at my task? Do you believe you are the first of your inferior species I've grilled?"

"The Imperium has . . . ah . . ."

The inquisitor clicked the switch. "Look up at me."

Cyrus complied.

"You have received pain twice. I cannot apply pain again except to kill you. You are inferior to me, but I sense a hidden agenda upon you. There is a stink of subterfuge in your words and possibly in your thoughts. You might be near to me in rank upon your strange vessel. It is why I allow you to look into my eyes. But this I know: You are no fighting creature. Chengal Ras marked you, and yet he allowed you to remain with the common ruck. Do you understand any of what I'm trying to tell you?"

"I don't think so," Cyrus admitted.

The inquisitor drummed his long fingers on the desk. "The Imperium—" He shook his elongated head. "Look down, invasion creature."

Cyrus hurried to obey.

The inquisitor clicked the switch again. Cyrus was certain the man turned a recording device on and off. He wondered why the alien bothered.

"What is the source of your illumination?" the inquisitor asked.

Cyrus had no idea how to answer because he didn't know what the man asked. He didn't know if he shouldn't ask for clarifications, either. So he said, "Captain Nagasaki ran the ship."

"You foolish creature, I am not asking about your commanding officers. Who gave direction? Who propounded the directives to give ultimate guidance?"

"Oh, I see what you're asking. Premier Lang—"

"Go on, finish your thought."

Cyrus recognized his mistake even as he made it. He spoke about Premier Lang, Sol's ruler. He needed to switch topics or at least make certain to leave out any mention of Sol. He mustn't ever give the aliens the route home.

"Premier Lang is our ruler," Cyrus said.

"What manner of being is he?"

"I'm not sure I understand you."

"The question is simple and direct. Is he a Web-Mind of the Imperium or—"

"What did you say?" Cyrus whispered. Web-Minds were cyborgs. Or Web-Minds had run the cyborgs a hundred years ago. Cyrus hadn't studied the Cyborg War like Captain Nagasaki, but everyone in Sol knew about Web-Minds. Could the alien's use of the word be a mistake?

The inquisitor stiffened and his skin darkened with mottled patches appearing unevenly on his face. "He has dared to query me," the man said to no one in particular. "I am a Rarified of the Third Order and he addresses me like a lackey of the Pits. I am soiled and he has profaned Chengal Ras. This insult cannot stand. He must undergo rehabilitation."

The inquisitor focused on the two soldiers.

Cyrus wasn't sure how to carry on, but he had to change tactics. The inquisitor was arrogant and unrelenting. Instead of being submissive to the man, maybe he should be arrogant in return. Yes, Cyrus decided to take a risk because the inquisitor had told him two pains were the maximum. Alien rehabilitation sounded bad, so what did he have to lose?

"I find your language tiresome and oddly constructed," Cyrus said, trying to talk like Dr. Wexx.

The inquisitor's attention snapped back onto him. "You profane Chengal Ras's gift?"

"Hardly," Cyrus said. "Is the tongue his native language?"

The inquisitor stared at Cyrus, and his skin darkened worse than before, increasing the spotted appearance of his features.

"I will be blunt," Cyrus said, thrusting his words like a knife, seeing an opening and taking it. "My rank aboard *Discovery* placed me high above the ordinary run of affairs. Earlier, you indicated I was near you in rank. I held my words in check because my shock forbade me from pointing out your gross error."

The inquisitor switched off the recording device. His words escaped as from a limp balloon. "You may be beyond rehabilitation."

Cyrus forced himself to laugh and shake his head. "How you strive to understand me. Your attempts are quite amusing."

One of the soldiers glanced at Cyrus. It was a momentary thing. Then the soldier became an automaton again, looking forward and awaiting orders.

The inquisitor's eyebrows twitched. Clearly, he noticed the Vomag's reaction. He clicked the switch back on and leaned minutely forward.

"The subterfuge in your brain whirls away in attempts to baffle our Illustrious One and the Glorious One Hundred. It is futile, as the Kresh are superior to all forms of human resistance. The defeat of your abnormal vessel proves the truth of my statement."

"The defeat was nothing more than an application of numbers," Cyrus said. "Ours was clearly the superior vessel."

The inquisitor's eyes seemed to glitter with malice as he narrowed them. "You will not hinder the investigation with your subterfuge. You will tell me what source gives you illumination or I will have no option but to send you away."

"Your phrases are like gongs and clashing cymbals in my mind," Cyrus said, wondering if he was laying it on too thickly. "They make noise, but it is difficult to decipher your meaning. If you would receive my answer, I need clarification."

The bleakest of smiles twitched at the corners of the inquisitor's lips. "You strive to compose your utterances. I am not deceived. There is something you hide but I have determined to root it from you despite your feeble trickery."

"Okay," Cyrus said. Trying to talk like Dr. Wexx was giving him a headache. "You win. I don't know how to talk like you and I don't know what you're asking me."

"The sun provides brilliance," the inquisitor said. "It illuminates existence. You understand that, yes? In a similar way the Kresh provide the Races with guidance."

"Who are the Kresh?"

The inquisitor blinked rapidly and his features mottled with dark splotches again. It appeared as if he would explode with rage, but slowly, he hooded his anger and whispered, "Chengal Ras is Kresh."

Cyrus shook his head.

"You doubt my words?" the inquisitor asked in obvious disbelief.

"No. I don't understand you."

The inquisitor put both palms on the desk. "I cannot tolerate any more of this deviousness and disrespect. It is beyond the pale and unacceptable. You will enter rehabilitation. I am marking you down for a full scope—"

The inquisitor stopped speaking and his eyes widened in shock. Then he looked down and bowed his head. At the same time, a soft sound occurred behind Cyrus.

He twisted his neck, looking back.

The wall had disappeared and a dry, musky odor almost made Cyrus gag. His eyes widened. The raptor-like alien towered in the spacious hall. The creature was huge but graceful. It was poised on the two large legs, each ending in curved talons. It wore metallic streamers from its waist and neck, and wore smaller streamers from its two arms. The arms ended in smaller talons like large fingers, three of them. The alien—the Kresh, Cyrus assumed—wore a belt around its dinosaur-like waist. A weapon one would presume was holstered on the belt, along with other devices.

"You speak of rehabilitation?" the Kresh hissed in an odd, snakelike manner.

Cyrus shuddered.

The crocodilian snout, teeth and the thick pick tongue—they moved and formulated words that he understood. The effect was much like seeing a crocodile rise from a lagoon and begin to speak intelligibly. It was horrifying and yet fascinating all at once.

The words transformed the inquisitor. He collapsed onto the desk, casting his arms and head on the metal.

"I am illuminated by your presence, Illustrious One," the inquisitor said in abject humility.

The soldiers no longer held Cyrus, but lay on the floor, covering their heads with their long, muscular arms.

In the high Gs, Cyrus shuffled around to regard the alien, the Illustrious One, the Kresh, he would suppose.

"You are intolerably vain," it said. "And you reek of defeat and stupidity." The Kresh turned its head. A small cylinder attached to its scaled neck sprayed a pink-colored mist. It inhaled with its nostrils on the end of its snout. The nine-foot frame shivered, with delight perhaps. The long tail swished, hitting the bulkheads of the corridor.

"Should I bow like the others?" Cyrus asked it.

The inquisitor raised his head. "You vicious freak of the void, cast yourself down in the glorious radiance of our Illustrious Master. Are you so lacking that you cannot feel the essence of supremacy in the mighty Chengal Ras?"

"Silence!" the Kresh hissed.

The inquisitor's head thumped back onto the desk.

Cyrus bent down onto one knee and he bowed his head before the raptor-like creature. One thing was obvious. The humanoids were subservient to the dinosaur-like Kresh. How had this occurred and when? No matter how it had happened, these humans needed freeing from the aliens. Hmm, was this the same alien that had been aboard *Discovery*?

"Creature," Chengal Ras said. "Your vessel achieved greater than light speed. Were you instrumental in the process?"

"No," Cyrus lied.

"You were in the . . . tele-chamber upon my arrival. Why were you there?"

217

So this *was* the same alien. Cyrus had tried to hurt it then, but failed. The alien must have tagged him somehow. Why had Chengal Ras put him back with the others? Maybe that was the wrong question. How did it know about the tele-chamber? Logically, one of *Discovery's* crew must have told a different inquisitor the right answers. No.

You're not thinking, Cyrus told himself. The aliens knew about the tele-chamber through Jasper when they had communicated.

"I have tolerated your insolence too long," Chengal Ras said. "You will administer answers or you will expire before your fellow herd beasts in a most excruciating manner. Your passing may teach them the cost of disobedience."

"Master, may I assist?" the inquisitor asked.

Chengal Ras shifted its attention to the inquisitor. "Speak, but if I find your words useless, you will expire for my amusement during the Docking Ceremony."

"It would be to my great delight if my passing could provide you with entertainment, Master," the inquisitor said. "Yet I hope my words may assist in your radiance."

"Speak, and do it quickly," Chengal Ras said.

"Master, I have found this one hiding a secret agenda. It reeks of subterfuge. If I could perform an extraction—"

"The Attack Talon lacks the facilities," Chengal Ras said.

"At High Station 3 I could—"

"Yes," Chengal Ras said. "You will extract his memories at High Station 3. He practices subterfuge and I detected a psionic assault upon my person in the alien tele-chamber. It may have come from him. Until we reach High Station 3, keep him in isolation. These creatures are not from the Imperium. That is decisively critical."

"Illustrious One, this is mighty news indeed," the inquisitor said.

"The Random Equation has fallen to the Hundred," Chengal Ras said, as if quoting a saying. "The time of our exaltation draws near. I have spoken."

Chengal Ras thereupon continued down the passageway, lurching in its raptor-like gait, causing another cloud of scented perfume to squirt from its neck tube.

"The inquiry is ended," the inquisitor said. "Return the outlander to his cell."

4

Cyrus began to plot as soon as the wall appeared behind him, locking him in the cell.

What could he do to change his fate? He didn't know. But he wasn't going to give these alien pricks any help defeating Sol or help them learn how to shift.

The days passed and the crushing acceleration never stopped. He exercised harder, doing squats until his knees ached. The Vomags had walked the passageways with ease. If he was going to escape, he would need to be able to do likewise.

Unfortunately, the impossibility of his plight nearly drove Cyrus to despair.

No, no, that's the wrong emotion. There's too much you don't understand. You have to keep trying until they kill you.

He made a mental list of things to give him hope. He needed hope. Once this particular journey ended, they would extract his memory. That sounded ominous.

Concentrate, Cyrus. Start using your brain.

He didn't know what was happening to the others, but he couldn't dwell on that. He needed to take what he had—the data, as Argon might have said—and see what conclusions he could reach.

From his time in the Teleship's observatory, he'd discovered that someone had carpet-nuked AS 412 III, the outermost Earth-like world. A ring of lasers around AS 412 II, the other Earth-like world, showed him the Kresh had ene-mies. The Imperium—whoever they were—had attacked New Eden from out-side the system, or so it appeared. This Imperium had Web-Minds. Now that could have been a coincidental turn of phrase, or it could mean that Sol-created cyborgs had attacked the Kresh.

Nagasaki had told them before that the cyborgs at the end of the Solar War had possessed proto-Teleships. If cyborgs had escaped Sol in a Teleship, might they have tried to set up an empire way out here? He couldn't know. But if they had, might they have encountered the Kresh?

Naturally, no one on Earth would have seen any of this. Probes traveled slower than the speed of light, and they sent messages back at light speed. The only way to find this was how they had, in a Teleship.

If the cyborgs attacked the Kresh that meant cyborgs had Teleships or something like Teleships. And from Chengal Ras's questions, the Kresh likely didn't have Teleships or shift technology.

How can any of that help you here?

Cyrus figured it helped by giving him something to think about other than his coming memory extraction. The rest of the time, he endured. He inspected every inch of the cell. He had no idea how they made the walls appear and disap-pear and he could see no way they recorded or watched him in here. Didn't they care what happened to him? Would they know if he tried to commit suicide?

Some of the time, he practiced mental exercises. He even used his psi-power aggressively, probing, trying to remove a wall. It didn't work. He tried to contact Jasper or Roxie and failed to sense either. He practiced using his mind shield. He squatted, did thousands of sit-ups, pushups and found his already whipcord frame becoming even more lean.

Once, a moment of weightlessness came unexpectedly. It was such a relief, but it didn't last long. If anything, the crushing Gs worsened afterward.

What does that tell you?

It wasn't hard to figure out. The ship had accelerated, building up velocity. Now it must have turned around and decelerated, slowing the velocity so it could dock at High Station 3.

Are we nearing one of the gas giants?

When he slept, his dreams worsened. Loneliness ate at him and his resolve hardened. He wasn't going to enter the memory-extractor. No. He would make them kill him first. Thoughts of his death made him listless, and for several sleeps he skipped his exercises.

What are you doing, Cyrus? You're giving up. Well, stop it! Get ready for the fight of your life. You may be the last one left from Discovery.

Sometimes, he wondered if he should just kill himself. No, he couldn't do that. He had to fight. He'd never given up as a child. Why should he give up now that he was mentally tougher and in the best physical shape of his life?

He ran in place for as long as he could. Each step jolted him so soon the back of his neck hurt. He went over plans, practiced jabs and kicks, and patiently waited.

What would a Kresh space station be like? *Chengal Ras called us herd beasts.* That meant something important. Cyrus lay on his cot and thought it through.

First, from what he'd seen, the Kresh treated their servants horribly. Second, the inquisitor wondered who gave Earthlings illumination. Might the man mean the Kresh gave the humans here guidance? That seemed right from what he'd seen. The Kresh figured humans were beasts. You didn't expect much from a beast, except that he or she acted like one. So they must think some other creatures ruled Earth's humans.

From his days in Level 40, Cyrus had learned that pride often came before a fall. The alien's arrogance might help him.

Three more successful seconds in the tele-chamber and I would be on my way home, a hero.

He hadn't thought about that for a while. He realized that now wasn't a good time to renew it.

The moment came when the acceleration lessened, lessened more, and then almost felt normal.

Are we almost there?

Cyrus felt mentally sluggish and he realized he'd been lax practicing his mind shield. Part of him never wanted to leave the cell because when he did leave, it would mean an ugly and brutal end. He started jeering himself, calling himself a coward and a weakling. Cowards deserved to die. If he were a man, he'd give the aliens something to remember.

He concentrated on the thought. He came up with a hundred scenarios about what he could do. That was funny in a way, because none of it happened how he expected.

He was lying on the cot, staring into space. His thoughts were empty, although his automatic mind shield was up. Maybe that's why he was aware of a subtle difference. It was a tiny thing, but he was so bored that he noticed it in a detached manner.

The wall he was staring at disappeared because the aliens did it and he happened to notice the mental procedure.

Oh, so that's *how they do it.* In that instant, he figured it out. Sure, it had to be the right kind of wall in order to do it. But now that he'd "seen" the aliens do it, he was sure he could duplicate the trick with his telekinesis.

He was so pleased with himself and his find that at first he didn't notice the inquisitor and Vomags standing in the corridor.

"Are you unhinged from reality?" the inquisitor asked.

Cyrus blinked in surprise, sitting up. The inquisitor looked like the same individual who had questioned him days or weeks ago. He had no idea how long it had been.

"Are we at High Station 3?" Cyrus asked.

The inquisitor stiffened and snapped his long fingers. The Vomags darted into the cell and dragged Cyrus to his feet. They gripped his arms just as they had last time. Their fingers felt like iron digging into his flesh.

"Proper decorum is critical at High Station 3," the inquisitor said. "Therefore, you will refrain from speech unless you are directly asked a question. Nod if you understand."

Cyrus nodded.

"Proceed," the inquisitor said, waving his long-fingered hand in a shooing motion.

The two soldiers marched down the passageway, taking Cyrus with them.

You'd better wake up and start thinking. This is it, and the aliens know it, too.

Instead of quailing at his plight—guarded by two fierce soldiers—Cyrus decided this was a good thing. It showed him escape must be possible. Otherwise, why bother with these precautions?

He began to observe, using his senses and thoughts to catalog the situation and to see what was there and what was missing. For instance, there was no background thrum. The engines must be offline. That would imply the ship had docked in some manner. Of course, that made sense if they'd reached High Station 3.

They entered the larger passageway and soon turned onto an even broader corridor, a huge passageway. Cyrus's heart leaped in his chest. He spied Argon, Dr. Wexx, and Captain Jones, each of them guarded by two Vomags and trailed by an inquisitor. None of the inquisitors wore *baans*.

Wexx squinted badly as if she could hardly see. The aliens must have stolen her sunglasses. Jones's features were slack as if he'd suffered brain damage. Argon glanced around and noticed him. Something powerful flashed in the chief monitor's eyes. Argon nodded at Cyrus. The trailing inquisitor gave the chief monitor a verbal reprimand.

Cyrus couldn't stop himself. "It's good to see you."

His Vomags tightened their grip.

"Silence, you fool," the inquisitor whispered. "This is the docking procedure. We give thanks for another successful journey into the void and back. You sully the purity of the moment."

"It's good to see you, Cyrus!" Argon shouted.

The inquisitor behind the seven-foot giant pointed a clenched fist at him, pressing a switch. The chief monitor groaned, with his head arching back. The two Vomags gripping the arms held up the big man. Argon's inquisitor relented and the chief monitor continued to march, but in subdued silence.

Cyrus seethed at the sight. He was sick of these aliens, sick of the Kresh and their arrogance. He wanted to strike back, to act. How could they have lost to these vicious bastards? It was as if he'd returned to a demented Level 40 Milan.

The Vomags marched their captives through the corridor until they reached a large hatch. When Cyrus's turn came, the soldiers marched him out of the ship and down steps into a monstrously huge, steel hanger.

Cyrus cataloged what he saw. Looking back, he noted that their vessel was a squat and bulbous ship about five stories high. It couldn't have been what had attacked *Discovery*, it was too small for that. No, this must be a massive shuttle. *Yeah, look at the size of the engine ports.*

He spied other bulbous shuttles. One moved on a sliding section of hanger, coming toward the others. The hanger was unbelievably massive. Lights went off into the distance farther than he could see. High Station 3 had to be the largest habitat he'd ever heard of. The number of vessels in here . . . he counted over three dozen.

The line of Sol captives and Vomag guards threaded toward a truck-sized entrance about half a kilometer away. There were other entrances, many vehicles, and humanoid workers.

Cyrus kept rubbernecking, looking around. Humans drove the various vehicles, hauling stuff from some massive shuttles and bringing containers to others. He didn't spy any Kresh doing work, just people, hordes of laboring people. Everyone wore a uniform and seemed Earth-normal in form. The most divergent people were the Vomags and the inquisitors.

What had his inquisitor called himself before, a Rarified of the Third Order? As Cyrus mulled that over, a raucous horn blew. Then several other horns blared mightily in a louder version of the first.

"They actually come," the inquisitor whispered. "Oh, this is exceptional. We are about to catch a glimpse of several Radiances together. This is glory, glory for their mighty feat of victory over you outlanders."

The Vomags gripping Cyrus released him. He flexed his arms. The two soldiers fell onto their bellies. So did the inquisitor.

Cyrus glanced around. Everywhere in the cavernous hanger, movement and work ceased. Truck-like vehicles screeched to a halt. Drivers leaped out and fell prostrate onto the metal deck plates. Those dragging massive hoses dropped the lines and fell onto their faces. Mechanics, techs, soldiers, inquisitors, pilots, every human aimed his head toward five Kresh. The towering aliens rode a lift descending from near the top of a shuttle.

"Cast yourself down!" the inquisitor hissed at Cyrus. "Bask in their radiance and fill your soul with their brilliance. I will never forget this day. Five move together, and one of them is a Hundred. Blessed is Chengal Ras, my master, the 109th in the arts of philosophical excellence."

Cyrus scanned the hanger. Dr. Wexx fell prostrate, so did Captain Jones. Argon hesitated. The chief monitor groaned then and sank to his knees, writhing onto his belly. Argon's inquisitor must have applied the pain device. Cyrus wondered why he didn't spy Roxie or Jasper.

"Are you daft?" the inquisitor asked Cyrus. "Why do you wait? Do you wish to be singled out as the prize of the Docking Ceremony?"

"What happens to the prize?" Cyrus asked.

"Base and foul creature of the stars, do you not understand? The Kresh will sacrifice to the Ultimate for another safe journey into the void. One soul must pay with blood for the success of the whole. It is a matter of unity, a rare occurrence among the masters. Do you not see, a Hundred offers Chengal Ras the slaying wand?"

Cyrus glanced around. Movement everywhere had stopped. Humans near and far lay on their bellies to these alien lizards. The Kresh's platform banged onto the deck plates. The five creatures strode off the platform and stalked toward the nearest clump of worshipful humans.

A screeching sound now reverberated through the hanger. It grew louder and abrasive, making Cyrus wince. The Vomags near him clapped their hands over their ears.

"Praise to the Ultimate," the inquisitor whispered. Then he too clapped his hands over his ears. The mechanical screeching intensified.

Cyrus Gant of Milan watched the five Kresh approach the prone humans. He'd reached High Station 3, was out of the cell and surrounded by motionless people. Deciding this was as good a moment as any, Cyrus turned and began striding away from the Vomags and inquisitor. He started walking for a side entrance where he'd seen a number of trucks enter.

Suddenly, the screeching stopped. A horn blared. Cyrus didn't bother looking back. Then the horn ceased.

"Human!" A Kresh spoke. "Human, abase yourself to the Ultimate."

Cyrus finally looked back. The five Kresh watched him. One of the creatures held a slender, seven-foot wand.

"Faithless creature," a Kresh said, "fall onto your belly!"

Cyrus raised his hand and gave the five aliens the finger. Then he turned away and began to sprint.

Another Kresh shout came, but he ignored it. He raced around a truck and used it to screen himself from them. He saw the driver looking up at him from on the floor. Then the man shut his eyes, pressing his forehead against the deck plates.

Cyrus kept sprinting. His endless days of running in place and doing squats had given him stamina. He neared the truck entrance.

A red light appeared above it. An automated muzzle thrust out of a slot. The tube had pitted edges, looking as if it had been used before. The thing tracked him as Cyrus concentrated, using telekinesis, shorting an electrical connection, and a red light above the muzzle turned dull.

In the distance from within the hanger a Kresh roared. At least, Cyrus assumed it must be a Kresh. He'd never heard a human make a sound like that. If they hadn't before, they must realize now that he had psi-powers.

Cyrus darted into the entrance. The people in here lay on their bellies, too. Air wheezed down his throat and into his lungs. He kept sprinting, looking for a door or other exit. He didn't know what he expected to find or how long he could keep out of their clutches. What he did remember from his youth was that big cities had slums. There, people could hide from the cops. That held true on Earth. Would it hold true on High Station 3?

Well, he was certainly going to try to find out. The Kresh had given him their language. Now, he was going to use it to his advantage.

5

Cyrus strode briskly through a warehouse that held thirty-foot shelves containing long tubes, assorted metal widgets, and plastic sheets. Behind him, an alarm blared. Workers driving alien forklifts glanced at him. They wore gray caps, most with single stars on the front and a few with three. Each wore a brown jacket with gray pants. Several workers frowned at him, but no one called out or asked what he was doing here.

I need to change my clothes and try to blend in.

Actually, he needed many things. A station map would be great. A haircut would help and a complete makeover would be best.

They must see I'm different and don't belong.

"No," he whispered. He needed to concentrate and act. He needed to find the station's slums, if it had one.

The overhead lights began to blink on and off. Speakers crackled and a moment later, a Kresh spoke: "Attention, High Station 3 personnel. This is a class five announcement. An unwarranted alien stalks the premises. Report any suspicious actions to your superior. The alien predator has mocked the Hundred and the Ultimate Magnificence. He will expire in the Grand Agonizer as a spectacle to rightness. This is an urgent summons to achievement. See that you obey and earn splendor and advancement in caste."

As workers listened to the announcement, Cyrus slipped into a deserted row. He checked to make sure no one saw him, leaped, and grabbed a shelf six feet up. He hauled himself onto it. While squatting, he moved into shadows. He lay on plastic sheets and peered around, watching for what would happen next.

Workers shut off their forklifts and eased onto the floor. They congregated and began to whisper among themselves. One man took off his cap and ran his fingers through his hair. He appeared nervous. The others urged him toward some sort of action. He replaced the cap and sidled to his forklift. The others glanced around and finally called to the man. Cyrus couldn't hear what they said. The worker at the forklift wore a bronze-colored badge on his jacket and his cap had three stars. He climbed into the seat and spoke into what must have been a communicator.

This was bad. The Kresh had just given him a death sentence. Cyrus shrugged moodily. Memory extracting would have probably been the same thing. Except . . . the Kresh said his death would be a spectacle in the Grand Agonizer. That didn't sound like a dignified ending, but more like dying on a cross like Spartacus had done.

Closing his eyes, Cyrus wondered if he should have waited for a better chance. No. He had no idea if another chance would have come. He'd seen one and he'd taken it.

He cocked his head. In the distance sounded cadenced feet clashing against the deck plates. What would the Kresh do next? If he were in their place, he'd send a regiment of Vomags to flush him out. Right. He couldn't hide here. This place was too open.

While crouching, he moved lengthwise down the shelf until he came to the end. He glanced about and risked it, jumping onto the floor. How much time did he have left?

Move, Cyrus. Get out of this warehouse.

He hurried with his eyes staring, searching for workers who might report him. His heart thudded. He saw a door. He had no idea where it led. He rushed to it and pulled. It wouldn't budge.

He concentrated and tweaked the locking mechanism with his telekinesis. He opened the door, stepped through, and shut it behind him. His knees threatened to unhinge. Leaning against a wall, he found himself trembling from the excitement.

You have to keep going. You need to get it together, Cyrus.

He was in a long corridor with dim lights on the ceiling. The corridor went off into the distance farther than he could see. It reminded him of looking into a mirror that faced other mirrors and trying to see how far the reflections went. He started walking. Was this a maintenance shaft?

I need a map so I know where I am and where I'm going.

He shook his head. He needed to use what he had, not wish for the moon. If he was going to wish, why not ask for a spaceship or that he could magically teleport back to Sol?

Thinking about the approaching, hunting Vomags and the Grand Agonizer, he ran, putting distance between him and the warehouse. It didn't take long for sweat to break out onto his skin. His breathing became harsh, and later his side ached. After a time, thirst began to torment him. Despite the exhaustion, or maybe because of it, he grinned savagely. He was tired and wanted to stop, but that would mean worse torture, so he kept running when normally he would have collapsed. He ran kilometer after kilometer and couldn't figure out why there were no more openings in the corridor. If there had been the one, there should be others, right?

Behind him, in the far distance, he heard an ominous clang. Were hunters in the corridor? If the Kresh truly wanted him, couldn't they use infrared tracking and follow his glowing footsteps?

The vanishing walls, he told himself.

Cyrus staggered to a halt and leaned against a wall. Sweat dripped from his chin and struck the metal floor. He panted, wiped stinging sweat out of his eyes, and panted more. Finally, his breathing returned to a semblance of normal.

He walked, and he searched with his psi-talent. Sixty steps later, he discovered an escape.

He did the trick with his telekinesis, and a headache exploded into being in his frontal lobe. He'd used his psi-talent one too many times in quick succession. He should have rested first.

Even so, a small section of wall vanished. He heard voices in the new, branching corridor, but he couldn't worry about that now. He moved through the opening and looked back. The smart move would be to hide where he'd left the straight corridor. He squeezed his eyes shut. The headache was bad, to use his telekinesis again so soon . . .

He willed himself to do it, and the wall reappeared.

Cyrus groaned as splotches appeared before his eyes. He clutched his knees and vomited the gruel in his stomach. He did it again, making grunting, gasping noises as the worsening headache pounded in his brain.

Finally, he used his sleeve and wiped his mouth. It was hard to see past the black spots in his vision, but he couldn't stop here.

Maybe I can never stop again, because when I do they'll catch me. What a thing. Maybe by the time they found him, he would be glad to rest.

He crouched for a moment and put his head between his knees. It felt as if his brain was about to explode, it throbbed so hard. He squeezed his knees against his temples and waited, breathing through his mouth.

I can't use my telekinesis for days now, maybe weeks.

He waited until the throbbing lessened. He stood afterward. He felt dizzy and waited for that to pass. Afterward, he found that he could see past some of the splotches in his vision.

The dim light of earlier remained and there were more branching corridors, a bewildering web of them. He kept going right, deciding any kind of process was better than random selection. He turned right, and he heard a scuffle of sound ahead.

His heart began pounding, and his vision cleared a little. A scuffle meant people, right?

I can't remain in these corridors forever. I need water and I need to eat.

Warily, Cyrus advanced toward the next corner. He cocked his head, listening, striving to hear a giveaway sound. He heard a voice in the distance, but couldn't decipher the words. What did it mean?

When Cyrus was five steps from the next intersection, a man stepped around the corner. The man was thick-shouldered, wore loose garments, and had a shaved head. He had a round tattoo with jagged edges on his forehead and he grinned nastily. He was missing some front teeth.

"You must be the alien predator," the man said. He drew a blade—a knife—from the folds of his garments. "I found him, Blas!" he shouted over his shoulder.

"Who are you?" Cyrus asked.

"Blas said a sneaky one like you would use the shafts," the man informed him. "I told him the odds were astronomical of us finding the alien. He said, 'All the more reason we should try.' I thought he was crazy, but will you look at this. You're our prize. The Kresh will reinstate us now. I'm sick of living in the Maze." The man's grin widened. "Blas! Hurry up. The predator looks antsy."

"Get out of my way," Cyrus said.

"Do you see this in my hand?" the man asked. He waved the knife. "I can gut you if you play foul like you did with the masters."

Cyrus weighed the odds. The corridor was narrow; two men could barely pass in it. It didn't give him much maneuvering room and it meant the man with a knife had every advantage. Maybe he should try to talk his way out.

"Do you want to keep being a slave to the aliens?" Cyrus asked.

The man laughed. "You sound like a chaosict, and everyone knows they're fools. The Kresh give us guidance. They give us meaning and help order our otherwise frenzied lives."

"They've made you slaves."

The man licked his lips. "You're a human-firster, hey? That won't do you any good here. I love the Kresh and this will prove it."

"Larl!" another man shouted. "Where are you?"

"Here!" the knife-man shouted. "You'd better hurry. The predator is working himself up to attack me."

Cyrus had nothing but his hands and he knew the foolishness of confronting a man with a knife. With fists, one had to punch hard to be effective. One needed speed and he had to hit the right spot. With a knife, it was different. You only needed to touch the other person and the blade did the work. It cut. The target bled, and in time, with the blood loss, came weakness. If he knew what he was doing, a man with a knife could beat an unarmed man ninety-nine times out of a hundred.

Cyrus backed away and tried to pull off his shirt. The fabric stuck to his sweaty skin, but a hard yank brought it off.

"What are you doing?" Larl asked.

Cyrus turned and ran.

"That ain't going to do you any good," Larl shouted. "Blas, he's taking off! Call the others."

Cyrus wrapped the shirt around his left hand. It wasn't much protection, but it was a little. He turned a corner and twisted around, facing it. He heard Larl coming after him. The man didn't run, but strode down the corridor. Larl turned the corner and his eyes widened in surprise.

"Tricky predator, ain't you?" Larl said. He thrust the tip of the knife at Cyrus.

It told Cyrus that Larl wasn't a professional knife-man, at least not of the Milan school of thinking. The man led with the knife, a critical mistake. Cyrus thrust his wrapped hand forward, taking the point. He shoved the knife back, and he stepped toward Larl, using the right, driving his fist against the man's gut. It was muscled and hard, and the loose clothing helped absorb some of the strike. Still, Cyrus knocked Larl back. He stepped forward, using both hands, and grabbed the knife wrist. Cyrus thrust forward again as he put a heel behind one of Larl's feet. He tripped the man, who went sprawling backward onto the floor. Larl's grip loosened and Cyrus ripped the blade free.

Cyrus hefted the knife to get its feel. From on the floor, Larl scrambled to his feet. Indecision filled the man's eyes. The knife had good balance.

"This ain't going to help you," Larl said.

"It doesn't hurt."

"Blas! He has my—"

Cyrus attacked as the man shouted. It wasn't a fair way to fight, but he didn't have a choice anymore. The man had hunted for him. Such a thing came with risks. Cyrus made a killing strike as Larl sucked air to shout for reinforcements. With the knife sticking through the man's throat, Cyrus eased Larl down gently, not wanting to alert this Blas.

It didn't make any difference.

"Well, well, well, Larl never did practice the blade enough. I told him it was going to get him in trouble someday."

Cyrus backed away, with the gory knife in his hand. Blood jetted from the corpse's throat, wetting the floor around it, no doubt making the floor slick. It was by observing the little things that one often won a fight.

Blas—if that's who this was—was a head taller than Larl. He had a gun in his right hand and an old scar running across his face. The left eye was white and appeared blind. He, too, had a shaved head, but without a tattoo. Instead of loose clothing, Blas wore leather or synthi-leather garments with metal clasps dotting the jacket.

"You're a cagey one, aren't you?" Blas asked. "Do you think you're cagey enough to take my gun the way you did Larl's blade?"

Before Cyrus could think of a reply, there came a sizzling sound. He'd heard the sound before on the alien ship when a Vomag had shot Argon. Cyrus didn't feel anything and he noticed that Blas still held his gun so it aimed at the deck plates. Then who had taken the shot?

Blas sank to his knees and color drained from his features. "That ain't right," he muttered. He began to turn his head. Another sizzling sound ended his attempt as Blas pitched face first onto the deck plates.

A Vomag soldier stood behind the man. He looked just like the others of his kind. No, there was something different about his Vomag, or there was something familiar. In either case, the soldier held a heat gun.

"Do I know you?" Cyrus asked.

"Yes. I am Skar 192 of the Tenth Cohort. I watched you baffle the Rarified during the questioning. It was impressive."

"How did you find me?"

"The third order Rarified gave me instructions as to where you would be."

"How could he know?" Cyrus asked.

"He knew because the Rarified are wise beyond understanding. It's what made your performance during the questioning all the more remarkable."

"So now what, you shoot me?" Cyrus asked.

"No," Skar said, holstering his weapon.

"I'm not going without a fight," Cyrus told him.

The Vomag cocked his head. "I see. You do not grasp the situation."

"You're wrong. I know I'm never going back to face the Grand Agonizer."

"Ah, then you do realize."

"Realize what?" Cyrus asked. "Why are you here if you're not going to shoot me and take me back to the Kresh?"

"I'm here to guide you to the Resisters," Skar said.

"What?" Cyrus asked.

"Come. We must hurry."

||||||||||

Before Cyrus went anywhere, he looted the corpses.

Skar watched impassively.

Cyrus took Blas's gun and found several extra magazines. There was also a hand-sized disc with a switch.

"Don't take that," Skar said. "It is a locator. The Kresh will use it to track you."

Cyrus hesitated before nodding, leaving the locator. He found a small package and opened it. It looked edible. So he nibbled at it before taking a bite. It tasted good. He devoured the bar before pulling out several small flat notes.

"What are these?" Cyrus asked.

"Toldecks."

"Toldecks for what?" Cyrus asked.

"For exchange," Skar said.

"Do you mean credits? You buy things with these?"

"Yes," Skar said. "They are toldecks."

Cyrus stuffed them away and found a few more on Larl. If the Maze was anything like the slums, one could always use cash as a bribe. He shrugged on Blas's synthi-leather clothing, having stripped the man. There were two heat holes in the back where the Vomag had shot Blas, but that couldn't be helped. The boots were too tight, but they fit after a fashion.

"A disguise is wise," Skar said. "Have you done this before?"

"On my own world. Who are the Resisters?" Cyrus asked.

"We will discuss such things later. Now we must reach the Maze before the Kresh gas these levels."

"Why haven't they gassed them already?"

Skar grabbed him by an elbow and dragged him along. The soldier was shorter than he was, but wider shouldered and bigger chested. He was also strong.

"Listen to my instructions," Skar said. "If I fall, you must go to the Crab Palace. There you must discover the Reacher. He will inform you."

"Inform me of what?"

"I am Skar 192 of the Tenth Cohort. I am a soldier. I am not privy to the Higher Learning. I fight. I conquer enemies."

"Yet you belong to the Resisters," Cyrus said.

They exited the corridors and entered a large chamber with machines lining the walls. Lights showed on some of the machines and electric sounds emanated from others. There was a small, wheel-less vehicle here, lying on its side.

Skar righted the vehicle and straddled it. "Climb behind me," the soldier said.

Skar bent lower, gripping handlebars. Cyrus climbed behind and almost yelped when the vehicle thrummed and lifted several inches off the floor.

"How does it do that?" Cyrus asked.

"I am a soldier, not a mechanic. Hang on."

The Vomag twisted a throttle, taking them across the floor much too fast. Cyrus grabbed the soldier's waist. The man seemed to be made of iron-hard muscle.

"Is this an antigravity cycle or does it do this through magnetic lift?" Cyrus asked.

"I must concentrate," Skar said. "So you must cease talking."

The next few minutes were wild. Skar shot through entrances and flashed across chambers. Several times, startled workers looked up. Twice, a man dived out of the way. One shouted angrily, shaking his fist.

"Get ready to jump," Skar said. "Now!" he shouted, springing off the levitating cycle.

Cyrus leaped and hit the deck plates tumbling. The cycle flashed toward a corridor, flying away out of sight.

"Where's it—"

A crash and an explosion ended Cyrus question of where the cycle went.

"Run," Skar said.

The soldier sprinted into a new set of corridors. Instead of metallic colored deck plates, the floor was black, with various red symbols painted in places. The soldier had short legs, but the Vomag moved with astonishing speed. It made the short-handled axe dangling on his belt bounce so it struck the left leg.

Cyrus concentrated on keeping up. He'd always been fast-footed, but this squat, short soldier would have beaten anyone he knew in a race. The soldier was too far ahead and darted around a corner out of sight.

"Wait up!" Cyrus called. He ran, turned the corner, and found the soldier waiting for him.

Skar ran slower afterward. "I forgot. You are not Vomag."

"Yeah, sure," Cyrus puffed. The Vomag reminded him of the marines. "How much longer are we going to keep running like this?"

"This way," Skar said, darting into a narrower corridor.

Their feet pounded on the metal floor. After what seemed like two more kilometers, Skar came to a sudden stop.

Cyrus barely halted in time. He panted and sweat dripped from him. He needed water soon or he was going to faint. To his disgust and surprise, Skar only showed a slight sheen of perspiration on his forehead.

"This is the spot," Skar said. He dug out a flat device from his belt and tapped a sequence of buttons. Before them, metal slid away to reveal a crawl space.

"It looks narrow," Cyrus said.

Skar studied him. "There are refreshments in the Maze. We must keep moving now before the Kresh realize you've been helped."

"How many people belong to the Resisters? Are you planning a revolt?"

"I am a soldier. I fight."

"Okay, okay, you don't know. I get it. Let's go."

Skar went in first. Cyrus followed, squeezing and twisting through. The edges of the opening tugged at his clothes, trying to tear them off. Soon, he was on his hands and knees in a tight space.

"Wait," Skar said. In the dim light, he aimed the flat device at the opening. The metal slid shut, casting them into pitch darkness.

"Do you have a light?" Cyrus asked. This place was already getting to him. He didn't like it in here.

"No. Now we must crawl. Remember, there are refreshments at the end of our journey."

"If I pass out are you going to drag me?"

"You cannot pass out," Skar said.

"Yeah, I get it. If you have to drag me, the game is over. Okay. This is better than I'd ever hoped to do. Lead the way. Let's go to the Crab Palace and talk to the Reacher."

They crawled in the darkness until Cyrus's hands and knees ached. The synthi-leather pants proved themselves. His other clothes would have worn through by now. He wrapped his hands in extra cloth and dreamed of stopping. He needed a drink. He badly needed to rest.

Would you rather be back aboard the shuttle on your cot?

Cyrus knew the answer to that. This was amazing. Despite his sluggishness, his mind kept whirling with questions. Humans resisted the aliens. That was good to know. Now he'd like to know where these humans came from. Why were they so different from each other? Soldiers like Skar seemed a different race compared to the Rarified, the inquisitor. Oh, right, right. The inquisitor had referred to "the Races" once. Was that different races of humans?

"The Rarified hated me," Cyrus said. "So how come it turns out he's helping me?"

"He belongs to the Resisters."

Despite his exhaustion, Cyrus grinned. "Do many people belong to the Resisters?"

"The Kresh exterminate all resistance."

"That's not much of an answer."

"Save your breath," Skar said. "We still have a long way to go."

The hours passed as they crawled. Cyrus had never been this tired in his life. Twice, he collapsed. Skar waited each time for what seemed like mere seconds. Then the soldier urged him to continue crawling.

"Where are we?" Cyrus wheezed.

"Near the Maze," Skar said.

"How big is High Station 3?"

"Huge," Skar said.

Cyrus didn't grin anymore, nor did he think much. He crawled, and sometimes he wished he were back in his cell. To lie on his cot and do nothing, that had been true glory.

Then light flooded around him and pain stung his eyes. He collapsed onto a new floor and closed his stinging orbs. He felt motion, a thud, a clang and wetness touched his lips. Greedily, Cyrus sucked at the wetness. It dampened his throat and took away some of the bone dryness.

"Slowly," someone whispered to him.

Cyrus endured until more moisture touched his lips. In time, he dragged his tongue over the moisture. Drips of water teased him. He sucked every particle of wetness. After a longer wait, cool metal touched his lips and water gushed into his mouth. He drank and choked on water.

With a groan, he sat up. His muscles jerked in a spasm. He threw up, spewing what Skar had trickled into his stomach.

"You must relax."

Cyrus opened an eye. A wall stood nearby, with garbage strewn on the ground. There were muffled sounds, many voices, although he didn't see anyone. Skar squatted beside him, holding a canteen and looking worried.

"Where are . . . ?" Cyrus whispered. He was too tired to keep talking.

"We have reached the Maze. You must take water, gain strength, and we must hurry to the Crab Palace."

"Move me . . . where I can . . . lean against something."

Skar dragged him near the wall, propping him against it. Cyrus looked up. The ceiling was three meters high and lights were embedded in it. The garbage stank. There were old wrappers, crumpled containers, and bones with bits of rotting meat clinging to them. Cyrus almost felt at home. This was too much like Level 40 Milan. For the first time, he really felt as if he had a chance. He knew how to survive in a slum.

"I'm ready for a drink," Cyrus said.

Skar trickled water into his mouth.

Closing his eyes, Cyrus let his body relax. It was hard, as different muscles kept twitching. This time, he kept the water down. Later, Skar trickled in more.

"Won't the Kresh gas the Maze?" Cyrus whispered.

"Yes," Skar said.

"So tell me how running here will help me stay out of their grasp."

"The Reacher will know."

"Have you ever met the Reacher?"

"No," Skar said.

"Is he a legend?"

"I do not know."

"How do you know about him?" Cyrus asked.

"The Rarified told me."

"Until then, you've never heard of the Reacher?"

"You speak truth," Skar said.

"Do you know how many people are in the Resisters?"

"The Rarified and me, and the Reacher," Skar said.

The Resisters must use a cell structure organization, Cyrus decided. Maybe there weren't that many resisters, but it was good to know a few humans at least didn't love the Kresh. Then he wondered why he felt so much better. Had there been something extra in the water?

"Why is he called the Reacher?"

"Are you ready?" Skar asked. "We must keep moving."

Cyrus blew out his cheeks. No, he was far from ready. However, thoughts of the Grand Agonizer gave him resolve. Remembering how Vomags had beaten Captain Nagasaki to death helped him to grit his teeth and climb to his feet with his final reserves of strength.

"Let's do it," Cyrus said. "Let's head to the Crab Palace."

The Maze lived up to its name. It was a warren of corridors, chambers such as the one they'd first entered, and hundreds of metal kiosks and open-air shops. Men, women, and children abounded. They mostly wore loose garments such as Larl had possessed. A few had the synthi-leather pants and jacket as Cyrus presently wore. People avoided looking at him and they stared anywhere but at Skar.

"You're a sore thumb," Cyrus said. "You're terrifying people. You should wear a disguise."

"I do not think there are any Vomags in the Maze except for me."

"That's not going to help us. Wait here."

"I must guard you."

"Wait here," Cyrus said. "I have to get you something." Seeing that Skar obeyed, Cyrus eased over several stalls and approached an old woman on matting. She had various articles spread out, including the loose robes so loved by many.

"Are those for sale?" Cyrus asked.

The old woman had a wrinkled face and lacked teeth. She squinted at him suspiciously. "I've never harmed you."

"I'm not talking about that. Are those clothes for sale?"

"Semper Fast protects me. If I whistle, he will come and fight you."

"What do you think I'm asking you?"

"You protectors are all alike, greedy thieves with murder in your heart."

Cyrus took out his toldecks, flashing them before the old woman's eyes. She stared at him in surprise.

"How much do you want for those robes?" he asked.

She bit her lip. "Why do you torment an old woman?"

Cyrus peeled a note from the others and let it flutter to her crossed knees. Then he scooped up the robe, wadding it in his arms.

"Are we even?" he asked.

She snatched up the note, staring at it in wonder. Then her eyes narrowed suspiciously. "Is this a prank?"

"It's an exchange, woman. I'm asking you if it's fair. Tell me yes or no."

"Yes," she said, making the note disappear.

"Then I'm taking this, too," Cyrus said. He grabbed a scarlet scarf.

"Yes. Now go," she said, "before I whistle for Semper Fast."

Cyrus took the clothing to Skar and talked the soldier into donning them.

"Wrap this around your face," Cyrus said, indicating the scarf.

"You are clever," Skar said.

"Let's hope so."

Soon, Cyrus purchased food and drink and they continued through the Maze. Now people glanced at Skar and they gave Cyrus a more critical study.

"Do you know what protectors are?" Cyrus asked the muffled Vomag. Only the soldier's eyes showed.

"I know the direction to the Crab Palace. I know the Maze is for outcasts and thieves. More than that, I do not know."

"You could have just said no."

"We must hurry," Skar said. "Soon, the Kresh will unleash the Guardians. If that occurs . . . Come, we must hurry while we can."

6

In despair, Jasper studied his watery surroundings and himself. He was stark naked except for an odd breathing mask. Every time he exhaled, bubbles wobbled to the top of the aquarium, the one he floated inside. He couldn't spy a tube from his mask to an oxygen tank or to an air cylinder outside. Perhaps the mask extracted the air directly from the water around him just as a fish did with its gills.

The aquarium appeared to be a ten meter square, with no surface water, no tiny air level.

They've trapped me in here. And he had no idea why. The only similarity was to the tank in the tele-chamber aboard *Discovery*. He wished he were back on the Teleship heading for Sol. He'd even accept an inhibitor in his mind, anything to escape these treacherous aliens. Why had he ever lowered his mind shield? That had been the worst mistake of his life.

I acted the part of a fool. They tricked me.

The mask had goggles and he swam near a flat, vertical surface. Looking through the glass, he found that he was in a large chamber with many strange machines. He didn't like their look or the cameras obviously monitoring him.

The inside of the aquarium was clean. If he defecated, a sweeper soon took the excess away.

He recalled little since the space battle. The aliens had taken control of Chief Monitor Argon. Jasper hadn't expected that. The chief monitor's plan of keeping him subdued had been a joke, well, almost a joke. Argon had a powerful mind shield, and it would have taken Jasper time to control the man. In that time, Argon might have pressed the switch to shock him.

Anyway, he'd wanted out of the New Eden system. The aliens had tricked him. They'd altered his thoughts. The idea had infuriated him then as it did now. He was the new breed, the god among the humans, but a god with feet of clay.

Now he was caught like a rat in a trap, or a fish in a barrel. He attempted to use his telepathy. A light flashed on the wall. It startled him, but it didn't halt his attempt.

Then a jolt of pain stunned him. He stopped his attempt. The aliens had rigged an anti-telepathy device in the aquarium.

Jasper swam from one wall to the next. Why had they taken his clothes? It was another strike against these evil bastards. He wished there was some way he could hurt them. That was the worst of it: He could do nothing to strike back at his tormenters.

After several minutes of swimming, Jasper noticed a door-shaped panel appear in one of the chamber's walls. The panel slid aside into a hall. A lean humanoid with a tall cranium and *baan* encircling his forehead entered. A nine-foot Kresh stalked behind the human.

Jasper blinked in surprise at his knowledge of the alien's race name. He recalled something new now: smaller humanoids had hooked him to a machine earlier and afterward, one of the Rarified had mentally force-fed him information.

The Kresh ruled Fenris. Within the star system, the Kresh fought the Chirr, and now they fought Web-Minds, raiders from interstellar space.

As he floated in the aquarium, Jasper watched smaller humans enter, going to the machines, turning them on and remaining to run them.

He knew other things. The Kresh were non-psionic, but the insect-like Chirr were psionic. The Kresh had modified humans, searching for psi-abilities. To control the psionic humans, the Kresh made the Rarified love them. It was an involved process that began at birth. If a Rarified showed non-love, the Kresh eradicated the offender. The Kresh had also built anti-psionic suits, which protected them from various psionic attacks.

Can you hear me? a Rarified asked. The tall humanoid standing before the aquarium wore a voluminous robe, with his hands hidden within the sleeves. When he spoke, he failed to move his mouth.

He's using telepathy.

I hear you, Jasper said, also using telepathy. This time, he didn't receive any shocks. In spite of the terrible situation, the strength of the humanoid's telepathy impressed Jasper. The humanoid's mental powers were nearly his equal.

You have the honor of floating before Chengal Ras, the 109th, the Rarified told him. *You belong to him now. Bow to acknowledge his superiority over you.*

Jasper's eyes flashed. The Kresh, this Chengal Ras, watched him keenly. The reptilian creature was big, and it was awful to witness the eyes studying him, realizing this thing with its crocodilian snout controlled his destiny.

It's a monster. It isn't my superior. It's an alien.

The tall human with his voluminous red robes stared at him, almost seeming to warn him with a look. The look asked a simple question: *Do you want to die here in this aquarium? It can happen like that.*

Jasper did not want to die. Reluctantly, as he floated in the ten-meter tank, Jasper bowed his masked head to the raptor-like alien.

You are tractable, the Rarified told him. *It proves you are wiser than your confederate.*

"I don't know what you're talking about," Jasper said.

The Rarified concentrated. An image appeared in Jasper's mind. He saw Cyrus sprinting for a large entrance. The young man ran past trucks as a Kresh shouted at him. Good for Cyrus. Jasper hoped the lad gave them hell.

You recognize him, the Rarified said.

We were on the ship together.

I sense greater union than that. You plotted together on your home planet.

Jasper clamped down on his shield, enraged that this tall freak could read some of his thoughts. Afterward, he managed a shrug.

You are powerful, Jasper. You are equal in strength to the greatest of the rarified. It is for this reason that Chengal Ras allows you your chaosict mannerisms, at least for now. Our master is a logician of amazing profundity. He climbs the ranks and will soon join the One Hundred.

They're the rulers of the Fenris System? Jasper asked.

Do not attempt to hold onto your antiquated concepts. That would be a mistake of the first order. You belong to Chengal Ras and must begin your life anew. Your former concepts . . . The Rarified shook his head. *I perceive that you come from a star system of wild humans. Their thoughts are loose and ill founded. It can be no other way, for they do not have the Kresh to guide them.*

We don't need the Kresh.

The Rarified smiled. It was a gesture of tolerance for a foolish statement. *Your unfocused reasoning will soon fall into line with your master. And these wild humans of the solar system, they will soon learn order and the harmony of living under Kresh guidance.*

You plan to conquer Sol?

Chengal Ras made a swift gesture with one of his smaller arms. It almost appeared to be one of annoyance.

His robes billowed as the Rarified turned to the Kresh and bowed low. The humanoid moved more slowly as he turned back to Jasper. *You absorbed a tremendous amount of information a short time ago. Even a powerful mind like yours needs time to sort the knowledge into the proper categories. Still, it is wise to know your place. You do not question a Kresh, any Kresh, and certainly, you do not question Chengal Ras the 109th, your master. That means you do not question me. Here in this chamber, I am the mouth of Chengal Ras.*

Jasper decided to bide his time. He needed to get out of this aquarium before he could think about anything else.

I understand, he said.

No, Jasper, I sense you do not understand. You are like your companion creature, the one you named as Cyrus. He broke ancient tradition by fleeing during the Docking Ceremony. He must die in a hideous manner to erase such blasphemy.

In spite of himself, Jasper grinned within his mask. If anyone had a chance on this mad world, it was the lad from Level 40.

You mock your master? the Rarified asked in amazement.

Chengal Ras made a hissing noise. In the background, one of the humans manning the machines threw a lever.

Shocks of pain bolted through the water and slammed against Jasper. He screamed and bubbles fled from his mask. He writhed in the water, a small fat man under assault.

Do you know what it feels like to drown? the Rarified asked.

I do not, Jasper gasped as the shocks subsided.

You may soon have the opportunity to learn if you continue in this useless resistance.

But I'm a powerful telepath, Jasper said. *You told me I am. Surely, the Kresh could use my talents. Therefore, it's a waste to harm me.*

Do not attempt to rate yourself. You are the property of Chengal Ras. Property can never mock its master. That is blasphemy against rightness. Do you wish to join your companion in the Grand Agonizer?

I do not.

Then cease all mockery and bend your thoughts toward love of Chengal Ras.

Jasper swallowed uneasily. *I will try.*

Your life hinges upon your success.

I understand.

The Rarified moistened his lips. He hesitated before saying, *You will now begin telling us all that you know about your companion.*

Jasper blinked several times. It was clear he should tell the alien everything. The creature held all the advantages. Only a fool would resist in such a situation. Yet Jasper found that the more he considered it, the more he admired Cyrus Gant. The young man had courage, and he'd managed to escape from the aliens who had tricked them all. It would be a pity to help these creatures find young Gant.

Are you refusing to aid your master? the Rarified asked.

Jasper didn't want to die. He didn't want to drown. *I'm not refusing. What do you wish to learn?*

Something shined in the humanoid's eyes. It was hard to tell what through the glass, the water, and the goggles. It seemed to be disappointment and maybe even a hint of contempt.

It caused Jasper to bristle. Who was this slave of the reptilian alien to have contempt for him?

You must tell me everything you can about the blasphemer Cyrus.

I—

Chengal Ras hissed, and he lashed his tail. With a sharp movement, he tore a metallic streamer from a talon and let it flutter to the floor.

The Rarified turned pale, and his shook head.

What's wrong? Jasper asked. *Did I do something wrong?*

You have failed to love, Jasper of Sol. Chengal Ras was curious to know if a wild of your power could learn the civilized arts. The techs have been monitoring you and I have detected falsity in your words.

Fear swept over Jasper. He blinked rapidly and found that his mouth was dry. *What . . . what are you going to do with me?*

Your query of me points to the truth of your barbarous manners. I told you that property never questions its master. Yet, you have disobeyed once again.

Give me a second chance, Jasper said. He swam closer to the glass and aimed his words at Chengal Ras. *Give me a second chance to show love.*

The Rarified shook his head. *Now you attempt to give orders. Chengal Ras was merciful before. With your barbarism you have spit in his face.*

What's wrong with you people? Jasper shouted. *I'm not like you. I haven't grown up kissing the tail of an alien. It takes time to learn that.*

You are barbarous, the Rarified said. *It has now become clear to your master that you cannot possibly learn obedience quickly enough to be of use. Therefore, we will continue with the original goal.*

What does that mean? Jasper asked.

You are in the first stage of the mind extractor. Since you are such a powerful telepath, Chengal Ras has deemed it unwise to use the rarefied to scour your thoughts. It would also take too much time. Instead, your master will sweep your thoughts and put them onto a memory spool.

Is that painful? Jasper asked.

The pain will cease to matter once your thoughts are on the spools. Then you will be a simple, mindless thing and quickly put out of its misery.

What?

If you believe in spiritual entities or some afterlife, prepare to meet him, them, or it.

In desperation and rage, Jasper shook a fist at the Rarified. Then he concentrated his telepathic powers and hurled a mind bolt at the mocking humanoid.

The tall rarefied clutched his head and screamed. He must not have been ready for such desperation. The humanoid staggered backward as his robes billowed once more. In a moment, his eyes rolled up into his head and he slumped onto the floor.

Jasper glanced around at his confinement one more time. There was no help coming for him. He was in a cage that he could never escape. Even gods could die, it seemed. But he would do this his way and he wouldn't give the aliens anything. It was a gesture. It had been his failure that had ruined the voyage for everyone involved, but especially for him.

It is time to die.

Jasper began ripping the breathing mask from his face. Chengal Ras roared, and the techs slapped buttons on their machines.

It was Jasper's turn to scream as pain slammed against him. Then a terrible thrumming began in his mind. He knew it was the beginning of the mind extraction. He pulled his mask harder and the pain shocked him into immobility.

I tried, Jasper thought. Then he endured pain as the first level of mind extraction began.

7

The Crab Palace neither served crabs nor was it a palace. It began in a larger chamber crammed with the most pitiful cases Cyrus had seen so far.

The crippled, diseased, and twisted lived in this chamber. They wore rags instead of robes and stank of pus, defecation, and urine. There was endless coughing, wheezing, and the last brays of the dying. The overhead lighting was spotty: shadowy in places and bright in others. The property limits seemed to be the extent of a person's rug or mat. Altogether, it was a depressing and disheartening place.

Skar led and picked his way through the packed throng. Some watched him. Others averted their gaze. The worst were the children who stared with the bulbous eyes of the starving.

Cyrus scowled. Skar had called these people outcasts. Didn't the Kresh care what happened here? Or was the Maze like a rat-hole? That would make these people rats, living in the crevices or in the insulation of the space station's outer walls. How many of the people were sick with radiation poisoning?

Skar headed toward a portal in the wall, surrounded by several metal kiosks. A gunman in synthi-leather stepped out of the first kiosk.

"Well?" the gunman asked. "Who are you from?"

"I have hunted in the stars," Skar said.

"What's that supposed to mean?"

"I am Vomag."

The gunman looked more closely, and he turned pale, re-gripping his weapon. "Look. I don't know what you're—"

"We seek the Reacher," Skar said.

The gunman froze.

"Is there a problem, Cast?" a bigger gunman asked, coming out from another kiosk. The man had a yellow scarf tied to his throat, with crusts of dried blood in it.

"No!" Cast said. "These two, take them back. They want crab."

The second gunman pulled out his weapon, aiming it at Skar.

Cast turned toward him. "I said no, you fool. He's Vomag."

"We're dead," the second gunman said listlessly. "We never should have listened to the old one. This was a bad—"

"Can't you think?" Cast asked. "If the masters wanted us dead, we'd already be dead. Take these two back and serve them crab."

The second gunman straightened his slumped shoulders. "Follow me," he said.

The man took them to the portal and tapped against the wall. He didn't use controls, but the portal opened. A fat woman in a draped robe sat on a stool within. Glowing controls on the wall illuminated her disease-spotted features. She must have opened the portal. Without a word or a nod, the gunman passed the woman and beckoned them to follow.

They walked past others sprawled on the deck plates, each on his or her rug. Soon, though, they walked through a narrow corridor of stainless steel. It branched and they turned left, right, and left. A slight thrum began, intensifying by degrees until Cyrus felt vibrations against his feet. They must be near engines of some kind. Finally, they walked through a dark corridor until the gunman tapped on a wall again.

A new hatch opened to a different place and the gunman said, "I hope this ain't a trick."

"Me too," Cyrus said.

Skar went through first and Cyrus followed. The gunman stayed behind and the hatch closed. A long maze of pipes and tubing ran for kilometers here and the machine noises were louder. They were in a vast, cavernous area, and it seemed to curve into the distance, almost to the horizon.

A short, bald woman with strange red eyes regarded them.

"I seek the Reacher," Skar said.

She turned without a word and they followed, marching for three hundred meters. "Is he the one?" the woman asked, pointing at Cyrus.

"I am a soldier," Skar said.

She halted and pointed at a closed portal. "The one you seek waits within." She stared at Cyrus. Her red eyes were unsettling and she seemed to measure him.

"You are strange," she said. "But you do not seem special."

Cyrus couldn't help but grin. "I am, though, Special Fourth Class, in fact."

"What does that mean?" she asked.

"We have no time," Skar said. "The Kresh hunt for him."

"Has he slain a master?" she asked in a hushed voice, her face alive with an eager hope.

"The Maze still survives," Skar said.

"Too bad," she said. "I wish you'd slain a master," she told Cyrus. "Once I loved them like everyone else. Now I hate the Kresh."

"Those are blasphemous words," Skar said.

"You should try them someday," the red-eyed woman said. "They are sweeter than honey."

Cyrus frowned as Skar led him toward the hatch, leaving the red-eyed woman behind. The gunman earlier had said something interesting: that he hoped this wasn't a trick. Had Skar used him? Was this an elaborate trick by the third order Rarified to find the Reacher?

Cyrus drew his heat gun and pointed it at Skar's back. He was tired, but he attempted to reason this through. If the Kresh knew the Reacher lived in the Maze, would they need an escaped Earthling as an excuse to find him? Maybe the trick went deeper. Maybe this was a setup to get him—Cyrus—to talk, to spill his guts to the Reacher, a Kresh puppet. Yet why would the aliens do that if they had a memory extractor?

Skar reached for the hatch. It slid open before he touched any controls. A psi-master regarded them. He wore a *baan* and a long white robe, although without a collar. Cyrus looked more closely. This one was old, with lines in his elongated face. The eyes—there was power in the man, and great weariness, too.

"Reacher?" Skar asked.

Cyrus readied the heat gun.

"You won't need that," the psi-master told Cyrus.

Skar turned around and spied the weapon. He looked up in surprise.

"I'm not sure if this is a trick or not," Cyrus explained.

Skar stared at him, and finally, he nodded. "That was a wise precaution. I should have expected it from one who could best a Rarified."

"Put away the gun," the psi-master said. "The soldier is genuine and so are the Resisters. You are from the alien vessel?"

"I am," Cyrus said. He hesitated but finally tucked the gun in his waistband.

"Enter," the psi-master told Cyrus. "Will you wait here, Vomag?"

"My life is at an end," Skar said. "I have no more purpose."

"That's not necessarily true," the psi-master said. "Remain here. You may soon have another task as honorable as the one you've just performed."

Skar paused before saying, "I will wait." He turned, crouched, and sat before the portal like a guard dog.

"Enter please," the psi-master told Cyrus. He turned and retreated into the room.

Cyrus followed, with the hatch closing behind him. The chamber was about the size of Venice's quarters aboard *Discovery* and was crammed with items. Some were old and worn—a stool, a table, and an old computer screen. Others looked new—a heat gun, a device with two prongs curving up and shiny discs on the end. There was another portal; Cyrus figured it must lead to a bedroom, as there was no place to sleep in here.

"You're the Reacher?" Cyrus asked.

The psi-master sat stiffly on a stool. The old man kept his spine erect. He indicated a softer, backed chair. Cyrus sank into it. The old man pointed at the table, indicting food and drink. Cyrus helped himself, guzzling bitter tasting water and devouring something like stale crackers.

"It is poor fare, I know," the psi-master said. "But it sustains me in the dark hours of existence."

"Why do you want to see me?" Cyrus asked.

"Questions, questions, so many questions," the psi-master said. "Yes, I am the Reacher. I suspect you have no idea what that means."

"I don't," Cyrus said, polishing off several more crackers. They reminded him of the gritty clots aboard the alien shuttle.

"I am the heart of the Resisters on High Station 3. My guile keeps me hidden from the Kresh." The psi-master laughed bitterly. "It is a vain belief, but it has sustained me for many lonely years. The Kresh care nothing about the Resisters or me. Hmm, that is incorrect. Ormdez Ree cares nothing about me. Some of the Hundred worry about us. The other Kresh believe those who worry have become addled."

"Uh, you're not making much sense," Cyrus said.

The old man studied him. "You are weary and have expended your mental powers. Still, you have escaped from the Kresh during the Docking Ceremony. It was an inelegant maneuver, but you took a chance and beat the masters for a moment in time. That is a feat for a human. Finder has told me about you. He was very excited."

"Finder?" Cyrus asked.

"The Rarified who interviewed you for the Kresh," the psi-master said.

"Oh. So what happens now?"

The old man continued to stare. Finally, he blinked and turned away. "For many, many years I have hoped for this day. Now it is here and I cannot believe it. Worse, I look at you and know it is impossible for us to defeat the Kresh even with Earth's help. Our Resistance is futile, but it has been better than bowing to the enslavers of humanity."

"How do you know about Earth?" Cyrus asked.

"That is a penetrating question, even though I do not think you understand our plight."

"If you won't answer that, tell me this: Where do you come from?"

"You wish to know my spawning place?"

"No, not you specifically," Cyrus said. "Where did all you humans come from? Why and how have the Kresh enslaved you?"

"We originally come from Earth, of course," the psi-master said. "How otherwise do I know about Earth and expect help from you?"

Cyrus laughed. It sounded shrill to his ears. "That's impossible. We're from Earth. *You* can't be from Earth, too."

The psi-master smiled sadly. "Why should it be impossible?"

"Do you have a Teleship?"

"What is that?"

Cyrus sat back in his chair and it creaked. How could this strange human be from Earth? Look at the man's head and body. No one on Earth had a similar shape.

"If you don't have Teleships and claim you're from Earth . . . when did you get here?"

" 'Here' meaning the Fenris System I presume," the psi-master said.

"Yeah," Cyrus said.

The psi-master closed his eyes and folded his arms. He seemed to be thinking deeply, almost as if he were retrieving stored knowledge. "Ah, yes," he said, opening his eyes. "We arrived according to the old calendar in 2225 A.D. That would be one hundred and seventy years ago. The Kresh enslaved us upon our arrival."

Cyrus stared at the man in shock. "So what happened to you?"

"Could you be more specific?"

"I don't know of anybody on Earth or in the Sol System that looks like you psi-masters."

"Psi-masters?" the old man asked.

"That's what we call you, ah, guys with the *baans*. Your bodies are quite different from the Vomags."

"Oh. I think I understand. We are the Bo Taws. The Kresh created us in their gene labs, just as they created the Vomags to storm the tunnels of the Chirr."

"The who?" Cyrus asked. This was too much information to sort through all at once.

The old psi-master or Bo Taw raised a long-fingered hand. It caused the wide sleeve to slide down, showing his bony, veiny arm. "We'll take forever if I randomly feed you bits and pieces of data. Let me start from the beginning. I think you'll understand better then. We lack time and soon you must leave or the Kresh will recapture you. We cannot afford that, as this is our greatest chance yet. Ah, I'm still confusing you, yes?"

"I'm for hurrying," Cyrus said. "The Kresh have threatened to put me in the Grand Agonizer."

"A horrible and sickening end," the psi-master said. "Therefore, I'll be as brief as I can. Still, I believe I should tell you the full story. You may never get another chance like this. Besides, we need Earth to know as much about us and the Kresh as possible."

"Ah . . ." *What was the best way to tell the Reacher the bad news? Maybe to just do it.* "I don't think Earth is going to find out about either of us for a long time."

"Fighting and struggling against an alien tyranny is much better than submitting," the Reacher said. "Our actions prove we are men. Now let me compose my thoughts. I want to get the facts right. My memory isn't what it used to be. Are you listening?"

"I sure am," Cyrus said. *Didn't he hear what I said about Earth?*

The old psi-master studied one of the walls, blinking slowly. He pinched the bridge of his nose with a long forefinger and even longer thumb. "I do not know all there is to know about the Great Trek. I have heard bits and pieces, and through my long and lonely years, I have connected the stories into a pattern, searching for the truth. We are scattered throughout the Fenris System, slaves to the Kresh.

"I know very little about the ancient Earth of long ago, its politics and the happenings that forced our ancestors to attempt the journey across time and space. There is an ancient tale of Bernard Attlee, an extraordinary visionary. How he knew about the Fenris System remains a mystery to this day. I suspect he had mental abilities, a clairvoyant perhaps who saw the Earth-like planets here in their pristine glory. In any case, he persuaded the leader of the expedition to chart a path to this system.

"The mighty starship *Winston Churchill* held eleven thousand desperate souls. It used nuclear bombs as fuel, an Orion vessel, building up velocity. Once out of the solar system and with sufficient speed, they turned on the Bussard ramjet. I do not know the specifics of such an engine. It is sufficient to say that it built up to near light speed. The journey took two hundred and thirty-seven years to complete, at least to an outside observer. Because of time dilation, much less time passed for the travelers. The hopes and dreams of beginning anew in what Bernard Attlee promised would be Earth-like conditions . . . there was great fanfare as the ship approached its destination."

"Didn't they use telescopes to study the system?" Cyrus asked. "Didn't they see it was already occupied?"

"That is a clever question," the Reacher said. "I should know the answer, but I don't. Hmm, that is interesting. In any case, the great visionary Attlee hadn't foreseen the Kresh, nor did the passengers discover them until too late. The Kresh inhabited the star system, had for countless generations as they battled their great enemy the Chirr. As far as I know, the Kresh never used star-drives like a Bussard ramjet. They never had or have psionic talents. They did have Attack Talons that dreadful day. The aliens attacked *Winston Churchill*, capturing what was left of the crew and passengers. Perhaps I should tell you a little about the Kresh. You've seen them, yes?"

"I have," Cyrus said.

"They're dinosaurs, or they look as we supposed dinosaurs must have in the olden times on Earth. Well, the Kresh are warm-blooded, so in that way they're unlike reptiles as the old books tell. They are inhuman in their thought patterns. Each Kresh strives for perfection in his or her chosen fields of study and contemplation. The hundred highest-ranked Kresh make up the Hundred, the ruling body, if one can call it that. Ormdez Ree, the Master of High Station 3, is ranked 30,231 in the Kresh hierarchy. That means in their way of looking at things, he is the 30,231st most impressive Kresh of the species. I estimate there to be something like eight or nine million Kresh in the Fenris System. So as you can see, Ormdez Ree is quite impressive indeed."

An odd smile flickered on and off the Reacher's face. "The Hundred view themselves as philosopher kings, and they are passionless, driven by cold reptilian logic. In any case, one hundred and seventy years ago, the Kresh captured a ship full of humans. Seven thousand people survived the journey and the battle. The Kresh tested them and found the humans intelligent enough to use. The Kresh scooped every female ovary clean of eggs and began their genetic warping.

"The Vomags they created became fodder for the war against the Chirr. The Chirr are intelligent insects and control the three inner planets. Before *Winston Churchill* arrived, the Kresh had annihilated the Chirr of the most inward planet. The Kresh personally fought in space, driving the Chirr spaceships from the void. On the planetary surfaces, the Kresh sent their fighting machines down to dig out the Chirr. But the so-called masters failed to drive the insects from any nest. With the coming of the Vomags, events changed radically. The soldiers in their millions—"

"Wait a minute," Cyrus said. "Millions, you're saying there were millions of Vomags?"

"The Kresh were busy in their gene labs, bringing eggs to maturity in record time. One hundred and seventy years have passed since we arrived in the Fenris System, but the Kresh have already bred hundreds of generations of mutated humans."

"That's disgusting," Cyrus said.

The Reacher shrugged. "Millions of Vomags have perished on the third planet. They drove deep into the nests, battling the Chirr in their underground hives. Finally, the Chirr exploded thousands of nuclear weapons, saturation-bombing their entire planet."

"They committed suicide?" Cyrus asked.

"No. The Chirr demolished thousands of Vomag bases, hundreds of thousands of combat flyers and tanks. They made a dead zone on the surface, no doubt burrowing deeper into the planet to escape the radiation."

"Chirr still live on the third planet?"

"Yes."

"Why don't the Chirr do the same thing on the second planet?" Cyrus asked.

"They try from time to time, but the Kresh space lasers are always tracking, always firing and destroying."

"It sounds like an alien war to the death," Cyrus said.

"The war is greater than that," the Reacher said. "But listen. Let me finish the tale. You must soon be on your way."

"Where are you expecting me to go?"

"Listen!" the Reacher said sternly. "I've not waited these long years for an impatient young man to ruin everything because he cannot listen. You are a link in a great chain. You must do your part."

Cyrus raised his eyebrows.

"The Vomag soldiers were simply one branch of humanity, a newly created race. The Bo Taw became another form of man. The Kresh do not possess psionic powers, as I said. Yet they tested the captured passengers and found that an infinitesimal number of humans do possess such talents."

"How did they know to test such a thing if they didn't have it themselves?" Cyrus asked.

"The Chirr are strongly psionic and have used their abilities against the Kresh for thousands of years."

Cyrus massaged his forehead. "This is incredible. It's too much to take in all at once."

"Let me speak the words. Your mind will work on sorting out the facts later."

"I guess," Cyrus said. He was comfortable in this chair. He doubted he would know such ease in the Grand Agonizer. "You're right. Keep talking."

"The Kresh bred the Bo Taw for psionic ability. There are hundreds of thousands of us now, and we are a special problem for the Kresh. I suspect that is when one of them came upon the solution, and that was *love*."

"What does love have to do with anything?" Cyrus asked.

"The Kresh do not love, but one among them deciphered its meaning in their alien symbols. He is high among the Hundred now, having gained rank through the discovery. That is how Kresh climb the hierarchy: through feats of mind, feats of rationality, anything that adds to their *Codex of All Knowledge*. I believe that is how he stumbled upon the human idea of love—the Kresh longing for greater knowledge. Their quest is a form of love, I suppose, though more like obsession. Most of them concentrate their minds and efforts on some area of expertise. They particularly prize practicality, the use of applied knowledge."

"I still don't understand what any of this has to do with love," Cyrus said.

"The Kresh wished to leash the Bo Taw to them. What better way than to make the psi-masters, as you put it, loyal creatures? They would enforce loyalty by making us love our masters. The Kresh rule us through devotion, and when needed, through harsh and brutal discipline."

"To gain love," Cyrus said, "doesn't one need to love also?"

"The Kresh argue they love us by giving us meaning, purpose, and most of all, order. In turn, they demand we obey and love them. Many Bo Taw and other lesser humans do love the masters, but many do not. The Resisters uses non-love—hatred, if you will—as the lever to pry people from their subservience to the Kresh."

"What does the rebellion look like?" Cyrus asked.

The Reacher shook his head. "I have much of the old wisdom, but there is much I do not know. Have slaves in Earth history ever risen up and successfully thrown off the yoke of their masters?"

"Yes," Cyrus said.

"Do you know this for a truth?"

"Yes, Moses led the Children of Israel out of Egypt, although Spartacus failed in the end."

"The old knowledge says slaves need outside assistance for victory."

"Legend says that God or the Creator helped Moses."

The Reacher nodded. "We have lacked the Creator's help, or anyone else's help for that matter. Thus, we have never revolted or rebelled, but merely resisted. Now, however, you are here to give us outside assistance."

"Me?" Cyrus asked. "What am I supposed to do?"

"Not just you, of course, but Earth. You are an earnest of Earth's good will."

"Surely you know that the Kresh captured our vessel."

"One ship, yes, this I do know," the Reacher said. "What about the others?"

"What others?"

The Reacher searched Cyrus's eyes. "You made the assault upon the Kresh System with a single warship? That strikes me as irrational."

"I think you have the wrong idea about us. We didn't know the Kresh were here. To the telescopes in the solar system, the Fenris System—or the Kresh System—looked empty. I believe the Kresh possess a machine that puts a false picture of this system out into the stars."

"But in your initial attack, some escaped."

"What initial attack?" Cyrus asked. "I have no idea what you're talking about."

The Reacher frowned. "There is a mystery here. Our minds are not linking. Nine years ago, Earth made the first assault."

"There's your mistake," Cyrus said. "No one from Earth even knew about—" He stopped suddenly, thinking.

"Ah. Your eyes, they show me you've had an epiphany."

"What are you talking about now?" Cyrus asked.

"Speak your thoughts, I beg you."

"Well . . . you're saying people from Earth attacked Fenris nine years ago. But nine years ago no one in the solar system even knew about Fenris."

"Yet nine years ago the Kresh captured humans or humanoid soldiers from Earth," the Reacher said.

"Yeah, I bet they did," Cyrus said. "Only they weren't from Earth, well, not directly anyway. If I'm right, they were cyborgs. We defeated the cyborgs over a hundred years ago, driving them from the Sol System."

"This is vitally important," the Reacher said. "Do you mind if I scan your thoughts?"

"Yeah, I'd mind it a whole lot," Cyrus said, bristling.

"Time is pressing. You must let me scan your memories."

Cyrus shook his head.

"I could force it," the Reacher said. For the first time, he seemed like a psi-master, with something of their arrogance. He stood straighter, and his eyes . . . the man's gaze bored into Cyrus.

"No you couldn't," Cyrus said. He drew his heat gun, aiming it at the old psi-master.

The Reacher's eyes tightened.

Cyrus winced. He felt the mind bolt, but his shield had been on automatic. He was too tired to try any telekinesis, but not too tired to shield his thoughts. "You aren't going to get your info like that," he panted.

The Reacher's eyes began to grow dull, turning a metallic color.

Cyrus groaned, but he fought, holding his mind shield. He stood and he aimed the heat gun at the man's tall forehead. "If you don't stop, you're dead."

"If you kill me, you will never leave the Crab Palace alive."

"Maybe, but I know you won't ever leave it either. I'll not be your slave."

The mind assault lasted a moment longer, and then stopped. With a stricken look, the Reacher turned away. "I shouldn't have done that."

"Would've could've should've," Cyrus muttered. He had another head-ache, the old bastard.

"Meaning what's done is done?" the Reacher asked.

"Sure."

With his back to Cyrus, the Reacher said, "Earth or Sol isn't sending more warships, are they?"

"This was a colonizing mission."

The old man took an audible breath. "I have revealed myself to you for nothing. All these long years . . . The Kresh will find us soon. I have played my last hand."

"You must have a way of escape from this place. Otherwise, why did you send for me?"

The Reacher faced him. "There is a vessel, yes, a tiny one. You will need the Vomag's help to reach it. I had thought you were a new path, but I see now I'm wrong. Perhaps . . . perhaps you are the Tracker. None of our own people has shown an aptitude for it. Ah, if you were the Tracker, yes, then the Dreams would still make sense. The road to freedom will still be a long one. Perhaps all isn't lost, though. Yes, you must go to Jassac."

"Do you mind telling me what the heck you're talking about?" Cyrus asked.

The Reacher smiled bleakly. "Many must die in order to mask your escape. There is no other way."

"Look. I don't think you realize what's really going on. We came in a ship that moves faster than light."

"That is impossible."

"It used to be impossible," Cyrus said. "We found a way to do it. The cyborgs know the way, too. Otherwise, they couldn't be out here this fast. What we can't allow is for the Kresh to figure out how to travel faster than light. We have to destroy our ship, the Sol ship, I mean, the Teleship."

"We cannot do that now. Perhaps once you find the Anointed One it will be possible."

"What Anointed One?" Cyrus asked.

"He is the one who will lead the rebellion, who will shake off the Kresh yoke."

"Who is he?"

"The Dreamer saw him, but she is long dead, slain in the Grand Agonizer many years ago. But she did not tell the Kresh enough to reveal the great hope."

"Who did she tell, or what did she tell?"

The Reacher smiled sadly. "As I said, you are the Tracker. You must find him and help him however you can."

"I don't know what you're talking about, and even if I did, how would any of this help destroy the Teleship?"

"I lead the Resisters on High Station 3. You say the Kresh might use your ship and learn this way of faster than light travel. If they find such a drive, surely they will go to Earth and defeat humanity at its core. I believe they hunger for more human genetic material to help fashion better and newer soldiers against the Chirr."

Cyrus thought about all the colonists in stasis aboard *Discovery*. The Kresh would use their DNA.

"We must stop the Kresh," the Reacher was saying. "The Resisters are too weak here. Instead, you must find the Anointed One. He can help both Earth and us here to defeat the Kresh."

"How can he do that?" Cyrus asked.

"I have no idea, but I think he will. You must find him and help him."

"Mister, you're crazy. Do you see me helping anyone?"

"I told you. I am the Reacher, not the Dreamer. I cannot see. I can only reach out and join the needed links."

"Sure," Cyrus said. The psi-master and the Dreamer . . . they were beginning to sound like lunatics.

The old man moved to the table and rummaged around. Finally, he handed Cyrus a crystal. "You must put this in a psi-reader later aboard the vessel."

"Uh . . . what vessel?" asked Cyrus.

"The Vomag and several Resister fighters will help you reach our hidden ship. With it, you must go to Jassac and find the Anointed One."

"Where's Jassac?"

"It is an Earth-viable moon orbiting Pulsar. That is the gas giant High Station 3 orbits."

"Okay. That I can understand. You also said something about many dying. What's that all about?"

A gong sounded from outside.

The Reacher's long features twisted with fear. "Our time is up. Guardians are in the Maze. The Kresh must know you entered. You must leave now. I wish you well, Tracker. Remember me."

"I will, and thanks."

"Show me your gratitude by freeing humanity from the Kresh."

"Sure," Cyrus said. The old man was crazy, but maybe hope was all he'd had left these many years hiding from the Kresh. What a miserable existence.

"Come," the Reacher said. "I must tell the Vomag what he needs to do."

8

Cyrus realized how exhausted he'd become as he followed Skar through the corridors. His legs were like lead and his mind was stuffy with fatigue.

Three gunmen from the Crab Palace had joined them along with the bald, red-eyed woman. Everyone wore synthi-leather jackets, following the protector Cast through the corridors.

The Reacher had spoken tersely with Skar, but the Vomag had brightened considerably.

"We have a mission," he told Cyrus, as if that was the greatest thing in the world. Maybe for a Vomag it was.

Cyrus was bone tired, but he tried to piece together what he'd just heard. The Dreamer, the Reacher, the Tracker, and the Anointed One—it sounded like a bad holo-vid from Milan, the ones he'd spent too much time watching as a kid. He'd loved the fantasy shows, with swordsmen, sorcerers, and vile monsters. The Reacher—the psi-masters in general—seemed like sorcerers to him. They wielded powers no one else possessed. Maybe the psi-talents caused them to act that way.

They could have called Venice "the Dreamer" for her clairvoyant warning. Yeah, maybe this Dreamer had been a clairvoyant. It wasn't anything crazy, just more psi-talents. The Kresh had tinkered with their humans. Maybe their scientists had discovered which genes caused the talents. Then it would have simply been a matter of flooding their lab creatures with the needed chromosomes.

Sure. Once upon a time, Earth scientists had warped normal people into the Highborn. Why couldn't the reptilian bastards have screwed with people enough to make the long-headed psi-masters? He had a small talent. Venice and Jasper had bigger talents and it had changed them. These psi-masters must think like holo-vid sorcerers. That's why they called people the Dreamer, the Reacher, and the Tracker.

I'm the Tracker, huh? I'm supposed to find the Anointed One on Jassac, a freaking Earth-sized moon. This is nuts.

At least he had allies. Maybe this Anointed One could help him free Jasper, Argon, Dr. Wexx, and the others. Maybe, if he could help stir up a system-wide rebellion, there would be a chance of recapturing *Discovery*. That meant he might be able to get back to Earth someday.

Would that be impossible? Probably, but it was a thousand times better than dying in the Grand Agonizer or sitting in the alien shuttle on the hard cot. He had purpose and he had friends, even if they were a strange band.

His friends might not be as friendly as he'd like, though. The Reacher had tried a psi-attack there at the end. The old man figured he could just bowl over the Earth lad.

"Not today, Reacher, not today."

"Did you speak?" Skar asked.

They climbed up pipes and large tubes, and everything around them thrummed. A few of the pipes had been hot, and one of the gunmen had badly burned his hand.

Cyrus looked down. He felt dizzy at the depth. Way down there the gunman with the burned hand looked all alone as he stood guard.

"Isn't there an easier way than this?" Cyrus asked.

"Climb," the red-eyed woman called down.

Cyrus climbed. This had to be the largest monkey-bar set in existence. He used pipes, hauling himself to another one, a second, a third and then he balanced precariously on a larger tube. Liquid surged through it. He felt it through the soles of his tight boots. Was it waste or water? He had no idea, but it reminded him of the algae plants in Level 40. He kept climbing, following Skar, who followed Cast, who followed the red-eyed woman. No one had told Cyrus her name. Maybe it was Climber.

After a time, Cyrus said, "Wait. I have to rest." His arms shook and he found it hard to grip the pipes anymore.

The red-eyed woman climbed down to him. The original floor had long ago faded into a bottomless pit. The top—it was nowhere in existence.

"You mustn't rest," she told him. "The Guardians are coming."

"If I keep climbing, I'm going to slip and fall off."

"Look into my eyes," she said.

He did, and it almost worked, her trick. He felt himself in his mind, falling, falling . . .

He turned his head. "Are you a psi-master, too?" he asked bitterly.

"I am a Null."

That piqued something in him. "What did you say?"

"I can hide from the Bo Taw, from their seekers."

"Can you show me how you do that?"

"Look into my eyes."

Cyrus wrapped his arms around a pipe, interlocking the fingers of both hands, and he leaned his back against a tube. "Okay, Lady. I hope this isn't a freaking trick."

He felt the falling feeling in his mind, and in a moment, he saw what she did to hide from psi-seekers. Her shield was different than his was; hers was camouflage.

You can do it, too. I sensed this in you. That is what I attempted to do.

Soon, Cyrus became aware of his surroundings again. "I don't feel any stronger."

"You're not," she said.

"I thought you were going to give me an energy boost, along with what you showed me," Cyrus said.

"The Reacher believed I should show you my ability," she said. "Since you needed to rest here, I decided this was as good a place as any for you to learn my secret."

"You aren't going with us to find the Anointed One?"

"We will see," she said. "I may join the quest."

"Did you help keep the Reacher hidden all these years with your null power?"

"Can you climb now?" she asked. "Have you rested long enough? The Guardians will be hunting and they do not wait for anyone."

Cyrus took a deep breath. "Yeah, sure, let's keep going."

Maybe ten minutes later, a distant cry drifted up.

"Guardians," Cast said, with fear making his eyes bulge. "It sounds like they killed Darter."

"You two," the woman said, "must stay here and fight the Guardians."

Cast looked as if he wanted to say something, but he nodded. "I hate the Kresh," he whispered.

The red-eyed woman grinned viciously. "I hate the Kresh." She turned to Skar. "We have little time left. Can you make him climb faster?"

Skar eased down beside Cyrus.

"I heard her," Cyrus said. "What's our goal anyway?"

"The outer hatch is near," the woman said. "We will use it to escape High Station 3."

"My hands don't have any strength left, but what the heck," Cyrus said. "Let's do this."

He climbed, and he looked down once and saw a silvery thing floating up. Shortly thereafter, the heat guns sizzled.

"They are useless against a Guardian," the woman said. "But it will—"

A dismal cry sounded, followed by a second, choking gurgle.

"Cast and Diebold are dead," the woman said. "The Guardian comes."

Fear gave Cyrus a burst of strength. He climbed, and he looked down into the depths of the pipe-tube monkey bars set. Then he saw it, the floating, fighting machine he'd seen in the tele-chamber. It was oval and it floated faster.

"There!" the red-eyed woman said. "We've reached the hatch. Quickly, don the suits and head aside."

"Where's the vessel?" Cyrus asked. "You'll have to show us."

"The Vomag knows. The Reacher told him."

"We can't let you face that thing alone," Cyrus said.

"You are the Tracker!" the woman shouted. "You are our last hope. You must find the one who will free humanity from the Kresh! Go, I beg you."

Cyrus's heart hammered and he chewed his lower lip in indecision. He'd faced a Guardian before and he'd defeated it, but with telekinetic power. He shook his head. He had nothing of the sort left to beat one now. But if he ran, he'd feel like a coward.

"Go!" the woman said. "Do not make our lives futile."

With a pang of shame, Cyrus climbed, heading for the hatch. Skar hurried ahead of him. "I never asked for this," Cyrus hissed.

He looked back. The Guardian shot a milky beam at the woman. The white ray stopped short centimeters from her body.

She can shield herself? I wish she'd shown me how to do that.

Cyrus might have stayed to look longer. Skar pulled him up to a platform and they dived through a hatch.

"It'll just follow us," Cyrus said. A muffled scream sounded through the closed hatch. "Now it's our turn, eh?"

"Quick," Skar said. "Put this on."

It was a space suit, a simple one. They stood in a small chamber with many suits hanging on the wall. There were kits and helmets, too.

Skar went to the hatch's control unit and smashed it with his fist until it began to hiss and smoke.

"Hurry!" Skar cried.

Although he was drunk with fatigue, Cyrus slid his feet into a space suit. He used magnetic clamps to close it. As he picked up a bubble helmet, something heavy clanged against the hatch.

Cyrus shouted and dropped his helmet so it hit the deck plates.

"I will stay back and fight it," Skar said.

"Wrong," Cyrus said. "We live or die together. Are you ready?"

Skar put on his helmet. Cyrus did likewise, and the Guardian slammed against the hatch again, obviously trying to beat it down. The Vomag slapped a switch on his suit and then on Cyrus's. He heard air hiss around him.

They opened the outer hatch, entered a tiny compression chamber, and pressed a switch. The hatch closed and a second later, another hatch opened to the stars.

A vast gas giant moved before them.

Skar clunked his helmet against Cyrus's helmet. "Turn on your boots." He didn't use a radio, but let the sound move through the plastic of their two helmets. It made Skar's voice sound far away.

Ah. Cyrus turned on his boots because he understood what he saw. The gas giant—Pulsar—moved before them because High Station 3 rotated to provide centrifugal force: pseudogravity to the occupants of the habitat. Once they walked on the outside, the centrifugal force would send them hurtling out into space. They needed their magnetic boots to anchor them.

Cyrus lifted one boot at a time. As it neared the space station's surface, the boot clanged down hard against the metal. He followed Skar, and the Vomag kept turning back around.

So did Cyrus. He saw it first. The Guardian floated out of the hatch. As it did, the fighting machine whipped outward because the surface moved and it didn't. Spray blew out of nozzles, slowing its movement away.

At that moment, the surface Cyrus stood on shuddered horribly. He began to shake and sway.

"What's going—?"

Before Cyrus could finish the question, he saw a fiery blast blow outward from the space station many kilometers away from them. Metal, debris, and then material, including people, blew outward into space. Another blast occurred, farther away. Cyrus didn't know if it came from the back or the front of High Station 3. What he assumed was that these explosions—bombs—were from the Resisters.

How long have they been saving these bombs?

Cyrus shuddered. How many people had just died to give him a chance to escape? He was like Spartacus escaping from the gladiatorial prison.

The Guardian—the floating, fighting machine—stopped spraying its jets. Did it go to investigate these blasts or had the bombs destroyed its guidance mechanism or link with its controller, if it had one?

Cyrus waited, but no more bombs went off. More people and things kept spewing into space. That was the air inside the habitat rushing out into the vacuum, taking people and things with it.

Were Argon, Wexx, and Jasper dead? Cyrus had no way of knowing. But he doubted the Kresh were stupid. Space stations would have accidents. Smart builders would have sealable compartments. It was also unlikely the Resisters would have been able to place bombs near critical Kresh locations. More likely, the bombs had been placed in the Maze or places like the Maze.

Cyrus's shoulders slumped. Had all these deaths occurred so he could escape? No. They'd occurred to help the Tracker, so he could help free enslaved humanity in the Fenris System.

I have to try. Yeah. I have to seek this Anointed One until I'm dead.

He followed Skar across the outer surface. They clanked to a depression on High Station 3. Then Cyrus saw the vessel as Skar caused a hatch to open. It was a black as sin shuttle, a tiny thing built like a needle. There would hardly be any room in there for them.

Cyrus followed the Vomag through the hatch. What a thing, a Resister spaceship. Well, for the moment at least he'd escaped the Grand Agonizer.

9

Skar 192 piloted the needle-ship. He sat in a swivel chair before a control panel, with a small window showing the stars and the color-banded gas giant. After reading a three-page manual, he switched polarity on the magnetics to repulsing, pushing them away from High Station 3.

They moved without an engine signature, merely a black object drifting away from the injured habitat. High Station 3 was a monstrously long cylinder, many kilometers wide. The gas giant Pulsar loomed over them. On the screen Cyrus used, he studied the positions of the gravitational system's moons and habs. One moon in particular dominated the Pulsar system. This moon was Jassac, Earth-sized and possessed of a breathable atmosphere.

Cyrus viewed their narrow ship. It had one chamber, which narrowed here at the piloting end. Bunks and exercise machines lined the bulkheads, but still it was only three times the size of Venice's quarters, making this a tiny ship.

Fortunately, it didn't look as if it would be a long journey to Jassac. Cyrus doubted it would take more than a week to reach there and possibly land.

He had found one very interesting machine. It was the amplifier device he'd seen the psi-master's use, the *baan*. The device had two curved prongs with two discs on the end to press against a *baan*. He'd found several of the *baans*.

Now he weighed the crystal Reacher had given him in his hand.

"Do you know what's recorded here?" Cyrus asked Skar.

The Vomag turned his swivel chair to face him as the chair squealed horribly. How long had this ship been here waiting?

"Yes," Skar said. "The Reacher wanted me to tell you it's all they have on the Anointed One. If you put the crystal in the device, don the *baan* and press against the amplifier discs, you will learn all the Reacher knew about him."

Cyrus didn't do it right away. He had to think about it. He rested, ate, slept, and found himself sitting before the amplifier again.

As he sat there, he felt something—a psi-master likely—searching for them.

Quickly, Cyrus composed himself and did what the red-eyed woman had shown him about being Null. He felt the psi-master reaching, searching, looking, and then there was nothing.

Cyrus opened his eyes and grinned. He could do it. He could hide from their psi-talents. He'd never let them catch him, and he would make these aliens pay for what they had done to *Discovery*. They'd thought to enslave him, not realizing he was a new day Spartacus.

With a nod, Cyrus decided he'd better learn whatever he could about this so-called Anointed One while he had the time.

Cyrus slipped the *baan* over his forehead. Immediately, he heard voices in his mind. He clamped down on them and used the Null, making himself vanish in the psionic world.

That was too close. Could this *baan* and amplifier be a trap?

Deliberately, before he could have second thoughts, Cyrus pressed the *baan* against the amplifier discs so the metal clicked. Next, he inserted the crystal into the obvious slot.

A green light flashed, and then Cyrus became disoriented. It felt as if he was falling, falling . . .

||||||||||

A voice spoke to him in his mind. It sounded like Reacher, but a mental recording of the man's thoughts.

"Where did the Kresh originate?" the recording asked. "I do not believe they are indigenous to the Fenris System. Their origins are unknown to me, although I believe the moon Jassac gives us the best clue."

As if watching a holo-vid, Cyrus viewed the largest moon orbiting Pulsar: the gas giant with many colorful bands. As if coming down from space, he spied the dusty, planet-sized moon comprised of red and black mountains. Like rotten teeth, the various mountains rose across high desert plains. There were deep chasm valleys here and there. On the highest plateaus sat squat, miles-long converters. They were black fortresses with vapors continuously billowing skyward.

Reacher said, "Ice haulers ship asteroids from New Saturn and from the outer asteroid belt and bring them down to Jassac. The ice is fed into the converters, I believe, in an attempt to reshape Jassac into the lost Kresh home world. The Kresh live in the deep valleys, and I believe that is what their home world must have most been like.

"The Kresh are loath to pass up any opportunity for the furtherance of the *Codex of All Knowledge*. In the wilds of Jassac, they have released genetically manipulated humans. These Stone Age primitives are large-lunged and large-hearted individuals able to live in the sparse regions. It is my belief the Kresh wonder how untamed humans will react in their natural state. The Kresh study everything from every possible angle.

"In pursuit of such knowledge, it is my contention that from time to time they place 'failed' specimens among the Jassac humans. The Anointed One appears to be such a human. In this, I believe the Kresh have made their greatest blunder. The following is a stolen recording of the Anointed One's entrance into Clan Tash-Toi."

Cyrus's awareness sped closer to the surface. He noticed something in the distance. Through the amplifying mechanism, a silent narrator embedded certain facts into Cyrus's thoughts. He understood what he witnessed, and he strove to view the proceedings carefully.

In harsh morning sunlight, with the vast banded moon—the gas giant Pulsar—high in the sky, a group of Tash-Toi warriors struggled over a jagged spine of red rocks. The warriors were thickly muscled men whose brown skin was burnt like cracked leather. Their eyes were hard and dark, their mouths mere slits and their large noses hooked. They wore rough garments of reddish leather and complex conical helmets of fur and black rock. Each man carried a leather shield, a stone-shod spear and a heavy flint dagger strapped against his chest.

Ahead of them, a baby cried. The sound emanated from a lone reed basket.

The warriors halted in suspicion, glancing around. Nothing but sand drifted in the breeze. They studied the sky, but no demons appeared or slid across the sky in their airborne cars.

Warily, seven warriors surrounded the basket and the baby. The creature appeared human, but had strange white skin. A red blanket covered his body. Bumps appeared where the babe flailed with his little fists under the blanket.

One of the warriors spoke up. He was a sneering, truculent-looking youth. "The creature's skin is pale and his eyes are demon blue. He must be diseased. Listen to him squeal. Kill him, I say." The youth produced a dagger.

"Wait," the largest Tash-Toi said. His helmet was more complex than the others were, signifying him as the hetman. He made a gesture to the others waiting by the jagged spine. A small figure rose up as if from the ground and limped toward the seven warriors. He was a twisted old man with a sun-wrinkled face and a riot of dark hair. He was dressed in skins and wore a crude metal badge clipped to his garments.

"Seeker," the hetman asked. "Why is this squealing thing here?"

The seeker squatted on skinny legs and peered at the baby. With his dirty fingers, the seeker made a fluttering-fingered gesture over the baby as it continued to cry.

"Kill it," the truculent youth said.

"Quiet," the hetman told him.

The big youth shifted from foot to foot, gazing sullenly at the baby.

"Seeker?" the hetman asked.

"It isn't a demon," the seeker whispered. "He smells of soap and has clean human skin."

The hetman grunted. The others remained silent. "What should be done to him?" the hetman asked.

"Bah!" the big youth said. "Look at him shiver in the summer air." The warrior reached down and jerked the blanket away, tossing it aside.

The naked and pink-skinned baby screamed even louder, waving his clenched fists and kicking his feet.

"Kill the weakling and be done with it," the young warrior said.

Two of the seven warriors grunted in agreement.

The seeker gasped. "Look!" he said.

The red blanket lying near the basket moved in jerks, stopped, and jerked again like a rock snake until it covered the exposed baby.

"It's demon-spawn!" the big youth shouted. He shoved the seeker aside and slashed down with his dagger. His flint edge chipped against the hardwood pole of the hetman's blocking spear. A flint chip struck the baby's nose and caused him to scream again.

With his free hand, the hetman clouted the youth on the side of the head. The young warrior sprawled across the red ground, unconscious.

With wounded dignity, the seeker picked himself up. He dusted his ragged garments.

"Well?" the hetman asked.

"The baby has power," the seeker said. "I want him for my apprentice."

"Yeg's son is your apprentice," one of the other warriors said.

"Still," the seeker said, "I want him. He has the power." Squatting, the old man rubbed the reed basket.

"Two apprentices are against custom," the older warrior replied.

The hetman glared at the fallen youth. "It is against custom," he said. "Even so, the white creature will be the seeker's second apprentice. I name him Klane. Klane will be under Yeg's son. And this rash fool must see that the babe receives his share of food." The hetman toed the unconscious youth.

The other warriors muttered among themselves. Soon, they nodded in agreement.

In glee, the seeker scooped up the baby boy called Klane. He limped to his youngest wife and handed him to her.

In such a way, the Anointed One entered Clan Tash-Toi.

The scene vanished into darkness, and the Reacher's voice came back. "It is all we know about the Anointed One, with the Tash-Toi Clan name of Klane. What happened to Klane? I do not know. There is a prophecy that points to the white one in the red sands. Surely, the old prophecy means Klane. We must find the Anointed One and learn what he knows. How will he free humanity from the Kresh? I do not know. But we must find him, and to do so we need a Tracker."

Cyrus drew back from the amplifier and removed the *baan* from his head.

"Did you learn what you needed?" Skar asked.

Cyrus glanced at the soldier. It was a good question. There was a baby among Stone Age warriors. The baby had clearly shown telekinetic power. *His name is Klane.* How could such a baby help humanity against the unbeatable Kresh?

"I am Spartacus," Cyrus whispered. He would seek this baby, this Anointed One. He would do whatever he could against the Kresh. He might not win, but that was better than surrendering to them.

"I learned something," Cyrus said.

"Good. Do you know where to go?"

"Yes, to Jassac. But where on the planet this Anointed One might be, I have no idea."

"If we find him, what do we do then?" Skar asked.

That was a good question. "Let's find him first," Cyrus said. "Can you make the needle-ship go faster?"

"I can, but now isn't the time. We have to get closer to Jassac. Otherwise, the Kresh might spot us."

Cyrus weighed the crystal in his hand. He needed to go back into it and study the terrain and the Tash-Toi. It was his only clue. What would Skar and he do once they found the baby Klane? He decided not to worry about that now. Finding the Anointed One was the problem. He would take each step one move at a time. While he did so, he would do what Spartacus had done, and that was hurt the slave-owning Romans.

I'm going to hurt the Kresh the best I know how.

Thinking that, Cyrus put the *baan* back on his forehead and the crystal back into the slot. He needed to learn as much as he could about Jassac while he had an opportunity.

"We're going to hurt the Kresh," Cyrus said.

"I hope you're right," Skar said.

"Or we'll die trying," Cyrus said.

Skar became grim-faced and turned back to the controls.

As the soldier did so, Cyrus clicked the *baan* against the amplifier. He would study everything with care this time. He needed more knowledge to help him in his bitter quest.

ACKNOWLEDGMENTS

Thank you, David Pomerico, for wanting to see the Doom Star universe continue in a new series. Thanks Brian Larson for giving me advice during the writing of the story and thank you David VanDyke for the first round of editing. Jennifer Smith-Gaynor, you gave me some "grim" editing advice later, but I believe your comments helped make the story better—thank you. A hearty thanks to the entire 47North team. You are an easy and enjoyable group of people to work with.

Thank you, Evan Gregory, for your advice on the business end. And I want to give a special thank you to my wife Cyndi Heppner and to Madison and Mackenzie: two of the nicest girls in the world.

ABOUT THE AUTHOR

2013 © CYNDI HEPPNER

Vaughn Heppner is the author of many science fiction and fantasy novels, including the "Invasion America" series and the "Doom Star" series. He is inspired by venerable sci-fi writers such as Jack Vance and Roger Zelazny, as well as by the *Night of the Long Knives* by Hans Hellmut Kirst. The original movie, "Spartacus," and its themes of slave rebellion, color much of his work. Among his contemporaries, BV Larson's military science fiction novels are most akin to *Alien Honor*. Canadian-born, Heppner now lives in Central California. Visit his website at www.vaughnheppner.com.